Kate's chin rose stubbornly.

A faint glimmer of amusement appeared in Jack's eyes.
She was calling his bluff, was she? After tossing that
coffeepot, she had a right to expect that he might want
to throttle her. And then she'd slapped him—slapped the
master of the house. So foolhardy. He could snap her in
two if he chose; she would surely know that. She wasn't
to know he'd never hurt a woman in his life. But did she
shrink back in fear? No, on she came, chin held defiantly
high. His amusement deepened. Such a little creature,
but with so much spirit.

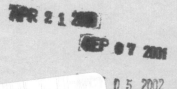

**Harlequin Historicals
is delighted to introduce
2000 RITA Award finalist Anne Gracie
and her North American debut book**

Gallant Waif
Harlequin Historical #557—April 2001

ANNE GRACIE

Gallant Waif

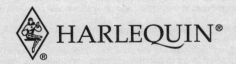

HARLEQUIN®

TORONTO • NEW YORK • LONDON
AMSTERDAM • PARIS • SYDNEY • HAMBURG
STOCKHOLM • ATHENS • TOKYO • MILAN • MADRID
PRAGUE • WARSAW • BUDAPEST • AUCKLAND

ISBN 0-373-29157-4

GALLANT WAIF

First North American Publication 2001

Visit us at www.eHarlequin.com

Printed in U.S.A.

Prologue

Kent, England. Late summer, 1812.

"No, no, Papa. I won't. You cannot make me!"

"Please, my sweet, I beg of you. It will not take long and I fear he will take no notice of me."

The tall dark-haired man waiting alone in the drawing-room reacted to the voices, which seemed to come from outside. He turned sharply and let out a soft expletive, his face tensed in pain. Moving more cautiously, he flexed his leg carefully, supporting himself with his cane. His sudden pallor gradually disappeared as the pain ebbed slowly away.

He glanced towards the sound of the voices and swallowed, tugging nervously at his cravat, thus ruining the effect that he'd taken hours to achieve. His clothes were of the finest quality, although somewhat out of date; they seemed to have been tailored for a slightly larger gentleman, for the coat that should have fitted snugly was loose everywhere except across the shoulders. The gentleman himself was rather striking to behold as he stood staring blankly out of the window, tall, broad-shouldered and darkly handsome, yet thin, almost to the point of gauntness.

Jack Carstairs had done enough waiting. It had been bad

enough being closed up in a carriage for hours upon end to get here...then to be left closeted in the front parlour for almost half an hour was too much for a man who'd spent the last three years out of doors, commanding troops under Wellington on the Peninsula. He opened the French doors on to the terrace and stepped outside into the cool, fresh air, and was immediately rewarded by the sweet, melodic tones of his beloved.

Jack stepped forward impatiently. Three years, and now the waiting was at an end. In just minutes he would hold her in his arms again, and the nightmare would be over. He limped eagerly towards the sound of the voices coming from the open French windows further along the terrace.

"No, Papa, you must tell him. I do not wish to see him." Julia's voice was petulant, sulky. Jack had never heard it so before.

"Now, now, my dear, I will speak to him and put him right, never fear, but you must see that it is necessary for you to at least come with me, for you know he will not believe me otherwise."

Jack froze. He had received a letter full of sweetness and love from Julia, only a month ago, just before he was wounded. It was in the same batch of letters that had told him of his father's death. Months after the event, as was all mail received on the Peninsula.

The lovely, well-remembered voice became more petulant, almost childish. "I don't want to see him, I don't. He's changed, I know, I saw him from the window."

Her father's voice was coaxing. He'd always been wax in the hands of his beautiful daughter, but for once he was standing relatively firm. "Well, now, my dear, you have to expect that. After all, he has been at war and war changes a man."

Julia made a small sound, which from anyone less exquisite would have been called a snort. "He…he's ugly now, Papa; his face is ruined."

Unconsciously Jack fingered the harsh, still livid scar that bisected his cheek from temple to mouth.

"And he can hardly even walk." Her voice grew soft and coaxing. "Please, Papa, do not make me speak to him. I cannot bear even to look at him, with his leg sticking out in that peculiar-looking way. It would have been better if he had died than to come back like that."

"My dear!" Her father sounded shocked.

"Oh, I know it seems hard," Julia continued, "but when I think of my beautiful Jack and how he is now I could weep. No, Papa, it's just not possible."

"Are you sure, my dear?"

"Of course I am sure. You told me yourself his father left him nothing. I cannot marry a pauper." She stamped her foot. "It makes me so angry to think of it—all that time wasted, *waiting*! And, in any case, he can barely walk without falling over, so you can be very sure that he will never dance with me again as he used to…"

Her voice tailed off as she recalled the magic moments she had spent on the dance floor, the cynosure of every eye, the envy of every other woman in the room. She stamped her foot again, angry at being deprived of all she had expected.

"No, Papa, it is quite impossible! I am glad now that you would not allow us to announce the betrothal formally, though I thought you monstrous cruel at the time."

Jack had heard enough. His face white and grim, he drew back the draperies which had concealed him and stepped into the room.

"I think that says it all, does it not?" he said in a soft, deadly voice.

There was a small flurry as the two absorbed what he might have heard. There was no telling how long he had been outside. Jack limped quietly to the door and pointedly held it open for Julia's father to make his exit.

"I believe your presence is no longer required, Sir Phillip," he said. "If you would be so good as to leave us alone, sir?"

Sir Phillip Davenport began to bluster. "Now see here, Carstairs, I won't be ordered about in my own house. I can see it must be a nasty shock for you, but you are no longer in a position to support my daugh—"

"Thank you, sir." Jack cut across him. "I understand what you are saying, but I believe I am owed the courtesy of a few moments alone with my betrothed."

The voice which had spent years commanding others had its usual effect. Julia's father began to look uncomfortable and took a few steps towards the door.

"Oh, but…" Julia began.

"As far as I am concerned our betrothal has not yet been dissolved and I believe I have the right to be told of it in person." Jack gestured again for her father to leave. Observing that gentleman's hesitation and concern, his lip curled superciliously. He added silkily, "I assure you, Davenport, that, while I may be changed in many respects, I am still a gentleman. Your daughter is safe with me."

Sir Phillip left, leaving his daughter looking embarrassed and angry. There was a long moment of silence. Julia took a quick, graceful turn about the room, the swishing of her skirts the only sound in the room. The practised movements displayed, as they were meant to do, the lush, perfect body encased in the finest gown London could provide, the fashionable golden coiffure, the finely wrought jewellery encircling her smooth white neck and dimpled wrists. Finally Julia spoke.

"I am sorry if you heard something that you didn't like, Jack, but you must know that eavesdroppers never hear any good of themselves." She shrugged elegantly, glided to the window and stood gazing out, seemingly absorbed in the view of the fashionably landscaped garden beyond the terrace.

Jack's face was grim, the scar twisting down his cheek standing out fresh and livid against his pallor.

"~~God damn~~ it, Julia, the least you could have done was told me to my face—what's left of it," he added bitterly. "It's partly because of you that I'm in this situation in the first place."

She turned, her lovely mouth pouting with indignation. "Well, really, Jack, how can you blame me for what has happened to you?"

His lips twisted sardonically and he shrugged, his powerful shoulders straining against the shabby, light, superfine coat.

"Perhaps not directly. But when my father ordered me to end our betrothal you cast yourself into my arms and begged me to stand firm. Which of course I did."

"But how was I to know that that horrid old man truly *would* disinherit you for disobeying him?"

His voice was cool, his eyes cold. "*That horrid old man* was my father, and I told you at the time he would."

"But he doted on you! I was sure he was only bluffing…trying to make you dance to his tune."

His voice was hard. "It's why I purchased a commission in the Guards, if you recall."

The beautiful eyes ran over his body, skipping distastefully over the scarred cheek and the stiffly extended leg.

"Yes, and it was the ruination of you!" She pouted, averting her eyes.

He was silent for a moment, remembering what she had said to her father. "I am told that I will never dance again. Or ride."

"Exactly," she agreed, oblivious to his hard gaze. "And will that horrid scar on your face go away too? I doubt it."

She suddenly seemed to notice the cruelty of what she had

said. "Oh, forgive me, Jack, but you used to be the handsomest man in London, before…that." She gestured distastefully towards the scar.

With every word she uttered, she revealed herself more and more, and the pain and disillusion and anger with himself was like a knife twisting in Jack's guts. For this beautiful, empty creature he had forever alienated his father. Like Julia, he had never in his heart of hearts believed his father would truly disinherit him, but it seemed his father had died with Jack unforgiven. It was that which hurt Jack so deeply; not the loss of his inheritance, but the loss of his father's love.

Feeling uncomfortable under Jack's harsh scrutiny, Julia took a few paces around the room, nervously picking up ornaments and elegant knick-knacks, putting them down and moving restlessly on.

Jack watched her, recalling how the memory of her grace and beauty had sustained him through some of the worst moments of his life. It had been like a dream then, in the heat and dust and blood of the Peninsula War, to think of this lovely, vital creature waiting for him. And that's all it was, he told himself harshly—a dream. The reality was this vain, beautiful, callous little bitch.

"Oh, be honest, Jack." She twirled and stopped in front of him. "You are no longer the man I agreed to marry. Can you give me the life we planned? No."

She shrugged. "I am sorry, Jack, but, painful though it is for both of us, you must see it is just not at all practical any more."

"Ahh, not practical?" he echoed sarcastically. "And what exactly is not practical? Is it my sudden lack of fortune? My ruined face? Or the idea of dancing with an ugly cripple and thereby becoming an object of ridicule? Is that it, eh?"

She cringed in fright at the savagery in his voice.

"No, it is not practical, is it?" he snarled. "And I thank God for it."

She stared as she took in the meaning of his last utterance.

"Do…do you mean to say *you* don't want to marry *me*?" Her voice squeaked in amazement and dawning indignation. It was for her to give *him* his *congé*, not the other way around.

He bowed ironically. "Not only do I not wish to marry you, I am almost grateful for the misfortunes which have opened my eyes and delivered me from that very fate."

She glared at him, her bosom heaving in a way that had once entranced him. "Mr Carstairs, you are no gentleman!"

He smiled back at her, a harsh, ugly grimace. "And you, Miss Davenport, are no lady. You are a shallow, greedy, cold little bitch, and I thank my lucky stars that I discovered the truth in time. God help the poor fool you eventually snare in your net."

She stamped her foot furiously. "How dare you? Leave this house at once…at once, do you hear me? Or crip— wounded or not, I'll have you thrown out!"

He limped two paces forward and she skittered back in fright.

"Just give me back my ring," he said wearily, "and your butler won't be put to the trouble and embarrassment of manhandling a cripple."

She snatched her left hand back against her breast and covered the large diamond ring with her other hand.

"Oh, but I am very attached to this ring, Jack," she said in a little-girl voice. "I did love you, you know. Surely you want me to have something to remember you by?"

He looked at her, disgust filling his throat, then turned and silently limped from the house.

Chapter One

London. Late autumn, 1812.

"Good God! Do you mean to tell me my grandson did not even receive you after you'd travelled I don't know how many miles to see him?" Lady Cahill frowned at her granddaughter. "Oh, for goodness' sake, Amelia, stop that crying at once and tell me the whole story! From the beginning!"

Amelia gulped back her sobs. "The house is shabby and quite horrid, though the stables seem well enough—"

"I care nothing for stables! What of my grandson?" Lady Cahill interrupted, exasperated.

"His manservant told me Jack saw no one."

The old lady frowned. "What do you mean, no one?"

"I mean no one, Grandmama, no one at all. He—Jack, that is—pretended to be indisposed. He sent a message thanking me for my concern and regretting his inability to offer me hospitality. Hospitality! His own sister!"

Amelia groped in her reticule for a fresh handkerchief, blotted her tears and continued, "Of course I insisted that I go up and tend him, but his man—a *foreigner*—would not even allow me up the stairs. I gathered from him that Jack was not ill...just...drunk! He won't see anyone. And, according to his manservant, he's been like that ever since he returned from Kent.''

There was a long pause while the old lady digested the import of this. ''Kent, eh? I wish to God he had never set eyes on that poisonous little Davenport baggage.'' She glanced up at her granddaughter. ''I take it, then, that the betrothal is definitely at an end.''

''Unfortunately, yes, Grandmama.''

''Good!'' said Lady Cahill vehemently. ''He's well rid of that little harpy and you know it.''

''But, Grandmama, it appears to have broken his heart.''

''Nonsense! He's got a fine strong heart. He's got my blood in him, hasn't he? When you're my age, you'll stop prating of broken hearts and other such nonsense. Bodies mend and so do hearts.''

There was a long silence.

''But that's just it, isn't it, Grandmama?'' Amelia said at last. ''Bodies don't always mend, do they? Jack's servant said that Jack's leg is still very bad and painful, although he can walk.''

Lady Cahill thought of the way her favourite grandson had looked when he'd come back from the wars in Spain. Such a fine tall, athletic lad he had been, too, before he left. But now…

She glared at her granddaughter. ''Don't let me ever hear you speaking such rubbish, do you hear me, gel? Never! That boy is as fine a lad as ever he was, you mark my words! He's got a fine fighting spirit in him.''

''I saw no fighting spirit, Grandmama.''

''Do you try to tell me, gel, that my grandson has had the stuffing knocked out of him and hides himself away from the world merely because his betrothal to that beautiful, heartless little viper is at an end? Faugh!'' Lady Cahill snorted. ''You'll not make me believe that, not in a month of Sundays.''

"No," said Amelia slowly. "But that, on top of everything else... He will never ride again, they say. And so many of his friends have been killed in the war... And, Grandmama, you *know* how much Papa's will hurt him—to be left with virtually nothing..."

"Lord knows what maggot was in your father's mind at the time," agreed Lady Cahill. "Bad enough to disinherit the boy, but to leave him 'whatever is found in my pockets on the day I die'"... Faugh! Utter folly! "Twas the veriest co-incidence that he died after a night of cards at White's. Had he not just won that deed to Sevenoakes, the boy would not even have a roof over his head!"

Lady Cahill snorted in disgust. Yes, Jack had taken some terrible blows, one on top of another. But even discounting Amelia's dramatics it seemed he was taking it badly. He could not be allowed to brood like that. He needed *something* to snap him out of it.

There was a soft knock at the door. "Yes, what is it, Fitcher?" the old lady snapped, her temper frayed by concern for her grandson.

"Pardon me, milady." The butler bowed. "This letter was delivered a few moments ago." He bowed again, proffering a letter on a silver salver.

Lady Cahill picked up the letter, wrinkling her nose in disdain at the undistinguished handwriting which gave her direction. "Humph," she muttered. "Not even franked."

She turned it over and broke the seal. She frowned over the letter, muttering crossly to herself as she did. Finally she threw it down in frustration.

"What is it, Grandmama?"

"Demmed if I can read the thing. Shockin' bad hand and the spelling is atrocious. Can't think who'd be sending me such rubbish. Toss it in the fire, girl!"

The young woman picked the letter up and smoothed it out. "Would you like me to try?"

Taking the snort she received from her grandmother to be assent, Amelia read it out, hesitating occasionally over misspellings and illegible words, of which there were many.

Milady I be right sorry to be addressing you like this it being above my station to be writing to Countesses but I cannot think of who else to turn to...

"A begging letter!" the Dowager Countess snapped in outrage. "On to the fire with it at once!"

"I think not, Grandmama," said Amelia, scanning ahead. "Let me finish."

...for my poor girl is now left all alone in the world with no kin to care what become of her but it do seem a right shame that the daughter of gentlefolk should have to skivvy to stay alive...

Lady Cahill's eyes kindled with anger. "By God, she's trying to palm one of your father's by-blows off on to us!"

"Grandmama!" Amelia blushed, horrified.

"Oh, don't be so mealy-mouthed, girl. You must know your father had any number of bits o' fluff after your dear mother died, and they didn't mean a thing, so don't pretend. But it's nothing to do with us. Your father would have left any base-born child well provided for. He was a gentleman, after all, even if he was a fool! Now toss that piece of impertinence in the fire at once, I say!"

But her granddaughter had forgotten her blushes and was avidly reading on. "No, wait, Grandmama, listen to this."

And being as I was her old nurse even if some as did say I wasn't good enough to be nurse to Vicar's daugh-

ter it falls to me to let you know what my girl has come
to being as you was godmother to Miss Maria her poor
sainted mother...

Lady Cahill sat up at this and leant forward, her eyes sharp
with interest.

...and her only remaining child so now there be nothing left for her but to Take Service her not willing to
be took in by myself and truth to tell there be little
enough for me alone so I beg ye Milady please help
Miss Kate for as the Lord is my witness there be no
other who can yours truly Martha Betts.

"Do you know any of these people, Grandmama?" said
Amelia curiously.

"I believe I do," said her grandmother slowly, picking up
the letter and scanning it again. "I think the girl must be the
daughter of my godchild Maria Farleigh—Maria Delacombe
as she used to be. She married a parson and died giving birth
to a daughter...must be nigh on twenty years ago. She had
two boys before that, can't recall their names now, and I lost
touch with the family after she died, but it could be the same
family."

She peered at the address. "Is that Bedfordshire I see?
Yes. Hmm. No kin? What can have happened to the gel's
father and brothers?" Lady Cahill frowned over the letter for
a short time, then tossed it decisively down on a side table.

"What do you mean to do, Grandmama?"

Lady Cahill rang for sherry and biscuits.

Amelia's husband arrived and they all went in to dinner.
Over cream of watercress soup, Lady Cahill announced her
decision.

"But, Grandmama, are you sure about this?" Amelia

looked distressed. "It's a very long journey. What if Jack won't receive you, either?"

Lady Cahill gave her granddaughter a look of magnificent scorn. "Don't be ridiculous, Amelia!" she snorted. "I have never in my life been denied *entrée* to any establishment in the kingdom. I go where I choose. I was a Montford, gel, before my marriage to your grandfather, and *no one*, not even my favourite grandson, tells me what I may or may not do!"

She dabbed her mouth delicately on a damask napkin and poured her sherry into the soup. "Tasteless rubbish!"

Later, as she pushed *cailles à la Turque* around her plate, she said, "I'll call upon Maria's gel on my way to visit Jack. I cannot let her starve and I'll not allow Maria Farleigh's child to enter into service! Faugh! The very idea of it. Maria's mother would turn in her grave. She was a fool to let her daughter marry a penniless parson." Lady Cahill's eyes narrowed as she considered the shocking mésalliance.

"The Farleighs were a fine old family," she admitted grudgingly, "but he was the last of his line and poor as a church mouse to boot. Church mouse. Parson! Ha!" She cackled, noticing her unintended pun, then fell silent.

She heaved a sigh and straightened her thin old shoulders wearily. She pushed her plate away and called for more sherry.

"Yes, I'll rouse the boy out of his megrims and keep him busy." Lady Cahill ignored the Scotch collops, the lumber pie, the buttered parsnips and the chine of salmon boiled with smelts. She helped herself to some lemon torte. "Can't leave him brooding himself into a decline up there in the wilds of Leicestershire with no one but servants to talk to." She shook her head in disgust. "Never did believe in servants anyhow!"

Amelia tried valiantly to repress a gasp of astonishment and met her husband's amused twinkle across the table. For a woman who considered a butler, dresser, cook, undercook, housekeeper, several housemaids and footmen, a scullery-maid, coachman and two grooms the bare minimum of service needed to keep one elderly woman in comfort, it was a remarkable statement.

"No, indeed, Grandmama," Amelia managed, bending her head low over her plate.

"Don't hunch over your dinner like that, girl," snapped the old woman. "Lord, I don't know how this generation got to be so rag-mannered. It wouldn't have been tolerated in my day."

The knocker sounded peremptorily, echoing through the small empty cottage. This was it, then, the moment she had been waiting for and dreading equally. The moment when she stopped being Kate Farleigh, Vicar Farleigh's hoydenish daughter, and became Farleigh, maidservant, invisible person.

Now that the moment had come, Kate was filled with the deepest trepidation. It was a point of no return. Her heart was pounding. It felt like she was about to jump off a cliff... The analogy was ridiculous, she told herself sternly. She wasn't jumping, she had been pushed long ago, and there was no other choice...

Squaring her shoulders, Kate took a deep breath and opened the door. Before her stood an imperious little old lady clad in sumptuous furs, staring at her with unnervingly bright blue eyes. Behind her was a stylish travelling coach.

"Can I help you?" Kate said, politely hiding her surprise. Nothing in Mrs Midgely's letter had led her to expect that her new employer would be so wealthy and aristocratic, or that she would collect Kate herself.

The old lady ignored her. With complete disregard for any of the usual social niceties, she surveyed Kate intently.

The girl was too thin to have any claim to beauty, Lady Cahill decided, but there was definitely something about the child that recalled her beautiful mother. Perhaps it was the bone structure and the almost translucent complexion. Certainly she had her mother's eyes. As for the rest... Lady Cahill frowned disparagingly. Her hair was medium brown, with not a hint of gold or bronze or red to lift it from the ordinary. At present it was tied back in a plain knot, unadorned by ringlets or curls or ribands, as was the fashion. Indeed, nothing about her indicated the slightest acquaintance with fashion, her black clothes being drab and dowdy, though spotlessly clean. They hung loosely upon a slight frame.

Kate flushed slightly under the beady blue gaze and put her chin up proudly. Was the old lady deaf? ''Can I help you?'' she repeated more loudly, a slight edge to her husky, boyish voice.

''Ha! Boot's on the other foot, more like!''

Kate stared at her in astonishment, trying to make sense of this peculiar greeting.

''Well, gel, don't keep me waiting here on the step for rustics and village idiots to gawp at! I'm not a fairground attraction, you know. Invite me in. Tush! The manners of this generation. I don't know what your mother would have said to it!''

Lady Cahill pushed past Kate and made her way into the front room. She looked around her, taking in the lack of furniture, the brighter patches on the wall where paintings had once hung, the shabby fittings and the lack of a fire which at this time of year should have been crackling in the grate.

Kate swallowed. It was going to be harder than she thought, learning humility in the face of such rudeness. But she could not afford to alienate her new employer, the only one who had seemed interested.

''I collect that I have the honour of addressing Mrs Midgely.''

The old lady snorted.

Kate, unsure of the exact meaning of the sound, decided

it was an affirmative. "I assume, since you've come in person, that you find me suitable for the post, ma'am."

"Humph! What experience do you have of such work?"

"A little, ma'am. I can dress hair and stitch a neat seam."
Neat? What a lie! Kate shrugged her conscience aside. Her stitchery was haphazard, true, but a good pressing with a hot flatiron soon hid most deficiencies. And she needed this job. She was sure she could be neat if she really, really tried.

"Your previous employer?"

"Until lately I kept house for my father and brothers. As you can see…" she gestured to her black clothes "…I am recently bereaved."

"But what of the rest of your family?"

This old woman was so arrogant and intrusive, she would doubtless be an extremely demanding employer. Kate gritted her teeth. This was her only alternative. She must endure the prying.

"I have no other family, ma'am."

"Hah! You seem an educated, genteel sort of girl. Why have you not applied for a post as companion or governess?"

"I am not correctly educated to be a governess." *I am barely educated at all.*

The old lady snorted again, then echoed Kate's thought uncannily. "Most governesses I have known could barely call themselves educated at all. A smattering of French or Italian, a little embroidery, the ability to dabble in watercolours and to tinkle a tune on a pianoforte or harp is all it takes. Don't tell me you can't manage that. Why, your father was a scholar!"

Yes, but I was just a girl and not worth educating in his eyes. In her efforts to control the anger at the cross-questioning she was receiving, it did not occur to Kate to wonder how the old woman would know of her father's scholarship. If Mrs Midgely wished Kate to be educated, Kate would not disappoint her. Some women enjoyed having an educated person in a menial position, thinking it added to their consequence.

"I know a little Greek and Latin from my brothers—" *the rude expressions* "—and I am acquainted with the rudiments of mathematics…" *I can haggle over the price of a chicken with the wiliest Portuguese peasant.* It suddenly occurred to Kate that perhaps Mrs Midgely had grandchildren she wished Kate to teach. Hurriedly Kate reverted to the truth. It would not do to be found out so easily.

"But I cannot imagine anyone offering a tutor's position to a female. I have no skill with paints and have never learnt to play a musical instrument…" No, the Vicar's unwanted daughter had been left to run wild as a weed and never learned to be a lady.

"I do speak a little French, Spanish and Portuguese."

"Why did you not seek work as a companion, then?"

Kate had tried and tried to find a position, writing letter after letter in answer to advertisements. But she had no one to vouch for her, no references. Someone from Lisbon had written to one of her female neighbours and suddenly she was *persona non grata* to people who had known her most of her life. It hadn't helped that the girl they remembered had been a wild hoyden, either. There were many who had predicted that the Vicar's daughter would come to a bad end. And they were right.

Life in service wouldn't be so bad, she told herself. As one of a number of servants in a big house, she would have companionship at least. A servant's life would be hard, harder than that of a companion, but it was not hard work Kate was afraid of—it was loneliness. And she was lonely. More lonely than she had ever thought possible.

Besides, a companion might be forced to socialise, and Kate had no desire to meet up with *anyone* from her previous life. She might be recognised, and that would be too painful, too humiliating. She had no wish to go through that again, but none of this could she explain to this autocratic old lady.

''I know of no one who would take on a companion or governess without a character from a previous employer, ma'am.''

''But surely your father had friends who would furnish you with such?''

''Possibly, ma'am. However, my father and I lived abroad for the last three years and I have no notion how to contact any of them, for all his papers were lost when...when he died.''

''Abroad!'' the old lady exclaimed in horror. ''Good God! With Bonaparte ravaging the land! How could your foolish father have taken such a risk? Although I suppose it was Greece or Mesopotamia or some outlandish classical site that you went to, and not the Continent?''

Kate's eyes glittered. Old harridan! She did not respond to the question, but returned to the main issue. ''So, do I have the position, ma'am?''

''As my maid? No, certainly not. I never heard of anything so ridiculous.''

Kate was stupefied.

''I never did need a maid anyway, or any other servant,'' the old lady continued. ''That's not what I came here for at all.''

''Then...then are you not Mrs Midgely, ma'am?'' Kate's fine features were lit by a rising flush and her eyes glittered with burgeoning indignation.

The old lady snorted again. ''No, most decidedly I am not.''

''Then, ma'am, may I ask who you are and by what right you have entered this house and questioned me in this most irregular fashion?'' Kate didn't bother to hide her anger.

Lady Cahill smiled. ''The right of a godmother, my dear.''

Kate did not return the smile. "My godmother died when I was a small child."

"I am Lady Cahill, child. Your mother was my goddaughter." She reached up and took the girl's chin in her hand. "You look remarkably like your mother at this age, especially around the eyes. They were her best feature, too. Only I don't like to see those dark shadows under yours. And you're far too thin. We'll have to do something about that."

Lady Cahill released Kate's chin and looked around her again. "Are you going to offer me a seat or not, young woman?"

This old lady knew her mother? It was more than Kate did. The subject had been forbidden in the Vicarage.

"I'm sorry, Lady Cahill, you took me by surprise. Please take a seat." Kate gestured to the worn settee. "I'm afraid I can't offer you any refresh—"

"Never mind about that. I didn't come here for refreshments," said the old lady briskly. "I'm travelling and I can't abide food when I'm travelling."

"Why did you come here, ma'am?" Kate asked. "You've had little contact with my family for a great many years. I am sure it cannot be chance that has brought you here just now."

Shrewd blue eyes appraised her. "Hmm. You don't beat around the bush, do you, young woman? But I like a bit of plain speaking myself, so I'll put it to you directly. You need my help, my girl."

The grey-green eyes flashed, but Kate said quietly enough, "What makes you think that, Lady Cahill?"

"Don't be foolish, girl, for I can't abide it! It's clear as the nose on your face that you haven't a farthing to call your own. You're dressed in a gown I wouldn't let my maid use as a duster. This house is empty of any comfort, you can't offer me refreshment— No, sit down, girl!"

Kate jumped to her feet, her eyes blazing. "Thank you for

your visit, Lady Cahill. I have no need to hear any more of this. You have no claim on me and no right to push your way into my home and speak to me in this grossly insulting way. I will thank you to leave!''

''Sit down, I said!'' The diminutive old lady spoke with freezing authority, her eyes snapping with anger. For a few moments they glared at each other. Slowly Kate sat, her thin body rigid with fury.

''I will listen to what you have to say, Lady Cahill, but only because good manners leave me no alternative. Since you refuse to leave, I must endure your company, it being unfitting for a girl of my years to lay hands on a woman so much my elder!''

The old lady glared back at her for a minute then, to Kate's astonishment, she burst into laughter, chuckling until the tears ran down her withered, carefully painted face.

''Oh, my dear, you've inherited you mother's temper as well as her eyes.'' Lady Cahill groped in her reticule, and found a delicate lace-edged wisp which she patted against her eyes, still chuckling.

The rigidity died out of Kate's pose, but she continued to watch her visitor rather stonily. Kate hated her eyes. She knew they were just like her mother's. Her father had taught her that…her father, whose daughter reminded him only that his beloved wife had died giving birth to a baby—a baby with grey-green eyes.

''Now, my child, don't be so stiff-necked and silly,'' Lady Cahill began. ''I know all about the fix you are in—''

''May I ask how, ma'am?''

''I received a letter from a Martha Betts, informing me in a roundabout and illiterate fashion that you were orphaned, destitute and without prospects.''

Kate's knuckles whitened. Her chin rose proudly. ''You've been misinformed, ma'am. Martha means well, ma'am, but she doesn't know the whole story.''

Lady Cahill eyed her shrewdly. "So you are not, in fact, orphaned, destitute and without prospects."

"I am indeed orphaned, ma'am, my father having died abroad several months since. My two brothers also died close to that time." Kate looked away, blinking fiercely to hide the sheen of tears.

"Accept my condolences, child." Lady Cahill leaned forward and gently patted her knee.

Kate nodded. "But I am not without prospects, ma'am, so I thank you for your kind concern and bid you farewell."

"I think not," said Lady Cahill softly. "I would hear more of your circumstances."

Kate's head came up at this. "By what right do you concern yourself in my private affairs?"

"By right of a promise I made to your mother."

Kate paused. Her mother. The mother whose life Kate had stolen. The mother who had taken her husband's heart to the grave with her... For a moment it seemed that Kate would argue, then she inclined her head in grudging acquiescence. "I suppose I must accept that, then."

"You are most gracious," said Lady Cahill dryly.

"Lady Cahill, it is really no concern of yours. I am well able to look after myself—"

"Pah! Mrs Midgely!"

"Yes, but—"

"Now, don't eat me, child!" said Lady Cahill. "I know I'm an outspoken old woman, but when one is my age one becomes accustomed to having one's own way. Child, try to use the brains God gave you. It is obvious to the meanest intelligence that any position offered by a Mrs Midgely is no suitable choice for Maria Farleigh's daughter. A maidservant, indeed! Faugh! It's not to be thought of. There's no help for it. You must come and live with me."

Come and live with an aristocratic old lady? Who from all appearances moved in the upper echelons of the *ton*? Who would take her to balls, masquerades, the opera—it had long been a dream, a dream for the old Kate…

It was the new Kate's nightmare.

For the offer to come now, when it was too late—it was a painful irony in a life she had already found too full of both pain and irony.

"I thank you for your kind offer, Lady Cahill, but I would not dream of so incommoding you."

"Foolish child! What maggot has got into your head? It's not an invitation you should throw back in my face without thought. Consider what such a proposal would involve. You will have a life appropriate to your birth and take your rightful position in society. I am not offering you a life of servitude and drudgery."

"I realise that, ma'am," said Kate in a low voice. Her *rightful position in society* was forfeited long ago, in Spain. "None the less, though I thank you for your concern, I cannot accept your very generous invitation."

"Don't you realise what I am offering you, you stupid girl?"

"Charity," said Kate baldly.

"Ah, tush!" said the old lady, angrily waving her hand. "What is charity but a foolish word?"

"Whether we name it or not, ma'am, the act remains the same," said the girl with quiet dignity. "I prefer to be beholden to no one. I will earn my own living, but I thank you for your offer."

Lady Cahill shook her head in disgust. "Gels of good family earnin' their own living, indeed! What rubbish! In my day, a gel did what her parents told her and not a peep out of her—and a *demmed* good whipping if there was!"

"But, Lady Cahill, you are *not* my parent. I *don't* have to listen to you."

"No, you don't, do you?" Lady Cahill's eyes narrowed thoughtfully. "Ah, well then, help me to stand, child. My

bones are stiff from being jolted along those shockin' tracks
that pass for roads in these parts.''

Kate, surprised but relieved at the old lady's sudden ca-
pitulation, darted forward. She helped Lady Cahill to her feet
and solicitously began to lead her to the door.

''Thank you, my dear.'' Lady Cahill stepped outside.
''Where does that lead?'' she asked, pointing to a well-worn
pathway.

''To the woods, ma'am, and also to the stream.''

''Very pleasant, very rural, no doubt, if you like that sort
of thing,'' said the born city-dweller.

''Yes, ma'am, I do,'' said Kate. ''I dearly love a walk
through the woods, particularly in the early morning when
the dew is still on the leaves and grass and the sun catches
it.''

Lady Cahill stared. ''Astonishing,'' she murmured. ''Well,
that's enough of that. It's demmed cold out here, almost as
cold as in that poky little cottage of yours. We'll resume our
discussion in my coach. At least there I can rest my feet on
hot bricks.''

Kate dropped her arm in surprise. ''But I thought…''

The blue eyes twinkled beadily. ''You thought you'd made
yourself clear?''

Kate nodded.

''And so you did, my dear. So you did. I heard every word
you said. Now, don't argue with me, girl. The discussion is
finished when I say it is and not before. Follow me!''

Gesturing imperiously, she led the way to the coach and
allowed the waiting footman to help her up the steps.
Swathed in furs, she supervised as Kate was similarly tucked
up with a luxurious fur travelling rug around her, her feet
resting snugly on a hot brick. Kate sighed. It seemed ridiculous, sitting in a coach like this, to discuss a proposal she
had no intention of accepting, but there was no denying it—
the coach was much warmer than the cottage.

"Comfortable?"

"Yes, I thank you," Kate responded politely. "Lady Cah—"

The old lady thumped on the roof of the coach with her cane. With a sudden lurch, the coach moved off.

"What on earth—?" Kate glanced wildly around as the cottage slipped past. For a moment it occurred to her to fling herself from the coach, but a second's reflection convinced her it was moving too fast for that.

"What are you doing? Where are you taking me? Who are you?"

The old woman laughed. "I am indeed Lady Cahill, child. You are in no danger, my dear."

"But what are you doing?" demanded Kate in bewilderment and anger.

"Isn't it obvious?" Lady Cahill beamed. "I've kidnapped you!"

Chapter Two

"**B**ut this is outrageous!" Kate gasped. "How dare you?"

The old lady shrugged. "Child, I can see you're as stubborn as your dear mother and, to be perfectly frank, I haven't the time to waste convincing you to come and stay with me instead of hiring yourself out as a maid or whatever nonsense you were about. I intend to reach my grandson's house in Leicestershire tonight and, as it is, we won't reach it until well after dark. Now, be a good girl, sit back, be quiet and let me sleep. Travelling is enough of a trial without having a foolish girl nattering at me." She pulled the furs more closely around her and, as if there was nothing more to be said, closed her eyes.

"But my house…my things…Martha…" Kate began.

One heavy-lidded eye opened and regarded her balefully. "Martha knows my intentions towards you. She was most relieved to hear that you would, in future, make your home with me until such time as a suitable husband is found for you. A footman is locking up your house and will convey the keys to Martha."

Kate opened her mouth to speak, but the blue eyes had closed implacably. She sat there, annoyed by the ease with which she had been tricked, and humiliated by the old lady's discovery of her desperate straits. She sighed. It was no use fighting. She would have to go wherever she was taken, and then see what could be done. The old lady meant well; she did not know how ill-placed her kindness was.

...until such time as a suitable husband is found for you. No. No decent man would have her now. Not even the man who'd said he loved her to distraction wanted her now. She stared out at the scenery, seeing none of it, only Harry, turning away from her, unable to conceal the revulsion and contempt in his eyes.

Harry, whom she'd loved for as long as she could remember. She'd been nine years old when she first met him, a tall, arrogant sixteen-year-old, surprisingly tolerant of the little tomboy tagging devotedly along at his heels, fetching and carrying for him and his best friend, her brother Jeremy. And when Kate was seventeen he'd proposed to her in the orchard just before he'd left to go to the wars, and laid his firm warm lips on hers.

But a few months ago it had been a totally different Harry, staring at her with the cold hard eyes of a stranger. Like all the others, he'd turned his back.

Kate bit her lip and tried to prevent the familiar surge of bitter misery rising to her throat. Never, ever would she put herself in that position again. It was simply too painful to love a man, when his love could simply disappear overnight and be replaced with cold disdain...

The coach hit a deep rut and the passengers lurched and bounced and clung to their straps. Kate glanced at Lady Cahill, but the old lady remained silently huddled in her furs, her eyes closed, her face dead white beneath the cosmetics. Kate returned to her reflections.

So she would never marry. So what? Many women never married and they managed to lead perfectly happy and useful lives. Kate would be one of them. All she needed was the chance to do so, and she would make that chance; she was determined. Maybe Lady Cahill would help her to get started…

Bright moonlight lit the way by the time the travelling chaise pulled into a long driveway leading to a large, gloomy house. No welcoming lights were visible.

In a dark, second-floor window a shadowy figure stood staring moodily. Jack Carstairs lifted a glass to his lips. He was in a foul temper. He knew full well that his grandmother would be exhausted. He couldn't turn her away. And she knew it, the manipulative old tartar, which was, of course, why she had sent her dresser on ahead to make things ready and timed her own arrival to darkness. Jack, in retaliation, had restricted his grandmother's retinue to her dresser, sending the rest off to stay in the village inn. That, if nothing else, would keep her visit short. His grandmother liked her comfort.

The chaise drew to a halt in front of a short flight of stairs. The front door opened and two servants, a man and a woman, came running. Before the coachman could dismount, the woman tugged down the steps and flung open the door. "Here you are at last, my lady. I've been in a terrible way, worrying about you."

Lady Cahill tottered unsteadily on her feet, looking utterly exhausted. Kate felt a sharp twinge of guilt. The old lady clearly wasn't a good traveller, but Kate's attempts to make her more comfortable had been shrugged aside with so little civility that, for most of the journey, Kate had ignored her.

Kate moved to help but the maidservant snapped, "Leave her be. I will take care of milady. I know just what needs to be done!" Scolding softly, she gently shepherded the old lady inside, the manservant assisting.

The chaise jerked as it moved off and Kate almost fell as she hastily scrambled out of it. She took a few wavering steps

Gallant Waif

but, to her horror, her head began to swim and she swirled into blackness.

The man watching from the window observed her fall impassively and waited uninterestedly for her to scramble to her feet. No doubt this was another blasted maid of his grandmother's. Jack took another drink.

Damned fool that he was, he'd clearly mishandled his sister, refusing to see her. He'd been heavily disguised at the time, of course. Even drunker than he was now. Good thing his grandmother hadn't asked to see him tonight. He'd have refused her too. Jack continued staring sourly out of the window, then leaned forward, intent. The small, crumpled figure remained motionless on the hard cold gravel.

What was wrong with the girl? Had she hurt herself? It was damned cold out there. Any more time on the damp ground and she'd take more than just a chill. Swearing, he moved away from the window and limped downstairs. There was no sign of anyone about. He heard the sound of voices upstairs—his grandmother was being tended to by the only available help. Jack strode into the night and bent awkwardly over the small, still figure.

''Are you all right?'' He laid his hand lightly on the cold cheek. She was unconscious. He had to get her out of the cold. Bending his stiff leg with difficulty, he scooped her against his chest. At least his arms still had their strength.

Good God! The girl weighed less than a bird. He cradled her more gently. Nothing but a bundle of bones!

Jack carried her into the sitting-room and laid her carefully on a settee. He lit a brace of candles and held them close to her face. She was pale and apparently lifeless. A faint, elusive fragrance hovered around her, clean and fresh. He laid a finger on her parted lips and waited. A soft flutter of warm breath caused his taut face to relax. His hands hovered over her, hesitating. What the deuce did you do with fainting females? His hands dropped. Ten to one she'd wake up and find him loosening her stays and set up some demented shrieking!

Jack went to the doorway. "Carlos!" No response. Dammit! He poured brandy into a glass and, slipping one arm around the girl, tipped a generous portion into her mouth. Instantly she came alive in his arms, coughing, hands flailing against him.

"Gently, gently," he said, irritated.

"What—?" Kate spluttered as he forced another mouthful of fiery golden liquid into her. She gasped as it burnt its way down her throat and glared indignantly at him.

"It's only brandy."

"Brandy!" She fought for breath.

"You needed something to bring you around."

"Bring me around?" Kate glanced round the strange room. She stared up at the shadowed face of the man who had an arm around her. Her pulse started to race. Blind panic gripped her and she tried to wrench herself away, to hit out against him. She was restrained by strong hands, gentle but implacable.

"You fainted outside." He held her a moment until she calmed slightly, then released her and stood back. "Mind you, if I'd known you were such a little wildcat I'd have thought twice about rescuing you from the cold, wet driveway and giving you my best brandy."

Kate stared blankly at him. Fainted? Rescue? Best brandy? She still felt decidedly peculiar. "I…I'm sorry… My nerves are a little jumpy these days…and I tend to overreact."

Especially when I awake to find myself in strange company, not knowing what has come before it. Her head was pounding. Had she fainted for just a few minutes, as he said, or would she find a gap in her memory of days or weeks, as she had once before? Her hand reached to touch the faint ridged scar at the base of her skull, then dropped to her lap. She glanced down and a wave of relief washed over her. She remembered putting on these clothes this morning…Lady Cahill…the long trip in the coach. It was all right. It wasn't like before…

But who was the man looming over her? She was aware of a black frown, a long, aquiline nose, a strong chin, and blue, blue eyes glinting in the candlelight. She blinked, mesmerised.

He shifted uncomfortably under her gaze and moved abruptly beyond the candleglow, his face suddenly hidden in shadows again.

"I…I really do beg your pardon," she said. "I didn't…I was confused." She tried to gather herself together. "It's just—"

"Are you ill?" His voice was very deep.

"No, I don't think so. It's just…it must be because I haven't eaten for several day—for several hours."

Jack frowned. The slip of the tongue was not lost on him.

Kate tried to sit up. Another wave of dizziness washed over her. Jack grasped her arm and thrust her firmly but gently back against the cushions. "Don't try to move," he ordered. "Just stay there. I'll return in a moment." He left the room.

Kate sat on the settee, one hand to her head. She felt weak and shaky. Brandy on such an empty stomach. She shook her head ruefully, then clasped it, moaning. She closed her eyes to stop the room from spinning around her.

"Here, this will make you feel better." The harsh deep voice jolted Kate out of her daze. She opened her eyes. Before her was a plate with a clumsily cut slice of bread and cold meat on it. It looked wonderful. She glanced quickly up at the man towering over her and smiled.

"Oh, thank you so much. It is very kind of you," she said, then added, blushing, "I'm afraid that brandy made me quite dizzy."

She applied herself carefully to her meal, forcing herself to eat with tiny bites, chewing slowly and delicately.

Jack watched her, still faintly dazzled by the sweetness of her smile. She was pretending uninterest in the food, he realised, even though she was starving. Well, who was he to quibble at pride? But she was certainly an enigma, with her pride and her shabby clothes.

''Who the devil are you?''

The sudden question jolted Kate out of the rapture of her first meal in days.

''My name is Kate Farleigh.'' She returned to the food.

''And who is Kate Farleigh when she's at home?''

Kate pondered as she chewed. Who was Kate Farleigh now? She was no longer the Reverend Mr Farleigh's daughter, nor Jeremy and Benjamin Farleigh's sister. She certainly wasn't Harry Lansdowne's betrothed any more. And she didn't even have a home.

''I don't suppose she's anyone at all,'' she replied in an attempt at lightness that failed dismally.

''Don't play games.'' The frown had returned to his face. ''Who are you and what are you doing here? I know you came with my grandmother.''

His grandmother? So this was the master of the house, Mr Jack Carstairs. His food was doing wonders for her spirits. She felt so much better. Kate almost smiled at his aggrieved tone. He obviously didn't want her here. Well, she hadn't asked to come.

''Oh, you mustn't blame me for that.'' She licked the last crumb delicately from her lips. ''It wasn't my choice to come, after all.''

''Why? What the deuce do you mean by that?'' He scowled, watching the movement of the pink tongue. ''What is your position in relation to my grandmother?''

What was her position? Kidnappee? Charity case? Spurious great-goddaughter? None of them would exactly delight a doting grandson. Besides, it would be very ungrateful of her to upset the man who'd fed her a delicious meal by calling his relative a kidnapper. Although the idea was very tempting.

"I'm not at all sure I can answer that. You will have to ask Lady Cahill." Kate got to her feet. "Thank you so much for your kind hospitality, sir. The meal was delicious and I was very hungry after my journey."

She took two steps towards the door, then faltered, belatedly realising she had nowhere to go. "Could you tell me, please, where I am to sleep?"

"How the deuce should I know?" he snapped. "I don't even know who you are, so why should I concern myself where you sleep?"

Rudeness obviously ran in the family, decided Kate. It mattered little. With a full stomach, she felt quite in charity with the whole world. She would find herself a bed without his assistance—having found billets all over Spain and Portugal she would be lacking indeed if she could not find a bed in one, not terribly large English country house.

"Very well, then, sir, I will bid you goodnight. Thank you once again for your hospit…" She paused, then corrected herself wryly, "For the food." She began to climb the stairs in a determined fashion. Halfway up, her knees buckled.

"Dammit!" Jack leapt stiffly towards the stairs and caught her against his chest as she fainted for the second time. He carried her into a nearby bedchamber and laid her gently on the bed. He stood looking down at her for a long moment. Who the devil was she?

In the soft light of a candle, he assessed her unconscious form. She was thin, far too thin. Clear delicate skin was stretched tightly over her cheekbones, leaving deep hollows beneath them. His gaze lingered where the neck of her shabby, too loose dress had slipped, revealing a smooth shoulder, hunched childlike against the chill of the night. Had he not chanced to be watching when she fainted, she would still be lying unconscious on the front driveway. It was an icy night. Doubtless she would not have survived.

He'd get no answers tonight. Best to tuck the girl up in bed and take himself off. He bent and removed her shoes, then stopped in perplexity. He was sure he should loosen her stays, but how to go about that with propriety? His mouth quirked. Propriety! It was quite improper enough for him to be in this girl's bedchamber. He shrugged and bent over the supine body, searching gingerly at her waist for stay laces. God, but the chit was thin! With relief he ascertained that she wore no stays, had no need of them, probably didn't even own any.

Carefully he covered her with warm blankets. She shifted restlessly and flung an arm outside the bedding. He bent again to cover it and as he did so her eyes opened. She blinked for a moment, then smiled sleepily and caressed his face with a cool, tender touch. "Night, Jemmy." Her eyelids fluttered closed.

Jack froze, his breath caught in his chest. Slowly he straightened. His hand crept up to his right cheek, to where she had touched him. As they had done a thousand times before, his fingers traced the path of the ugly scar.

He grimaced and left the room.

The thunder of galloping hooves woke Kate at dawn next morning. She stared around the strange room, gathering her thoughts. It was a large chamber. The once rich furnishings were faded, dusty and worn.

She sat up, surprised to find herself fully clad except for her shoes. How did she get here? She recalled some of the previous night, but some of it didn't make sense. It was a frightening, familiar feeling.

Kate could have sworn she saw her brother Jemmy last night. She vaguely remembered his poor, ravaged face look-

ing intently into hers. Only that could not be, for Jemmy lay
cold and deep in a field in Spain. Not here in Lady Cahill's
grandson's house. She got out of bed and walked to the window, shivering in the early morning chill.

The view was beautiful, bare and bleak. The ground glittered silver-gilt with sun-touched frost. Nothing moved, except for a few hardy birds twittering in the pale morning
sunlight. Immediately below her window was a stretch of
rough grass. A trail of hoof prints broke the silvery surface
of the frost.

Her eyes followed the trail and widened as she saw a
riderless horse galloping free, saddled, reins dangling around
its neck. It seemed to be heading towards a small forest of
oaks. It must have escaped its restraints. She could sympathise. She too would love to be out in that clear, crisp air,
galloping towards the forest, free and wild in the chill of
dawn. How she missed her little Spanish mare and her early
morning rides, that feeling of absolute exhilaration as the
wind streamed through her as if she were flying. Dawn was
the only time she could ride as fast and as wildly as she
liked. Her father was never an early riser.

Turning, Kate caught a glimpse of herself in the glass that
hung on one wall. She giggled. It looked as if she'd been
dragged through a haystack backwards. Wild brown curls
tumbled in every direction. *The veriest gypsy urchin*—how
many times had she been called that? Swiftly she pulled out
the remaining pins from her hair and redid it in her customary
simple style. She brushed down her clothes, pulling a wry
face at the wrinkles. She looked around for a pitcher of water
with which to wash, but there was nothing in sight.

Walking softly, so as not to disturb the sleeping household,
she left her room and went downstairs in search of the
kitchen. There was not a soul around. A house of this size
should surely have many servants up and about their duties
at this hour, in preparation for when their master woke.

The more she saw, the more Kate goggled with surprise. What kind of establishment had Lady Cahill brought her to? The floors were gritty underfoot. Dustballs drifted along skirting boards and under furniture. The furniture, no longer fashionable, was covered in a thick layer of dust. The early morning sunshine was barely able to penetrate the few grime-encrusted windows which were not shrouded by faded curtain drapery. She shuddered at the number of cobwebs she saw festooned across every corner—she loathed spiders. Everything spoke of neglect and abandonment, yet the house was, apparently, inhabited.

This shabby, dirty, rambling house did not at all fit in with the impression given to her by Lady Cahill's manner, clothes, and servants. It was her grandson's home. Why did he not command the same sort of elegant living his grandmother so obviously took for granted? Kate shrugged. The mystery would be solved sooner or later; in the meantime she needed hot water and something to eat.

Finally Kate discovered the kitchen. She looked around in disgust. The place was a pigsty. The floor hadn't been swept in weeks, there was no fire burning in the grate and cold ashes mingled with the detritus on the floor. The remains of past meals had been inadequately cleared away and piles of dirty dishes lay in the scullery.

It might be the oddest gentleman's establishment she'd ever had the doubtful privilege of visiting, but here was one way she could earn the large breakfast she planned to eat. Kate rolled up her sleeves and set to work. It was ironic, she thought, clearing the ashes from the grate and setting a new fire—the misdeeds of her youth had given her the one truly feminine skill she possessed.

The only time Reverend Farleigh had spoken to his hoydenish daughter had been when she'd misbehaved. Kate's crimes had been many and various: climbing trees; riding astride—bareback—hitting cricket balls through windows;

coming home in a straggle of mud with skinned knees, tangled hair and a string of illegal fish. Her father had soon learned it was not enough to confine his wild and errant daughter to her bedchamber—she simply climbed out of the window. He'd learned it was more effective to give her into the custody of the housekeeper, who'd set her to work, cleaning and cooking.

The youthful Kate had despised the work, but years later she'd become grateful for knowledge generally considered unnecessary and unbecoming to a girl of her class. It had proven invaluable. Most girls of her station in life would have recoiled with genteel disgust at the task she faced, but Kate's experiences in the Peninsula War had inured her to the horrors of filth and squalor.

This kitchen was nothing compared to some of the unspeakable hovels where she and her father and brothers had been billeted during Wellington's campaigns. In those hovels, the Vicar's impossible daughter had discovered an ability to create a clean and comfortable environment for her family, wherever they were. And had glowed in the knowledge that for once she, Kate, had been truly *needed*.

Her skills were needed here, too, she could see.

Almost an hour and a half later Kate looked around the room with some satisfaction. The kitchen now looked clean, though the floor could do with a good scrub. She'd washed, dried and put away all the crockery, glasses, pots and pans. She'd used sand, soap and water to scrub the table and benches. And she'd even taken her courage in both hands, tackling the worst spiderwebs and killing two spiders with a broom. A fire now burned merrily in the grate and a huge iron kettle steamed gently. She poured hot water into a bowl in the scullery and swiftly made her ablutions.

A rapid search of the provision shelves unearthed a dozen or so eggs. Kate checked them for freshness, putting them in a large bowl of water to see if they sank to the bottom. One floated; she tossed it out. A flitch of bacon she found hanging up in the cool room. And, joy of joys, a bag of coffee beans. Kate hugged them to her chest. It had been months since she had tasted coffee.

She roasted the beans over the fire, then used a mortar and pestle to crush them, inhaling the aroma delightedly as she did so. She mixed them with water and set it over the fire to heat. She sizzled some fat in a pan, then added two thick rashers of bacon and an egg.

The floor did need scrubbing, Kate decided. She would do it after breakfast. She went to the scullery to fetch a large can of water to heat. The largest can she could find was wedged under a shelf, stuck fast. She tugged and pulled and cursed under her breath, then the heavenly aromas of bacon, egg and coffee reached her nostrils. Oh, no! Her breakfast would be ruined! She raced into the kitchen and came to a sudden halt.

Lady Cahill's grandson sat at the table, his back and broad shoulders partly towards her. He was tucking into her breakfast with every evidence of enjoyment.

''What do you think you're doing?'' Kate gasped crossly.

He didn't stop eating. ''I'll have another two eggs and four rashers of bacon. And some more of that excellent coffee, if you would be so good.'' He lifted his empty cup without even turning to face her.

Kate stared in growing indignation.

''More coffee, girl, didn't you hear me?'' He snapped his fingers impatiently, still not bothering to turn around.

Arrogance obviously ran in the family too! ''There's only enough for one more cup,'' she said.

''That's all I want.'' He finished the last bite of bacon.

''Oh, is it, indeed?'' Kate said, pulling a face at his impervious back. The exquisite scent of the coffee had been tantalising her for long enough. She'd cleaned and washed his filthy kitchen. All morning her mouth had been watering in anticipation of bacon and eggs and coffee. And he'd just walked in and without so much as a by-your-leave had devoured the lot!

"There's only enough for me," she said. "You'll have to wait. I'll make a fresh pot in a few minutes."

He swung around to face her. "What the deuce do you mean—only enough for you?"

Jack was outraged. To his recollection, he'd never even heard a kitchen maid speak, let alone answer him back in such a damned impertinent manner. And yet who else would cook and scrub at this hour of the morning?

She stared defiantly back at him, hands on hips, cheeks flushed, soft pink lips pursed stubbornly. One hand moved possessively towards the coffee pot and her small chin jutted pugnaciously. She was a far cry from the pale, exhausted girl he'd met by candlelight the night before.

Despite his annoyance, his mouth twitched with amusement—there was a wide smear of soot reaching from her cheek to her temple. She stared him down like a small grubby duchess. Her eyes weren't grey, after all, but a sort of greeny-grey, quite unusual. He felt his breath catch for a moment as he stared into them, and then realised she was examining his own face just as intently. He stiffened, half turned away from her, keeping his scarred side to the wall, and unconsciously braced himself for her reaction.

She poured the last of the coffee into her own cup and proceeded to sip it, with every evidence of enjoyment.

Jack was flabbergasted. He was not used to being ignored—let alone by a dowdy little maidservant with a dirty face. And in his own kitchen! He opened his mouth to deliver a crashing reprimand, but she met his eye again and something held him back.

"I think I've earned it, don't you?" She gestured at the sparkling kitchen.

He frowned again. What else did kitchen maids do but clean and scrub? Did the chit expect to be thanked? Did she realise who she was addressing? He opened his mouth to inform her, then hesitated uncertainly, a novel sensation for Major Carstairs, late of the Coldstream Guards.

How the devil did one introduce oneself to a kitchen maid? Servants knew who one was, and acted accordingly. But this one didn't seem to know the rules. And somehow it just didn't seem right to roar at this pert little urchin when only a few hours before he had held her in his arms and felt just how frail she was. Despite her effrontery.

He cleared his throat. "Do you know who I am?"

"Lady Cahill's grandson, Mr Carstairs, I presume?"

He grunted.

Why had he mentioned it? Kate looked gravely at the tall dark man leaning back in his chair. He didn't look particularly out of place in the kitchen, sprawled at the large scrubbed table, his long booted legs crossed in front of him. He was very handsome, she realised. Maybe he felt it would not be appropriate to eat in here with her when they had not been properly introduced.

"Would you rather I brought your breakfast to another room? A breakfast parlour, perhaps?"

His scowl deepened. "I'll eat it here." Long brown fingers started to drum out an impatient tattoo on the wooden surface of the table.

"Please try to be patient. I'll finish my coffee, then cook enough bacon and eggs for both of us."

Jack stared at her, debating whether to dismiss her instantly or wait until she'd cooked the rest of his breakfast. The egg had been cooked just how he liked it, the bacon had been crisped to perfection and she did make the best coffee he'd tasted in months. But he was not some scrubby schoolboy, as she seemed to imagine—he was the master of the house!

Jack's lips twitched with reluctant amusement. His man-servant's cooking had, he perceived ruefully, seriously un-dermined his authority and his resolution. The men in his brigade would have boggled at his acceptance of this little chit's effrontery, but they had neither drunk her coffee nor looked into those speaking grey-green eyes. Nor had they carried her up a flight of stairs and felt the fragile bones and known she had been starving. He couldn't dismiss her—he could as soon rescue a half-drowned kitten then kick it.

She sat down opposite him at the kitchen table. He stiff-ened awkwardly as her gaze fixed on his face.

"So," she said, "it was you in my bedchamber last night."

His mouth tightened abruptly, his face dark with bitter cyn-icism. What was she going to accuse him of?

"When I woke up this morning I couldn't quite remember how I got to bed. I thought I remembered seeing Jemmy, but now that I see you, of course, that explains it."

Kate didn't notice the stiffening of his body and the way his eyes turned to flint.

"Jemmy caught a bayonet wound, too, in just the same place, only his became terribly infected. Yours has healed beautifully, hasn't it?"

She stood up, stretched luxuriously and smiled. "Isn't cof-fee wonderful? I feel like a new woman, so I'll forgive your barefaced breakfast piracy and cook some more for both of us."

He stared at her in stunned silence. Who the devil was this impertinent, shabby, amazingly self-possessed girl with the wide, lovely eyes? And how could she recognise a bayonet wound and, what was more, refer to his shattered cheek so calmly when every other blasted female who had laid eyes on it had shuddered in horror, or wept, or ostentatiously avoided looking at it? He had the evidence of his own mirror that it was not a pretty sight.

And, he thought, watching her slight body move competently around the kitchen, who the devil was this Jemmy she kept mentioning? Jemmy with the scars, who was not, apparently, out of place in her bedchamber!

They were just finishing the last bacon and eggs and coffee, when the outside door opened and in walked a dark, stockily built man. He took one comprehensive look at Kate and smiled, a dazzling white smile which lit his swarthy face.

"Señorita."

Kate smiled slightly and inclined her head.

He sniffed the air and let out a long, soulful sigh. "Ah, coffee."

Kate chuckled. "Would you care for a cup, sir?"

"The *señorita* is very kind." The white smile widened in the dark face and he bowed again.

Kate dimpled. "Then please be seated, sir, and I will fetch you a cup directly." She went to fetch the coffee pot.

The two men began to converse in Spanish. Kate slowly stiffened. Three years in Spain and Portugal had resulted in a certain amount of fluency in both languages. She could understand every word the men said. And she was not impressed.

"So, Major Jack, who is the little brown mouse with the pretty eyes, the terrible clothes and the dirty face?"

Kate peered at her reflection in a spoon, then scrubbed at her face with a clean dishcloth.

"Damned if I know, Carlos. Some servant of my grandmother's." His tone was indifferent, bored.

A chair scraped on the floor and footsteps came towards her. Kate bent over the pots, then jumped nervously as a warm hand touched her lightly on the shoulder. She turned quickly and found a pair of dark blue eyes regarding her from a great height, a glimmer of amusement in their depths. Did he find it amusing to give her a fright? Or had he noticed the clean face? She blushed.

"If you would be so good…" He waved her aside, bent, took a burning twig from the fire, lit a cheroot and returned to the table, limping heavily.

"Jumpy, isn't she, the little mouse?" said Carlos in Spanish.

Kate could almost feel the shrug of the broad shoulders.

"Skinny too."

"Probably hasn't had a square meal in a good few weeks," the deep voice agreed. "I don't know what my grandmother could want with such a little waif."

Kate flushed in mortification. Was it that obvious?

Carlos continued, "Pretty, though. Those eyes are beautiful. Needs some meat on her bones yet. Me, I like a woman to feel like a woman."

Jack Carstairs grunted. "You think too much about women."

"Ah, Major Jack, do not say so, you, with your fine handsome face and wicked blue eyes that all the ladies sigh over."

Jack's hand went unconsciously to the shattered cheek.

"Ah, Major Jack, that little scratch will never make you safe from the ladies' attentions. It will only—"

"Hold your tongue, Carlos," Jack snapped brusquely.

There was a short silence. Kate pushed some more sticks into the fire, her face rosy.

"Yes," Carlos continued, "that little bird is as flat as a board at the moment, but with some of your good solid English beef in her the curves will grow—oh, yes, they will grow most deliciously."

His soft laughter washed over Kate's rigid body. How dared they discuss her like that? She was no innocent, not any longer, but they did not know it.

No one who had travelled with an army could retain the total innocence of men that was so necessary for an unmarried English lady. Still, for most of that time she'd had the protection of her father and brothers and the broader protection of the soldiers who knew them. Kate had walked freely among the troops, tending wounds, writing letters to loved ones and doling out soup and cheerful greetings, secure in the knowledge that not one of them would offer her the sort of insult that she was now having to endure in the home of a so-called English gentleman! Even if it was in a foreign tongue.

Of course, given how she had left the Peninsula, she should be inured to this sort of insult by now—but these men knew nothing of that. And she was *not* inured to insult and never would be!

Carlos's voice penetrated her consciousness again. "And when those curves do grow, Major Jack, I will be there to worship them. I, Carlos Miguel Riviera."

"That's enough!" Jack's voice was suddenly harsh. "You'll do no such thing."

"Ah, Major Jack…" the other smiled with dawning comprehension "…you fancy the little mouse yourself, do you?"

"Not at all," snapped Jack furiously. "I have no interest in tumbling scrawny kitchen maids. But I won't have you sniffing around her. She's…she's my grandmother's servant and you're not to go near her, understand?"

The men of the Coldstream Guards all knew that particular tone and not one of them would have dreamed of answering back or disobeying. Carlos's hands rose in a placatory fashion. "No, no, of course not, Major Jack. I will have nothing to do with the girl, nothing, I promise you." His voice was soothing, conciliatory, then his evil genius prompted him to add, "She is all yours, Major Jack, all yours."

Jack sat up and glared at Carlos, but a clatter from the other end of the kitchen distracted him. Both men turned to look at Kate.

The small body was rigid with fury, the grey-green eyes

blazing tempestuously. "Your coffee, *gentlemen*." She emphasised the last word sarcastically, then, to both men's utter amazement, she lifted the coffee pot and hurled it straight at them.

Chapter Three

Reactions honed by years of fighting sent both men instantly diving out of the way, but nothing could save them from being splattered with hot coffee as the earthenware pot shattered against the wall behind them. They cursed and swore in a fluent mixture of Spanish, Portuguese and English and turned to face the source of their anger. But there was no one to be seen. Kate had not waited to see the results of her action, but had stormed out of the kitchen while they were still ducking for cover.

"Blast the wench!" Jack growled. "What the hell's the matter with her? Damned coffee all over me." He pulled off his shirt, now sodden with brown coffee, and used it to mop down his dripping face and chest.

Carlos, similarly engaged with the aid of a drying cloth, looked across at him. "You think, Major Jack, that maybe she understand what we were saying?"

Jack stared at him. "An English kitchen maid, in the middle of Leicestershire, understand Spanish?" His tone was incredulous. "Impossible! Though she did clean that soot off her face."

He absent-mindedly rubbed the shirt over his arms and chest, then shook his head. "No. Ridiculous. She's English."

He stood up and roughly towelled the remains of the coffee from his unruly black hair.

"Unless she has Spanish blood in her." He considered her clear, pale skin, the grey-green eyes and the curly, nut-brown hair, then he shook his head again. "Hasn't got the colouring for it."

Carlos shrugged. "Then why?" His hands spread out eloquently, indicating the devastated coffee pot.

"How the hell should I know why?" Jack growled. "The chit ought to be in Bedlam for all I know. Damn her, but she'll not get away with it this time!"

"This time?" queried Carlos, the beginnings of a grin appearing on his broad face. "Do you say, Major Jack, that the little mouse has crossed you before?"

A pair of icy-blue eyes turned on him. "Clean up this mess at once," snapped the crisp voice so familiar to the men of the Coldstreams.

"*Sí, sí.* At once, Major Jack, at once." Carlos bent to the task instantly as Jack strode from the room with a frown like a black thundercloud on his face.

"Oho, little mouse, you've roused the lion in him, to be sure," Carlos muttered. "I hope you've hidden yourself safe away, for Major Jack is greatly to be feared when he has the devil in him."

Jack entered the hallway and glanced swiftly around. No sign of the chit. His hands clenched into fists. He'd give the little hussy a good shaking before he sent her packing! The chill morning air quivered against his bare skin, and with a muttered curse he moved quickly up the stairs towards his room, favouring his stiff leg quite heavily. Turning the corner on the landing, he ran smack into Kate storming along the corridor. They collided with such force he had to grab her to steady himself.

Kate, too, reached out instinctively and found herself clasped against a broad, strong, very naked male torso. His chest was deep and lightly sprinkled with dark hair, his shoulders broad and powerfully muscled. His skin was warm and smooth and his scent, the scent of a powerful male, surrounded her, filling her awareness.

"Oh!" she gasped, and tried to pull away.

"Not so fast, my girl!" he grated. "How dare you toss that thing at us? You could have caused a serious injury."

"Nonsense," she scoffed, tugging at his grip, "I've played cricket for years—I'm an excellent shot and I aimed to miss."

"Cricket? Rubbish! Girls don't play cricket. You need a lesson in behaviour, young woman!"

"Let go of me," she spat, struggling in his arms. "How dare you?" She wriggled and writhed, but he held her effortlessly. It was no use trying to fight him, she realised; the big brute was far too strong. He chuckled, a low rumbling from deep inside his chest.

"If you keep wriggling against me like that, little spitfire, I just might begin to enjoy this," he murmured into her ear.

Kate froze. The wretch was seeking to put her to the blush—she would have to use other tactics.

"Ohh, ohh, you're hurting me...ohh..." She sighed dramatically and sagged abruptly in his arms.

"Bloody hell!" he muttered.

Kate felt the hard grip on her arms instantly gentle.

"Hell and damnation," he muttered again. The girl was so small and frail. And he had caused her to faint. A wave of remorse passed over him. He felt a brute, a savage. He'd known she was half starved. There was no need to frighten her to death, even if she had hurled a pot of hot coffee at his head. He'd have to carry her to her room, he supposed. His grip shifted and he bent to swing her into his arms.

Instantly Kate moved. In a flash she escaped his arms and dealt him a smart slap across the face. "Brains before brute force every time!'' she flashed, and took to her heels down the corridor.

As she reached her room, she turned. ''And girls do play cricket!'' She slammed the door behind her, turned the key and leant against it panting, laughing, oddly exhilarated.

He stared after her, frustrated, cursing her in English and Spanish. Then he turned and limped as quickly as he could towards his grandmother's room, his face black as thunder.

''Grandmama!'' He burst into her room. ''Who the devil is that…that little hell-cat?''

The beady blue eyes examined her grandson's face closely. He was in a fierce temper—it was positively blazing from his eyes. Splendid! Lady Cahill thought. No sign of the lack-lustre absence of spirit that Amelia spoke of. Something, or rather someone, by the sounds of it, had stirred him up beautifully. And his loving grandmother would continue the process.

She glared at him. ''What the devil do *you* mean, sir, to come storming into my boudoir at this time of day, cursing and swearing and raising your voice?'' The blue eyes were frosty with displeasure. ''In *my* day, no gentleman would dream of entering a lady's presence in such indecent attire, or should I say lack of it? Be off with you, boy, and don't return until you are properly clothed! I am shocked and appalled, Jack, shocked and appalled!'' She turned her head from his naked chest in a pained, offended manner.

Jack opened his mouth, then shut it with a snap. Blast it, he could hardly give her a piece of his mind. She was his grandmother, dammit. He glared at her, fully aware of her game. She was the most outrageous old lady he knew—he would bet his last guinea that she was no more shocked at seeing a man without a shirt than he was. And as for his swearing…the old hypocrite, peppering almost every phrase she uttered with oaths, then pretending to blush at his! He was damned if he'd stay and let his grandmother rake him over the coals for the entertainment of herself and her dresser! Jack bowed ironically and left the room.

He slammed the door and Lady Cahill relaxed back against the pillows, grinning in a most unladylike way.

"Oh, how shocking, milady," said the hovering woman dressed severely in grey.

"Oh, don't be such a ninny, Smithers. You've seen a man without his shirt before, haven't you?" Lady Cahill cast a quick glance at her poker-faced maid. "Well, perhaps not. It'll widen your education in that case."

"Milady!" said Smithers indignantly.

"Oh, fetch me my wrap," said the old lady. "I'm getting up."

"Before eleven!" gasped Smithers.

Lady Cahill regarded the shocked face of her maid in amusement. "Perhaps not," she decided. "You can fetch that child I brought with me. Ask her to come and take hot chocolate with me here, if such a thing can be found in this benighted place."

Her maid stiffened in displeasure. "That…that shabby young person, milady?"

The old lady's voice turned to ice. "That 'shabby young person', as you refer to her, is the daughter of my beloved goddaughter, Maria Farleigh, and as such, Smithers, is to be treated as my honoured guest. Do you understand?"

The woman curtseyed. "Yes, milady," she murmured humbly.

Kate stiffened at the knock on her door. She hunched her shoulder away from it and remained curled up on the bed. The knock sounded again. "Go away!" she said.

There was a short silence.

"Miss?" The voice was unmistakably female. Kate slipped off the bed and ran to the door. The disapproving face of Smithers met her eye. "Lady Cahill invites you to join her in her bedchamber to take chocolate." The cold, pale eyes ran quickly over Kate's shabby outfit and the long nose twitched almost imperceptibly in disdain.

Kate's chin rose. "Have you prepared the chocolate?" she asked bluntly.

The stare grew contemptuous. "I am her ladyship's dresser, not the cook. I will direct Mr Carstairs's man to arrange for the cook to prepare it immediately." The cold stare informed Kate that even a guttersnipe would know better than to expect an important personage like Lady Cahill's dresser to lower herself with the preparation of foodstuffs.

Kate repressed a grin and took two steps in the direction indicated by Smithers. She would have liked to see this woman's face when she realised there was no one to prepare breakfast for herself or Lady Cahill. Then a stab of compunction halted her. Lady Cahill was an elderly lady who had been exhausted by her journey into the country. And Kate knew that she had eaten nothing at all during the trip.

"Please inform Lady Cahill that I will join her directly. I will see to her ladyship's breakfast first."

The eyebrows rose in displeasure. The prim mouth opened. "But her ladyship gave me the clearest instructions—"

"If you would be so good as to convey my message to Lady Cahill," Kate interrupted in a cool voice which, despite its soft huskiness, left no room for argument.

"Very good, miss." The woman sniffed disparagingly, but left without argument, hiding her surprise. Despite her hideous clothing, this girl had some breeding in her.

Kate ran downstairs, keeping a wary eye open for the two men, but they were nowhere to be seen. In the kitchen she quickly built up the fire and set the kettle to boil. There was no chocolate to be had. She surveyed the barren storeroom ruefully and shrugged. She'd just have to do the best she could.

She found a large tray and set it with a cloth. In a few minutes it bore crockery, a pot of tea, two soft boiled eggs and some lightly buttered toast. It was not what Lady Cahill was used to, no doubt, but it would have to do. She carried the heavy tray upstairs.

"Ah, my dear," said Lady Cahill. "But what are you doing carrying that heavy tray, you foolish child? Get one of the servants to do that for you."

Kate deftly set the tray down on a table beside Lady Cahill's bed. "Good morning, ma'am," she said cheerfully. "I trust you slept well."

The old lady grimaced. "In this bed? My dear, how could I?" She gestured towards the shabby hangings and worn furniture. "I suppose I must be grateful that I have a chamber at all, since my dear grandson refused even to see his sister. Thank heavens Smithers had the forethought to pack bedding. I don't know what sort of place my grandson is running here, but I can tell you—I intend to have words with him on the subject."

The old lady twinkled beadily at her and Kate found herself smiling back. She poured the tea.

"Tea?" said the old lady pettishly. "I told Smithers chocolate."

"I fear there is none to be had in the house."

"No chocolate?" said the old lady incredulously. "I know the countryside is uncivilised, but this is ridiculous." She pouted. "I suppose there are no fresh pastries either?"

Kate shook her head. "No, indeed, ma'am. But I did get you some freshly boiled eggs and a little toast. Here, eat it while it is still hot," she coaxed.

Ignoring the old woman's *moue* of distaste, Kate placed the food before her. After some grumbling, Lady Cahill consumed the repast, pretending all the while that she was only doing it to please Kate. Finally she sat back against her pillows and regarded Kate speculatively. "Now, missy," she said. "I gather you've met my grandson."

"What did he say about me?" Kate asked warily.

The old lady chuckled. "Nothing much, really."

"Oh," said Kate. Clearly Lady Cahill did not intend to enlighten her. "He...he doesn't know who I am, does he, ma'am?"

The old lady noted with interest the faint colour that rose on Kate's cheeks. "Didn't he ask you?"

Kate looked slightly embarrassed. "No...I mean, yes, he asked me, and of course I told him my name. But I don't think he understands my position."

"What did you tell him?"

Kate looked uncomfortable. "I told him to ask you." She was annoyed to find that her voice had taken on a faintly defensive tone and added boldly, "Indeed, ma'am, I could not answer him, having been kidnapped! I do not know why you have brought me to this place or what you intend me to do."

Lady Cahill acknowledged her point with a slow nod. "Truth to tell, child, I had no clear intention at the time, except to get you away from that dreadful cottage and prevent you from ruining your life."

"Ruining my life? How so, ma'am?"

"Tush, girl. Don't poker up like that! Once you'd been in service that would have been the end of any possibility for an eligible alliance."

"An eligible alliance!" Kate spoke in tones of loathing.

"Yes, indeed, miss!" snapped Lady Cahill. "You're not on the shelf yet. You have good blood, good bones and you have no business giving up on life in such a stubborn fashion!"

"Giving up on life? I'm not giving up on life. I am endeavouring to make my way in it. And I fully intend to do so—in the way *I* choose to do it!"

Kate jumped up from her seat at the end of the bed and began to pace around the room. It was vital that she get Lady Cahill to understand. It was simply not possible for Kate to make an eligible alliance any longer. She was ruined and, even if she attempted to hide the fact, it must come out eventually. But she had no desire to explain the whole sordid tale to this autocratic old lady whose sharp tongue hid a kind heart. It was cowardly, she knew, but if she could retain this old lady's respect, even by false means, she would. She must convince her some other way.

"I know you mean well by your charity, but I cannot bring myself to accept it. I have been too long accustomed to running my father's household, and have had responsibilities far in excess of other girls of my age and station."

"Charity be damned!" snapped Lady Cahill.

"Ma'am, just look at me. Look at my clothes. You say you wish me to live with you as your guest, to take me into society. Can you see me paying morning visits and attending balls in this?" She gestured angrily at her shabby garments.

Lady Cahill stared at her incredulously. "Well, of course not, you ridiculous child! I wouldn't dress my lowest skivvy in those rags." She leant back in the bed, shaking her head at the folly of the girl. "Naturally I will provide you with all that you will need—dresses, gowns, gloves, hats, parasols, trinkets—all the fal-lals that you could wish for. "

"Exactly, ma'am. I would have to ask you for each little thing, and that I could not bear."

"Ah, bah!" snorted Lady Cahill.

"Besides, ma'am, I have no social skills to speak of. You seem to have overlooked the fact of my upbringing. I have no musical skills, I have never learnt to paint watercolours, I can patch and darn anything, and have even sewn up wounds, but I cannot do fancy embroidery. I can dance, but I do not know how to chat of nothing day in and day out. I have worked for most of my life, ma'am, and that is what I do best. I simply do not have it in me to act the social butterfly and that is what you want me to do."

Oh, Lord, Kate prayed, let me not have to tell her the truth.

Her arguments were valid enough; it would be difficult for
Kate to accept charity—that was true. She knew herself to
be overly stiff-necked about such things. But to attend routs
and balls, to learn her way in society, to bury herself in frivolity for a time—a foolish part of Kate longed for those
very things.

Lady Cahill stared, utterly appalled. "Child, child, you
have no idea what you are saying. Most of those things are
not necessary and the others you can learn. Entering society
does not mean becoming a social butterfly and chatting of
nothing—though, I grant you, a great many people do little
else. But there are fools in every stratum of society."

She fell silent for a moment, then waved her hand at the
girl sitting so silently at the end of the bed. "You fatigue
me, child, with your foolish intractability. I must give this
matter further consideration. Leave me now. We will talk of
this further."

Kate rose, feeling a trifle guilty for causing the old lady
distress. It was not her fault, she told herself defensively. She
had not asked to be brought here. She had the right to make
decisions for her own life and she owed Lady Cahill nothing
except politeness. So why did she feel that she was in the
wrong? Was it wrong to wish to owe nothing to anybody?
Was it wrong to want to earn her own money, to refuse
dependence on others? No, it wasn't wrong…it just felt
wrong when she had to refuse an old lady's kindness, she
reluctantly acknowledged.

She picked up the breakfast tray and left, closing the door
softly behind her. A door ahead of her opened and Jack Carstairs appeared in the hall. Kate halted abruptly. He was between her and the stairs. She could flee to her own room,
return to Lady Cahill's bedchamber or face him out.

Folding his arms, Jack leaned against the wall and awaited
her arrival, a sardonic look on his face.

Kate's chin rose stubbornly. She would not be intimidated

by mere brute force! Even if he was over six feet and with shoulders as wide as…well, as wide as any shoulders had a right to be. But she wasn't nervous of him. Certainly not! She gripped the heavy tray more tightly in her hands, taking obscure comfort in the fact that it was between them, and walked forward, her head high.

A faint glimmer of amusement appeared in Jack's eyes. She was calling his bluff, was she? After tossing that coffee pot, she had a right to expect that he might want to throttle her. And then she'd slapped him—slapped the master of the house. So foolhardy. He could snap her in two if he chose; she would surely know that. She wasn't to know he'd never hurt a woman in his life. But did she quail? No, on she came, chin held defiantly high. His amusement deepened. Such a little creature, but with so much spirit.

Even if she didn't fear violence from him, after that outrageous act of hers in the kitchen, she must surely expect to be dismissed without a character. It was, he knew, a servant's biggest dread, for it meant they were unlikely ever to gain employment again. She must know that. Her dreadful shabby black clothes, clearly made for another woman and adapted to her thin frame, showed she was well acquainted with poverty. And starvation was obviously a recent experience.

But her precarious position hadn't stopped her hurling that pot of hot coffee straight at his head. Or over his head, as she claimed. Cricket, indeed! He almost snorted. But why had she thrown it in the first place? Unlikely though it seemed, perhaps this little English kitchen maid did speak Spanish. Jack decided to test the theory. He remained leaning casually against the wall, watching her.

Kate swept past him, apparently indifferently, though her heart was beating rather faster than usual. She reached the steps, and he said in Spanish, "*Señorita*, there is an enormous black spider caught in your hair. Allow me to remove it for you."

He waited for her to turn around, to scream, to start tearing at her hair or to continue, ignorant of what he had said.

She simply froze. Jack waited for a moment, puzzled, and then strode towards her. *"Señorita?"*

She did not move. Jack touched her shoulder. Good God! The girl was shaking like a leaf. He could hear the crockery on the tea tray rattling faintly.

Swiftly he turned her around to face him and was appalled to see naked terror in her eyes. Her face was dead white and the clear smooth forehead was beginning to bead with perspiration. She was swallowing convulsively. Through dry, pale lips she whispered piteously, "Please get it off me."

Jack stared at her for a few seconds, stunned by the unexpected intensity of her reaction.

"Please," she whispered again, shuddering under his hands.

"My poor girl. I'm so sorry," he said remorsefully. "There is no spider. None at all."

He took the tray from her unresisting hands and laid it on a nearby table, not taking his eyes off her.

She stared at him, uncomprehending. He placed his hands on her shoulders again and gave her a tiny shake to jolt her out of her trance-like terror.

"There is no spider. I made it up," he explained apologetically. "It was a trick."

Her mouth opened and she started to breathe again in deep, agonised gasps.

"I'm sorry," he repeated. "I wanted to see if you understood Spanish."

She looked up at him in confusion, her mind still numbed by the remnants of her uncontrollable fear of spiders.

"I spoke in Spanish, you see." His hands rested warmly on her shoulders. She was still trembling and, despite himself, he was moved. Not knowing what else to do to atone, he drew her against him, wrapped her in his arms and held her tight against him, uttering soothing noises in her ear. He inhaled slowly. What was that fragrance she wore? It was hauntingly familiar. His arms tightened.

It did not occur to him that it was utterly inappropriate for him to be behaving in this way with a mere kitchen maid. As a boy, Jack had frequently brought home creatures in distress—half-drowned kittens, injured birds—and if he had thought of it now he would have explained to anyone who asked that he was merely offering comfort and reassurance. And she felt so right just where she was.

Kate's cheek was pressed against his chest, her head tucked in the hollow between his chin and his throat. She could feel the warmth of his breath, the roughness of his unshaven cheek catching in the silk of her hair as he moved his face gently against it. She heard the steady thud of his heart. His strong body cradled hers, protecting, calming.

It had been so long since Kate had been held so comfortingly, the impulse just to let herself be held was irresistible. She felt his broad, strong hand moving soothingly up and down her spine and a shiver of awareness passed through her.

Gradually, Kate realised just who was holding her and why. She tried to wriggle out of the strong arms. He did not immediately release her, so with all the strength she possessed she thrust hard at his chest and emerged from his embrace dishevelled and panting, her face rosy with embarrassment.

''I suppose this is another one of your tricks!'' She tried to smooth her hair and brushed down her clothes.

Jack felt his guilt intensify at her words and, unreasonably, anger flooded him.

''No, it damn well isn't, you little shrew! I'm not in the habit of entertaining myself with scruffy kitchen maids. I was merely offering comfort.''

She glared at him, not knowing which made her angrier, his actions of the past few minutes or his description of her.

"Well, I don't need your sort of comfort and I wouldn't have needed comforting in the first place if you hadn't played that beastly trick on me!"

"How was I to know you'd make such a devilish to-do about a spider?"

Kate's temper died abruptly and she looked away. She had always been deeply ashamed of her fear of spiders and had tried valiantly to conquer it, to no avail. Her brain might tell her that the horrid creatures were small and for the most part harmless, but the moment she was confronted with one she panicked. It was a weakness in herself she despised.

"You're right," she muttered stiffly. "I'm sorry I made such a fuss. It won't happen again." She turned to pick up the tray.

"Not so fast, my girl," he said, and his hand shot out to grip her wrist. He turned her to face him again. "Who the devil are you?" he said slowly, his eyes boring into her.

"I told you my name last night. It is Kate Farleigh, in case you have forgotten," she retorted, twisting her arm to escape his grip. "Will you please release my hand?"

"I haven't finished with you yet."

Kate pursed her lips in annoyance. "I suppose you think your position entitles you to make game of others!"

"What?" He frowned down at her in puzzlement.

"Evidently you consider you're perfectly entitled to treat those less fortunate than yourself in any fashion you care to! Well, I take leave to dispute you on that. No matter who I am, I have the right to go about my concerns as I see fit, without interference from you or any other member of your family!" Kate looked pointedly down at her wrist, imprisoned by his large strong hand.

He noted the short, blunt, unpolished nails, so different from the smooth, polished ovals on every lady of his acquaintance. He turned her hand over and his large thumb moved gently back and forth over the work-roughened skin. There was no doubt that this girl was accustomed to menial work, but she was an enigma all the same.

"You are the damnedest kitchen maid!" he murmured at last, shaking his head. "How the devil did you come to be brought here by my grandmother?"

Kate looked up at him in surprise. The dark head was still frowning over her hand. She repressed a rueful grin. She supposed she couldn't blame him for that. She was surely dressed for the part and he had seen her working in the kitchen, obviously at home. Well, if the master of the house insisted on calling Kate a kitchen maid, Kate would oblige him—and serve him right! She had an imaginary spider to pay him back for, after all!

"Sir." She tugged at her hand.

His thumb still absently caressed her.

"I must get back to my duties, sir. The kitchen floor needs scrubbing." She tried to pull her hand free again, becoming increasingly unsettled by the gentle motion of his thumb on her skin.

"But where on earth did you learn to speak like a lady?"

Oh, drat the man! Would he never leave off? Kate's sense of humour got the best of her. "A lady, sir?" She goggled in mock-surprise, and did her best to simper. "I never thought I sounded like a real lady." She pronounced it "loidy".

"I kept house for an old gentleman for a long time and he insisted I learn to speak proper-like. He was a true scholar, sir, and a Reverend he was, too, and he hated what he called the mangling of the English language."

He did not appear to notice that her accent had broadened considerably during this speech, a fact which Kate found immensely encouraging. She twisted her hands awkwardly, as she imagined a rustic wench would, when confronted by a handsome gentleman.

"He taught me to read and write and cipher an' all," she added ingenuously, regarding him with wide, innocent eyes—which she was tempted for a moment to cross, but didn't.

"But you understand Spanish," Jack persisted. "Where does a kitchen maid come to know a foreign tongue like that?"

"I imagine there are hundreds of kitchen maids in Spain," she responded pertly, her eyes downcast to hide the mischief in them.

"Don't be impertinent, girl; you know perfectly well I was asking how an English kitchen maid like you came to know Spanish. It's obvious to me that you have no Spanish blood."

She beamed up at him foolishly. "You're absolutely right, sir—no Spanish blood at all. You are a clever gentleman. Coo, so you are."

The chit was playing games with him again! He was hard put to it not to laugh—except that he had an equally strong impulse to turn her over his knee. How on earth had this cheeky little miss survived this long without being strangled, let alone kept a position in a household? He couldn't imagine his grandmother putting up with this type of cheek from a maidservant. His mouth quirked in some amusement. His grandmother would not take kindly to competition in the art of impertinence and this little baggage was every bit her equal.

"Enough of your sauce, girl. I asked you how an English maid came to understand Spanish."

"Oh, the gentleman did a lot of foreign travel and it were easier for him to take me than leave me behind, so a'course I was bound to pick up some of the lingo, wasn't I? Will that be all, sir?" she asked humbly, her head bent to hide her laughter.

She could see perfectly well that she hadn't satisfied his curiosity, and that he didn't like it. He was used to being in control. Well, he wasn't going to control her. He'd be furious when he found out who she really was, but it served him right for jumping to conclusions. And for the spider.

"Hmm. Yes, all right," he mumbled ungraciously.

Kate bobbed him the sort of rustic curtsey her old nurse used to make to her father, and picked up the tray. She stepped lightly down the stairs, her mouth trembling on the verge of laughter as she imagined his face when his grandmother finally explained who she was.

Jack watched her slight figure disappear, then turned and knocked at his grandmother's door.

Chapter Four

"**W**here the devil did you find that girl, Grandmama?" he demanded on entry.

His grandmother regarded him coolly. "I am very well, Jack, thank you for asking."

"Dammit, Grandmama…" he began, then, noting the light of battle in the beady blue eyes, decided it would be politic to capitulate. His grandmother, Jack knew from long experience, was quite capable of parrying his questions all day. Curse it, he sighed, what had he done to be plagued with such females? Only a few days ago, life had been so peaceful.

He sat himself down on the edge of her bed, his stiff leg out before him, ignoring the strangled gasp of horror from his grandmother's maid at the impropriety.

"Oh, get out, Smithers, get out if you cannot stomach the sight of a man seated on my bed!" snapped Lady Cahill. She waited until the maid removed herself, after having favoured her mistress with a look of deep reproof.

"Stupid woman!" muttered the old lady. "But she's worth her weight in gold at *la toilette*. Makes an old woman like me look less of an old hag."

Jack smiled, his good humour restored. "Old hag, indeed! What a shocking untruth, Grandmama. As if you haven't remained an acknowledged beauty all your life. You've clearly recovered from the ordeal of the journey, for I must tell you that you are in great looks, positively blooming in fact.''

"Oh, pish tush!" said his grandmother in delight. "You're a wicked boy and I know perfectly well that you're only trying to turn me up sweet."

Jack's lips twitched, as he recalled the time his grandmother had read his sister a blistering lecture for using exactly that piece of slang. "Turn you up sweet, indeed?" he quizzed her. "Good God, Grandmama. What a vulgar expression. I'm shocked!"

"Don't criticise your elders and betters, young man," she retorted, her twinkling eyes revealing she was fully aware of her inconsistency. "Now, what's all this I've heard about you falling into the megrims? It's not like you, Jack, and I won't have it!"

Jack took a deep breath, struggling to overcome the surge of annoyance that rose within him at her blunt statement. "As you see, Grandmama," he responded lightly, "your sources have misinformed you. I'm in the pink of health despite being a cripple."

Lady Cahill frowned at him. "You're no more a cripple than I am," she snapped. "What's a stiff leg? Your grandfather had one for years as a result of a hunting accident and it never stopped him from doing anything he wanted to."

"As I recall, ma'am, my grandfather was still able to ride to hounds until shortly before his death."

A short silence fell. Lady Cahill considered the cruel irony of her grandson's injury. A noted rider to hounds until his injury, Jack had received as his only inheritance a house in one of the most famous hunting shires in the country. Now, when he was unable even to sit a horse.

Jack stood up awkwardly. He still found it hard to face discussion of his wounds. "Can one enquire as to what brought you to my humble home?'' he asked, changing the subject.

"You may well ask that," she said crossly.

"Yes, I just did," he murmured irrepressibly.

"Don't be cheeky, boy! I came to find out what was happening to you. Now, tell me, sir, what did you mean by denying your own sister hospitality?"

"Grandmama, you can see for yourself that this place is not yet fit to receive guests... Besides, I was castaway at the time. I do regret it, but I've had enough of women weeping and sighing over my...my disfigurement," he finished stiffly.

"Disfigurement, my foot!" She snorted inelegantly. Her eyes wandered to the scar on his right cheek. "If you are referring to that little scratch on your face, well, you were always far too good-looking for your own good. You look a great deal more manly now, not so much of a pretty boy."

He bowed ironically. "I thank you, ma'am."

"Oh, tush!" she said. "I think I will get up now, so take yourself off and get one of those lazy servants of yours to bring me up some hot water."

"I regret it, ma'am, but I cannot."

"What do you mean, boy?"

He shrugged indifferently. "I don't employ any indoor servants."

Lady Cahill sat up in bed, deeply shocked. "What? No servants?" she gasped. "Impossible! You must have servants!"

"I have no interest in the house. I've bivouacked in enough dam—dashed uncomfortable places in the last few years and now it's enough for me to have a roof over my head and a bed to sleep in. I have no intention of forking out a small fortune for a horde of indoor servants, merely to see to my comfort, even if I had a small fortune to fork out, which as you know I do not."

Lady Cahill was appalled. "*No* indoor servants?"

He shrugged again. "None but my man, Carlos, and he sees to my horses as well." He held up his hand, forestalling any further comment from her. "There are only those servants you brought with you yourself. I'm afraid you'll have to get them to wait on you. Only I sent them to stay in the village at the inn—all except for your dresser and maid. They can see to your needs as best they can."

Lady Cahill snorted. "You won't see Smithers demeaning herself by heating water."

He shrugged. "Get your other maid to do it. She seems capable enough."

"What other maid? What are you talking about, boy?"

Jack sighed. "Grandmama, don't you think it's time you stopped calling me 'boy'? I am past thirty, you know."

"Don't be ridiculous, boy! And stop changing the subject. What other maid are you talking about?"

"The little thin creature in the dreadful black clothes. I must say, Grandmama, that I am surprised that you haven't noticed them. You're usually so fastidious about your servants' appearance. And how is it—" his voice deepened with indignation "—that you allowed the girl to almost starve herself to death? She swooned last night in the driveway and there was no one to assist her."

"Swooned?" said Lady Cahill, watching him narrowly.

"Fell down in a dead faint. From hunger, unless I miss my guess. She's nothing but skin and bones, with the most enormous eyes. Pale skin, curly brown hair, looks as if a breeze would blow right through her, a tongue on her like a wasp but, apparently, scared stiff of spiders."

Jack halted, suddenly aware that he had said far too much. He knew from past experience that his grandmother could add two and two and come up with five.

"Frightened of spiders, is she? That surprises me. I wouldn't have said that that young woman was afraid of much at all. I would've said she has a deal of courage. But she's not my maid,'' Lady Cahill added finally. ''Is that what she told you?''

Jack frowned. ''No,'' he said slowly, thinking back. ''I suppose I rather jumped to that conclusion.'' His eyes narrowed, recalling Kate's performance of a few minutes ago. ''If she isn't your maid, who is she?''

''Her name is Kate Farleigh.''

''I know that, ma'am. She did inform me of that. But what is she doing here?'' Jack hung on to his patience.

His grandmother shrugged vaguely. ''Now, how should I know what she is doing, Jack? You know perfectly well I haven't left this room since I arrived last night. She could be picking flowers or taking tea. How the deuce should I know what she is doing, silly boy?''

Jack gritted his teeth. ''Grandmama, why has this girl come to my house?''

The old lady smiled guilelessly up at him. ''Oh, well, as to that, dear boy, she had no choice. No choice at all.''

''Grandmother!'' Jack's lips thinned.

''Now don't get tetchy with me, boy; it doesn't work. Your grandfather used to rant and rave at me all the time.''

''I fully understand why, and heartily sympathise with him!'' her undutiful grandson snapped. ''Now enough of this nonsense, Grandmama. Who is she?''

''Her name is Kate Farleigh and she is the only daughter of my goddaughter, the late Maria Farleigh, *née* Delacombe.'' In a few pithy sentences, Lady Cahill put Jack in possession of the bare bones of Kate's story, as she knew it.

He frowned. ''Then she is a lady.''

''Of course.''

''Well, she doesn't behave like one.''

''I saw no sign of any lack of breeding,'' said his grandmother. ''A temper, yes. Glared at me out of those big blue eyes of hers—''

''Not blue. A sort of grey-green.''

The old woman repressed a grin. So he had noticed the colour of her eyes, had he? "Whatever you say," she agreed. "The gel glared at me, but there was no sign of panic—stayed as cool as you please as I whisked her off to heaven-knew-where."

His eyebrows rose at this. "What do you mean, you whisked her off?"

"Oh, don't look like that, Jack. It was the only possible thing. You said yourself the girl was on the verge of starvation. She was in dire straits. She is an orphan with no blood kin to turn to and has not a penny left in the world, unless I miss my guess."

Jack frowned, stretching his bad leg reflectively. "I still don't understand."

"The girl has far more than her share of stubborn foolish pride. Just like her dratted father in that respect. Maria's family wanted to make a huge settlement on her when she married him, Maria being their only child, but he would have none of it. Didn't want it to be thought he was marrying her for her money. And look what has come of it! His own daughter dressed in rags and almost starving! Faugh! I have no patience with the man!"

"But Kate…er…Miss Farleigh, Grandmama," he prompted.

"Said she wasn't interested in taking charity from me or anyone else. Well, I had no time to stand around bandying words with her in her poky little hovel. So I kidnapped her."

"You *what*?" Jack stared at his grandmother in amazement. Truly, she was an outrageous old lady. His lips twitched and suddenly he couldn't help himself; the chuckles welled up from somewhere deep inside him. He collapsed on the bed and laughed till his sides hurt.

His grandmother watched him, deeply pleased. It was the first glimpse she'd had of the beloved grandson who had gone off to the wars. A scarred, silent, cynical stranger had returned in his place, and until she saw him laughing now, with such abandon, she had not realised how frightened she'd been that the old Jack had truly perished for ever in the wars.

Something had shattered the deep reserve he'd adopted since he came home from the Peninsula War, crippled, disinherited, then jilted. He'd remained unnaturally calm, seeming not to care, not to react. Except that he'd withdrawn into himself and become a recluse.

Now, in the space of an hour or so, Lady Cahill had seen her grandson boiling with fury, then laughing uninhibitedly. And a slip of a girl seemed to have caused it all. Lady Cahill thanked heaven for the impulse that had caused her to call on Kate on the way to Leicestershire. The girl could not be allowed to disappear now.

The old lady pushed at Jack's shoulders, which were still heaving with mirth. "Oh, get out of here, boy. I've had enough of you and your foolishness this morning." She spoke gruffly to cover her emotion.

"It's time I got dressed or Smithers will be having hysterics. It's clear to me that this place of yours needs a woman to set things in order, so I suppose I must shift myself and set to work. See if you can get me some hot water, there's a good boy. Now move, Jack, or I will get out of bed in my nightgown right now and that would most certainly cause Smithers to fall in a fit and foam at the mouth!''

Jack grinned at her. "You are, without doubt, the most scandalous old lady of my acquaintance. I'm surprised that poor woman hasn't died of shock long since." He rose from the bed and, still chuckling, limped from the room.

Jack headed downstairs, the laughter dying from his face. Now to find Miss Kate Farleigh without delay and put her straight on one or two things. A kitchen maid? Hah! Only interested in scrubbing the floor? Hah! To think he'd been worried about her! No doubt the little wretch was sitting somewhere with her feet up, laughing up her shabby sleeve at the fine trick she had played on him.

Entering the kitchen, he came to a dead halt. Kate was down on hands and knees, vigorously scrubbing the large flagstones of the kitchen floor, exactly as she'd said she would.

"What the *devil* do you think you're doing?" he roared.

Kate jumped, then turned, laid down the hard-bristled scrubbing brush and sat back on her heels. She noted the black frown, the clenched fists and the outrage. Her eyes twinkled. So, he had finally discovered who she was. And was feeling rather grumpy about it. She pressed her lips firmly together to stop them quivering with laughter.

Jack's violent reaction to the sight of her scrubbing his floor confused him. He battled with anger and an equally strong desire to lift her up and whisk her upstairs. She looked so small and delicate. She had no business attempting such a dirty and demeaning task. "I said, what do you think you're doing?"

She glanced at the floor, still swimming with dirty water, then at the discarded scrubbing brush. "It's called scrubbing the floor," she explained helpfully, unable to resist teasing him a little. "I would have thought a man of your age—"

"Don't play games with me, girl!" he growled. "What the devil is my grandmother's guest doing scrubbing my floors and cooking my breakfast?" He glared at her. "I won't have it, do you hear me? I won't have it!"

Kate, kneeling in a pool of scummy water, endeavoured to look soulful. "But you did, don't you remember? Three eggs, six rashers of bacon, and almost a whole pot of coffee."

"Dammit, I'm not talking about that—"

"But you were. You accused me of cooking your breakfast and then said you wouldn't have it," she interrupted gently. " I'm sorry if you didn't like my food."

She attempted to make her lower lip quiver sorrowfully, but abandoned the effort and rattled on, well aware that she was fanning his temper to flames and oddly excited by the prospect. "If you prefer, I won't cook your breakfast again. Indeed, I hadn't intended to do so, for it was my own breakfast I was cooking and you stol—commandeered it."

With a grubby hand she pushed a straggling curl off her face, leaving a smear of dirt in its place. Unaware, she continued, "I gather you didn't like it after all. But I dare say you are one of those people to whom the mere thought of breakfast is anathema. Perhaps the consumption of food at such an early hour made you feel...unwell? Certainly, if you'd been drinking the night before... I do seem to recall..." She lowered her eyelashes discreetly.

"I...that's not...I wasn't... The breakfast was very goo—" Jack glared at her again. The interview was not going at all as he had planned it. The cheeky little urchin. She was tying him into knots with a flow of polite-seeming nonsense, for all the world as if she were sitting in his grandmother's drawing-room, instead of at his feet in a puddle of water with dirt on her face.

"Why are *you* scrubbing this floor?" He bit out each word.

"I thought it was the best way to clean it. Perhaps there's a more modern method you would prefer?" She looked up at him as if for enlightenment, her gaze wide-eyed and artless.

"No, there isn't!" he snapped, infuriated.

"Well, in that case..." Kate hid a grin and picked up the scrubbing brush.

"Put down that blasted thing!" he roared.

Kate obligingly put it down, in the manner of humouring a lunatic. "I see. You don't wish me to use the brush. Perhaps you would like me to use another implement?" She looked around the room, apparently seeking an alternative.

"I don't wish you to use anything!" he growled.

"But how else can I clean the floor?"

"I don't wish you to clean the floor at all!" he snapped.

Kate's eyebrows rose. "Oh, I see. You *like* it dirty." She shook her head in amazement. "Well, if you *prefer* to live in filth…"

"I prefer nothing of the sort," he roared, goaded beyond endurance. Bending down, he grasped her shoulders and dragged her to her feet.

"You impudent little baggage! Don't bandy words with me! I won't have you scrubbing my floors. Curse it, you're my grandmother's guest! Guests do *not* scrub floors!" He shook her in frustration. "Do you understand me?"

It was one thing, Kate found, to tease him into losing his temper. It was quite another to be hauled unceremoniously to her feet and treated like a naughty child.

"Let go of me!" she gasped angrily, struggling in the iron grip. She swung back her foot, ready to kick him in order to free herself, but he was ready for her.

"No, you don't, you little vixen!" He lifted her at arm's length; her feet dangled six inches from the floor. "My grandmother said you were a lady but, by God, she doesn't have any idea of what a shrew you really are!"

"Well, no doubt your grandmother is also under the impression that you are a gentleman!" Kate flashed back. "I'm sure she has no knowledge of your…your manhandling habits!"

She freed herself at last with a final twist and darted behind the kitchen table.

"My what?" he said wrathfully.

"Well, what else would you call it?" she responded, pushing back several more curls which had come loose in the struggle. She glared at him, eyes bright, cheeks flushed, panting. "I haven't been in this house above a day and on several occasions you have…have used violence on me!"

"Violence?" he repeated incredulously. "And who threw a pot of hot coffee at my head not an hour ago?"

"And who deserved it, and more, for sitting there discussing me so horridly, as if I was...was...a...?" Kate flushed.

Jack looked uncomfortable. "Well, how was I to know you understood what we were saying?"

"A gentleman would never have put me in that position."

"A lady would never have been in the kitchen in the first place!"

"Oh, so I'm a lady now, am I? Pity you didn't think of it earlier."

"My grandmother told me about you."

"And you're prepared to take your grandmother's word on it, are you?" she said dryly.

"Are you calling my grandmother a liar?" he said in the soft tone that would have been a warning to anyone who knew him well.

"She's undoubtedly a kidnapper, so why not a liar?"

It was a complete facer, Jack had to admit it. His grandmother had confessed to kidnapping Kate without a shred of self-consciousness or guilt. He called down a silent curse on all women, particularly those currently under his roof.

"We will not discuss my grandmother," he said with dignity. "The fact remains that it was *your* behaviour which led me to assume you were a kitchen maid and treat you as such."

"Oh, so it's perfectly respectable to insult honest kitchen maids, is it? Pray forgive me for not understanding the finer points of a gentleman's code of conduct!"

Jack's hands clenched in frustration. "Of course it isn't, you little shrew! How in hel— Hades was I to know you understood Spanish?"

"Oh, so that makes it my fault too, does it?" Kate had been unsuccessfully trying to twist her hair back into its usual simple style; she tugged at the knot in frustration, bringing the rest of her hair tumbling over her shoulder.

''Then perhaps I'd better warn you that I also speak Portuguese, French, Latin and Greek, in case you ever find yourself wishing to insult me in those languages!''

''I didn't mean that and well you know it!'' snapped Jack, his gaze following the glossy tumbled curls. Her hair smelled of that faint fresh fragrance that so eluded him, but her comment had put him in mind of another grievance. ''And how did you learn to speak those languages in the first place?''

''I told you!'' said Kate.

''You told me some faradiddle about working for some eccentric old gentleman—''

''My father!'' snapped Kate. ''And it was no faradiddle! Everything I told you was true.''

''Including the nonsense about being a poor little kitchen maid?'' He leaned forward over the table.

''Well, no,'' she admitted, ''I was my father's housekeeper. I never told you I was a kitchen maid—you jumped to that conclusion. I merely did not contradict your assumption.'' A gleam of pure mischief shone in the green-grey eyes. ''Besides, it was quite entertaining. I simply couldn't resist.''

He suddenly lunged forward across the table and caught her hand before she knew what he was doing. She struggled to snatch it back but his grip was firm. He turned her hand over and examined it, gently rubbing a red mark caused by the scrubbing brush.

Kate, embarrassed, tried again to pull her hand away. ''I know I don't have a lady's hands. I never have. In fact, as I told your grandmother, I doubt very much I can even be called a lady. What I allowed you to believe wasn't so far from the truth. Soon I will indeed be the maid you took me for.''

His grip on her hand tightened. ''Nonsense!''

"It is not nonsense," she said quietly. "Now, if you would please release my hand—again."

He dropped it as if it were a hot coal. "So, what do you intend to do?"

"Finish washing the floor," said Kate, ignoring his real meaning.

"For the last time, girl, you will *not* scrub that floor!" He thumped a clenched fist onto the table.

Kate shrugged. "I refuse to cook in a pigsty."

"You're not going to do any cooking at all! Good God, woman, don't you *ever* do what you're told?" said the harassed erstwhile Major of the Coldstream Guards, running a hand through his unruly dark locks.

"Not when I'm told such foolish nonsense," she answered composedly.

Calm grey-green eyes met fiery blue ones.

"Tell me, Mr Carstairs, who is to make luncheon for your grandmother if I do not?"

Jack's mouth opened, then closed. Kate's eyes twinkled.

"Exactly. Stale bread and cold meat will not do for her ladyship. On the other hand, neither my father nor my brothers ever had any cause to complain about my culinary skills, therefore I will prepare luncheon for your grandmother and, of course, the rest of the household. But I will *not* cook in such dirty surroundings, and so…" She bent gracefully to pick up the dish of water and the scrubbing brush.

"You will *not* scrub that floor! Carlos will do it. It's bad enough that I must accept your offer to prepare luncheon for my grandmother, but I won't allow you to sully your hands any more with such menial and degrading tasks! Don't argue with me, girl!" he growled, seeing her mouth open.

"I'll see to it at once!" He stormed to the door, which opened on to the courtyard. "Carlos!" he bellowed. There was no answer, so with a muttered oath Jack stepped outside, preparing to search for his servant. Then he halted, remembering something. He stood for a moment, seemingly a little embarrassed.

"My...er...grandmother is...er...in need of some hot water... Could you please...er...would you mind setting some on to heat?"

"Of course," said Kate. He closed the door behind him. Kate turned to fetch the water. She jumped as the door crashed open again.

"And don't even *think* of carrying it up to her, you hear me?" he roared at her.

Kate stared at him in surprise.

"I'll take it up. It's too heavy for you," he mumbled, and left again.

"I cannot stay here in these primitive conditions," Lady Cahill announced.

Jack repressed a jubilant grin. He'd hoped to be rid of her and it seemed that his prayers were about to be answered. "I did warn you, Grandmama, that this house is not fit for guests."

"No need to sound proud of it, boy," she snapped. "I have directed Smithers to get my things ready. I will stay a sennight or so at Alderby, before returning home."

"Well, if you wish to reach Alderby in good time, you should leave here by two o'clock." He rose.

"Sit down, boy. I haven't finished with you yet. I need to discuss that gel."

Jack frowned, then a look of complete indifference settled on his face. He shrugged. "I thought she was to go and live with you. Changed your mind, have you?"

"No, I haven't! It is still my most ardent wish that she come and live with me and make her entrance into society, as is her birthright."

"Well, then, it's settled." He stretched his long, lean frame.

"It's no such thing!" said the old lady tartly. Her grandson turned and raised his eyebrows in enquiry.

"The stupid gel will have none of the scheme."

The thick dark brows came together in a frown. "What? You mean that girl out there—" he jerked his head in the direction of the door "—that half-starved little ragamuffin has turned you down?" His voice was incredulous. "Refused an offer to be fed and clothed in the first style of elegance and taken to all the most fashionable places?" He ran his hands through his tousled dark hair. "I don't believe it."

"It's true enough!" said his grandmother acidly. "Turned me down on no less than two separate occasions."

"Does she know what she's refusing?" he said. "Did you explain it to her? Describe to her what her life could be like?"

He received a withering look in reply.

"Yes, yes, I suppose you did," he muttered, shaking his head in amazement. He could imagine no female of his acquaintance even considering the rejection of such a magnificent offer, let alone a girl in such dire straits as this one. Women, in his experience, were after all they could get.

"Lord, the chit must have bats in her belfry."

"No," said his grandmother dryly. "She suffers from the same complaint as you."

He stiffened and looked down his nose at her. "And what is that, may I ask?"

"Excessive, stubborn, stiff-necked pride."

"Excessive...er...pride?" he exclaimed stiffly. "I don't know what you are talking about."

He could feel the knowing blue gaze boring into him and clenched his teeth. She was referring to her offer to finance him, made when he'd first returned to England. He had refused it in no uncertain terms then and was damned if he was going to give her the satisfaction of discussing it now.

"The two situations have nothing in common." He ignored the disbelieving arch of her elegantly pencilled brows. "In any case, what has her situation to do with me?"

"The girl intends to hire herself out as a maidservant."

"What?" His voice thundered. Kate had mentioned it earlier, but naturally he hadn't believed her. For a gently born girl to seriously consider such a thing was unheard of, particularly if she had other options.

"That's utterly ridiculous!" Aware of his revealing overreaction, he lowered his voice. "She can't be serious. What's the chit playing at?"

"Of course it's ridiculous," said his grandmother, "but I do believe she means it. She intends to earn her own way. When I first met her she took me for her new employer."

"Well, then, if she is so determined to ruin her life, what can you do?" he said in a show of indifference that deceived no one.

Lady Cahill smiled the sort of smile which had always made her family uneasy in the past. Jack watched her suspiciously.

"I intend to provide her with the kind of position she says she wants."

"As your maid?" Jack was incredulous. "I must say, Grandmama, that seems rather shabby to me—"

"Not as my maid," the old lady interrupted. Jack's eyes narrowed, dark suspicion forming even as she spoke. "As yours."

"Mine!" he exploded. "I'm damn—"

"As your housekeeper, I should have said," continued his grandmother imperturbably. "It's as clear as daylight to me that you need someone to prevent this house from crumbling into complete barbarism, and you have told me yourself that you are not willing to waste your money employing anyone to do it. I, however, am not prepared to allow a member of my family to live in such a disgraceful state. And you must admit this admirably solves the two problems."

"I'll admit nothing of the sort!" he said angrily. "I won't tolerate such unwarranted interference in my affairs, Grandmama!"

"So you don't wish to help the girl?"

"Help her? To social ruin by employing her as my maid...housekeeper? I don't think—"

"No, Jack, you don't think. Naturally I will send some respectable woman to act as her chaperon. And I'm not considering any ordinary terms of employment. I intend to put this to the girl: if she will consent to run your household for six months, turn it into a gentleman's establishment instead of a ramshackle place where a lady cannot even get a cup of chocolate to break her fast, then I will consider—and, what's more to the point, so will *she*—that she will thereby have earned my sponsorship for a season in London. *She* can keep her pride, *you* can live like a moderately civilised human being and *I* can introduce Maria's gel to society."

Lady Cahill sat back and regarded her grandson with some satisfaction. "And, in the meantime, it will give me some time to have someone look into the matter of Kate's finances. I cannot believe that she's been left completely destitute. So, she stays here while I organise things. And setting this house in order will keep her nicely occupied, so that's settled."

"It is *not* settled."

"Jack, if you say no to this scheme, it will mean the end of that girl, for I tell you she is as stubborn and foolish as you are and she tells me she will not accept charity from me, or from anyone else."

Jack met her level glance.

"Ah! Dammit!" He slammed his hand down on the table in frustration.

His grandmother smiled. She reached up and patted his chin. "I knew you'd agree with me in the end."

"I don't," he snapped.

"But you will have her here."

"It is the most ridiculous, ill-considered, inconvenient and damnably outrageous scheme I have ever heard of!"

"Good, then you'll do it!" nodded his grandmother complacently.

He glared at her and clenched his hair with his fingers.

"Yes, all right, you leave me no choice, though without doubt I should be clapped up in Bedlam for agreeing to it!"

"Don't be silly, boy," she said, suddenly businesslike again. "Now send that man into the village to tell my coachman to come and collect my baggage. Oh, and before you do fetch young Kate here. I'll just explain to her what it is you want her to do."

"What *I* want?" he began. Fortuitously, he noticed the provocative glint in his grandmother's eye. "Yes," he said, goaded, "you do that, Grandmama," and strode from the room, slamming the door after him.

"And so, my dear Kate, you can see that my grandson's domestic circumstances are in a shocking state and yet Jack has no one to see to the smooth running of the house." Lady Cahill applied a delicate wisp of lace to a wrinkled eyelid to emphasise her distress.

Kate became thoughtful. Lady Cahill had not resumed her arguments in favour of taking Kate to London with her and presenting her to society. Kate felt equal measures of disappointment and relief at that. A very small part of her, the wild, rebellious, frivolous part of her that her father had tried so hard to crush, wistfully longed for the prospect of a London season. Kate ruthlessly suppressed it. It was too late for all that.

An idea occurred to Kate. This could be her chance. Her domestic skills might once more be the saving of her. With Lady Cahill's backing, Kate might be able to carve herself a niche in this household and earn herself a home, a living, some security.

''Ma'am,'' she said hesitantly, ''if you wish...I mean, if you think I am suitable...I could become the housekeeper here.''

''*You*, child? Don't be ridiculous! You couldn't possibly act as my grandson's housekeeper!'' said the dowager spider to her youthful fly.

''Indeed I could, ma'am. I'm young, but I've had a great deal of experience. I was my father's housekeeper for many years. And it would be a better position than I would be likely to find elsewhere.'' Kate fought to keep the eagerness out of her voice. ''I would take good care of your grandson, and you could rest assured that I was safe and in a secure position.''

Lady Cahill tapped her finger thoughtfully on the small table in front of her, then grimaced at the dust it had collected.

''Faugh!'' she exclaimed in disgust. ''This place is a disgrace! And you think you can improve it, do you?'' She looked at Kate. ''It won't do, you know.''

''Ma'am?'' said Kate, a worried pucker between her brows.

''Oh, I don't doubt you could do the job,'' she added, seeing Kate's readiness to argue the point. ''But I could not possibly pay Maria Delacombe's daughter a *wage*!'' She made a wage sound like some unspeakable insult.

Kate's heart sank. She could not survive without money.

''I must confess, however, that I'd worry about my grandson a lot less if I could be sure someone sensible were here to look after him. ''Tis bad enough he will never ride again—that I must accept, as he must...''

Kate frowned. Jack's limp was bad, to be sure, but she had observed it closely. It seemed to her no worse than Jemmy's limp had been... Perhaps— Lady Cahill's voice cut into her thoughts.

"But allow him to sink into sloth and misery I will not."
The old lady looked at Kate speculatively.

Kate held her breath.

"All right, Kate Farleigh, I'll strike a bargain with you.
You work here as my grandson's housekeeper for the next
six months without wages. At the end of the six months you
come to live with me in London and I'll present you to society."

Kate blinked at the old lady in surprise. It was a magnificent offer. Too magnificent, she realised slowly, and utterly
impossible. She opened her mouth to refuse.

"Well, child, what do you say? Do I rest easy tonight,
knowing my grandson is in good hands, or not?" Lady Cahill
touched Kate's hand gently, confidingly. "My dear, I know
that living with an old woman like me in London isn't what
every young girl would want, but I do like a bit of youth
about me. You'd be doing an old widow a great favour."

A lump in Kate's throat threatened to choke her. She had
never thought to find such kindness again. It was almost too
much to bear. Yet she could not take advantage of the old
lady's ignorance.

Lady Cahill had made the offer without knowing the real
reason why Kate could never enter society, would never be
able to marry, why no decent man would have her. Kate
would have to tell her, explain once and for all. And afterwards she would no doubt have to leave and return to the
life she had planned for herself before Lady Cahill's well-
meaning interference.

Chapter Five

"Lady Cahill," said Kate, "I do thank you, but your offer is made in ignorance of my circumstances. If I were to accept, you would surely despise me once you learned the truth. And society would condemn you or think you a fool to have been so taken in."

When Lady Cahill saw the look on Kate's face she bit back the pithy comment she had been about to make on her complete indifference to society's opinions on anything.

"May I ask why, child?"

Kate was very nervous. She didn't want to tell Lady Cahill, didn't want to lose her affection and her respect. But there was no choice. The story would eventually come out—it always did. Better to get it over with, instead of having the threat hanging over her.

"I am not regarded as fit for marriage," said Kate at last.

"Will you tell me why, child?"

"It's a long story," said Kate. "When my brothers, Jemmy and Ben, went to the war on the Peninsula, my father and I accompanied them. I've spent the last three years living with the army."

"Child. How dreadful for you!" Lady Cahill looked appalled.

Kate shook her head. "No, ma'am, it wasn't at all. In fact those three years, while the boys and my father were alive, were the best years of my life."

Lady Cahill made a shocked sound of disbelief and Kate smiled ruefully. "I'm afraid it's true. I...I've always been a bit of a hoyden, you understand, and I found the life suited me—much better than at the vicarage. I was never lonely and...and my father valued me as he never had before." She looked down at her hands. "You see, when my mother died, Papa blamed me—she died giving birth to me."

"But, child, that was not your—"

"Oh, I know, but Papa could never see that... You said I had my mother's eyes... Papa was a good man, but when he looked at me all he could see was my dead mother...so he never looked at me. *Never.*' Kate choked on the word.

"Oh, my dear..."

"But somehow, on the Peninsula, things changed. Perhaps, with death and danger all around us, everything else faded into insignificance. I don't know... And because, in such a difficult situation, comfort comes to mean a great deal..." Kate looked at Lady Cahill. "I became quite a good housekeeper, you see. And hot food at almost any hour, a warm, dry place to sleep and clean clothing mean a lot to men at war..."

She sighed. "They truly needed me and I was happier than I have ever been in my life...until poor Ben was killed at Ciudad Rodrigo..." She fell silent for a moment, then continued, "And then everything fell apart at Salamanca."

Lady Cahill frowned. Jack had been wounded at Salamanca.

As she spoke, Kate's hands unknowingly began to pleat the stuff of her skirt in tiny, deliberate folds. "Last July, our army was retreating from the Douro River, back towards Salamanca—you may have read of it; the newspapers hate it when we retreat. The French were close behind us. At times they were even parallel with us and so close that you could see them through the swirling clouds of dust.'' She gulped.

''Jemmy was hit in the chest... We got him on to our cart...but with all the dust and confusion we fell a long way behind.''

She turned the wad of pleated skirt over and methodically began to unpleat it. Her voice was flat, bleak. ''Then Papa was hit. In the stomach. I...I managed to get him and Jemmy away to a deserted building. It was half destroyed, but at least it was shelter... Jemmy died the first night...Papa lasted two more days... I had a little laudanum and at least I...I was able to ease his passing...''

Lady Cahill leaned forward. ''You poor child—''

''I didn't remember anything after that...until more than a month later.'' She straightened her skirt with shaking hands, smoothing out the wrinkles. ''I awoke one morning and found myself in a French camp. An officer, Henri Du Croix, was interrogating several recently captured prisoners—English prisoners. I had no idea how I got there.''

She shivered and continued, ''It was the most terrifying feeling... Later, I learned that the officer, Henri, had found me wandering after Salamanca. I had been wounded—on the head.'' Her hand crept unconsciously to the scar almost hidden by her hairline. ''Apparently I was unable to remember my name or anything, although he knew, of course, that I was English. I became his prisoner...and his mistress.''

Kate flushed at the small sound from Lady Cahill. She could not look at the old lady. Her hands began their intricate pleating again.

''I discovered that for the last month I had lived with him, slept with him in his tent...'' Kate swallowed in embarrassment, and forced the words out ''...living as man and wife.'' She flushed a darker rose colour and added, ''I know it was true—I remember it. You must not think he was a totally wicked man—in his own way, I think he was fond of me…but I swear to you I did not realise what had happened until a month after Salamanca…when it was too late.''

She took a deep shaky breath and continued, determined to get it all out in the open. ''In Lisbon afterwards they called me the Frenchman's whore…and a traitress.''

Lady Cahill made a shocked sound.

''Traitress, because I'd tended the wounds of French soldiers. I have some small skill with injuries, you see. And though they were the enemy I see no wrong in what I did. They were only men, like our men—tired, hungry, in pain, and longing to be with their loved ones, not fighting this dreadful war. That part, I do not regret…''

She shrugged, her eyes downcast. ''So, now you know.''

The material of her skirt was crushed and twisted. Her voice rose again in distress. ''But I did *not* consent to be Henri's mistress—he told me he was my *husband* and I *believed* him. I found a ring on my finger, though I did not know how it got there. I could not even remember my own name at the time, and so I believed him! He was very convincing. He said I was his English wife. I never knowingly—''

''Hush now, child! Do not distress yourself. I don't doubt your word,'' interrupted Lady Cahill

Huge, swimming grey-green eyes regarded her doubtfully.

''Oh, tush, child,'' the old lady said gruffly, patting Kate's knee. ''As if I did not know you are the soul of honour.''

Kate inhaled, a long, tremulous breath. Tears trembled on her lashes. ''Then you are very singular, ma'am, for few others believed me. They thought me a wanton, a liar, a traitress.''

''Lud, child. Anyone with a grain of sense could see you are none of those. As far as I am concerned, you did nothing wrong. And I respect you for tending their wounded. Tell me, how did you return to English territory?''

''Well, as I said, my memory came back to me when Henri

was interrogating English prisoners—perhaps it was the sound of English being spoken that caused it to return. It took me a day or two to find out what happened and make my plans to escape. Then I stole a horse and rode into Allied territory. It was not difficult to pass from behind the French lines—a woman is not so suspect as a man.'' She flushed. ''But you see why I cannot possibly enter society, or marry.''

''I see nothing of the sort,'' said Lady Cahill. ''There is no reason for anyone to know of this—''

''It is a matter of public record,'' said Kate regretfully. ''I returned to the English forces almost six weeks after my father's death. Naturally I was interviewed, in case I was a spy. Some of the officers who interviewed me didn't believe I'd lost my memory. Others were only interested in what I could tell them about the French. It was supposed to be kept secret, but when I reached Lisbon everybody there knew the worst,'' she concluded bitterly.

There was a long silence. ''It is not mere wilfulness or false pride preventing me from seeking a husband, you know,'' Kate added. ''Ever since I was a little girl I've dreamt of my wedding day, waited for the man whom I could love for ever…and played with other people's children, preparing myself for the day when I had children of my own.'' She smoothed twisted fabric with unknowing hands.

''I have put this dream away…but *not* of my own volition.''

Lady Cahill opened her mouth to argue, but Kate continued, ''In Lisbon I received a taste of what would face me if I ever again tried to enter society. Ma'am, I was shunned, reviled…even *spat* on—by English ladies, some of whom I'd regarded as friends…'' Her throat swelled and tightened, remembering whispers and sidelong glances, prurient curiosity and outright hostility.

''And men whom I thought I knew, whom I thought were

decent Christian gentlemen, tried to *touch* me, made obscene suggestions.'' *The Frenchman's whore*—she was fair game.

"Even Harry...my betrothed..." Kate shuddered. Harry's eyes had run over her body in a way they never had before. The realisation had entered Kate's heart like a blade of ice. He was no different from the rest.

"It was unspeakably vile...and I could not bear to face it again." She looked wearily at Lady Cahill. "That is why I cannot accept your very kind offer, why I cannot seek a husband or go about in society. I could not bear to meet someone who knows what happened."

She tried to smile. "It is not so very bad, you know. I cannot miss what I've never had. I've not had the sort of upbringing that other girls have. And I'm young and healthy and—" she wiped her eyes "—generally not such a dreadful watering pot. If I could only find a position as a children's nurse or companion... You could help me with that, could you not?"

Lady Cahill was deeply moved. Kate had been badly wounded, she could see that. There was no point in pushing her to agree to any plans at present. She was still too vulnerable to risk her heart and her hopes again—she needed time to recover. Lady Cahill would help Kate, but not to a position as a children's nurse. No, if an old woman had any say in the matter, Maria Delacombe's child would have her dream. She reached out and took Kate's hand in a tight grasp.

"Of course I will help you, child. Try to put the whole horrid business behind you. You found yourself in a difficult situation, but you conducted yourself with honour as a true Christian lady. I am sure that both your father and your mother would have been very proud of you. I know I am."

Tears spilled from Kate's eyes. Kindness, she suddenly found, was so much harder to withstand than cruelty. The old woman gathered the girl into her arms and held her tightly for a moment or two.

"Lady Cahill, you see—"

"I see nothing at all at the moment," Lady Cahill interrupted, wiping her eyes. "This dratted face paint has run and I refuse to do or say another word until it is repaired. Fetch my maid to me, and in the meantime go and wash your face and comb your hair. Return to me in twenty minutes."

Kate stared at her, dumbfounded. Suddenly laughter began to well up inside her and she sat back and laughed until the tears came again.

Sympathy and warm, wicked humour gleamed back at her from the admittedly smudged face of the old woman. "That's right, my girl. A good cry and a good laugh. That's what the doctor ordered. Now," she continued briskly, "fetch Smithers to me and go and wash your face. You look a sight!"

Later that afternoon Kate helped the old lady climb into her travelling chaise, and stood in the driveway, waving her off. Lady Cahill had promised to "do what I can to help Maria's gel", and Kate felt sure that she would find her a position as a children's nurse in some quiet, pleasant household.

In return, Kate's job was relatively simple—she had to put Mr Jack Carstairs's house in order. That was well within her capabilities. She might not enjoy housework very much, but there was no doubt that Sevenoaks was badly in need of attention, and there would be real satisfaction gained from restoring a ramshackle house to a graceful residence. And her old nurse, Martha, was to come and live here. That would be wonderful, thought Kate. Martha was a dear and would keep Kate from feeling too lonely. Martha had also known and loved Jemmy and Ben.

Moreover, Kate thought, mentally ticking off her advantages, she was surrounded by lovely countryside and could go for long rambles whenever she wanted to. In fact, she could do whatever she wanted, whenever she wanted to. She was her own mistress and she meant to enjoy that rare freedom while she had it.

And she was needed.

Kate had no doubt whatsoever that Lady Cahill's grandson needed her skills, and that once he saw how much easier his life would be with Kate as housekeeper he would be grateful. Perhaps she could also use her healing skills—possibly even help him to strengthen his injured leg and reduce that dreadful limp. They might even become friends, she thought optimistically. To be sure, he had proved a trifle autocratic and difficult to get along with at first, but that was largely her own fault for teasing and tricking him.

Kate felt sure that Jack Carstairs would prove to be exactly like Papa and the boys and all the other men she had ever known—as long as his surroundings were clean and comfortable and his stomach was full of good cooking, he wouldn't care what she did.

Carlos grinned as he heard the sound of his master's voice raised yet again, this time from the direction of the breakfast-room. He crept closer to peer in at the open window.

"I've told you before, I *won't* have you scrubbing floors!" The deep, angry voice was raised in frustration.

"Ah, yes, I'd forgotten your preference for dirt." Kate's voice was dry.

"Oh, don't be ridiculous!" snapped Jack.

"Then what would you have me do?" she retorted crossly. "You can see for yourself that these floors need scrubbing. Someone must do it and you know perfectly well that Martha is too old to do such a task. I am young and strong and, no matter what you may say, if something needs scrubbing, then I will scrub."

"It is not fitting!"

"Now you are being ridiculous!" Kate said, exasperated. "Tell me, what is fitting for a housekeeper? When I take down the curtains to wash them, you roar and forbid me to do it! If I clean the windows, so I can see out of them instead of gazing at a view of dirt, you appear out of nowhere and bellow that it is not for me to be doing that! Your interference is quite insupportable! Please, Mr Carstairs, go away and let me get on with my work!''

''I said, I will not have you scrubbing! Look at you, you're a mess! You've got dirt on your chin, a smudge of something else on your nose and your hair is falling all over the place!''

''Oh, yes, mock me for doing honest work!'' Kate scrubbed furiously at her face with one hand, dashing curls from her eyes with the other.

''You missed a spot.'' He reached out and flicked her small tip-tilted nose, his lips twitching with reluctant amusement.

Kate made an infuriated noise and returned to her scrubbing, ignoring the man standing in front of her.

''I said I *won't* have you scrubbing.''

Carlos grinned. He knew that tone. There would be fireworks if Señorita Kate didn't do as she was bid. He moved closer for a better view, then ducked hastily as a bucket was flung through the window.

''Oh, for goodness' sake!'' exclaimed Kate. ''How very childish!''

Carlos's eyes widened. To answer back to Major Jack! In that mood! And call him childish! Carlos cautiously raised his head to look in again, then ducked as he noticed his master striding towards the window. Desperate not to be caught eavesdropping, he dived into a nearby bush.

''Carlos!'' yelled Jack, thrusting his head out of the window. ''Carlos!''

''Er…*sí*, Major Jack,'' mumbled Carlos, sheepishly emerging from the bush.

''What the devil are you doing down there?''

Carlos opened his mouth. ''Er…''

"Oh, never mind. There's a bucket out there somewhere. Fetch it and fill it with hot water. Then get in here and scrub this floor. On the double!"

Carlos's mouth drooped. "*Sí, sí*, Major Jack, at once," he muttered. Scrubbing! Again! Dolefully he fetched the bucket and headed for the scullery. Scrubbing was no job for a man! Señorita Kate wanted to do it, so why did Major Jack not let her do it?

"On the double, I said!" came the bellow from the window.

"*Sí, sí*, at once, Major Jack." Carlos scurried away to do his master's bidding.

Kate got to her feet. She could not scrub without water, and in truth she would be relieved to have Carlos do it—she loathed scrubbing. In any case, she could do nothing while Jack Carstairs stood guard over the scrubbing brush.

She glared at his handsome profile, in two minds about his bossiness. He had no business interfering with her work. On the other hand, he kept saving her from chores she hated. It was very confusing. Papa and the boys never minded what she did. Jack Carstairs was almost a stranger, and yet he was oddly...she could only call it protective.

That reminded her. "Er...Mr Carstairs," she said diffidently.

"What the devil do you want now?"

"I...I want to thank you."

Jack's head whipped around in amazement.

"Yesterday I found Carlos in my room."

Jack's brows snapped together.

"He said it was on your orders."

Suddenly Jack knew what she was going to say. "Oh, that," he mumbled gruffly, and turned to go.

Her hand on his arm stopped him. "He was there to clean away all the cobwebs and kill any spiders. And I believe you told him to do the same with all the other rooms. It was a very kind and thoughtful gesture and it would be remiss of me not to thank you, and I do so, very much.''

Jack felt a rush of warmth as he looked down at the sweet face. He gazed into the clear eyes and felt the soft pressure of her hand on his arm. He could smell that faint elusive scent she had, unlike any lady's perfume he knew of, but oddly familiar, nevertheless.

''What *is* the name of that perfume you wear?'' he asked abruptly.

Kate dropped his arm and stepped back a little. Jack was annoyed to see a faint trace of wariness in her eyes.

''I wear no perfume. I cannot afford it.''

''But I can smell it whenever I stand close to you, some faint fragrance.''

Kate blushed slightly. ''It's only rosemary.''

''Who?''

''The fragrance you have noticed. It is rosemary, a herb. I make a rinse of it for my hair, and put sprigs of it in my clothes to keep them fresh. It grows plentifully and is free and I am very fond of its scent. Obviously I am too lavish with it,'' she said defensively. Definitely too lavish, she thought, if he could talk to her about the way she smelled.

He stared at her thoughtfully. ''No, not too lavish. It's very nice.''

''Carlos. That farm you visit,'' said Jack later that afternoon.

''Farm?'' said Carlos cautiously.

''The one you visit so frequently. The one with all the daughters,'' said Jack impatiently. ''I want you to go there at once.''

''*Sí*, Major Jack.'' Carlos brightened visibly.

''Bring back a couple of girls.''

Carlos goggled at his employer.

"Wipe that ridiculous look from your face, you fool! I want those girls to come here to work."

Carlos hesitated. "To scrub, you mean, sir?"

"Yes, and whatever else needs doing. Miss Farleigh cannot do all the work that she seems to think necessary."

A grin split the dark face. "*Sí*, Major Jack! I will fetch them at once!" Carlos moved with alacrity.

"And, Carlos—" His master's voice halted him. "There will be no fraternising with the wenches while they are employed here, understand?"

"*Sí*, Major Jack," sighed Carlos dolefully.

He headed off towards a nearby cottage where the unfortunate farmer had seven daughters to feed, clothe and somehow marry off. There would be no trouble in persuading two of them to come and work for a gentleman like Major Jack.

Trudging across damp, muddy fields, Carlos gradually brightened. He might not be allowed to fraternise with the girls, but at least he would no longer have to demean himself scrubbing floors. And, if Miss Kate had a couple of girls to help her with the work, she would not be making Major Jack so angry all the time.

"What the devil do you mean, you wouldn't wear them?"

"Mr Carstairs, you must realise that I cannot accept clothing from you." Kate's tone was mild but her chin was defiantly high.

"Why the devil not?"

"It isn't proper," said Kate composedly. "And besides, I have sufficient clothing for my needs here. Martha brought the trunk containing my things."

"Balderdash!" he exploded. "You are the stubbornest female it has ever been my misfortune to meet! You know perfectly well that those rags you wear are fit only for burning!"

Kate bit her lip on the retort that had risen to her tongue.

There was some truth in his statement. The trunk containing all the clothes she had worn in Spain, as well as all her father's papers and things, had been lost when she had been captured by the French. The clothes she'd left in England were from a time when she was a young, carefree girl. Faced with total poverty, Kate had sold all clothes with any claim to fashion and style. Those that remained were old and worn and now dyed black for mourning.

"My clothes may not meet with your approval, sir, nevertheless, they are perfectly adequate for my position."

"That they are not! You are my grandmother's ward!"

"No, Mr Carstairs, I am housekeeper here!"

Jack ran his hand through his hair in frustration. The chit opposed him at every turn! "Do you think I wish it said that I pay you so poorly that you cannot afford to dress like a civilised human being?"

"As you have no visitors and virtually no contact with anyone, I cannot imagine that anyone will have anything to say about it, so it need not concern you," Kate retorted. "Besides, you do not pay me at all."

"Not for want of trying!"

"Mr Carstairs, I was put in this position by your grandmother, not you. It has nothing to do with you, and you must see that I could not accept money from you under any circumstances. Your grandmother and I have an agreement, and that is my last word on the subject." Kate turned to walk out of the room, but Jack caught her arm and pulled her close. He glared down at her and spoke in a low and furious voice.

"All right, Miss Katherine Farleigh, then here is *my* last word—if you won't accept a wage and you refuse my offer of new clothes, then I'll have no alternative but to dismiss you!"

Uncomfortably aware of his firm grip on her arm and the proximity of his warm body to hers, Kate had to force herself to look up at him. For a moment of two she stared into his glittering blue eyes, only a few inches from her own. She felt his hand tighten and her pulse quickened at the suddenly intent look in his eyes. His effect on her was most unsettling—she had to fight it. She pulled free of him, and brushed down her skirt, buying a few seconds in which to compose herself, aware that his unnerving gaze had not altered.

''You cannot dismiss me. You haven't the power.''

''The devil I haven't!''

He took a few steps towards her. Kate retreated rapidly to the door. ''My agreement is with Lady Cahill, not you, and only *she* can dismiss me.'' She poked her tongue out at him, then slipped out the door and down the stairs as fast as she could.

It was a kind offer, Kate thought, but he knew as well as she did that it would be most improper for him to buy her clothing. A man only did that for his wife...or his mistress. Kate bit her lip. It was probably the grossest hypocrisy for the ex-mistress of a French officer to be quibbling about such a thing. But it was precisely because she was so vulnerable to accusation that she had to maintain the highest level of propriety.

Propriety was a frail web of protection at best, but without it she would be crushed. Propriety was what kept her feeling like the Reverend Mr Farleigh's daughter instead of a fallen woman. Without it, she would never be able to go about her daily work with a light heart, feeling free to tease and provoke Jack Carstairs if she felt like it, defying him when his bossiness became too provoking and arguing with him if she disagreed with his pronouncements.

She was thinking a little too much about Jack Carstairs these days, she realised. He was the first thing she thought of when she awoke...and the last, before she went to sleep. Even their frequent quarrels she found exhilarating. And, even when he was infuriating her with his interference, deep down she could not help feeling touched by his concern for her…warmed by it. And feeling warm feelings towards him in return…such feelings were dangerous.

Nothing could come of them. She would only hurt herself if she allowed herself to weaken. If—no, *when* he learned about her background, Jack Carstairs would be no different from any other man.

Jack glared at the closed door and clenched his fist at it, swearing softly. The chit had defied him yet again, blast it! But she wouldn't get the better of him this time. She might think she had won the battle, but Major Jack Carstairs knew it was just a preliminary skirmish. And he had served under the Beau, the Marquis of Wellington, the ultimate master at turning retreat into victory.

A slow smile appeared on his lean face and he limped towards the writing desk, sat down and began to pen a letter to his grandmother.

Chapter Six

"S̃eñorita Kate," called Carlos from the hallway. "Something here for you."

Kate stepped back from her task, and glanced around her with some satisfaction. With the aid of Millie and Florence, the girls from the farm, she had wrought a remarkable improvement in the room. The old, mismatched furniture looked infinitely better, gleaming softly from vigorous applications of beeswax. The dusty curtains had been taken down and laundered and brilliant late autumn sunshine streamed through the newly washed windows. The oak floor was freshly polished, and the old Persian carpet had been taken out and ruthlessly beaten until the rich colours glowed.

Housework might not be Kate's favourite activity, but at least it showed results she could be proud of. The room looked warm and inviting, a far cry from when Lady Cahill had snorted at it so disparagingly. All that was needed now was a bowl of flowers or leaves. Perhaps she could find some in the tangled garden. Kate gathered up her cleaning rags and stepped into the hall.

"What is it, Carlos?"

"These arrive for you, *señorita*." He gestured towards a large number of bulky packages resting on the long hall table.

"For me?"

"You like me to carry them upstairs for you, *señorita*?"
Carlos offered politely. These days he treated her with the
utmost respect. Once he might have thought her a skinny
little mouse of a thing, with her huge greeny eyes and her
shabby clothes, respected only because he was ordered to.
But no one who had seen this little creature coolly stand up
to his master would need to feign respect. Carlos had not
forgotten the coffee pot, either.

"That would be very kind of you, Carlos," Kate murmured abstractedly, puzzling over these unexpected and mysterious items. She followed him upstairs to her room, her
arms full of parcels, and he even more heavily laden.

When he left, Kate opened the packages, slowly at first,
then faster and faster, her head in a whirl. They contained
everything she could ever think of needing. A wonderful
warm merino pelisse. No cold winter wind would dare penetrate that to send her shaking and shivering. Dresses, in fine
warm cloth, the colours dark—lavender, grey, black and a
beautiful soft dove—nothing to offend her state of mourning.

And underclothing, some of fine, soft linen, trimmed with
lace, some of silk and satin, the like of which Kate had never
in her life seen or felt. Surely it would be positively sinful
to wear garments such as these exquisite things next to your
skin? As for the nightgowns and chemises—they bore no
earthly resemblance to the patched, sturdy, voluminous garments Kate had worn most of her life.

She stared dumbfounded at the tumble of lovely things
spread out across her bed. Jack had bought them, of course.
He hadn't listened to a word she'd said… But, oh, they were
so beautiful. It had been so long since she'd had anything
new, and these were of the finest quality. She wouldn't wear
them, but it wouldn't hurt, surely, to hold them up against
herself and look in the mirror and imagine, just for a moment,
that they were hers.

She lifted the dove-coloured dress and stood in front of the mirror, holding it against her. It was very elegant—high-waisted, with a border of embroidered leaves around the hem—simply but beautifully cut. And the material felt so light and yet so warm. She rubbed her cheek against its soft folds and inhaled, savouring its new, delicious smell.

One after another, Kate held the dresses against her slender frame, draping them this way and that, trying to imagine how they would look if she were to wear them—which, of course, she could not.

She picked up a nightgown. Fine silk slipped through her fingers like water. She held it up, imagining herself wearing it, and blushed. It was…would be quite immodest. The Reverend Mr Farleigh's daughter had never owned, or even imagined, such a garment. It was so fine that surely you could see through it. She slipped her fingers inside the nightgown and, sure enough, her skin glowed pinkly through the delicate fabric. She blushed a deeper rose and hastily put it down and then picked up the dove dress again.

''That colour suits you,'' said a deep voice from the doorway.

Kate gasped and whirled around, clutching the dove frock against her, for all the world as if she were naked. Jack Carstairs stood in the open doorway, leaning casually against the door frame.

''H-how long have you been there?'' she stuttered.

He did not respond, but a slow smile told her the answer and her blush deepened. He'd seen her looking at the nightgown.

''I've brought you a letter.'' He glanced down at the welter of clothes that covered the bed and the lurking smile widened. Kate followed his gaze. He was looking at the underclothes and nightgowns. Hurriedly she snatched them up and thrust them under the dresses, her cheeks burning.

''Wh...what did you say you wanted?'' she muttered, unable to meet his eyes.

''A letter has arrived for you,'' he said softly. ''And I see that that's not all.''

Jack couldn't resist teasing her. The sight of that nightgown sliding sensuously over her skin had caused his body to tighten, imagining her clothed in nothing but that fine translucent silk. And the blush that rose so easily to her cheeks would no doubt be repeated elsewhere on her body. He knew it. And she knew he knew it; he could tell by her loss of composure. Kate Farleigh wasn't easily rattled, and by God he was going to enjoy it while he could. The little termagant was adorable like this, flushed and embarrassed and uncertain.

''Please give me the letter,'' said Kate, still flustered by the amusement in his deep voice. He held it out. She reached for it, but he swiftly raised it out of reach.

''Say 'thank you' first,'' he drawled, still grinning.

''Give it to me, please,'' she repeated, annoyed. The big lummox! Did he think she was going to grapple with him for it? She had been teased by experts—her brothers—and she wasn't so foolish as to think she could get the better of him by trying to snatch the letter. He was far too tall, for one thing.

In any case, she'd sworn never to let him get his hands on her again. Her encounters with Jack Carstairs were nothing like the tussles she'd had with her brothers. His touch had no brotherly feel about it at all; it made her feel oddly helpless and fluttery inside and it took all her will-power to break away from him.

''I've come all the way upstairs to bring it to you. Don't I deserve something?'' he teased, enjoying her discomfiture.

''You deserve something, all right,'' she muttered beneath her breath.

He heard her and laughed. "Little wildcat. Here's your letter, then." He tossed it on to the bed.

"Thank you. Now please leave." Kate went pointedly to the door. "And you can take all of your things with you,"

He looked at her in mock-amazement. "My things? What ever do you mean, Miss Farleigh?"

Kate nodded at the pile of clothing on her bed. "All of those. I told you before, I cannot accept such gifts from you."

He stared at her in exaggerated surprise. "My things? You think these are *my* things? My dear Miss Farleigh..." He bent and, before Kate could see what he was about, drew the silk nightgown from its hiding place. He held it up against his lean, strong frame.

"You think that *this* is *mine*?" His blue eyes quizzed her wickedly. Kate fought against the rising tide of embarrassment that threatened her again.

"Oh, don't be ridiculous!" she snapped, trying not to smile. The frail wisp of silk only served to emphasise the masculinity of the man. "You know exactly what I mean."

He let the delicate silk trail through his long brown fingers, then tossed the offending garment to one side. "But *I* haven't offered you these."

"But—"

"You'll find that this letter from my grandmother explains everything," he interrupted smoothly. "It arrived with the rest of these things. It wasn't *my* taste that selected these...although for once in my life I find myself in total accord with my grandmother." He smiled, a slow, teasing smile that had Kate fighting those fluttery inner feelings again.

"Your grandmother?"

"Yes. She told me in my letter that she'd sent you some clothing more suited to your position."

"You mean you didn't send me all of this?"

"No, indeed. I hope, as a gentleman, I wouldn't dream of so insulting you." He added piously, "A lady could certainly not accept such gifts from a gentleman, Miss Farleigh. I am shocked you would even suggest it." He pursed his mouth primly, his eyes twinkling wickedly.

Kate tried to avoid his gaze. She had been made to feel very foolish. He'd known very well that after their previous discussion of her wardrobe she would jump to the conclusion that he'd sent these things. He might not have actually sent them himself, she realised, but he most certainly was behind his grandmother's charitable actions.

"But I cannot—"

"I hope you're not suggesting there is any impropriety attached to an elderly lady buying a few bits and pieces for the daughter of her godchild?" he interrupted in a cool voice. "Her own mantua-maker made them from measurements Smithers took from your old clothes."

Kate hadn't realised Lady Cahill had taken so much trouble. She felt a little embarrassed, but she didn't want to back down while he was standing over her like this. "No...but...it is too much...too generous..."

His face hardened, his eyes lost their twinkle.

"Understand me, Miss Farleigh. These things are from my grandmother and you can and will accept them!"

Kate resented his tone. "You have no right to tell me what I may or may not accept."

"I care nothing for that. You will oblige me by appearing in one of these dresses within the half-hour." Lord! The chit was stubborn.

"I will do nothing of the sort," Kate responded defiantly. "I resent your high-handed manner, sir, and take leave to tell you I will *not* wear these clothes."

He took two menacing steps towards her and she skittered away out of his reach. "Understand me, miss! You will wear these new clothes and burn the old ones!"

"Oh, will I, indeed?" She pulled a face.

Jack took his watch out of his pocket and glanced at it. "You'll dress yourself in one of those new dresses within the half-hour, or..."

"Or what?"

"Or, Miss Katherine Farleigh, I will come in here and dress you myself." There was a hard glitter in his eyes that suggested he was not jesting.

She wrinkled her nose at him. "You wouldn't dare!"

"Just try me, missie!" he snapped. "You have half an hour."

He left the room.

Kate locked the door firmly after him and sat down on the bed. He'd thrown down the gauntlet and naturally she'd picked it up. It was time Jack Carstairs learned once and for all that he was *not* her master. He had no authority over her whatsoever. If she didn't choose to wear these clothes, she wouldn't, and no bossy great interfering man would tell her otherwise.

A little over half an hour later there was a knock on her door. "Who...who is it?" Kate called, annoyed at the involuntary quaver in her voice.

"It's me, miss, Millie."

Kate unlocked the door. "Come in, Mil—"

Millie stood twisting her apron nervously. Jack Carstairs loomed darkly behind her. Kate drew herself up straight and stared defiantly at him. He snapped his fingers at the maid.

Millie swallowed. "I'm here to collect your old clothes, miss."

"That won't be necessary," replied Kate smoothly.

Millie looked doubtfully back at Jack. "But Mr Carstairs—"

"Mr Carstairs has nothing to do with it, Millie. My clothes belong to me, not Mr Carstairs."

"Excuse me, Millie," said Jack softly. He moved past her

and approached Kate determinedly. Mistrusting the look in his eye, she skipped around to the other side of the bed. He opened the door of the wardrobe and started to drag her old clothes from it, tossing them to Millie.

"Stop that at once!" snapped Kate, outraged. He ignored her and moved next to the chest, which he similarly emptied into Millie's waiting arms.

"How dare you?" cried Kate, and ran to restrain him. He whirled and took her shoulders in a firm grip. Their eyes locked for a moment. Slowly his hands slid down her arms and he held her wrists in a light but unbreakable grip.

"Let me go, you big bully!"

"I thought I made my instructions clear to you before." He looked meaningfully down at the shabby old dress she was still wearing in defiance of his orders.

Kate's mouth grew dry. He could not surely mean to carry out his threat to dress her in the new clothes himself? She struggled to escape, but to no avail. He was a very powerful man and she had no hope of pitting her strength against his.

"That will be all, Millie," he said.

"Don't leave, Millie," cried Kate.

"I said, that will be all, Millie. Take those rags outside and burn 'em. Carlos has a fire ready."

"*Burn* them?" The Reverend Mr Farleigh's daughter was appalled. "But that's a shocking waste of perfectly good clothing—"

He snorted.

"But it is," she persisted. "I am very sure that the vicar's wife would be glad of them for some of her poorer parishioners. You have no idea how difficult it is to ensure that people are adequately clothed."

He raised an ironic eyebrow. "Believe me, Miss Farleigh, my appreciation of that particular problem grows hourly."

Kate stamped her foot in frustration.

Jack grinned. "Take 'em to the parson's wife, Millie, with

my comp—'' he glanced at Kate's face and changed his mind ''—with Miss Farleigh's compliments.''

''At least leave me one of the old dresses,'' Kate cried. ''I cannot possibly carry out some of my duties in such elegant outfits as those.''

''What sort of duties do you mean?'' enquired Jack silkily.

''Well, things like scrub—'' Kate floundered to a halt and glared at him, realising the full extent of his trickery.

''Exactly,'' he concluded, enjoying his victory. ''Take 'em out, Millie.''

Millie did not dare disobey. ''I'm sorry, miss,'' she muttered, casting a sympathetic look at Kate. She left, taking Kate's clothes with her.

Kate struggled in Jack's grip for a moment longer and then changed her tactics. She held herself stiffly and forced herself to meet the angry blue eyes.

''Unhand me, sir,'' she demanded, her eyes glittering with haughty indignation.

''I told you,'' he grated. ''You had half an hour. The time is up.''

''How dare you steal all my clothes?''

''Not quite all, I think.'' He glanced down at the dress she was wearing. ''I did warn you.''

At that she started to struggle again, but he effortlessly held her arms behind her and then held them in the grip of one large strong hand. She was pressed hard against him, chest to chest. She could feel his heart thudding. He seemed to be breathing rather harder than usual.

''And now, Miss Katherine Farleigh,'' he said softly, his breath warm against her ear, ''will you agree to accept these clothes from my grandmother or not?''

''No, and you cannot make me!''

''Oh, no?'' His free hand went behind her and to her horror she felt his hand tug free a button at her neck. He looked at her, and one long, strong finger gently stroked the soft skin of her nape. Kate stared defiantly back, struggling to maintain her composure, willing her body not to respond to the delightful sensation.

He undid a second button and waited, stroking, circling, smoothing her skin. His eyes darkened. His body seemed to surround her and it took every bit of Kate's self-discipline not to lean into him. And he knew it, the beast, she told herself, desperately resisting the tiny seductive caresses. His tactics were utterly unfair, totally despicable, Kate decided, so she tried to kick him. Her legs were restrained by the pressure of his powerful thighs. He reached for the third button, but Kate had had enough.

"Yes, all right, then, I accept the clothing," she snapped, adding under her breath, "You big bully!"

He heard her and chuckled. "This time, Miss Farleigh, I believe brawn has won the day." He released her and stood back triumphantly. "You'd better mean it," he added, "for if you defy me once more—"

"You need not go on about it so—I gave you my word," she muttered crossly.

"So you did." His eyes mocked her anger.

Kate glared at him, wishing she could think of something—anything to wipe that infuriating grin off the wretched man's face. "Get out of my room," she ordered.

His grin grew wider. "Sore loser," he said softly, and left.

In a whirl of temper Kate flung off her old clothes and donned new ones—new underclothing, the soft, warm, dove-grey dress she had liked so much and a grey spencer, smartly frogged with black and gold braid. The sensual pleasure of the fine new clothes did nothing to alleviate her annoyance with Jack Carstairs. He had no right to force her to accept them...after all, she was entitled to choose what she wore, wasn't she? She wasn't his slave or anything, was she? If they truly did come from Lady Cahill, she supposed she had no moral qualms about accepting them. But whether she did so or not was *her* choice—not his!

Oh, but the man was infuriating—always sticking his nose in where it was neither needed nor wanted! She kicked her old clothes into a heap in the corner, wishing they were Jack Carstairs instead.

A short time later there was a knock on the door.

"What do you want now?" she exploded. There was a brief silence.

"If you please, miss," said Millie's hesitant voice, "Mr Carstairs sent me up to fetch the rest of the things to go to the parson."

Kate handed the bundle to Millie and watched as the girl took the last remaining remnants of her old life.

It was not such a bad thing, she realised suddenly. Her old clothes had carried old associations—and none of them good. Some had been given to her after she'd escaped from the French—reluctant charity to a disgraced woman. Some dated from her girlhood before they all went to war. All of them were dyed black with grief. She had put those times behind her now, and was building a new life. The new clothes were symbolic of that.

She smoothed down the long woollen sleeve of the grey spencer. Never had she worn such lovely, fashionable, expensive clothing. She noticed Millie's sidelong glance as she did so and smiled a little ruefully.

Millie grinned back at her. "Aye, "tis sad to lose old clothes—some seem like old friends, don't they, miss? But, well, it's a beautiful jacket, miss. And all the rest. The old lady sent them, I hear." There was a question in her voice, and Kate hastened to reassure her.

"Yes, Lady Cahill. It was very kind of her."

Millie nodded. "Ah, well, that be all right, then." She paused. "Like a cup of tea, miss?"

Kate hesitated.

"It's all right," said Millie, reading her thoughts accurately. "Mr Carstairs is off up the Bull."

"I beg your pardon?"

"The Bull, miss—the Bull and Boar Tavern. He'll not be back till late, I reckon."

"Oh, well, then, in that case, yes, I'd love one."

Later that evening Kate donned one of her new nightgowns and slipped into bed, shivering. The nights were getting very cold—soon she'd have to think about heating a brick to take to bed with her. Or perhaps using that bedwarmer she'd found. She burrowed down into the bedclothes, enjoying the feel of the soft linen nightgown against her skin. She had taken out the silk one and looked at it for a moment of two, then put it wistfully away. She could not imagine a time when she might have a use for it. Such a garment was not meant as clothing to warm a girl at night—rather, it aimed to warm a man...

For the first time in months, Kate thought of Henri and the things he had done to her in the privacy of his tent. She had not disliked them...but any pleasant memories had been driven out by the realisation that she was not wed to him after all, that he was a stranger who'd lied to her, tricked her, taken marital rights illicitly. And she'd felt used and angry and guilty...

She wondered what it would be like to share those pleasures with Jack. She thought of the silken nightgown—as it had looked draped incongruously against his big, masculine body. Having seen the creamy silk sliding through his fingers, it was easy to imagine the same creamy silk sliding over her body, and those same tanned fingers stroking, caressing, exploring...

Suddenly her face flamed in the dark. Such thoughts! It was shocking. She knew now why girls were kept so ignorant until marriage—the whole thing was far too unsettling. She burrowed her face into the pillow, cooling her cheeks on the cold linen.

She'd been blaming that quarrel over the clothes on Jack Carstairs but, in truth, she'd provoked most of it herself. It had been Kate who'd thrown down the gauntlet, not him—she'd known very well how he would react if she refused the clothes, and he had. Giving her the excuse to defy him...

She squirmed in mortification as she realised it was she who had first laid hands on him, she who had provoked that whole physical tussle. Worse, she'd enjoyed it, had liked the feeling of being in his arms, had wanted him to keep touching, stroking, caressing...imagining Jack doing to her what Henri had done...

Bleakly Kate faced the truth: those women in Lisbon were not so wrong about her after all—she *was* a wanton hussy—she'd just proved it. Miserably she pulled the covers over her head and tried to think pure thoughts. It didn't work. All she could think of was the way she had felt when Jack Carstairs held her. Kate curled herself into a ball in the big bed. The only thing to do was to recite every psalm, prayer and passage from the Bible that she knew and hope they would drive the thoughts from her head. It would take a long time, for she had frequently been made to memorise passages from the Bible as a punishment. And she had been a *very* naughty child...

At the Bull and Boar Tavern, Jack sat nursing a brandy, staring into the fire, oblivious of the noise of his fellow drinkers.

His face softened into a half-smile as he recalled the way she'd boldly faced him down, a stubborn little ragamuffin in her dreadful black hand-me-down dresses, sternly rejecting the clothes she desired so badly. And she did desire them; there was no doubt about it in his mind.

He could tell by the way she'd touched her cheek to the

material, like a child caressing a puppy or kitten, by the way she'd slid her fingers through the silk of that nightgown, as if she'd never even imagined such a garment was possible.

Only Kate was no child. He'd been unable to resist teasing her, flirting, flustering her...

He tossed down the last of the brandy and signalled to the landlord to bring him another. A buxom tavern wench brought it instead, pressing up against him invitingly as she did so. Jack's eyes automatically went to the gaping neckline that was presented for his enjoyment and he registered that she was both attractive and willing. He glanced up and shook his head, smiling to soften his rejection. No, a tumble with a willing tavern wench would not solve his problems.

He recalled the dreamy way Kate had draped the fine silk nightgown against her soft skin and felt his body tighten again, imagining her in it.

Impossible...unthinkable...

Perhaps he should take up the tavern wench's offer after all... He glanced across at her again, but somehow she seemed too buxom, too willing, too... He realised the way his thoughts were heading and tried to quash them firmly.

Bloody hell! Was *that* what that scene in her bedroom had been all about? He couldn't deny that he had been aroused by the sight of her with that damned silk thing. Was that what had prompted him to go so far, undoing the very buttons at her back? He recalled the feel of the warm silken skin of her nape and the scent of her body and swore darkly.

What the hell was he going to do? If he wasn't more careful, things with Kate Farleigh would get out of hand. They almost had. Her teasing sense of fun, the wholehearted way she threw herself into a quarrel, her very defiance spurred him to want to push it further with her each time. He felt entirely too stimulated by her very presence. If she'd been a different sort of woman, he'd have no hesitation in making her his mistress—and what a mistress she'd make, he thought. All fire and passion and silky limbs and hair. He felt aroused just thinking about it.

But Kate was no kitchen maid, nor a tavern wench—she was a respectable lady, and after Julia Davenport he'd forsworn all dealings with respectable ladies for ever.

Damn it all to hell and back!

He wondered how his grandmother was faring with her enquiries into Kate's situation. He hoped it was going well. The sooner she was out of his hair the better—for both of them.

He called for another drink.

Chapter Seven

Kate awoke very early one morning. She slid out of bed, padded across the chilly floor and peered outside. It was almost dawn, faint shards of morning light dimming the last of the stars. Winter had begun—outside it looked cold, but inviting. For the last week she had worked unceasingly indoors, and she was feeling stale and housebound. A good brisk walk was what she needed.

The house seemed deserted as she slipped out of the back door. Her boots crunched across the frosted grass. As the pure, cold air bit into her lungs, Kate felt a surge of exhilaration. The rich earthy scent of rotting leaves and the sharp contrast of pine was in the air and it felt good to be alive. Suddenly she felt free of all the constraints of her life—her poverty, her past, her concerns about the future, her problems with Jack Carstairs.

It had been more difficult than she'd expected, working in such close proximity, feeling as she did about him. Such shameless, entirely inappropriate feelings, too. Every night. Sometimes *even during the day*. It was dreadful. Kate had done her best to fight them with passages from the Bible, but even that failed to eradicate the problem. It was very lowering to discover how steeped in depravity she had become.

She told herself a thousand times a day that such dreams were foolish, as well as wicked. She was a disgraced woman. She could never enter his world. He would be disgusted if he ever found out about Henri.

Such dreams were impractical, too—even had she been as pure as the day she was born, she was still poor and Jack needed to marry an heiress to make up for the fortune he had lost when his father had disinherited him.

In fact, she told herself severely, Kate Farleigh had no business to be thinking anything at all about Jack Carstairs except what she would cook him for dinner. She knew the correct behaviour for a woman in her position and, even if she couldn't make her feelings behave, she could try.

So she'd tried to keep out of his way, tried to keep a formal barrier between them, tried to follow Lady Cahill's instructions to ensure her grandson lived in a civilised fashion, tried in all ways to be the perfect, invisible housekeeper.

But all her good resolutions had been ruthlessly undermined by Jack Carstairs himself. He always seemed to be watching her—appearing from nowhere, opening doors, seating her at table as if she were a fine lady. Glaring gimlet-eyed if he found her doing anything he deemed "inappropriate", storming off in a temper when she pointed out in the most reasonable of tones that she knew what she was doing.

And she'd tried, so very hard, to resent it.

He was being ridiculous, she'd told herself. What did a man know about housekeeping anyway? He had no business interfering with things which were none of his domain. He was a bossy, meddlesome, arrogant pest!

But it was more difficult than she'd imagined. Her strength of mind was weakened by the realisation that he was concerned for her welfare, that he cared whether she was comfortable, that he wished to shelter her from the harshness of her everyday life. Even if he was just being gentlemanly and polite, even if he treated all his housekeepers like this, it was still very…weakening.

And that, combined with her own wanton tendencies, made life with Jack Carstairs very dangerous.

Kate sighed, then rallied herself—listing his character defects was a useful strategy. She did so as she marched down the garden path, enjoying the cold air, the droplets of dew still shivering on the plants as she passed. He was frightfully bossy, even for a major in His Majesty's Coldstream Guards. And arrogant. Stubborn. Yes, indeed—worse than any mule she had wrangled with on the Peninsula. And infuriating, especially when he had trapped her in some misdeed, then laughed at her with those wicked blue eyes.

And moody. Some days he would be warm and friendly, then, from out of nowhere, a blaze of intensity would emanate from him. His blue gaze would seem to burn right into her, then just as suddenly he'd turn away and storm out of the room in cold, bitter withdrawal.

Mornings were the worst; he usually slammed into the kitchen from outside, flinging himself down at the table, surly and uncommunicative for some time, drinking cup after cup of her coffee. Sometimes he would refuse to eat the breakfast she'd cooked, and limp straight through the kitchen, grey-faced and grim. On those days he would retire upstairs to his private parlour where, Kate gathered, he quietly drank himself into oblivion, preferring to drown his demons rather than face them.

On those days his unhappiness ate away at her, burning away all her good resolutions like acid. On those days it was hardest of all to remember that she was only his housekeeper, there on sufferance…she wanted to be so much more… She longed to have the right to put her arms around him, to comfort him and to coax and tease him out of his black depressions. But she had no right.

On those days she threw herself into the jobs she hated

most, the hard, dirty, filthy jobs—rendering mutton fat, cleaning and black-leading the grates, sifting wood ash and boiling it up to make lye. Boiling the cottons and linens in a big copper boiler, filling the laundry with steam. Tossing other clothes in flour and then beating them until clouds of flour flew, leaving them clean and sweet-smelling but her hair and nostrils clogged.

In spite of it all, Kate found herself dreaming about him day and night—even when making soap, when the stink of the sheep fat and home-made lye made her eyes water! He was so impossibly attractive, particularly when he looked at her with that smile lurking wickedly in his eyes, inviting her to share his amusement. And when his voice deepened and took on that low resonance it shivered though her bones, turning them to honey…

Kate headed towards the forest. It was magical. Dawn was stealing over the hushed landscape, highlighting the purity of the bare, frost-etched branches. Her breath escaped in misty tendrils and hung in the motionless chill. Far away she could hear a cockerel crowing, and beyond that a dog barking. It was as if she was the only person astir in the world. Kate hugged the delightful sensation to her and strode on.

Suddenly she heard the sound of rapid hoofbeats close behind her—too close. She dived off the narrow pathway just as a riderless horse pounded past her, reins dangling free, stirrups flapping.

Shaken, she clambered out of the tangled underbrush, smoothing her skirts and brushing mud from her hands. Someone had had an accident—a rider had been thrown. Should she go back and see if they were all right, or should she try to catch the horse first? If its reins got tangled or caught, it could injure itself. She ran along the path and came to a stile, where a large roan stallion stood, snorting and tossing his head, unable to go any further. Calmly Kate approached, talking quietly and coaxingly, while he watched her in suspicion, poised for flight.

It was one of Jack's horses, she was sure, though why he should keep so many horses when he couldn't ride was beyond her comprehension. It was the same horse she'd seen on her first morning at Sevenoakes. Clearly he was a rogue, and one in need of more exercise than he was currently receiving. She had seen him running free several times before, Carlos in hot pursuit.

Had a thief tried to ride it? If so, he'd made a big mistake—that particular horse had only ever been ridden by Jack, according to Carlos. Jack had bred the horse himself, broken him to bridle and trained him to do his every bidding. He'd even taken the horse to war with him. And now no one rode him at all. Jack should have sold the horse, she thought, not kept it here, under his eye, where every sight of it was a bitter, festering reminder that he could no longer ride.

"Come on, there…good boy…there, there…" she murmured, wishing she'd brought an apple with her. She held out her hand as if offering something and continued slowly and deliberately to approach the horse. Curiously, it thrust out its neck, sniffing to see what titbit she was holding. Kate deftly and calmly took hold of the dangling reins.

The big horse tried to jerk away, but she held him firmly, soothing him with murmured endearments and steady hands. She'd always loved horses, and they seemed to know it. Jack's roan was no exception—under Kate's calming influence he stopped his nervous trembling, and was soon blowing affectionate snuffles into the front of her dress. She quickly checked him over, running experienced hands down his legs, and was relieved to find no sign of damage. Now to see if he would accept her on his back.

With some difficulty, for he was still nervous of any other rider, and she was hampered by her long skirts, Kate managed to mount the big horse, using the stile as a mounting block. He reared up and snorted in fear at first, but Kate clung on tightly, and her firm hands and low, soothing voice soon had him under control again. Then, sidling and dancing under her unaccustomed light weight, the roan headed back down the narrow pathway at a brisk trot, shying skittishly at every falling leaf or shifting shadow.

For the first few moments, Kate was wholly engrossed in controlling her mount, then, as it became clear that the stallion accepted her mastery, pleasure filled her—it was so long since she had ridden a horse. And this was such a fine horse. She could understand why Jack had been unable to bring himself to sell the animal. The thought occurred to her that perhaps she could ask if she might exercise him. He certainly needed it.

As the path opened out, she saw a trail of hoofprints crossing the field nearest the house, and remembered her task. Someone might be hurt, even if it was a thief who deserved punishment! Castigating herself at her selfish pleasure in the ride, she urged the stallion into a canter. Rounding the back of the stable, she saw a prone figure lying on the frozen ground.

Kate's heart missed a beat. No, surely not. She urged the horse closer, then flung herself off, retaining just enough presence of mind to tie it to a nearby bush. The figure on the ground was ominously still.

Breathing hard, she fell on her knees beside him, heedless of the cold, wet mud, and gently turned him over. Dear Lord, she prayed, let him not be badly hurt!

"Jack. Are you all right?" There was no answer. She laid her cheek to his chest. His heart was beating steadily. Thank God! Swiftly she ran her hands over his limbs. Nothing was broken. She gently examined his head but could find no extraordinary bump or cut. He was as white as a corpse, and almost as cold.

Kate whipped off her pelisse and tucked it around him,

then eased his head and shoulders into her lap, abandoning all modesty, surrounding his body with her legs. She would ensure his warmth, at least. Later, if he did not regain consciousness, she would have to leave him and go for help. But while he was so pale and frozen and helpless she could not leave him.

She held him close, praying silently that he would be all right and that someone would come soon to help them. One hand cupped his rough, stubbled chin, tenderly cradling his head against her breast, the other smoothed his hair back off his forehead. She murmured soothing words in his ear, her breath mingling with his in the crispy air.

She was just deciding reluctantly that she might have to leave him to fetch help when Jack's eyes flickered open. He stared up at her blankly for a moment or two and muttered, "You?" in a tone of bemusement, then closed his eyes again.

"How do you feel?" Kate asked softly, his head still against her breast.

"Bloody," he muttered, still with his eyes closed.

"Oh, no, there is no blood," she assured him.

One blue eye opened and regarded her sardonically. "Good." He lay heavily against her for another few moments, then, seeming to become aware of just how intimately he was lying against her, he sat up, groaning. He swore as a sudden wave of pain shot through his leg, and he stilled his movements suddenly, bending to examine his leg more closely.

"You haven't broken anything either," Kate said reassuringly.

"And you'd know, I suppose," he said.

Kate didn't allow herself to rise to his bait. "Well, yes, I would know, but I don't expect you to believe me. Now, it's extremely cold on this ground and you'd better move if it's at all possible."

He glanced at her again, and a frown darkened his forehead

as he noticed that she was shivering. Then his eyes fell to her pelisse, tucked securely around him. He swore, dragging it off him and almost angrily thrusting it at her. ''Put that on at once, you little fool! Do you want to catch your death?''

Kate ignored him. ''Do you think you can stand up?''

Jack moved his bad leg a little and groaned. ''I think I can manage to walk, but the question is, can your ears bear the bad language that will doubtless result from the effort?''

Kate laughed aloud at this. As if he did not already curse with almost every breath he took! ''Here, put your arm across my shoulder and see if you can stand.''

He sat up and she wedged her shoulder under his armpit. Using his good leg and herself as a lever, he slowly rose to his feet. His lips were tightly compressed, but he did not utter a word. By the time he was upright, he looked exhausted. White lines around his mouth told Kate he was in considerable pain.

''Do you really think you should be trying to walk on your bad leg?'' said Kate hesitantly. ''I could easily run for help and fetch someone to carry you on a litter.''

''I'll be damned if I'll let the blasted thing make me a cripple,'' he muttered bitterly.

''Oh, well, that's a relief,'' murmured Kate provocatively.

He shot her a look of hard enquiry.

Her lips twitched with amusement. ''I feared the strain would be too much for you.''

''I fail to understand what you find to amuse you in this situation,'' he grated.

''Oh, nothing, to be sure, sir,'' she said. ''Only that I feared that your effort to refrain from cursing would be too much for you. However, I perceive that your tongue is in its usual fine form, so I need feel no anxiety on your behalf.''

He stared for a few seconds and then recalled his use of the word ''damned''. Despite himself, his lips twitched. Leaning heavily on her, he began to move slowly towards the house. After a few minutes he glanced down at her. "You really are the oddest girl."

"What makes you say so?"

"Ninety-nine women out of a hundred would be turning this into a major dramatic occasion, weeping and having hysterics over me, and here you are, having the audacity to tease me about bad language."

"Would you prefer me to have hysterics, then, sir?" Kate pretended to consider it seriously. "I must confess that I haven't had a great deal of experience in the matter, but if it would make you more comfortable, then I'm sure that I could undertake to stage a very convincing bout of hysterics. If you prefer it, that is." Her eyes danced mischievously, but all the time she urged him onward, hoping her nonsense would distract him from the pain.

He threw back his head and laughed outright at that. "Good God, no! Heaven preserve me from hysterical females!"

They continued their laboured progress for a few more minutes, then stopped for a brief respite.

"You have no idea how refreshing it is to have a sensible female to deal with," he said earnestly.

At this Kate was forced to lower her head and compress her lips to prevent herself laughing out loud.

He noticed, however. "What is it now?" he asked and, when she did not respond, he put a hand under her chin and turned her face up to his. Finding it brimful of suppressed merriment, he frowned in suspicion.

"Well, what have I said to cause this?" With a light finger he flicked at the dimple which peeped elusively out.

Her eyes danced irrepressibly. "For weeks now you have been calling me 'the stubbornest, most infuriating female it has ever been my misfortune to meet'!" she growled in a deep gruff voice. Then she allowed her mouth to droop mournfully. "And *now*, when you call me *a sensible female*, alas, there are no witnesses!"

His lips twitched. "Well, most of the time..." he began.

Kate burst into peals of infectious laughter and reluctantly he joined in. As they laughed, she met his eye and felt the jolt of warm good humour pass through her. Slowly the laughter died in his eyes and she felt his gaze intensify. Suddenly Kate became hotly aware of the intimacy of their position, her body held tightly under his arm, wedged firmly against his hard, warm body, his mouth only inches away from hers. For a moment they stood there, their eyes locked, then she felt, rather than saw, his mouth moving down towards hers. Abruptly she turned her head away, her heart racing, her mouth dry.

"Come on now," she murmured. "We'd best keep moving and get you in out of this chilly morning. Your leg will need to be examined by the doctor." She felt him withdraw as they moved off.

"I'm not having any damned leech or sawbones maul me around any more. I had enough of them to serve me a lifetime on the Peninsula."

"Oh, but surely you cannot compare the physicians we have here in England with some of the butchers that passed for surgeons during wartime?" Kate said incautiously.

Jack stopped and looked at her in surprise. "Do you know, you're the first person in England that I've ever heard with an accurate notion of some of those bloody devils? Apart from anyone who was there, I mean. You sound as if you actually have an inkling of what it was like."

Kate smiled slightly. "Do I, indeed?" Her face sobered. "Well, I did have two brothers and a father who died there. Now, have you had enough of a rest to continue, or do you wish to rest a moment or two more?"

That got him moving again. Kate was relieved, but, more

than that, he'd given her the opening she'd wanted. "Not all doctors are butchers, you know," she said after a time.

He snorted.

"It's true," she insisted. "I once met the most wonderful physician, descended from a long line of physicians, right back to the Moors, who used methods of treatment that enabled some terrible wounds to heal almost like new."

"Humph!"

"For instance, with a bad leg like yours," she persisted, "where the wound had healed, but the muscles had lost their strength, he would order that the leg be massaged three times daily with hot oils, the oil being rubbed well in and each part of the leg stretched and pummelled."

"Ah…" he said ironically. "A torturer. I have heard that some of those oriental types have the most subtle and fiendish methods."

"I know it sounds like that, but it is truly efficacious, though it is not at all comfortable at first." Kate remembered the groans of anguish that her brother Jemmy had uttered when the treatment first began, and how it had taken all her will-power to continue the treatment.

"After a few short weeks, the limb begins to strengthen and, with added exercise, I believe that almost full power can be returned in some cases."

"Rubbish!" he snapped curtly. "Unscrupulous leeches preying on credulous fools."

Kate understood his hostility. Hope could be very painful.

"Possibly," she said quietly. "I suppose it depends on the wound, but this treatment had my brother walking after our English doctors had told him he would never be without crutches again."

She paused to let that sink in. "And his wound was very bad, enough to have them planning to amputate."

Kate would never forget frantically clinging to the surgeon's arm, begging him to wait for another opinion, and then the final relief when her father had burst into the tent and wrested the saw from the man's drunken hand.

"Perhaps the method may help your leg."

"I doubt it!"

"It could not hurt to try, surely?" she coaxed.

"Dammit! You know nothing about it, girl! I have been mauled enough by incompetents from the medical fraternity and I will have nothing to do with any more quack cures, especially those dreamed up by mysterious oriental fakirs!"

Kate felt a wave of frustration surge through her. It was perfectly obvious to her that he had been attempting to ride his horse in defiance of the medical prognosis he had been given and despite the pain his leg was so clearly giving him. It was sheer insanity to attempt to use a barely healed limb for strenuous exercise.

"Don't be so stupid. You cannot simply ignore damage done to muscles and sinews and ride by will-power alone. You are just a man, with a man's body. You were dreadfully injured and I am sorry for it, but you must face the fact of your injury, instead of pretending it does not exist."

"What the devil would you know about it? I'm damned if I'll give in to it," he growled, attempting to thrust her away.

Kate glared right back at him. "And who said you should give in to it?" she demanded. "Not I—I said face facts, not give in."

"Dammit, girl, you go too far. This is none of your concern!"

"Well, if you wish to ride that horse instead of falling off it all the time, you will have to do something differently," Kate said furiously. "You may be able to walk on that leg, but it is so stiff and weak you cannot grip on to a horse. And if you keep doing what you are doing you will end up giving yourself a much more serious injury. You need to retrain your muscles and exercise them. The treatment I spoke of is specifically aimed to restore flexibility and muscle strength…''

The words died on her tongue. Jack was staring at her with such a mixture of humiliation, outraged pride and sheer fury that she recoiled, thinking for a moment that he might strike her.

''Damn you to hell and back, girl! Mind your own blasted business!'' he exploded. ''I don't need your damned unwanted advice, I don't need your blasted quack miracle cures and I don't need your damned assistance. I can make my own way to the house!''

Kate knew she should stop, but she had to have one last try, using an analogy he might accept. ''What would you think of a trainer, who, after a horse had fallen and injured itself, put it straight at the highest jump, and expected it to succeed? Would you not think him a fool?''

He was silent. Not knowing whether to feel encouraged or not, Kate continued, ''A man who wants such a horse to jump again would surely walk it over low jumps, gradually raising them until it is strong enough and confident enough to jump anything. Well, wouldn't he? Think about it, Mr Carstairs.''

He stared at her, and for a moment Kate thought her argument might have reached him. But, gritting his teeth against the pain, Jack pushed her roughly away and began to stump painfully towards the house.

''You stupid stubborn man!'' raged Kate, going after him and inserting her shoulder under his again. ''If you don't want to listen to what I say, well, of course, that is your right, short-sighted as it may be… No, I *won't* be pushed away! How ridiculously…'' she cast around for an adequate adjective ''…manlike…to reject my practical assistance when you know you need it.''

Jack stopped and glared furiously down at her, his fingers biting into her shoulder.

"All right," she said hastily, meeting that fiery blue gaze. "I have said my piece now and I promise you I will say nothing more on the subject." She began to head once more towards the house, forcing him to move too.

They made slow, painful progress to the house, Kate silently cursing her runaway tongue. For the first time ever, they'd been completely easy with each other, even joking and laughing, despite his awkwardness at being discovered, helpless on the ground. And then she'd ruined it. Knowing what she knew.

As she'd sat on the cold ground, cradling his head against her, the whole picture had come together—the sound of a galloping horse when she first arrived, hoofprints on frosted grass, day after day, his early morning bad temper, white lines of pain around his mouth.

He'd been doing this for weeks, sneaking out before dawn to try and learn to ride again. His mental anguish, the desperation that drove him to try to ride, secretly, day after day, *knowing* he would fall—Kate's heart contracted at the thought. It had taken courage—mad, proud, stubborn courage. But without treatment he would never be able to do it. And sooner or later he was bound to do himself a grave injury.

It need not be that way, she was sure of it, and so she had spoken—too much. Offending the very pride she admired. He would never listen to her now, never forgive her. She was only his housekeeper, existing, not to put too fine a point on it, on the goodwill of his family. *When* would she learn to accept it?

Finally they reached the house and she helped him to a chair in the kitchen. "I'll fetch Carlos," she said quietly, and moved towards the door.

He did not acknowledge her; he just sat there, his face a white and bitter mask.

Chapter Eight

"What's this? Looks delicious."

Before Kate could say a word, Jack had scooped a fingerful of the creamy mixture and popped it in his mouth. She clapped a hand over her mouth, attempting unsuccessfully to repress her mirth. Giggles escaped her as his eyes filled first with disbelief, and then with disgust. He rushed outside and she heard the sounds of vigorous spitting, as he attempted to rid his mouth of the foul taste of her latest domestic effort.

Kate collapsed in a chair, and laughed until the tears rolled down her cheeks. It served him right. He had been hanging around the kitchen all day, popping in and out for no apparent reason—lurking! Several times she'd asked him if there was anything he wanted, but he'd almost snapped her nose off! It was his kitchen, wasn't it? Well, of course it was, the silly man! She knew that!

Normally it wouldn't have bothered Kate so much, but today was proving to be one of those days; first a bird's nest had fallen down the chimney right into the bouillon which had just reached aromatic perfection. And it was baking day, but the dough stubbornly refused to rise. And the kitchen had been cluttered with damp washing for days.

And she'd been sleeping badly, ever since the accident. That was his fault, too!

Kate saw him only at breakfast. She would not have admitted it to a soul, but she knew she only really started to breathe each morning when he limped through the kitchen door, those tell-tale white lines of pain around his mouth. It was only a matter of time before he injured himself seriously, and they both knew it, but the man was so stubborn!

Last night she'd slept even worse than usual, alternately dreaming of him and worrying about him. She'd awakened feeling scratchy and irritable. And then the wretched man had lurked! Underfoot! All day! Observing each disaster!

So now justice was served, and the sounds of his violent expectorations were as music to her ears. Still chuckling, Kate wiped her eyes with a corner of her apron. He re-entered the kitchen, wiping his mouth, which was still puckered at the lingering after-taste.

"Are you trying to poison me?" He grimaced again and scrubbed at his mouth with his handkerchief. "What the hell was that foul stuff anyway?"

"Spermacetti oil, white wax, almond oil," she said, between giggles. "I haven't yet added the lemon oil and lemon juice."

He choked. "Spermacetti oil? You were planning to feed me *whale oil*? That's for burning in lamps!"

Kate giggled again. It was a new recipe she was trying—guaranteed to remove freckles. "I do not usually feed my cold cream to gentlemen, no matter how hungry—or greedy—they are."

"Cold cream?"

"Cold cream."

"Hrmph!" He turned away. His ears turned slightly pink. Another giggle escaped her.

He continued to fidget for some minutes, then finally he

spoke. "Pour yourself a cup of coffee and sit down, Miss Farleigh. I wish to talk to you." His voice was serious.

She fetched two cups and placed them on the table, still trying to keep a straight face. Eventually she met his gaze. He looked away, and the laughter died in her eyes. This really was serious.

"That brother of yours—you say he was able to regain the use of his leg?"

"Yes, completely," she murmured, her pulse beginning to race.

"Because of the treatment you described to me?"

"Yes," she confirmed, trying hard to suppress her rising jubilation.

"And you think my leg may benefit from similar treatment?"

"I am no medical expert but, yes, I think it would help." She swallowed convulsively. "At least...I cannot say if your leg will be completely restored, but I firmly believe there would be significant improvement."

"Because of your brother."

There was considerable scepticism in his voice, but Kate detected a grain of hopefulness. It was time to tell him the truth. It might cost her his respect, but if he could be convinced to try the treatment he might regain full use of his leg. Faced with that option, there was no choice but to risk it.

"Not only because of my brother—there were many others."

"Others?"

"Yes, I saw this treatment used on many of our soldiers and, in almost every case, it brought some improvement."

"And naturally there were hundreds of wounded soldiers in the village in...where did you say my grandmother found you—Bedfordshire?"

"No, of course not, but I saw hundreds of wounded soldiers in Spain and Portugal."

He was incredulous. "*You* were in Spain and Portugal?"

She nodded.

"In wartime?"

"Yes."

"When?"

"For the last three years."

"On your own?"

She flushed. "With my father. And my brothers, where possible."

"What was your father doing there? Surely he was too old to be in the army."

"My father felt he was needed more on the Peninsula than in his parish in Bedfordshire."

"So he just packed up his Bible and went?" he said sceptically.

"Yes, indeed. Though you would have to have known my father to understand. Once he had made up his mind there was no gainsaying him."

"But what of you?"

She looked at him in mild surprise. "I went with him, of course. He was a brilliant scholar, but hopelessly impractical in the domestic field. He had no notion at all of how to procure lodgings or food or any of the other things so necessary to life in a country torn by war."

"And you had?"

She looked at him in surprise. "Yes, of course." She flushed, realising she must sound boastful. "Well, not at first, but I soon learned. And once I was able to speak some of the language it became much easier."

"Incredible. You were—how old—seventeen, eighteen?"

"At first, yes."

"And you did not mind?"

She opened her eyes at that. "No, I did not mind." She

grimaced wryly. "Remember my unladylike hands? They're a sign of a terrible hoyden, I'm afraid. I had some of the best times of my life travelling with the army… I see I've shocked you."

"No, not at all. But…did you not experience a great deal of hardship?" Jack knew several officers' wives who had gone to war, but all of them had had servants to see to everything. And a husband to protect them. A girl who wore the sort of clothes Kate had arrived in certainly would not have had many servants.

"Oh, naturally there were times I wished we were not having to sleep in a dirty, vermin-infested village, or ride for hour after hour in the pouring rain or the sweltering heat—I am not unnatural, you know! But at least it was never dull. There was always something to be done and someone to talk to."

She could not explain to him how she'd almost welcomed such discomforts because they highlighted her usefulness to her father, making him value her for the first time in her life.

"But the danger. Did your father not consider that?"

"Oh, yes, of course!" She was indignant at the slur. "Why, at Badajoz he kept me virtually confined to my tent for more than a week."

Jack gasped. "You were at *Badajoz*?" He could not believe it. That bloody siege with its even bloodier aftermath! And her father had protected her from blood-crazed rampaging troops with a piece of canvas!

"Yes, and at Ciudad Rodrigo and all the other battles that are now famous, but always I was well to the rear during the fighting," she said crossly, "for several officers spoke to him and after that Papa was most insistent about it."

"I should think so too!" he muttered, his hair raising on his scalp as he recalled some of the bloodier incidents in his experience of the war.

"Yes, but it was very impractical, for how could I tend the wounded when I was so far to the rear all the time?"

"Tend the wounded?" His tone was incredulous.

Kate flushed, knowing the reason for his surprise. He thought her immodest. Harry too had been incredulous when he had discovered that she had been helping wounded soldiers, not simply her brothers. He had been furious, forbidding her to do anything so indelicate again. Her refusal had caused him to thin his lips and walk off angrily. Obviously Jack Carstairs felt the same—well, his good opinion of her was a small thing to risk, if it meant he might ride again.

"Well, I had to do something to help—there was so much need. And that is how I came to know the Moorish doctor." She looked earnestly at him. "And why I have such a strong belief in his methods of treatment."

He reached across the table and took her small hand in his large one, his thumb rubbing gently over the skin of her small, grubby "hoyden's hands'. He gazed at her face, noting the delicacy of her features, the small tip-tilted nose, the wide, innocent-looking eyes that had witnessed so much hardship and suffering. "You truly are the most amazing girl."

Suddenly she became acutely aware of the warmth of his hand, the large brown thumb that was moving caressingly back and forth across her skin, and she flushed and awkwardly pulled her hand away.

"Nonsense," she muttered gruffly. She started clearing away the cups, intensely aware of his eyes following her every movement. "Would you like me to prepare the hot oils for the treatment? It is not difficult—it only takes persistence."

Now it was his turn to look awkward. "Can you not explain to Carlos what is required?"

"It would be better if I did it myself," Kate said. "I can show Carlos once I have ascertained the treatment needed—

it is not difficult, but there are a few tricks to it that are better demonstrated than explained.''

Kate saw the look on his face and flushed. He *was* shocked at her indelicacy. Well, there was no need for him to be concerned—she was no delicate flower—but it was very difficult to force herself to disillusion him.

''It is...I...'' she began, stumbling over the words. With her face averted she continued woodenly, ''Mr Carstairs, I am not the innocent you seem to believe me. I have seen the male form before, have cared for a number of wounded men, not only my brother, so, you see, you have nothing to be concerned about.'' She avoided his eye, her cheeks rosy. ''So, shall I prepare the oils now?''

''No, no, I was only enquiring out of interest,'' he said hurriedly, unnerved by her willingness to begin at once.

''But you will think on it.''

He smiled faintly at her intensity. ''I shall,'' he agreed, ''but I have much to do today.''

He stood up and left the room. Kate watched him go, a frown on her face. He had nothing at all to do, she knew. He would probably spend the remainder of the day brooding. Drinking. The man had suffered more than physical damage. It was almost as if he was afraid to hope. Well, she could hope enough for two.

That evening, however, Jack did not retire in his customary solitude, but invited Kate and Martha to join him in the parlour where Carlos had lit a fire. He had a bottle of port beside him when they arrived, but he was not drunk. He poured Kate and Martha a glass of sherry, and they settled down in front of the cosy fire and chatted. Kate, initially wary of his motives, soon relaxed, perceiving he was making a genuine effort to play the polite host.

Gradually Jack turned the conversation around to more recent events. Her tale of being with the army had stunned him. He had to know more.

"So tell me, why did your father drag you off to travel in the tail of an army?" Jack tried to keep the anger out of his voice. It was ill to think badly of a man he had never met, a man who was dead and gone, what was more, but he could not forgive Kate's father for exposing such an innocent young girl to the horrors of war, valiant little creature though she might be.

"In the tail?" Kate grinned. "You can't think I would be so poor-spirited as to travel at the tail with all the heavy baggage and complaining wives and impedimenta! Nothing so dreary, I'm glad to say. Jemmy found me a charming little Spanish mare and I was able to go where I wanted."

"Good God!" he muttered, appalled. Had none of her family recollected she was a sheltered young girl of eighteen or so?

"Oh, it was much more convenient, for then I was free to ride back and forth, keeping an eye on Papa, for he was dreadfully absent-minded at times, and also the baggage, which travelled with Luis, our Portuguese servant. And then, you know, I was always on hand to snaffle a good spot when we stopped for the night and make sure everything was comfortable for them and a hot meal ready."

She smiled as she sipped her sherry. "We were lucky—Jemmy was hunting mad. Even when we were returning to Portugal after Talavera, and food was so scarce that almost everyone was starving, he managed to shoot a hare or something for the pot, just when I thought my stomach was going to stick to my backbone." She rubbed her stomach reminiscently. "Jemmy could turn even a retreat into a hunting trip."

Jack moved uncontrollably in his chair, flooded with anger, fighting an impulse to sweep her into his embrace. He, too, had fought at Talavera. He recalled only too well the horrors of that retreat, the starving men, the sheer bloody hell of being unable to provide enough food. That she should ever have been put in such a frightful position! How many times had this little creature faced starvation? He would never forget how thin and frail she had felt in his arms the first time he met her! How he wished he had known her earlier. He would have ensured she was never in danger, or frightened or hungry.

Kate blushed suddenly. "I'm sorry, I know it is unladylike to mention such things."

Jack was amazed. She could casually refer to the experience of living through a frightful battle and retreating with an exhausted and starving army, then blush because it was unladylike to mention such a thing as a stomach. His eyes caressed her. She was unique, this little Kate.

"I was at Talavera," he said quietly.

"Then you will recall that dreadful trip back into Portugal too." She nodded. "Were the Coldstreams at Busaco? Jemmy was wounded there. Was that where you caught your facial wound?"

"No." His hand crept up to his ravaged cheekbone. "This is a souvenir of Badajoz."

They both fell silent, remembering Badajoz. The fire crackled loudly as a knot of sap burst. A log fell and sparks twirled madly up the chimney. In her comfortable wing chair, Martha stirred, then returned to her heavy doze. Kate regarded her with compunction. She was an old woman, and she should not be dozing uncomfortably in a chair at this hour, but tucked up warmly in bed. But none of Kate's arguments could shift her—she was Kate's chaperon, and her reputation would be safely guarded by her old nurse. Even though Martha knew there was no reputation to guard.

"You seem remarkably calm, relating your experiences." Jack's deep low voice pulled Kate out of her reverie. "Were you never frightened before a battle, for instance?"

"Lord, yes, utterly terrified," she said simply. "Before every battle I was a mess—unable to eat, leaping six feet at every sound...even a little grumpy."

His warm chuckle washed over her. "Grumpy? Now why do I not find that difficult to believe?"

Kate wrinkled her nose. "Yes, fear brings out the virago in me. I used to snap at Ben for being such a big, slow stupid!"

She paused and stared into the flames for a moment. "Ben was the eldest. He was the sort of person you could not for one moment imagine in a hurry, or a flap, about anything. Yet he invariably got things done just as fast and with none of the drama that Jemmy or I seemed to cause."

She said in a slow, gruff voice, "'This sweaty haste doth make my head spin all the day'—Ben was always saying that to Jemmy or me, and Father would always take him to task about mangling Shakespeare and mentioning sweat in front of me." Her voice quavered a little.

Jack watched her from the shadows, his eyes unreadable. A father who didn't want her ears sullied with the word "sweat', but who took her into situations where she was surrounded by blood, sweat and far, far worse.

"Jemmy used to roast Ben about his unflappability too, but he was a wonderful brother. They were so different, those two—like quicksilver and stone... No, I don't mean stone precisely because that suggests Ben was cold and he wasn't—he was a big darling." Her eyes blinked rapidly and her lips quivered with emotion.

Jack wanted to gather her into his arms and kiss her grief and distress away. Poor, gallant little waif.

"Ben never saw Badajoz. He was killed at Ciudad Rodrigo... Were you at Ciudad Rodrigo?"

He shook his head.

She continued, "I remember that first day there so clearly. It was terribly cold, and the snow was frozen and crunchy underfoot from the frost that night. But the morning was so still and perfect—simply beautiful, you know, the sort of day when you long to go for a good gallop, then come home to a lovely hot breakfast...

"And then the big guns shattered the morning, pounding and pounding until I thought my eardrums would shatter too, though I was a long way from them, you know. And I stuffed my ears with rags to stop the noise... Ben was killed the next day. I suppose you could say he was lucky, for he caught a ball in the temple and probably didn't know what hit him before he was dead."

She bit her lip. "You probably think I am unnaturally cold to say he was lucky, but there are so many more terrible ways for a man to—"

He could restrain himself no longer. He had to touch her. He reached across and took her small, cold hands in a warm grip.

"He *was* lucky, Kate. There couldn't be a better way to go than instantly, in the open air, in the heat of action." His hands enveloped hers in warmth.

They lapsed into silence. The only sounds were the crackling of the fire and the slow, rhythmic sound of Martha sleeping. His thumbs stroked back and forth across her skin. Soothing, wordless reassurance.

"How did Jemmy and your father die?"

She blinked the tears back for a few moments, then said softly, "They were both caught by snipers on the way to Salamanca. You recall the way our army and the French were travelling parallel and exchanging shots every now and then to relieve the tedium?"

He nodded. They had been in so many of the same places and yet their paths had never crossed.

"Jemmy was wounded in the chest and, a short time later, Papa was caught in the stomach. Both wounds were fatal.

They could not bear the jolting of the cart, so I found a deserted farmhouse and stayed with them until they died.''

The simple statement hid a world of grief and Jack felt his heart stir. ''I think it is time you took yourself to bed.'' He rose, reached down a hand to help her up, then, without conscious volition, drew her into his arms, cradling her securely against his big warm body.

There was little passion in the embrace, just warm, protective, comforting strength, and she nestled against him, listening to the pounding of his heart, wishing the moment could last for ever. Kate had not expected to be held like this again in her life, and she clung to him, desperately, revelling in his warmth and strength and tenderness.

He reached down and gently tipped her face up to his and they gazed into each other's eyes, then his dark head bent over hers and their lips met in a long, tender kiss.

Martha snorted in her sleep and stirred, awakening, and in moments the two were standing in separate parts of the room, Kate bending over her old nurse, assisting her to stand, Jack leaning casually against the wall, his face in shadow again.

It was probably the port anyway, Kate told herself for the umpteenth time as she separated curds from whey in the kitchen, making cottage cheese. They'd barely spoken since that night. In fact, he'd obviously been going out of his way to avoid her. Kate realised he was regretting the impulse which had caused him to kiss her. And, though she could never regret anything so magical, she knew she *should*.

So she had decided to forget the conversation by the fire, the wonderful embrace that had sent her to bed floating on air. It was not an easy resolution, but she was managing quite well, the memory of his kiss occurring to her no more than a dozen times a day before being firmly banished. It was very wearing, being wanton.

''Señorita Kate, Major Jack, he say he is ready for your

torture treatment to begin. This morning.'' Carlos grinned. ''He no try to ride today, no hurt himself.''

Kate was stunned. Jack had listened to her after all! He was prepared to trust her. She grinned back at Carlos, delighted, then hastened to prepare everything before Jack could change his mind.

Holding the small pot of hot, aromatic oil carefully, she mounted the stairs and walked slowly with Carlos towards Jack's bedroom door. She was absurdly nervous. Don't be ridiculous, she told herself. You've done this a dozen times or more. There's no reason to behave in this missish fashion, just because you're in an English country house and not a Portuguese cottage or a tent in Spain.

Yes, a small voice answered her silently. But this is Jack...

She pushed open the door. Jack lay on the bed, dressed in a nightshirt, his lower body swathed in a sheet. He looked at her, glanced down at the sheet, clutched it more firmly around himself and his colour darkened.

''This is a damned stupid idea. I've changed my mind,'' he announced. ''Leave the stuff with Carlos. I'm sure we can work out what needs to be done.''

Kate perceived he was thoroughly embarrassed by her presence. All her nervousness dissolved like magic and she tried not to smile. ''Now don't be foolish. I told you before, it is not simply a matter of rubbing in a few oils. It is a special technique that must be taught.''

She noted his heightened colour and said softly, ''You must not worry that I am here. I have performed many much more difficult tasks. Try to imagine that I am simply one of those who tended your wounds in Spain.''

He snorted. His imagination could not do it. Kate was small and slender, with a smooth, clear complexion, and soft pink lips. The last person to touch his wound in Spain had been a big brawny soldier, bald, toothless, tattooed and with thē most extensive vocabulary of obscenities that Jack had ever encountered.

He braced himself as she reached for the sheet and clutched it tighter.

"Now don't be silly," she said firmly. "I must be able to see the leg, if I am to apply these oils to it in the proper way." She flushed slightly and said in a lower tone, "I told you before, I am not unacquainted with the male form. It will not embarrass me to view your leg."

Jack found he could not release the sheet. It was not so much that he was worried about offending her maidenly modesty, he realised, it was not wanting to see her look of revulsion when she saw the mess that was his leg.

Briskly she twitched the sheet away. Jack clenched his teeth, awaiting her disgusted reaction. She bent over it silently. The leg was white and hideously criss-crossed with violent red and purplish scars. The muscles were shrunken and slightly twisted in places, as if pulled out of alignment by the puckered scarring.

She examined it carefully, not letting her feelings show. He truly had been mauled about but, apart from the dreadful scarring, it didn't look too bad. She ran her hand gently down the leg, feeling the lines of the muscles. She felt him flinch under her touch and quickly met his gaze.

"Did that hurt?"

He was watching her, an odd look in his eyes. She had shown no sign of horror or disgust, no sign of sympathy or pity either.

"Did I hurt you, sir?" she repeated.

"Er…your hands are cold. I did not expect it, that's all."

"Oh." Kate continued to examine the leg.

"Now, Carlos," she said, "I am going to work first on these muscles." Carlos bent his head over the leg curiously. "See how they are pulled tight by the scarring here. That is what makes it so hard to bend. Now, a little of this oil just so, and then…'' She applied it to the leg and began to massage it in. Jack Carstairs groaned slightly and shifted awkwardly.

"Is the oil too hot, sir?"

"No, no…it's not that," he muttered, not meeting her gaze.

Kate continued the treatment, explaining softly to Carlos all the time. Her small strong fingers rubbed and pummelled and pushed at the shrunken muscles. Jack lay on the bed, his face a mask of control. Kate alternated small intensive localised movements with long, soothing strokes up and down the whole leg, pulling and pushing with a strong, smooth, rhythmic action. During one of these movements Jack uttered a muffled moan. Kate's head went up abruptly. This action was meant to be soothing and relaxing, not painful.

"Am I hurting you, sir?"

Jack flushed. "No, no…er…don't you think Carlos can take over now?"

"No, sir, not yet. I thought it would be best if I took him through a complete treatment first. It should take no more than fifteen or twenty minutes."

"Oh, God!" groaned Jack, and shifted under the sheet again.

"I must be hurting you," Kate said, distressed. "I am so sorry. This part of the treatment should not hurt at all. Perhaps there is something I have missed. Can you tell me exactly where the pain is located?"

He glared at her for a moment, examining her face for any sign of mischief. She looked back, troubled grey-green eyes innocently meeting his gaze. She really had no idea what her touch was doing to him.

"Dammit! No!" Jack growled crossly. "You're not hurting me at all. Just get it over with as quickly as possible!" His eyes darted past her, over her shoulder, to where Carlos was standing; Kate felt a spurt of surprise at the withering look Carlos received.

Kate bit her lip. Of course she was hurting him, or why was he moaning? Men were so stubborn at times. She didn't mind if he cursed or groaned, but she did need to know if the treatment was hurting or not and where. She continued in silence. He was getting tenser and tenser under her hands. It was puzzling. He should be relaxing. She redoubled her efforts, rubbing in the warm, aromatic oils with firm, rhythmical strokes along the length of his leg. Suddenly he groaned again and with a surge of sheets he turned over on to his stomach, sending Kate sprawling on the bed.

She sat up, flustered and astonished. "What on earth do you think you are doing?" she demanded crossly. "Turn over, please; I haven't finished there yet."

"Oh, yes, you have, Miss Farleigh," came the uncompromising reply, slightly muffled by the pillow. "That's quite enough from you."

Kate shrugged. "Oh, well, I suppose I can work on the back of the leg as well as the front." She reached out and began to rub it again.

"Damn and blast it, woman!" The words exploded from the pillow. He jerked his leg away from her and tried to thrust it back under the sheet. "Out, Miss Farleigh, now!"

"But—" Kate began.

"Carlos!"

Kate felt Carlos's hand on her shoulder. "Please, Señorita Kate," the man said. "You must go now."

"But I have not finished showing you everything."

Carlos grinned. "Oh, *señorita*, you have shown me plenty, I think."

"Carlos!" the deep angry voice from the pillow growled warningly.

"At once, Major Jack!" Carlos said hurriedly. His eyes glinting with private amusement, he turned back to Kate again. "It is certain that Major Jack can bear no more of your treatment today. Perhaps another time in the future…"

"Carlos!" There was no mistaking that tone.

"*Sí, sí*, Major Jack. Now, *señorita, por favor*." He ushered Kate rapidly out of the room and shut the door behind them.

Kate stopped on the landing. "I don't understand it at all," she said worriedly. "What I was doing should not have hurt him so much. He's not the sort of man who would complain of a little pain. His leg must be worse than I thought."

Carlos grinned down at her wickedly. "It was not his leg which was troubling him, *señorita*," he said meaningfully.

"What do you mean?"

Carlos shrugged. The English were so prudish about things such as this. She had brazenly entered Major Jack's bedroom and bared his leg without so much as a blush, so she was no innocent.

"Señorita Kate, it is a long time since the Major has been with a woman, and when you touched him…" He shrugged. "Well, he is a man, after all…"

Kate stared at him a moment, assimilating what he was telling her. Then a fiery blush surged up over her face and she was flooded with embarrassment. "Oh," she gasped, and fled.

Chapter Nine

For perhaps the twentieth time that evening Carlos glanced towards Kate with foreboding. The little mouse was behaving more like a cat tonight, pacing back and forth, clearly disturbed about something, and from the looks that she was casting towards the ceiling it concerned Major Jack.

Naturally. Carlos sighed gently. If she was touchy and moody, it was nothing to what his master had been. Ever since Major Jack had been unable to disguise his body's response to her.

Carlos shook his head. It was the simplest matter in the world. These English made such a fuss over things. So the Major was attracted to the little mouse. It would be something to be concerned about if he was not, in Carlos's opinion, for she had blossomed lately and was looking very pretty. But instead the Major must go to all lengths to avoid her, even having Carlos sneak around heating oils in secret, in case she found out he was continuing the massage treatment without her. Such foolishness.

Kate kicked one of the logs in the fire angrily, releasing a shower of sparks up into the chimney. How could he give up after only one attempt? she asked herself for the hundredth time. She was utterly convinced that massage would improve his leg, possibly even enable him to ride again.

Obviously he didn't have her faith. But to try it only once and then give up! Merely because he was affected by lust.

That was what was so upsetting. It was partly her fault—men were unable to control their baser natures, she'd been told. They took their lead from women, she'd been told. And she'd behaved so indelicately.

Assuring him she was not embarrassed to see his leg! Telling him she was no innocent! That she was well acquainted with the male form! No wonder he'd reacted as he had.

It was clearly eating away at him, for every evening since he had retired to the upstairs parlour and commenced to drink himself into oblivion. He even seemed to have given up on his morning attempts to ride.

Well, she would not stand for it any longer. There were two faces to guilt, she knew—it could fester inside a person, or it could be got rid of, by turning it outward, by turning it to anger. And a healthy dose of anger, Kate decided, was exactly what Mr Jack Carstairs was going to receive.

Carlos eyed the slender, pacing figure with misgiving. If she had a tail she would be lashing it. A wise man would hide himself discreetly away until the fireworks were over. Stealthily he rose. His movement caught Kate's eye. She stopped and turned towards him, decision and resolution in every inch of her. Carlos's heart sank. Too late, he thought mournfully.

"Carlos, come with me if you please. And bring that large bucket from the scullery." Dolefully he did so and followed her out of the room. She marched upstairs to Jack's private parlour. Carlos felt his hands growing damp. Surely she would know better than to disturb Major Jack at this time of night, when he would be in his blackest, bitterest mood—he would have consumed two bottles, maybe, by now. *Ay de mí!* It was madness.

* * *

Jack lay sprawled in a chair before the fire, a glass of brandy dangling perilously from his long, strong fingers. He gazed into the dancing flames, his eyes half-closed. Damn her. Damn her. Damn her! It had been so much easier before she had come into his life. So much easier...and so much duller. He should have forced her to go off with his grandmother.

She wouldn't have been here long enough to plague him, to provoke him, to insinuate herself into his...life.

She had no business being here, scrubbing his floors, cooking his meals, with no one to talk to in the evenings but a foolish old woman, a rascally Spanish groom, two illiterate farm girls and a crippled wreck. She should be in a ballroom, dressed in silk and satin, swirling round the floor as light as thistledown, engaging in light social *badinage* with a score of men hanging on her every word.

Six months! How would he ever stand it? It was hard enough to keep his hands off her as it was. She was like no woman he'd ever met. She'd been through so much. And yet, to look at her, see that fresh, sweet face, no one could believe she had spent three years at war, seen death, destruction, men at their worst, while in the process losing her entire family.

Curse her father! What the devil did he think he was about, taking a young girl into that hell-hole? Getting himself killed so that she had nobody to look after her, nobody to call her own. Jack lit a cheroot and puffed sullenly, brooding on the iniquities of the Reverend Mr Farleigh. His grandmother had said the damned fool had even refused to let Kate's grand-parents settle money on Kate's mother. Stiff-necked bloody idiot. Pride was one thing—but to leave his daughter in such straits! Good thing he was dead, Jack thought, or he'd prob-ably have throttled the man...

Dammit, his grandmother had no business leaving her here. She should be in London, finding herself a rich hus-band, some titled fellow who would pamper her and protect her for the rest of her life, who could give her all the fine things she had been denied. Any man should be grateful to win her... His mouth twisted at the unpalatable thought.

She was so damn naïve. She had no idea what her touch had done to him that time when she was massaging him. She was so full of unconscious sensuality and unawakened passion. Would probably fall for the first handsome face she saw. The *ton* was infested with damned blackguards. He would have to speak to his grandmother about it. Make certain she protected her from the wrong type, make sure she chose well for little Kate.

He drained the glass, then carelessly refilled it, slopping brandy on to the fine polish of the table at his elbow. Whatever he did, he was going to have to get her out of his house and up to London soon, for, the Lord knew, he was having the devil's own job keeping away from her. And that simply would not do. She was too fine a person to get herself chained to a poverty-stricken, embittered cripple. Scrubbing his floors the rest of her life. He thought of those small, work-roughened hands. No. If it killed him, he would get her out of here and into a fine London drawing-room.

He drank deeply again, and his mood darkened, recalling each and every time he had touched her. His body responded even at the memory and his mouth curled cynically. He had to stop this, had to get her out of his mind and out of his life. He was finished with women, finished with ladies anyway—even floor-scrubbing ladies with tender, beguiling eyes who smelt so sweet and fresh. They were a trap. Women thought differently from men.

Even the best of them wanted a man for what they could get.

He thought of Julia and the heavy bitterness rose inside him again. Was Kate any different? What would a penniless, homeless orphan want with him—a crippled wreck—an ugly, crippled wreck...? A home, perhaps? Even a run-down one like this might look good to a homeless waif. And, while he might consider himself poor, his sort of poverty was relative; he would never be in danger of starvation—she had already experienced that, several times. No, he would never be in danger of having nowhere to go, no one to turn to.

He had a home, a family and he was his grandmother's heir. It didn't take a genius to realise that all of that would look good to a girl with nothing. And if the price was having to live with a broken-down ruin of a man, well, Kate was a girl full to overflowing with good Christian virtues—charity, selflessness, pity… Yes, it wasn't hard to see what Kate might see in him. A girl could put up with a lot for the sake of a home, security and family…

"Señorita," Carlos whispered tentatively. "I do not think this is a good idea."

Kate glanced at him scornfully. "No, naturally you would not," she snapped. "You are the one who purchases those bottles of poison he pours down his throat every night."

Carlos shrugged. "He is my master, after all."

"Well, if you had any concern for your master, you would refuse to do his bidding in this. Can you not see, he is destroying himself?" She stamped her foot. "Well, I won't have it! I am employed by his grandmother to see to his welfare and I will put a stop to this right now." She stepped towards the door.

"Señorita, I beg you, it is not a good time." Carlos grabbed her sleeve in desperation. "Please, wait until morning."

"By morning, he will have consumed a great deal more of that filthy stuff," she responded briskly. "Now, let go of me, Carlos." She flung open the door.

"Señorita, it is too dangerous to cross him when he is like this," Carlos hissed urgently.

"Coward!" Kate flung off his hand and strode boldly into

the room. She lit a brace of candles from the flickering fire and, placing them on the carved wooden mantelpiece, turned to face Jack. He remained silent and motionless, the glittering eyes regarding her broodingly from under heavy dark brows. She noted the glass balanced carelessly between long, elegant fingers, the half-empty decanters on the low mahogany table by his chair, the splatters where he had spilled the liquor while pouring it with unsteady hands, the mess of half-smoked cheroots where he had stubbed them out in a particularly beautiful china bowl.

"Carlos," she said. "Bring the bucket here at once if you please."

Reluctantly, Carlos shuffled forward, irritating Kate by throwing a sheepish grimace of apology towards Jack as he did so.

"Hold it up," she ordered, and before Carlos or Jack had any idea of what she was planning she hurled the decanters and bottles into the bucket. The sound of smashing crystal echoed shockingly in the silence. With a sweeping movement she tossed in the cheroot stubs and ash and finally nipped the glass from out of Jack's hand and tossed it into the mess in the bucket.

"There, that's better," she said, brushing her hands together. "That will be all, Carlos."

"*Madre de Dios!* It will indeed," he mumbled, and fled the battlefield.

Kate took two steps back. Jack was beginning to recover from his astonishment, exhibiting all the signs of a man in the beginnings of the black throes of rage. Kate hid her satisfaction.

"What the devil do you think you're doing, woman?" he roared, rising from his chair and moving purposefully towards her.

"What I should have done a long time ago," she answered composedly, and skipped behind a chaise longue. Her heart was beating fast, but although she was a little nervous of what he might do to her in his drunken state she didn't think he would actually kill her, despite the fury in his eyes. And besides, there was something exhilarating about confronting him like this, just the two of them in the darkened room.

"You must know it is very bad for you to be up here like this, night after night, brooding and being miserable and drinking yourself into a stupor." She moved from behind the chaise longue to a small refectory table. "So I decided it was time you stopped drinking."

"Oh, did you, indeed?" he growled, and made a swipe to grab her. She darted from the shelter of the refectory table to that of a wing chair. "And just what the hell business is it of yours what I do, madam?"

She watched him warily. "Your grandmother employed me to look after you—"

"The meddlesome old harpy foisted you upon me to drive me insane!" he roared, and made another grab in her direction. She eluded him just in time. "And, by God, she has succeeded beyond her wildest expectations!"

"Oh, nonsense!" responded Kate sensibly. "If you feel a trifle put out just now, I can understand that, but you are undoubtedly finding the effect worse because of all that brandy or port or whatever the horrid stuff is you've been drinking!"

He stopped and stared at her in stupefied fury. *"A trifle put out? A trifle put out?* I'll show you a trifle put out! I'm going to teach you a lesson, my girl, a lesson that damned father of yours should have taught you a long, long time ago, about not interfering with a gentleman's pleasures!" He lunged clumsily forward again.

"Don't be rude about my father," snapped Kate.

"I'll do whatever I please in my own damned house, my girl, and that includes giving you that beating that your father should have given you the first time you treated him to the first taste of your damned impudence!''

''I was never impudent to my father in my life!'' Kate lied indignantly, resolutely ignoring the dozens of birchings she had received for impudence and worse. ''And how dare you threaten me, you big bully? If you dare to lay one finger on me, I...I'll scream.''

''And who will rescue you, pray tell?'' He grinned evilly. ''If I know Carlos, he'll be as far away as possible from this little fracas, Millie and Florence will be home by now, and as for Martha—'' he grinned even wider ''—well, you know as well as I do that I can do no wrong in Martha's eyes. She will probably egg me on.''

Kate gritted her teeth. Within minutes of stepping over the threshold of Jack Carstairs's house, Martha had conceived the absurdest *tendre* for him. And he dared to make mention of it! Boast of it, even! Kate glared at him across a bowl of greenery that she'd placed there only that morning.

''I don't need to scream,'' she panted, ''I can protect myself.'' She picked up the bowl and flung it. It missed him, smashing on the wall behind, but the foliage and water hit their target most satisfactorily. Kate grinned triumphantly.

Jack plucked greenery from his hair and dashed the water from his face. ''Ha! Missed, little vixen! So much for cricket.''

''That was deliberate,'' she said airily, ''but I promise you, I won't miss next time.''

He leaned over the table. ''You certainly enjoy throwing things, don't you? I suppose I ought to be grateful that there is not a pot of boiling oil to hand, or no doubt you would fling that at me, wouldn't you?''

''Probably.''

''Well, just for that, I'm going to give you the biggest beating you've ever had in your life.''

There was amusement in his eyes, despite his anger. Kate

resolved to remove it—she was certainly not going to let this deteriorate into a game.

"Well, at least now you've got an ambition in life! And about time too."

Jack stiffened. "And just what do you mean by that?"

Kate's chin lifted defiantly. She hadn't meant to be quite so blunt—it had just slipped out—but she couldn't back down and ruin the effect she had worked so hard to achieve.

"I said, at least you have an ambition in life now," she enunciated, quailing inwardly as she did so. "I mean, of course, apart from that of drinking yourself to death! Not that threatening to beat a woman is exactly an ambition to be proud of..."

Jack's face whitened with rage and shock. "How dare you? I've never beaten a woman in my life!" he grated. "Now, get out of my house now—before I break your neck and throw you down the stairs," he added, sublimely unaware of his inconsistency. His long fingers dug into the back of the Queen Anne chair between them. Kate could hear the fine old brocade shredding under the pressure.

Kate was shaking, her pulse was pounding with excitement, unsure whether she was thrilled or terrified. It looked as if he really did want to kill her, now. But something deep inside her told her that, no matter how he was behaving and what he threatened, he would not actually harm her. Not really.

"Oh, yes, that would suit you very well, wouldn't it?" she taunted, dancing from behind one piece of furniture to the next. "Get rid of me and there would be no one to prod you out of your shell again. Well, if you want me out of here, you will have to throw me out, Mr Carstairs, for I will not leave here unless of my own free will and I do not choose to go just yet."

He made a lunge for her and as Kate skipped out of his

way her foot caught on a loose rug. Without hesitation his arm shot out, preventing her from falling.

"I have you now, little vixen," he growled, drawing her closer. Kate struggled against the unbreakable grip and he stared down at her, his eyes blazing. Effortlessly he pressed her back against a nearby table, imprisoning her legs with one muscular thigh and enclosing her narrow wrists in one large hand. Ignoring her struggles, he pulled her hard against him, chest to chest, breathing heavily, causing a light, tantalising friction. Silence fell, except for the sounds of their breathing and the crackling fire.

"I really ought to beat you, you know," he murmured at last, his eyes darkening.

Kate knew she was in no such danger. His hold on her might be unbreakable, but it was also quite gentle. Almost possessive. It was another kind of danger altogether she was in. She gazed up at him for a long moment, her eyes clinging to his, then dropping to his mouth. She should not encourage this, should not allow it. She might want it with all her heart, but it was not proper to want it. "Please..." she gasped, and wriggled, meaning him to release her.

He looked down at her enigmatically and groaned. "If you must look at me like that with those eyes..." he muttered, and lowered his mouth to hers.

It was no gentle embrace and Kate had never experienced anything like it. She struggled half-heartedly against the invasion of her self-possession, but his lips, at first hard and demanding, softened and were tenderly teasing and coaxing hers until, without conscious volition, she responded to their demands and her lips parted.

Fire shot through her with such force that she let out a small whimper. His grip instantly gentled and he lifted his face and stared into hers. Kate was helpless—his muscular arms were all that kept her from sliding to the floor, her head was thrown back and her damp lips remained parted.

"What did you mean about my eyes?" she finally said.

"Only that every time I look into them I want to do this—"

He lowered his mouth to hers again in a long, passionate kiss.

Kate's senses were reeling but, more, she could not believe what he had said—her eyes made him want to kiss her? *Her eyes?*

He lifted his head back and smiled into her dazed face. She knew she should do something, say something, but she could not. Her eyes clung to his and he seemed to see the silent message in them for he murmured, "See—you're doing it again," and lowered his mouth, with agonising tenderness, to hers.

Without warning, he brushed his fingers across her breasts. Kate gasped and arched her back in response. Her nipples were unbearably tender as his hands rubbed the material of her frock and chemise across them. Her body was racked with wave after wave of the most exquisite shudders, and she could not help but push herself against him. At the same time, his mouth, lips and tongue were creating the most amazing sensations, intensifying the feeling she had of needing to get closer to him, to feel him against, around, inside her.

She could taste the brandy he had been consuming, the tobacco he had smoked, but also, something indefinable, the maleness and uniqueness of Jack. She wanted to touch him, taste him, feel him. One of her hands embedded itself in his thick, crisp dark hair, while the other cupped his jaw, rubbing tenderly back and forth, revelling in the texture of his unshaven chin. His mouth moved away from hers for a moment and she whimpered softly in protest at the deprivation and followed it.

His body was pressing against hers, moving in a slow, rhythmical motion, male to female, holding, tasting, wanting. His arms moved around to her back, and Kate thrust forward into the circle of his body, rubbing her breasts against the hardness of his chest. She felt him withdraw from her in some indefinable way, then gradually became aware of a growing draught at her back.

Abruptly she realised that Jack was unfastening her dress, trying to slip it from her shoulders. She pulled back, uttering a small exclamation of surprise, and found herself clutching her dress to her and staring him wordlessly in the face.

''Jack...'' she whispered, an unanswerable question in her eyes.

His gaze fixed on her face for a moment. He swore and thrust her away. Running a hand through his hair, he turned and headed for the table where he habitually kept the brandy. He pulled up short and swore again, recalling its recent fate. He dug his hands into his pockets and stared moodily into the fire. He kicked it once with his bad leg and sparks flew and danced like whirling dervishes up the chimney, while the pain brought him to his senses.

Kate hurriedly fastened up her dress as best she could, then waited for Jack to turn around. They stood there for long, silent minutes, Jack staring into the fire, his chest heaving, an unreadable look on his face, Kate, her face delicately flushed in the candlelight, wide-eyed and nervous.

Jack clenched his jaw. One tender word from him now and she would be in his arms again. And this time there would be no stopping him. He was poised on a knife-edge as it was. He'd never wanted any woman in his life as much as he wanted her.

But Kate was a lady, and if he touched her now they would be calling the banns next Sunday in church, and he couldn't do that to her: tie her for life to a miserable wreck when, with his grandmother's help, she could have almost anyone, and a life of ease and pleasure. No, he wasn't much of a gentleman, but he had enough pride not to speak that tender word and snare her with her own kindness.

"Get out of here before I really do give you a beating," he growled. "Lord, didn't your father ever teach you not to throw yourself at a man like that? If I didn't know you to be an innocent..." He ran his hand through his hair. "It's provocation of the worst sort. Do you not understand? It is asking to be used like the lowest sort of woman!"

The colour slowly drained from Kate's face. She opened her mouth, but the words would not come.

...asking to be used like the lowest sort of woman! He was accusing her of wantonness, she thought despairingly. Blaming her, like all the rest... Throwing herself at a man... *If I didn't know you to be an innocent...* But he didn't know her as well as he thought he did. And what would he think, once he did know her better? That she'd provoked Henri, too? That she'd asked to be a Frenchman's whore?

She would die if Jack ever looked at her the way those men in Lisbon had.

She stared at him numbly. It was true. She had provoked him.

Provoked...the argument. Provoked his anger, that was all. But Jack had grabbed her first. And he had kissed her when she had no thought of it—well, not much. Oh, yes, she had kissed him back, but he had started it, kissing her in that devastating... And *he* had been the one who had begun to undo her dress! But, like the people in Lisbon, he held her responsible...

Well, if *she* was wanton, then so was *he!*

Suddenly anger bubbled up in her, anger not only for what Jack had said, but for what men had said about her in Portugal and Spain. Blaming her!

Hypocrites!

This time she would not tamely accept the blame for what a man had done to her. She would retrieve her position. And give him the response he deserved!

She stared up at him, her face a white mask. Unconsciously his hand reached out towards her and in a flash she slapped him hard across the face. He stood there stupidly, unmoving, and, in utter silence, she turned and exited, quietly closing the door behind her.

Jack stood staring at the door a long time. After a while his hand came up and rubbed his cheek bemusedly. It was no light slap. His little Kate packed a good wallop. He sat down again and gazed into the fire, his hand still covering the cheek she had slapped, although the sting had long since faded.

How had it got so far out of hand?

Bloody hell, one minute she was driving him crazy, provoking his retaliation—sweeping in like some small avenging angel to wrest his drink out of his hands. He'd been justifiably angry with her then as she danced from chair to chair, flinging insults and bowls of greenery at him—cheeky little imp. Then his anger had started to change. It had become a hunt. And when he'd caught her, felt her small, panting body against his, all his frustrations had come to the fore...

Hell, she needed a lesson, but he'd never intended to hurt her like that. He couldn't get the memory of her eyes out of his mind. For a moment, before she had taken in what he had said, he had glimpsed the shyest, sweetest glow in her eyes as they had blinked up at him, her senses still reeling from the impact of his embrace. Jack would never forget the way that tender glow had died, replaced by anguish and deepest hurt...

She hadn't deserved that. He clenched his fist and slammed it down on the arm of the chair. Hell and damnation, she should have known better than to accost him when he was drunk. But she had felt so sweet in his arms, so sweet and warm and trusting. And he hadn't been able to bear it, knowing that it was impossible. So he had turned nasty to drive her away before it was too late. He groaned again.

He punched the arm of the chair once more, then punched his leg, taking bitter satisfaction in the pain it caused him.

In the sanctuary of her bedchamber, Kate lay across the counterpane, a damp and crumpled handkerchief bearing testimony to bitter tears. She lay, staring at the faded wallpaper, her breath racked by an occasional shudder—all that remained of her terrible weeping bout. She felt oddly calm now, the calm after the storm.

For the best part of the year now she had done her utmost to remain quite aloof from other people, cutting herself off from feeling more than the most superficial day-to-day emotions. The decision, she now realised, had been rooted in fear, fear of being hurt again, fear of being rejected.

And she had been right to fear.

What did you mean about my eyes?

Only that every time I look into them I want to do this—

And his kisses were everything she'd ever dreamed of—and more. For better or worse she was irrevocably in love with Jack Carstairs.

All her resolutions, all her biblical recitations, all her frantic planning to the contrary had been nothing but desperate attempts to deny the truth to herself. She recognised it now. The damage had been done well before she was truly aware of it.

At first, she hadn't seen the danger in him, despite his attractiveness. She'd just felt happy that her skills were needed at Sevenoakes. But his interfering ways had unsettled her—their quarrels had left her exhilarated, infuriated and gloriously alive. But it was more than just physical attraction, she knew. The quarrels were due to his protectiveness. She'd tried to reject it but, for a girl who'd rarely experienced it, protectiveness was a very endearing quality in a man. And when she'd recognised his pain she couldn't help but respond to it despite her resolutions to stay aloof. And by the time she'd realised how deeply entangled with him her emotions had become it was far, far too late.

She had tried...but then he'd kissed her. And with the inevitability of a flower responding to the warmth of the sun she'd opened her heart and let herself feel things for him that she had never felt for another person.

She loved him.

...every time I look into them I want to do this— Jack could not know how much those words had meant to her. When anyone else looked into her eyes, they saw her dead mother—her father, her brothers, Martha. Even Lady Cahill looked at Kate and saw her mother.

But Jack only saw her, living, breathing Kate. And with Jack, only with Jack, her eyes brought her kisses. And in his arms, being kissed, she had offered all that she was and all that she could be...

And he had thrown it back in her face.

It hurt, unbearably badly. She felt utterly crushed.

Chapter Ten

Next morning Kate rose early and went down to the kitchen to prepare breakfast as usual. She had come to several firm decisions in the night. She had allowed herself too much freedom with Jack—she was only his housekeeper. She should not have tried to interfere with his life, no matter how good her intentions. She should never have allowed herself to feel any emotion for him—it was inevitable that she would get hurt. She'd been living in a dream world and it had to stop.

She was *never* going to let anyone—not Jack Carstairs, not anyone—affect her emotions like that again. She would control it all much better in future, rebuild the walls of ice she had made around her heart in Lisbon. She had allowed Jack Carstairs to melt them. This time, she would build them stronger. She had already started the process during the long, sleepless night which had just passed. She could feel the chill of it surrounding her already. Inches thick. It might be cold, but it was also painless.

Kate put the coffee on, then stiffened as she heard unmistakable uneven footsteps coming towards the kitchen door. The door opened. There was a long silence. She could feel his eyes boring into her. Taking a deep breath, she turned to face him.

"I owe you an apology, Miss Farleigh," said Jack. "I had no business saying those things to you. I did not mean them and I regret them very deeply. I also forced myself upon you in the most disgraceful manner. It was unforgivable." Kate blinked. Damn him, damn him, damn him! He was utterly sincere. She felt a distant sensation of ice melting all around her. Oh, damn him!

He continued, "I do not ask you to forgive me, but I do hope you will at least accept my humble apologies. I assure you, nothing of that kind will happen again."

Kate had a lump in her throat. "Mr Carstairs, it was not entirely your fault. It…it is no business of mine whether you choose to spend your evenings drinking or not." Her voice grew huskier than ever. "My interference was unwarranted, so whatever you may have said or done I have only myself to blame."

Oh, Lord, she thought, why did I do that? She'd had no intention of apologising. It shouldn't matter to her what he thought, said or did. So what was she doing? More apologising, apparently. "I also said some terrible things to you and I did not mean them…or, at least, I should not have…"

She floundered to a halt. She could feel his warm gaze resting on her. A long, tense moment passed, then the coffee boiled over.

"The coffee! Oh, goodness!" exclaimed Kate, and rushed to rescue it. "Ouch!" She gasped and flinched, having incautiously grabbed the hot cast-iron handle and burnt her hand. She stepped back from the stove, sucking her hand.

"Let me see."

"It's nothing," she said dismissively, cradling her hand protectively nevertheless.

"Here," he said authoritatively. "Show it to me." He gently took her hand in his and bent over it, examining the burn carefully. Kate looked at the dark head bent over her hand and felt herself tremble. She longed so much to place her hand on it and run her fingers through the thick, unruly hair. Ice, she thought. Think ice!

"It's not serious," she said quietly. "I've had much worse burns than this."

"Well, you shouldn't have."

Kate was astonished at the suppressed anger in his voice.

"You shouldn't be in a position where you keep burning yourself."

It was that protectiveness again. Unnerved, she tried to pull her hand away. His head came up and he stared into her eyes.

"Oh, damn it all to hell!" he muttered, and pulled her into his arms. His mouth came down on hers, hard, and Kate could feel the passion pouring from him. Ice cracked all around her, turning instantly to steam.

The kiss was over in seconds. Jack pushed her away and left the room, heading outdoors. Kate sagged against the table, the pain of her hand almost forgotten. Moments later he entered again, carrying a bowl of water in which large chunks of ice and snow floated.

"Here you are," he said gruffly. "Put your hand in that. Cold is the best thing for burns, the colder the better."

Her burnt hand seemed utterly irrelevant now. Kate blinked at him, bemused. It was too late—no walls of ice could withstand this man. She loved him. The only ice she could feel were the few chunks in the bowl. Everywhere else around her was warm. Very warm. She glowed.

"Oh, for God's sake, don't look at me like that," he groaned. "Put your hand in the damned bowl and forget what just happened. I...I must still be drunk from last night."

He ran his fingers through his hair. Kate watched them. He saw her watching and swore again.

"I said stop it, damn you, Kate! It was an aberration, a

mistake. I'm sorry. It won't happen again. You have my word on it. Just stop looking at me like that, will you?''

''It won't happen again?'' Kate whispered. If she couldn't build walls against him, then why resist?

''No, it damned well won't.''

''Then I'm sorry too.''

He clenched his fists, unable to believe what he had just heard. ''Oh, for God's sake!'' he muttered. ''I can't take much more of this.'' And he limped quietly from the room.

She shouldn't have said it, Kate knew. It was not what a respectable girl should do, but since she wasn't considered respectable any more, then...

And she liked his kisses, more than liked them.

Never had she experienced anything like the emotions she felt whenever Jack Carstairs took her in his arms and lowered his mouth to hers. His kisses left her feeling so devastated, alive, exultant, vulnerable and...most gloriously invaded.

And she wanted more.

''I'm going to write to my grandmother asking her to take you into her house immediately,'' Jack announced, entering the library where Kate was busy dusting books.

She whirled from her task. ''But why?'' she whispered, her eyes wide with distress.

He could see she'd been working hard; her hair was starting to fall out of its knot, she had a smudge of dust on her chin and a blur of beeswax over her right eyebrow. Lord, was there ever a chit so unsuited to a domestic occupation? She needed to marry a rich man, if only to keep her face clean. He tried to keep the amusement out of his eyes, forcing himself not to soften towards her.

''We can't go on like this.''

''Like what?''

His eyes grew hard. ''Like this morning and the evening before.''

She flushed and clutched the book she had been dusting to her chest. "Well, I do not wish to go to London to stay with your grandmother."

"That's beside the point. If you stay here, this will get out of hand."

Kate's eyes were fixed on him. "Will it?" she asked softly.

Jack swore under his breath and turned away. Dammit! Those big grey-green eyes made him lose all resolution. He had to make her understand once and for all.

"God deliver me from naïve virgins!" he growled in frustration.

Kate stiffened, but he didn't notice.

"You don't realise the danger you're in," he said.

Oh, don't I? Kate thought.

"Men have needs, Miss Farleigh, carnal needs. They are not like women. If the need is upon him, a man will turn to a woman to fulfil those needs. Do you understand me? I said *a* woman, any woman, whichever woman is available to fulfil those carnal needs."

Kate bit her lip.

Jack cursed again. Dammit, he had no choice but to be as brutal as he could to her, to stop that soft glow that shone in her eyes every time they rested on him. He had no future to offer her. God's truth, but he could not even dance with her, and if anyone was born to dance it was Kate Farleigh, thistledown maiden. He couldn't allow her to bury herself in obscure poverty, especially since she had no idea of what she was missing.

She had never been to London, never danced until the wee small hours at a glittering ball in the arms of a succession of handsome blades, never attended the Opera, Covent Garden, Drury Lane, Almack's. She had seen death, far too much of it, but never experienced the sort of life which London and his grandmother could offer her. She could have a splendid future; if brutal words were what it took to get her to London, then he would speak them.

"I am no exception. I may be a disfigured cripple—" Kate flinched at the raw self-hate in his voice "—but I am still a man, with a man's needs." He paused to let his words sink in. "And it has been a long time since I had a woman, Kate. A very long time. And that is what…this is. That's *all* it is. Do you understand me? I would never have touched you, never have kissed you, but I was drunk and it has been too long since I had a woman and I got carried away." He turned away from her so he wouldn't have to look at her face.

Kate stared at the cloth in her hand and slowly crumpled it. She began to polish the shelf nearest to her. He had to be *drunk* to wish to touch her? That was what he was telling her? She was *any* woman to him? A mere available female? The words were harsh, biting, but, she eventually realised, they hadn't upset her as much as they should have.

Because, deep down, she didn't believe him.

If it was an available female he wanted, then why hadn't he bothered Millie or Florence? Or the barmaid at the tavern he frequented—from all accounts she was no better than she ought to be. No, whatever Jack Carstairs thought of her, it wasn't as any available female. And it wasn't the fault of his drinking either—all that did was exacerbate the problem.

"You will make the preparations necessary to go to London at the end of the week." His words seemed to come from a long way away.

Kate stopped her mindless polishing. "No, I won't," she said over her shoulder. She had no intention of running the gauntlet of London society. Not while she had a choice. And besides, she had made a promise to his grandmother.

He was incredulous. "Did I hear you say no?"

"You did," she answered quietly. "I have no intention of leaving."

"Have you no sense, woman?" he growled. "After what I just told you? You intend to stay? And risk being ruined?"

Her lips twisted ironically and she folded the dustcloth into a hard little package. Could one be ruined twice? It was a moot point.

"Didn't you hear what I said, you foolish chit?" He grabbed her shoulder and swung her around to face him. "You risk losing your virtue by staying here! What the devil is the matter with you?"

She wrenched herself out of his hard grasp and stood there, smoothing down her skirt like a bird who had just escaped a cat.

His eyes narrowed and his face hardened. "Perhaps that is your plan."

"What do you mean?"

"Seduce me and try to trap me into marriage," he said slowly.

"Seduce you?" she gasped indignantly.

"Isn't that what has been happening here? No doubt my grandmother's cunning claw is somewhere in the plot too." He laughed harshly. "Yes, I'm sure it is. No doubt you two planned it nicely between you."

"How dare you?"

He ignored her and continued. "Oh, God, what a fool I've been. It's as plain as the nose on my face. My grandmother, concerned I may never marry, now that my betrothal to Julia is at an end, appears out of nowhere. She dumps poor little lost Kate on me, hoping I will conveniently scoop her up and make her mine, thus dealing with two problems at once. Ha!" He glared at her. "Only it won't work, for I'm wise to your plot. You'll not trap me so easily, Miss Farleigh; I have no intention of wedding you."

"And I have absolutely *no* intention of wedding you either, Mr Carstairs!" Kate's temper had her firmly in its grip by now. "I would never, *ever* stoop to such a shabby plot and you have a...a colossal impertinence suggesting such a thing. It's utterly preposterous and I demand an apology at once—for me and for your grandmother too, for I am sure she would never scheme so sordidly!''

''Not sordidly, I agree; incessantly is a far better word.''

Kate ignored his interjection. ''And how dare you accuse me of trying to seduce you? It is *you* who have been grabbing and manhandling me, ever since I got here, plaguing me continually, when all I have tried to do is to get this house in order,'' she finished virtuously, if inaccurately.

''Oh, so I've been plaguing and manhandling you, have I? And who was it who accosted me in my room in the middle of the night?''

Kate stamped her foot. ''I did no such thing! How dare you even suggest it?''

''The upstairs parlour, then. And you came slinking in, knowing I was three sheets to the wind, and proceeded to seduce me.''

''I did not slink! I never slink!'' Kate spat. ''And you were not 'three sheets to the wind', as you so poetically put it, you were *drunk!* A sot! And if you imagine I was trying to seduce you by removing that poison you were swilling, then you have a very odd idea of what is seductive and no wonder this Julia, whoever she was, jilted you!''

''Leave her out of this,'' he snarled.

''Gladly.'' Kate tossed her head, wishing she knew more about his erstwhile fiancée.

''And these so-called *manhandling habits* you apparently object to so much—I haven't exactly noticed you valiantly resisting them. And I seem to recall myself calling a halt to proceedings each time, not you.''

Kate, blushing furiously, could think of no adequate reply. Of course she hadn't called a halt to his embraces. He knew perfectly well that his kisses left her with about as much resolution as a blancmange, leaving her with no desire to call a halt to anything. But how...how *scurrilous* of him to taunt her with it. She stood there glowering helplessly.

A slight, knowing smile appeared on his face.

"Oh, you are so infuriating!" she snapped. "For your information, I have *no* intention of marrying. Not you! Not anyone! Not ever!"

"Rubbish!"

"It is not rubbish, it happens to be true."

He watched her from under thunderous black brows. It wasn't the first time he'd heard her refer to this nonsense. He could no more imagine Kate Farleigh going through life as a lonely spinster than he could fly.

"And why not, Miss Farleigh? I have heard you assert it, but you have yet to offer one convincing reason. I know what women want—" Jack could not keep the sneer out of his voice "—wealth, a fine home, position, admiration and some poor besotted sap to hand it to them on a platter. There isn't a woman born who doesn't scheme after that."

Kate winced at his cynical view of marriage. Was he speaking from personal experience? Someone had hurt him; she could see that clearly. Julia? Kate couldn't speak for all women, of course, but, for herself, none of those things mattered—only love. But Henri had stolen Kate's right to be respected; without respect, there could be no love. So she could not marry. Lisbon had taught her that. Lisbon and Harry, her betrothed.

"You are wrong about most women, but I can see you will not listen. All I can do is repeat that I have no intention of marrying. As for my reasons, they are very personal and private. Your grandmother knows and that is why she did not press me to accompany her back to London, why she found me this temporary position as your housekeeper instead."

He snorted. "Balderdash! My grandmother only offered you this position because you are too blasted stubborn to know what is good for you. This position was nothing but a temporary sop to your pride. She has every intention of introducing you to society. There is no reason on earth why you cannot marry some rich, respectable fool.''

He stared down at her, his eyes hard and glittering, his mouth compressed with anger. ''You just have to get yourself out of my hair and up to London, flutter those long eyelashes at whichever gentleman meets your requirements, murmur softly in his ear in that smoky soft voice, smile and swish that delectable little body in front of him. Before the poor fool can say 'boo' you will be walking up the aisle on his arm and, no doubt, within a year or two you will be dandling his heir damply on your knee.''

His long hard fingers bit into her shoulders and he shook her as he spoke. Kate's mouth quivered with anguish at his unconscious cruelty. To hear the impossible, put into words like that, painting such a cosy, utterly unattainable picture...

Jack could feel every breath entering and leaving her body, smell the sweet clean fragrance of rosemary in her hair. She quivered under his hands and he took a long, rasping breath.

''And if he proves a touch reluctant in popping the question, then just you look at him like that and the poor idiot won't be able to help himself.'' With a groan he planted his mouth on hers and she was swept again into the maelstrom of emotion that was becoming so dear and so wondrously familiar to her.

Eventually he released her mouth and stood looming over her, breathing hard. Kate, her senses still reeling under the impact of his embrace, clutched his shoulders and arms, leaning against his warm, heaving chest for support.

Shakily she gathered together the tattered remains of her self-control and pushed against the powerful chest and arms that enclosed her.

Instantly he released her and stepped back. Kate was conscious of a feeling of isolation so intense that it threatened to shatter her resolution. She wanted to lean back into that hard, wonderful embrace again, but she could not. She retreated to the other side of the room and stood there, gathering her composure.

Kate, with every reason in the world to insist on complete propriety, had failed to do so. If that was what was bothering him, she would ensure that the kisses stopped. She was sure she could manage it, especially if the consequence for failure was for her to be sent away to London. Away from him.

After a few moments she said shakily, ''You are mistaken about a great many things, Mr Carstairs, but you are quite correct about one—this behaviour must stop.'' She took a deep breath and continued in a cold little voice, ''I apologise for my part in any impropriety that has taken place. Rest assured, it will not occur again. You will have my full co-operation in that. But I will not go to London.''

Jack stood and watched her, his eyes sombre. He nodded briefly and left, shutting the door quietly behind him.

Kate picked up her dust rag. Tears began to spill from her eyes.

The days passed, but there was no more mention of sending Kate to Lady Cahill. There was little mention of anything at all, for she and Jack rarely spoke unless they couldn't help it.

Christmas came and went as if it were just another day. But it wasn't, not for Kate. After church, she went to some trouble to make an especially good dinner, but Jack did not join them, so it was a very subdued meal with just Martha and Carlos attending. The farm girls had been given the day off, and in any case it was too bitterly cold to do much else but huddle near the fire.

For Kate it was a day of intense, searing loneliness, recalling Christmases past with her brothers playing all sorts of silly tricks and games...

She tried to be strong about it, to tell herself that it wasn't so bad really, that she had food, and shelter, and was better off than many. But this was only the first in a lifetime of solitary Christmases facing her. The realisation seeped into her bones, leaving her feeling chilled and forsaken, despite the roaring fire.

Eventually, at the end of a long, miserable day, she crept into bed, and allowed herself the luxury of crying herself to sleep.

Jack, returning from a day passed in self-imposed isolation at a local tavern, heard the muffled sobbing as he passed her door. He froze, listening. Every fibre of his body urged him to enter her room, to take her into his arms, still the sobbing with his mouth. To hold her, comfort her, lo— But he could not. Even drunk as he was, he knew that to go to her was to ruin her life for ever. He leaned against her door in anguish, each sob reverberating silently in his body, until at last silence fell and he knew she slept.

One morning, well into the new year, as Kate stood taking her customary view out of the window to greet the dawn as it lit the snow-covered landscape, she heard the muffled thunder of hoofs beneath her window. Her heart leapt into her mouth. Would he be thrown again? She flung open the window and leaned out into the chill air, straining to see. The big roan stallion galloped past her, his mane streaming in the breeze. Clinging firmly to his back was Jack Carstairs, riding adequately, if not as stylishly as he once must have done. Kate's hand crept to her cheek, her eyes filling with tears as she realised what he had accomplished.

It was the end of his humiliation. He could ride. Jack Carstairs would once again ride with the Quorn or any other hunt. She watched him as he galloped over the small rise and then slowly she washed and dressed. It was a great day. He would probably not even mention it to her, but she would celebrate the occasion by cooking him an especially delicious breakfast.

Kate was out fetching eggs when she heard the clatter of hoofs on the cobblestones behind her. She whirled and almost dropped the basket of eggs as the roan clattered to a halt in front of her, held firmly in check by a masterful hand. He grinned elatedly down at her, slid off the big horse and grabbed her with eager hands.

"Did you see me, Kate? I can ride again. And it's all thanks to you." Without warning he swept her up into his arms and whirled her around and around, laughing delightedly. Kate laughed too, wishing she had put down the basket so she could hug him back. Finally he slowed and, still holding her above him, looked up into her face.

"Well, Kate? Shall we call pax? I am too pleased with the world today to continue our armed truce."

Her heart too full to speak, she blinked back tears.

"What's this?" he said. "Tears?" The smile died from his face and he slowly let her slide down to the ground, still holding her hard against his body.

"Oh, no," she mumbled, putting down the basket and groping for a handkerchief. "I...I often cry when I'm happy. It...it is the most ridiculous thing."

He smiled down at her. "It is, indeed," he said softly, "but then, that's Kate, isn't it?"

She looked up, startled at the warmth in his voice.

"Never does anything the commonplace way," he murmured. "Here, allow me." Taking the handkerchief from her unresisting grasp, he proceeded to dry her eyes and cheeks with one hand, the other gently cupping the back of her head.

Kate found she couldn't move. She was overwhelmed by the sensation of his hard, strong body against hers, the warm breath of him on her cheeks, his soft, deep voice murmuring in her ear. She knew she should move away from him. Her inner voice told her so, but she could not bring herself to

move. Eventually he finished drying her cheeks and they
stood still, unmoving, in silence. Kate found she could not
look at him. She was oddly breathless and stared at the buttons on his shirt, totally aware of the warmth and strength of
his embrace. Finally he placed a gentle finger under her chin
and lifted it until their eyes met.

"Thank you, Kate," he said softly, and bent his mouth to
hers, his tenderness undermining every resolve she had made
to push him away. At first his lips were soft and warm and
gentle, then, as she opened her mouth beneath the pressure
of his, he groaned deep in his throat and the kiss deepened.
Kate gave herself up completely to the delicious, disturbing
sensation of his tongue seeking, caressing, entwining with
hers. She pressed her body hard against his and ran her hands
up through his thick dark hair, clutching it in mindless
delight. With a groan, he lifted his head and stared down into
her face, her eyes dazed with pleasure, his almost black with
passion. "Oh, God," he muttered, and kissed her again, a
hard, long, passionate kiss, which sent shudders of sensation
coursing through her body.

Suddenly Kate found herself abruptly released. Dazed, she
slowly became aware of voices and footsteps clattering over
the cobbles. As Millie and Florence rounded the corner of
the house, Jack was collecting the reins of the roan stallion.
Kate was still standing where he had left her, trying to collect
her wits after the onslaught on her senses.

"Good morning, Miss Kate, Mr Carstairs," they chorused.
"Father says it be going to snow terrible bad again soon."

Jack chatted easily with the girls and Kate marvelled at
his cool composure. Perhaps he hadn't experienced what she
had, she concluded. He couldn't have, if he was able to talk
and chat so casually. Lust seemed to do different things to a
man than to a woman. But it wasn't only lust on her part—
it was love too. Perhaps that was the difference. She forced
herself to greet the two girls and then walked with shaky legs

to the kitchen, where she sat on the nearest chair and tried to collect her thoughts.

She'd tried so very hard to evict Jack Carstairs from her heart, but it seemed he was embedded there irrevocably and for ever. Nothing seemed to work. She had spent weeks trying to harden her heart against him. And as soon as she felt it was under control he would look at her with those wickedly twinkling blue eyes, and all resolution would melt. Or he would say something in the deep voice that never failed to go straight into her bones. Or he'd carelessly touch her in passing—a light hand on the shoulder, the brush of a thigh against her skirts—the most harmless contact shot sensation through her.

And then there was that kiss just now…

In his joy at being able to ride once more, he was utterly irresistible. In moments like that she was willing to fling all caution, all propriety, everything to the wind and give herself to him for as long as he wanted her. And moments like that occurred all too often.

The only solution she could think of was the one he had suggested and that she had rejected so strongly—to physically remove herself from his presence—and that she could not bring herself to do. It would happen in a few months anyway, so she would stay close to him while she could…

By the time the girls entered the room, carrying fresh milk from the farm, Kate had herself under control again. She managed to get through the morning without seeing Jack again, except in the distance. For the rest of the day she found excuses to avoid his presence.

But that evening he was in too exuberant a frame of mind to dine alone, insisting on turning their evening meal into a celebration, pouring wine for them all, Millie and Florence included, and talking the most ridiculous nonsense that had them all in stitches. Kate was fascinated, never having seen this side of him before. Carlos, too, was in fine form, a wide grin lightening his dark face as he egged Jack on to further and further extremes of silly banter with the girls and Martha, causing riotous giggles to fill the room.

It appeared that all this time Jack had had Carlos heating oils and making up unguents, continuing Kate's treatment in secret. Some of the stories of the near-misses and narrow escapes from Kate's discovery had them all whooping and shrieking helplessly as Jack mimicked first Carlos, then Kate, then Martha, then the stuffy village apothecary.

He was utterly charming in this mood, Kate thought, wiping tears of laughter from her eyes. She suddenly realised that this was probably how he had been before the war.

This was the Jack that must have been betrothed to Julia, she realised with a sinking feeling—witty, handsome and vital. A man who was at home in the upper reaches of the *ton*. Who would have all the women eating out of his hand, from the lowest born like Millie and Florence and Martha, to the highest like Julia, whoever she was, and his grandmother.

It was clear to Kate now that he was almost well enough in body and spirit to return to the world he had renounced. A world where he would be amongst his peers and in his own element. She wondered dully if he would go back to Julia, now that he seemed to have climbed out of his pit of misery.

She should be happy for him, she told herself. And she was—for him.

Chapter Eleven

One afternoon in late February, in a period of clear weather which signalled the impending demise of winter, a smart curricle drew up at the front door of Sevenoakes. It was followed moments later by another, even smarter than the first, then an elegant travelling phaeton and several grooms leading a string of fine horses. From the sporting style of the vehicles, it was clear that they were driven by young men of substance and fashion. Three gentlemen alighted from the various vehicles and strode up the front steps, shouting merrily for ''Mad Jack' and exchanging good-natured insults concerning each other's driving prowess or lack of it.

Kate opened the front door, and froze. She had not expected visitors, particularly not *tonnish* ones like these. She stood like a statue, barely noticing their hearty exuberance. A short, round-faced man rushed straight past her, tossing her a heavy, many-caped driving coat and a high-brimmed hat as he went. Peering up the stairs, he shouted, ''Hey, Jack! Mad Jack Carstairs! Come out from wherever you're hiding, man, and give us a drink!''

A tall, lanky fellow passed her another many-caped greatcoat and a curly-brimmed beaver and, laughing, followed his friend. The last handed her a heavily frogged greatcoat of military cut and said calmly, ''Sir Toby Fenwick, Mr Lennox and Colonel Masterton to see Mr Carstairs.''

Colonel Masterton? A soldier? *From the Peninsula?* Kate tried desperately to bring the panic under control. He could not see her properly—she was almost invisible under three heavy coats. ''Please wait in the drawing-room to your left, sir; I will endeavour to find Mr Carstairs.''

The gentleman raised a quizzing glass to his eye. Kate huddled more firmly behind the coats. Having finished his inspection, he smiled faintly and strolled languidly into the room Kate had indicated. She backed out of the entrance hall, tossed the coats on to a chair and collapsed on top of them, her pulse racing.

She was overreacting, she told herself sternly. There was absolutely no reason to think he might recognise her. Merely because he was a colonel. No doubt hundreds of colonels had never even been to the Peninsula. And hundreds more who'd never even heard of Kate Farleigh. It was ridiculous to expect that this one might have recognised her. She certainly did not recognise him, nor any of the others.

Controlling her anxiety, Kate sent Millie out to fetch Jack while she put out simple refreshments of wine, brandy and bread and butter. She sent Florence into the drawing-room to light the fire. Florence emerged hurriedly, blushing and giggling. Kate's lips thinned. She was being a coward, making the girls put up with that. She would have to face Jack's visitors sometime.

Suddenly she thought of something. She flew upstairs and raced to her room. After rummaging in a large oaken chest she emerged, triumphantly brandishing a white spinster's cap she had noticed some weeks before. She put it on, carefully tucking in every last curl and tying it firmly under her chin with the tapes provided. She looked at herself in the mirror. Perfect. The cap was dreadfully ugly and much too large for her head. It was embellished with lace, knots of ribbon and a frill which hung almost to her eyelashes. In this, she could face any soldier visitors, secure in the belief that she was unlikely to be recognised. She glanced at her reflection in the mirror and giggled—she almost didn't recognise herself.

She hurried downstairs, ignored Millie and Florence's looks of amazement and Martha's gasp of horror, picked up the tray of refreshments and marched into the drawing-room, her head held high. It had to be—she could not see from under the frill otherwise.

"Brandy—this is more like it." The tallest gentleman leaped forward from where he had been warming himself at the fire and lifted the decanter and a glass from her tray.

"Ho, you blackguard!" shouted the chubby young man. "Don't think you are going to make off with that. Here, pour some for me!" He too snatched a glass from the tray and pursued his friend. It occurred to Kate that the two were, as her brothers used to phrase it, a trifle foxed.

The third gentleman sauntered up to her. Kate held her breath. "Allow me," he said, taking the tray from her grasp and setting it on a nearby table. He glanced briefly at her cap as he straightened up, then followed her gaze to where the other two were carelessly filling their glasses, slopping brandy on to the surface so carefully polished by Kate only that morning.

"You are perfectly right, ma'am." he said, observing her pursed lips. "I fear that we stayed a trifle too long at the excellent hostelry a short distance from here. My friends are indeed a trifle…er…exuberant."

"So I see," said Kate dryly.

"And you, mà'am, we have not had the pleasure. Colonel Francis Masterton, late of the 95th Rifles, at your service." He bowed. "And you are…?" He paused.

"Er…Kate Farleigh," mumbled Kate. His lightly uttered words had flustered her badly. The 95th Rifles? He *was* from the Peninsula. Pray God he knows nothing of me, she thought frantically. And oh, heavens! Why did I tell him my name? I should have changed it. Oh, Lord! She held out her hand automatically, then, remembering, she pulled it back awkwardly. Servants did not shake hands. ''I am the housekeeper here.''

''Indeed?'' he said on a long note of surprise. She glanced up at him from under the frill. Heavy-lidded grey eyes regarded her shrewdly. ''You surprise me, ma'am,'' he said, and stunned Kate by reaching for her hand and bowing over it politely, carrying it lightly to his lips.

She flushed and pulled her hand away. ''I...I will see if Mr Carstairs is available.'' Oh, Lord, what did he mean by kissing her hand? Was he mocking her? Did it mean he knew of her? He certainly thought her no servant. Did he think her Jack's mistress?

''Mr Carstairs is indeed available,'' came a deep voice from the doorway. Jack stood there and, by the glint in his vivid blue eyes, Kate knew he had seen the Colonel kiss her hand. She turned to leave. Jack's hand restrained her.

''Don't leave us yet, Miss Farleigh,'' he said, frowning at her cap. ''I'd like you to meet my guests, all of whom have recently returned from battling Boney's forces on the Peninsula.''

Oh, Lord, Kate thought—*all* of them? Not just the Colonel?

He turned her to face them. Kate was pale and rigid.

Jack spoke with cold formality. ''This is Sir Toby Fenwick and Mr Andrew Lennox, both late of the 14th, the Duchess of York's Own Light Dragoons, and I gather you've just met Colonel Francis Masterton who has, I collect, recently sold out of the 95th Rifles.''

The two younger gentlemen stared at him, surprised.

''Dash it, Jack,'' said chubby Sir Toby, ''what's all the formality? Formal introductions to servants now, eh?'' He laughed and raised his glass to his lips. "Introduce me to that other little blonde—"

Kate, mortified, tried to pull away from Jack's hold.

Jack ignored her and spoke with paralysing chill. "Miss Katherine Farleigh is the ward of my maternal grandmother, Lady Cahill. Miss Farleigh and her companion, Mrs Betts, called here on their way to join my grandmother in London, but they took pity on a poor bachelor and kindly offered to assist me to get this house in order. You will have no idea of the enormous debt of gratitude I owe to this lady and her companion."

One of Colonel Masterton's mobile brows was raised slightly, but he did not otherwise react. The other two came sheepishly forward under Jack's flinty gaze and held out their hands.

"Sorry, ma'am," said lanky Andrew Lennox. "Took you for one of the servants."

"Er...yes, dam—dashed sorry," mumbled Sir Toby. "Er...you'll have to excuse...er...taken rather too much... er... Delighted to meet you, ma'am." Pink with embarrassment, he took Kate's hand in a damp grip and shook it vigorously.

Kate's fear inflamed her temper. Jack had no right to embarrass her or his guests with this charade, introducing his housekeeper as his grandmother's ward. It was a deliberate ploy to force her into the role she had told him a dozen times she wanted none of. And he'd discomfited his guests on purpose, to declare her off limits.

But he was unwittingly playing with fire. If indeed any of them recognised her later, they would be furious if they thought they had been tricked into apologising to a disgraced woman. And they would blame Jack. They would not know of his ignorance—she must and would repudiate his introduction and clarify her position.

"There is no need to apologise, sir," she said firmly, "for

Mr Carstairs exaggerates. I am, in fact, the housekeeper, placed here by Lady Cahill, whose ward I am *not*. She was godmother to my late mother, and that is the full extent of the connection.''

''Dammit, woman, don't contradict me. You are my guest!'' Jack roared, furious to hear her demean herself like that.

Mr Lennox and Sir Toby recoiled at his tone. They were well acquainted with his temper. Colonel Masterton raised an eyebrow yet again.

''I say, steady on, old chap,'' began Mr Lennox, laying a tentative hand on Jack's arm.

Jack ignored him. He shook Kate's arm and glared at her cap. ''You are *not* a servant here, dammit! You are my guest!''

His friends cast wary looks at Kate, as if expecting her to burst into tears at any moment. But Kate was made of stronger stuff. She shook herself free of his hold with an infuriated squeak, and smoothed down her skirt.

''You just bellowed and swore at me, Mr Carstairs,'' she said dulcetly. ''No *gentleman* would bellow or swear at a *guest*—particularly in front of other guests. Such behaviour is invariably reserved for mere servants, who are in *no* position to answer back.'' She sailed victoriously out of the room, leaving a stunned and breathless audience behind her.

''In no position to answer back!'' snorted Jack. ''The little vixen always has the last word.'' He turned to face his friends.

Colonel Masterton was convulsed with silent mirth. Mr Lennox was gazing at the closed door, his eyes filled with admiration, and Sir Toby Fenwick stood, his mouth hanging open in stupefaction. He turned to Lennox. ''See what I saw, Lennox, old chap?''

Lennox grinned. ''I saw a female, no bigger than your

thumb, give Mad Jack Carstairs the neatest set-down he's had in years.''

Sir Toby nodded vigorously. "That's what I saw too. Never thought I'd see the day. What an amazin' girl! And the chit's the housekeeper, you say?''

"No, you fool, I told you—oh, to hell with it!'' snapped Jack, annoyed. "What the devil are you doing here in the first place, Tubby?''

Sir Toby looked self-conscious. "Oh, well...heard a rumour...you'd stuck your spoon in the wall, or close to.''

"So you decided to come up and see whether I was dead or not.''

The others looked vaguely uncomfortable.

"I'm glad you did,'' said Jack, surprising himself as he realised that, for the first time in months, the prospect of visitors did not fill him with repugnance. "Of course,'' he added, "I must warn you, the standard of hospitality here isn't what you've previously enjoyed in my company. Conditions here at Sevenoaks are quite spartan.''

He smiled wryly and looked them up and down. "In fact, I'm not certain that three such prodigiously elegant sprigs of fashion will be able to bear the lack of amenities at this establishment.''

This brought about a spate of heated denial and much good-natured chaffing.

"Hang it all, man, we've bivouacked with the best of them, in beastly little holes all over the Peninsula, and if you're saying I can't take it any more, then you can dashed well eat your words!'' asserted Sir Toby. He peered boskily around the room, taking in the glowing furniture, the roaring fire, the soft, faded colours.

"And besides, this ain't such a bad place as we were led to believe. In fact, dammit, it looks positively cosy. Much more comfortable than that damned cold barracks of a place my ancestors saw fit to build in the dim dark past.'' He sank into a chair with a sigh of satisfaction and took a deep draft of his glass.

Kate retired to the kitchen, shaking. She had not intended to draw attention to herself like that. Deny her status as his grandmother's ward—yes. But be drawn into what could only be called a spat with Jack! And in front of his friends! Oh, her wretched, wretched temper! Servants were, by and large, invisible to gentlemen like Jack's friends. That and her cap were her only defences against discovery. But now she'd let her temper ruin everything. No true servant would answer her master back so impudently. Far from being invisible, she'd made herself a source of interest to them. Oh, what a careless fool she was!

All her earlier decisions about seeking employment with folk not of the gentry came back to her in a mocking I-told-you-so. She would never have behaved in such a way had she taken a position with people who were not of her milieu. She would never have let down her guard enough.

She had let herself become complacent, comfortable, secure.

She'd stopped fearing discovery with every stranger—because she met no strangers. The effects of Jack's self-imposed isolation and the unusually severe winter had ensured that. They had existed, in the months she'd been here, as if in a cocoon, or on an island. And in that cocoon Kate had felt safe.

But now Jack had regained his strength, the spring thaw was coming and the protective isolation had been ripped away. The man whom she could hear now, laughing with his friends, bore little resemblance to the embittered recluse she'd encountered when she'd first arrived at Sevenoakes. The world could come to Jack Carstairs now and he would welcome it. She, however, was exposed to strangers' eyes and dependent on the vagaries of their memories...

There was no use worrying—she should concentrate on preparing dinner out of what she had available. She sent Carlos to kill two more chickens, and prepared a pie from the remains of yesterday's roast beef. It would be a plain but substantial meal. And Carlos would serve it.

After dinner the gentlemen sat over their port.

Kate sat in the adjoining room, her chair pushed as near as was decent to the connecting door. Some sewing lay in her lap, but her fingers weren't moving. She was eavesdropping. She had been unable to endure the strain any longer— she had to know whether any of the men had recognised her. From where she was sitting she could hear every word in the next room.

"Pos'tively cosy li'l place you have here, Jack," said Sir Toby. "Good dinner, good wine, roaring fire, good companions—all a man could want, right here. And right smack bang in the middle of some of the best damned hunting country in the world! You're a lucky man, Jack Carstairs."

At his words an awkward hush fell over the room.

"Oh, God, Jack, I'm a clumsy oaf! I'm sorry. I didn't mean—"

"Just shut up, Tubby!" hissed Andrew Lennox. "You've said quite enough."

"I didn't mean…" Sir Toby trailed off miserably.

There was a short silence.

"There's no need to treat me with kid gloves, you know," said Jack. "In fact, you don't need to feel sorry for me at all."

Colonel Masterton leaned forward into the light and stared hard at his friend. "So…" he said on a long note of discovery.

Jack grinned."You always were as sharp as a razor, Francis." He found his hand seized and wrung in a powerful grip.

The other two stared in bewilderment.

"What the devil are you two talking about?" said Andrew Lennox. "I can only think of one thing..." He stared hard at Jack, read the truth in his eyes, then he too leapt forward and seized Jack's hand, pumping it fervently.

"Will somebody please tell me what's going on?" complained Sir Toby. "Why is everybody shaking Jack's hand and what are you all being so damned mysterious about? Found an heiress, Jack, have you?"

The others laughed.

"Well, I'd planned to keep it as a surprise for tomorrow, Tubby, but I can ride again. Of course I'm not quite up to hunting yet, but I will be soon."

Sir Toby stared, dumbfounded, for a moment, then leapt from his chair, spilling his drink, and seized Jack's hand, shaking it until Jack thought it would drop off.

"'S marvellous, old man, simply marvellous!" he kept repeating. He glared round at his two friends still seated in their respective chairs. "Don't you un'erstand, you two idiots? Jack can ride! Ain't you going to congratulate him?"

The others roared with laughter. When the tumult had died down and a fresh round of drinks had been poured, Francis said to Jack, "I don't understand. The surgeons swore you'd never ride again, didn't they?"

"They did. Miss Farleigh disagreed."

"Miss Farleigh?" said Mr Lennox.

In the next room, Kate froze. Oh, no, no, she prayed silently. Do not tell them; please do not.

"Yes, her brother had been cured of a similar sort of injury by some Eastern doctor," continued Jack. "She told me her brother regained almost full strength...unfortunately."

"What?"

Jack explained. "Miss Farleigh lost her father and both her brothers in the war. Her brothers were in the 83rd, I believe. She is now utterly alone in the world, except for my grandmother, who has become her guardian."

Kate sagged in her seat. The 83rd. She could not have been more clearly identified. If any of them had heard anything of her, their memories would be well and truly jogged now.

"Yes, that's one point that I must confess quite eludes me. Do, pray, explain, dear boy. I know a little of Miss Farleigh's story…"

Kate leapt from her chair. She stole to the door and leaned against it, breathless with fear. The Colonel *did* know her. He would tell Jack everything. Kate chewed her lip worriedly. She would have to leave. She couldn't bear to see Jack's face when he knew.

"Knew her brothers and met her father on several occasions. In Spain, you understand. And I have met Miss Farleigh once before, though she looked a little different then… But your grandmother's ward? I never heard that you were related to Farleighs, Jack."

"We're not, of course. No blood relation at all as far as I know. She—my grandmother, I mean—was Miss Farleigh's mother's godmother."

"Ah," murmured Francis ironically. "A close family connection, I see."

Oh, for goodness' sake, get on with it! thought Kate. The tension was killing her.

Jack shrugged ruefully. "Well, you all know my grandmother—if she decides the connection is a close one then neither mortal man nor woman, can shift her."

"No, indeed," agreed Andrew. "Nor the immortals, I'd wager."

Sir Toby interrupted. "I don't understand what your grandmother's got to do with this, Jack. Terrifying old woman! Treats me like a scrubby schoolboy every time I have the misfortune to run into her. As far as I'm concerned, the further she stays out of everything the better." He paused a moment, then said with deepening suspicion, "I say! She's not here, is she? Lurkin' upstairs somewhere?"

Kate could have screamed with frustration.

"Oh, shut up, Tubby, you fool!" chuckled Andrew good-naturedly. "Let Jack finish his story. The oriental doctor, Jack," he prompted.

"Well, as I said," continued Jack, "Miss Farleigh's brother regained full use of his limb, and she told me about it, though, like the fool I was, I wouldn't listen to her... Damn near bit her head off for trying."

"I can well imagine," said Sir Toby frankly. "And, what's more, you can be devilish unpleasant to be around when you're like that, Jack; take my word for it. Wouldn't have come uninvited like this, except Francis made me. Expected to see you snarling round the place like a bad-tempered wolf. Had to stop for a few quick ones on the way. Wasn't going to tackle you sober! So what'd she do? Whisper sweet nothings, eh?"

Kate clenched her fists.

Jack chuckled. "On the contrary, she told me that if I wanted to spend the rest of my life being a cripple and falling off horses, to go right ahead doing what I was doing!"

"She didn't?" gasped Sir Toby.

"She did. Told me to my head I was wallowing in self-pity, too."

"Good God!" said Francis.

"You didn't hit her, did you, Jack?" said Sir Toby.

"Oh, don't be so stupid, Tubby," said Andrew.

"No, Tubby, but she certainly got blasted for her efforts, as I expect you can imagine. But the words stuck in my mind and finally bored their way into what was left of my sanity. So I eventually swallowed my pride, sought her assistance, and to cut a long story short I can ride. It's not a pretty sight, but nevertheless I stay on. I've not ridden to hounds yet, but it won't be long before I'm up to it. So, Tubby, old fellow, you were quite right after all; I am a lucky man—thanks to Miss Farleigh."

Kate relaxed briefly against the wall. Tears glimmered in her eyes. She'd given him something good to remember her by, at least. When he knew the truth, perhaps his condemnation would be tempered by the memory of her help with his leg.

The men in the next room fell silent for a while, only the occasional clink of a glass or the crackling of the fire could be heard. Then Andrew Lennox spoke, and at his words tension raced through Kate once more.

"You said you'd met Miss Farleigh before, Francis?"

"Indeed, I have," he affirmed. "Though it took me a moment or two to place where I'd first seen her."

"Where was it?" enquired Andrew.

Kate closed her eyes and held her breath.

"At the final siege of Badajoz," the Colonel announced coolly.

Kate's eyes flew open. *Badajoz?*

"Badajoz? You cannot be serious! Explain yourself, Francis," demanded Andrew.

"Do you mean to say that that chit was at Badajoz?" spluttered Sir Toby in amazement. "Not possible, is it? I mean, no women at Badajoz...well...I mean women, yes... that was part of the prob...but not ladies...er...you know what I mean."

"Indeed there was, Toby, one undoubted lady at least, for which my aunt Charlotte will be eternally grateful," said Francis.

There was a short stunned silence.

"Your aunt Charlotte? Gammon!" snorted Sir Toby. "Can't tell me your aunt Charlotte was at Badajoz, for I won't believe it. Stuffiest woman in the world, your aunt! Never been out of the country. Hardly ever been out of London. I'd wager my best hunter on it."

Francis chuckled softly. "True, old chap, but whom, above all others, does my aunt value in this world?"

After a short pause Andrew said, "Er, your cousin Arnold?"

"Exactly—my cousin Arnold," agreed Francis.

"What the devil are you talking about?" demanded Sir Toby. "I don't understand why we're talking about everyone's dratted relatives. It was bad enough with Jack's grandmother, but now you must rabbit on about your aunt and your cousin Arnold. I was glad to see the back of him after Badajoz, and I damned well don't ever want to see or talk—"

"What happened to Arnold at Badajoz, Toby?" interrupted Francis sweetly.

"Got shot or wounded in some damned way or other and lost his wits and blethered on and on and on about an angel saving him, or some such nonsense."

Jack exclaimed aloud at this.

"Quite true, old chap," explained Sir Toby. "Drove us all batty with his tales of his angel. By the time he was sent home I for one was ready to finish the work that some damned-fool Frog had obviously botched."

"Tubby, old son," said Francis, "that was no angel—that was Jack's Miss Farleigh."

Kate's knees almost gave way.

"What?" The exclamation came from three throats in unison.

"Quite true. Miss Farleigh was over there with her father and made it her practice to venture in, often quite close to the fighting, and tend the wounded. Came across Cousin Arnold with a ruddy great gash in his arm that wouldn't stop bleeding. Tied it up so tight that the blood couldn't get through. Surgeon who finally got to treat him said she'd saved his life. Would have bled to death for certain. Touch-and-go for a while there as it was."

Kate leaned against the door jamb, her eyes closed. That poor boy was Francis's cousin? In the other room there was a long silence, broken only by the quiet crackling of the logs burning in the hearth.

"She told me her father had confined her to a tent for a week after Badajoz," growled Jack furiously. "My God, when I think of the bloody atrocities…"

"I do believe he did," said Francis. "After he discovered her saving Arnold."

There was another long silence.

"Gal's a damned little heroine," said Toby at last.

"Too true," agreed Francis quietly. "And, from what I can make out, Arnold was only one of many she saved."

In the next room Kate sank silently on to the chair. She felt dizzy with relief. Francis did not know the rest of her story—she was safe for a time. She had been so frightened…but he thought her a heroine! She did not need to hear any more. A *heroine*—he wouldn't say that if he knew about Henri. The relief was overwhelming. She was exhausted. Silently she slipped from the room and went upstairs to bed.

"Arnold's angel, you say? Good Gad!" mumbled Sir Toby. "Not the sort of thing one expects a lady to…to…"

"No, indeed," agreed Andrew warmly. "Most ladies would faint dead away if we even told them one-tenth of the things that could happen in war, let alone…" His voice died away as all four men stared into the fire, recalling how the blood-crazed troops had gone mad after the long siege and storming of Badajoz. The raping, the plundering, the pillaging. It was horrific to imagine Kate in the midst of it all.

After a few moments Andrew raised his voice in a rallying tone.

"And why are we sitting here brooding in such a melancholy fashion? We're all here, alive and well, drinking this excellent port, reunited at last. And Jack, back from the dead, with the best of all possible news."

"Yes, by Gad!" said Sir Toby. He raised his glass. "Here's to Mad Jack and the Hunt! Back together at last!"

"Yes, indeed," agreed Francis. "Jack and the Hunt, let's drink to it!"

"And to Miss Farleigh," said Jack quietly, raising his glass. With one accord the others rose to their feet and drank the toast.

"To Miss Farleigh."

"Arnold's angel."

Chapter Twelve

Kate yawned as she set the table in the breakfast parlour next morning. She had slept poorly, worrying about what to do. The very idea of leaving Sevenoakes, and Jack, pained her deeply, but she knew she ought to do it. The arrival of his friends had shown her what thin ice she was skating on. All Jack's friends were soldiers; there would be more visitors, more soldiers. They'd come for the hunting as well as Jack's company. And with more visitors there would be more chance of discovery, more chance of denouncement. It was just a matter of time.

But if she wasn't here there would be no reason for any of Jack's visitors to speak of a well-born English girl who'd lived in sin with a French officer. She wanted to stay near him for the rest of her life, but if the price of that was to have him look at her in disgust, then the price was too high. Better by far to leave him in ignorance, thinking well of her.

She stood back, regarding the table setting. As she did so, her hand went to her head, and she flipped at the irritating frill. She probably didn't need to wear her disguise any more, but better safe than sorry. Jack's introduction of her as a guest had given her another reason to wear it. The cap was the sort of thing a spinsterish housekeeper might wear and it, better than anything, would make her position clear.

Finally she heard male voices and footsteps and swiftly began the last-minute preparations needed to serve hot breakfasts. She had thick home-cured ham and fresh-laid eggs sizzling softly in a pan, slices of bread toasting gently, a jug of ale poured and the tantalising aroma of coffee filling the air when Jack entered the kitchen.

"What the devil are you doing in that thing again?"

"I have no idea what you are talking about, and if you wish to converse with me then I warn you that breakfast will be ruined. I am doing four things at once as it is, and if you expect me to bandy words with you at the same time, then you will be disappointed." Kate was pleased—she was doing a very good imitation of her previous behaviour; he would not suspect anything was wrong.

"Please wait in the breakfast parlour and I'll bring everything in to you and your friends directly." She glanced up at him. "I take it they are all downstairs?"

"What the devil are you doing in that abomination?"

Kate stamped her foot. "I know nothing of abominations; I haven't got time for them. What I want to know is how many to serve breakfast to. Are all your friends arisen?"

"Yes," he snapped. "Why are you doing all this yourself? Where are those girls and that good-for-nothing man of mine? Carlos!" he bellowed.

"Kindly do not deafen me with your shouting." She whisked a slice of toast off the grill just in time to stop it burning. "Carlos and the girls have gone to the village to purchase additional supplies needed for your friends' visit."

"Need they all have gone? Surely one would have been enough."

"Mr Carstairs!" Kate whirled around and glared at him, her resolutions forgotten. "If you must come in here and pick quarrels with me at this hour, it is your prerogative to do so—but do not expect to have an edible breakfast at the same time!''

The coffee smelt delicious. The ham and eggs superb. Some toast was beginning to smoke. It was a tactical retreat, Jack told himself.

The decision had nothing to do with his rumbling stomach. Besides, he had a responsibility to his guests. He would deal with her later.

Breakfast arrived with no further disturbance. Jack's friends instantly hailed Kate as Arnold's angel. Relief swamped her anew. They saw her as a heroine, not a traitor and a whore. A heroine! She couldn't help but laugh. They insisted that Kate join them for breakfast and set themselves to entertain her further.

After a time Kate became very aware of Jack glowering at her cap. She had noticed his friends blink at it each time she brushed the frill from her eyes, but they were all far too well-mannered to comment. Jack, she felt with a sinking heart, was not similarly inclined. She put her chin up stubbornly and continued to ignore his black looks.

Francis's eyes began to glimmer with humour. He'd noticed Jack's foul mood the instant he had returned from the kitchen. He now perceived there was a silent battle of wills taking place across the table. She was not at all the angel his cousin had named her, but a vibrant little minx who gave as good as she got. She was perfect for Jack.

At the conclusion of the meal, Kate rose and gathered up the dishes while the others made plans for the day. Jack murmured his excuses and followed her.

Francis observed Jack's hasty exit. Unless he missed his guess, there was about to be another confrontation between Miss Farleigh and his friend. He had no qualms about following them—it was certain to prove entertaining. Hearing the voices raised in conflict, he slid unobtrusively into the kitchen.

"And now, Miss Farleigh, I will have my answer at last. What the devil is that atrocity on your head?"

"What atrocity?"

"That white thing." Jack gestured disdainfully.

"It is a cap."

"I know what it is! What the devil do you mean by wearing it?"

"Is it not obvious?"

"Not to me. That sort of thing is usually worn by dowdy old maids well past their prayers, and then only if they have something to hide. You are still a girl and your hair is too pretty to hide."

The compliment took Kate by surprise, but she rallied. "It is kind of you to say so, but I am not a young girl. I am a spinster, and as such I will wear this cap."

Jack snorted in disgust. "You are no spinster, so take it off at once and do not let me see the damned thing again."

"I am indeed a spinster and I have every intention of wearing this cap, whether you like it or not." Kate glared at Jack, hands on her hips.

"Oh, do you, indeed?"

Francis smiled, recognising the signs—Jack was in a fine temper, but doing his best to hold it back. Jack moved closer. Kate backed away warily, clutching the cap to her head protectively. Francis decided it was time to make his move.

"Pray forgive my interruption—no, no, continue, do. I would hate to spoil your conversation." He seated himself, clearly with every expectation of being entertained. "I think you were about to make a dive for Miss Farleigh's cap, old man," he prompted helpfully.

Kate glanced from Francis's polite expression to Jack's black frown and began to giggle. Francis's smile broadened into a grin. Jack dashed his hand angrily through his hair.

"Damn you, Francis," he swore, then his sense of humour began to get the better of him. The twitching of his lips, so clearly at odds with his black frown, provoked his observers to further mirth, and finally he too joined in the laughter.

At last Kate stood up, and immediately Francis and Jack rose to their feet. "Please excuse me," she said, "but I have things to do."

"So do I," agreed Jack, and before she knew what he was about he had snatched the offending cap off her head and tossed it into the fire. "That's better." He grinned triumphantly.

"Oh! You wretch!" exclaimed Kate.

"It was an abomination and the only thing to do with abominations is to burn them. Don't you agree, Francis?"

Francis bowed towards Kate. "Forgive my perfidy, Miss Farleigh, but, much as I deplore his crude methods, that cap was indeed an abomination and not, therefore, to be borne by any man with an eye for beauty. Your hair is quite, quite lovely and should never be hidden."

Kate blushed.

Jack looked at his friend through narrowed eyes. "Yes, well, I think you have said quite enough, Francis. It is time you took yourself off. Er...isn't that Toby calling you?"

Francis smiled. "Wonderful hearing you must have, dear boy," he murmured. "I didn't hear a thing."

Jack glowered and thrust him out the door. He turned to Kate, but encountered such a fiery look from the sparkling grey-green eyes that he decided his duty lay with his guests. He followed Francis out to the hall, where they found Mr Lennox.

"Fine morning for a ride, Jack, don't you think?"

"Excellent idea," Jack agreed, his good mood restored, and, after shouting for Sir Toby to join them, the foursome headed towards the stables.

It was a crisp, sunny morning, ideal for riding. Wisps of fog and remnants of snow lingered in the shadowy hollows, waiting to be burnt up when the bright sun finally discovered them. The horses were in fine fettle and snorted and pranced, eager to be out and moving, but Francis, Sir Toby and Mr Lennox kept their mounts well reined in, unsure of Jack's capabilities and not wanting him to strain his leg. After several minutes of the dreary pace they'd set, Jack became aware of his friends' strategy.

"Come on, you sluggards!" he shouted. "Race you to the top of that hill." Recklessly he urged his horse into a gallop. Shouting and laughing, the others followed. It was a mad race and by the end of it all four of them were flushed and breathing heavily.

"By Jove, Jack!" exclaimed Sir Toby excitedly. "I would never have thought it; stap me if you're not riding damn near as well as ever you did. S'a marvel, I tell you, a marvel!"

"Not quite as well as I used to, I fear," responded Jack, grinning from ear to ear nevertheless. He stretched his bad leg a little awkwardly and the others became aware of white lines around his mouth, a sign that he was in some pain.

"I say, Jack, you haven't overdone it, have you?" said Mr Lennox.

"No, no." He met his friend's doubting look and grinned ruefully. "Well, perhaps a little, but I couldn't have you three keeping me wrapped in cotton wool, now could I? Such a pace you'd set, I'd have died of boredom." The others laughed. "Now, you all ride on, don't worry about me," he said. "I'll take it a little slower now that my blood's moving again."

"Yes, go on, you two," agreed Francis. "I'll keep Jack company for a bit. My head's still a trifle delicate from last night, and any more riding like the last episode and I fear the wretched thing will fall off." The other two laughed as they rode away, but Jack turned and regarded his friend sceptically.

"My poor Francis," he said in mock-sympathy. "And I always thought you had the hardest head of anyone I knew."

Francis smiled blandly back at him. "Ah, well, you have the advantage of me by several years, you know. I am nigh on thirty-five."

They moved forward at a slow canter, chatting as they did so. After some time, the talk ceased and they walked their horses in companionable silence, enjoying the morning, each man absorbed in his own thoughts.

Then Francis chuckled to himself.

Jack turned his head. "What is it?"

Francis shook his head in amusement. "Never thought I'd see you setting up as a milliner."

"What the hell do you...? Oh, that. Stubble it, will you?" mumbled Jack.

But Francis had no intention of dropping it. "It was an ugly enough cap, to be sure, and it made that pretty little thing look like a dowdy, but you acted as if she deliberately wore it to annoy you."

Jack harrumphed. "She did."

"Oho...so it's like that, is it?"

Jack glowered. "Like what? She's my grandmother's ward, that's all."

"And naturally you must supervise her headgear," agreed Francis sympathetically.

"She was foisted on me by that meddlesome old witch. I had no choice in the matter."

"Ahh." Francis nodded his head wisely.

"Ahh nothing!" snapped Jack. "You have added two and two and come up with five. The girl means nothing to me. She's a damned nuisance, if you want to know the truth!"

"Mmm," agreed Francis infuriatingly.

Jack ground his teeth. "Damn your eyes, Francis."

His friend chuckled softly. After a few minutes he spoke again. "Well, dear boy, since you have no interest in little Miss Farleigh, you'll have no objection if I pursue her myself."

Jack wrenched his horse to a halt, slewed round in the saddle and glared at his friend. "What the devil do you mean by that? You'll do nothing of the sort. She...she's my grandmother's ward."

Francis's eyebrows rose extravagantly at his tone. "I would court her honourably, of course—you could have no objection to that."

Jack had dozens of objections, but he couldn't think of a single thing to say. It was one thing to urge Kate to take up his grandmother's offer and go to London to find herself a husband. Jack had envisaged some gentle, fatherly soul who would pamper Kate and smother her in luxury. He glanced at his friend and frowned. Not a handsome, worldly, elegant...rake!

"Why the devil would you be wanting to court someone like Kate?" he demanded. "Dammit, man, you're a notorious rake!"

"A notorious rake?" Francis laughed. "And what of you, Jack? The man who put all the matchmaking mamas in a flutter to protect their chicks— Ah, no, you settled down, didn't you? The Divine Julia. Whatever happened to her?" He noticed Jack's frown and clucked sympathetically. "Still carrying a torch, are you? Well, I can see how little Kate, charming as she is, could not compare with the fair Julia."

"I'm not carrying a torch and I will thank you not to mention Kate's name and hers in the same breath."

Francis smiled in spurious sympathy. "Ah, so the goddess is still enshrined in your heart, then?"

"The goddess, as you so mistakenly call her, is nothing but a shallow, self-centred harpy, and if you think for one minute, Francis, that she...she..." Jack was so angry, he was lost for words. "If you don't know that Julia Davenport is not worth Kate Farleigh's little finger, then...then...I don't know what you are," he finished lamely.

Francis controlled his urge to grin. Jack was responding

beautifully. "No need to convince me, old man. I was never one of the Davenport's admirers. I am the one, don't forget, who may court little Miss Farleigh with a view to marriage."

Jack gritted his teeth. His friend's habit of referring to Kate as "little Miss Farleigh' was starting to annoy him very much. "Never thought you'd be one for parson's mousetrap. What's brought it on?"

"Oh, well, there comes a time in a chap's life when it's time to settle down. I've been keeping my eyes open for a while now and somehow the idea of one of the schoolgirls on the marriage mart doesn't really appeal. A man wants to settle down with a woman who'll make him comfortable, a woman of sense."

Jack was revolted by this description of Kate. "It sounds to me like you are more interested in taking a comfortable old chair to wife," he said sourly.

Francis chuckled. "No, indeed. I most certainly don't think of Miss Farleigh as a comfortable old chair. Why, the very notion is offensive." He paused delicately. "Ah, perhaps you haven't noticed, old man, but little Miss Farleigh is quite a pretty little thing, with an eminently kissable mouth. Even that smut of flour on her nose this morning looked quite delicious."

He ignored Jack's growl.

"And have you noticed her dimple? It hardly ever appears, but when it does it's utterly charming. Add to that her extraordinary voice and her delightful laugh, and you have in one small package a very cosy armful indeed, very cosy."

Jack was appalled at the vision his words conjured up. Kate nestled in Francis's arms. He felt positively sick. "You know she has not a penny in the world."

Francis shrugged. "I'm not hanging out for a rich wife."

"Are you in love with her, then?" Jack's mouth was dry as he waited for the answer.

"Good heavens, no." Francis laughed carelessly. "A chap

doesn't have to be in love with his wife to have a happy marriage. As long as she loves him, it will work.''

''And you think she loves you, do you?'' Jack growled.

''No, dear boy, not yet.'' Francis smiled complacently. ''But the marriage bed has a way of taking care of that, does it not? By the end of the honeymoon she will love me.'' He winked. ''I'm told I am rather a good lover, you see. And, besides, I intend to be a kind and indulgent husband. Women like that, you know. And I do believe young Kate has had very little indulgence in her life...''

Observing Jack's face, Francis deemed it prudent to join Sir Toby and Mr Lennox. He reached across and patted Jack's leg. ''You look as if your leg is paining you, dear boy. Why don't you take yourself home and I'll meet you back at the house?'' Unable to keep a straight face any longer, Francis galloped away, putting the greatest possible distance between them before his mirth escaped him.

He left Jack staring after him, his face a mixture of fury, chagrin and despair. It was true. Francis would make Kate a fine husband. So why did the thought make him feel so sick inside? It was very confusing. Reason forced him to admit Francis would make someone an excellent husband. Only...not Kate.

Jack entered the house from the side entrance nearest the stables and paused, hearing voices coming from the front parlour: Kate and a man whose voice he did not recognise. He entered the room.

Kate was seated on a lounge sofa, smiling happily at a complete stranger. Jack frowned. The stranger was holding both of Kate's hands in his, and she was making no attempt to remove them from his grasp. She turned and beamed at Jack.

''Oh, Ja— Mr Carstairs, isn't it wonderful? This is Mr Jeremiah Cole.''

Cold blue eyes swept over Mr Cole's person and one eyebrow rose sardonically. His hard stare shifted pointedly from Cole to Kate's hands. Cole immediately released them.

"Forgive me, Miss Farleigh—" Jack's tone was frigid "—but I do not immediately perceive what is so wonderful. Who is this person?" His eyebrow rose again as his gaze swept over the man before him.

To his annoyance, Kate did not even seem to register his arctic reception of her guest. She laughed.

"Oh, I'm sorry. I must confess Mr Cole's unexpected appearance has put me in somewhat of a fluster." She turned and beamed at the stranger again. "A very welcome appearance and a very happy fluster, but it has made me forget my manners."

She rose and immediately the stranger did the same. Jack's eyes grew even flintier as he noted that the Cole fellow was almost as tall as he, solidly built and modishly dressed.

Kate continued, "Mr Carstairs, I have much pleasure in presenting a distant and until now unknown cousin of mine, Mr Jeremiah Cole. Mr Cole, Mr Jack Carstairs, my..." She hesitated. Mr Cole's eyebrows rose slightly.

Jack instantly recognised her difficulty. "Miss Farleigh is the ward of my grandmother, Lady Cahill. My grandmother prevailed upon Miss Farleigh and her companion, Mrs Betts, to assist a poor bachelor in setting this house to rights."

A speculative look came on to Mr Cole's face, so Jack added, "She will shortly be taking up residence with Lady Cahill and making her entrance to society under her aegis." That should stop the fellow's suspicious mind, he thought, for what grandmother would sponsor her grandson's mistress into society?

"Delighted to meet you," said Cole affably. "I must say, I was bowled over when I found that my little cousin had survived the terrors of war after all. And when I arrived here and discovered what a very charming and delightful little cousin she was too I was bowled over even more thoroughly.'' He kissed her hand.

Jack watched balefully as Kate blushed. She was making no attempt to pull her hands out of the fellow's sweaty grasp.

"Tell me, Cole," he said, "how did you discover Miss Farleigh's whereabouts? Not many know she is here."

Cole turned, still retaining Kate's hand. "I was contacted by Lady Cahill's man, Phillips. My late father was executor of the Delacombe estate, you know, and their property came to him, as closest living male relative. It passed therefore to me on his death two months ago." He smiled at Kate, an oily smirk to Jack's jaundiced eye. He patted her hand and then grew solemn.

"You can imagine my joy when I discovered that I was not, in fact, all alone in the world, and that my cousin was alive and well—not perished at the hands of the dastardly French along with her father and brothers." He squeezed Kate's hand sympathetically. "Naturally I came post-haste to meet her. And of course to make my condolences on the loss of her loved ones."

"It was very kind of you, Mr Cole," said Kate softly.

"Please," he said, "Mr Cole sounds so formal. I am your only living relative, even if rather distant. Could you not bring yourself to call me Cousin Jeremiah, and allow me to call you Cousin Katherine?"

"Cousin Kate will do nicely, Cousin Jeremiah." She smiled at him and he kissed her hand again.

Jack stared at the little display, revolted. Could Kate not see the fellow was an oily Cit? He might be well dressed and passably good-looking, if you liked biggish men with sandy hair and regular features, but he was a deal too smooth for Jack's liking, and as for his continual flattery of Kate and that incessant groping and kissing of her hand...

Jack itched to take the impertinent fellow by his elegantly tailored collar and toss him out on his ear, but he knew Kate would never allow it. He regarded her sourly. She was completely taken in. She obviously took the fellow at his word and even seemed to enjoy him pawing and slobbering over her hand. She allowed it at any rate. And smiled.

"So you are the heir." Jack interrupted before the fellow could kiss Kate's hand for the third time.

"Yes, indeed," agreed Mr Cole. "Though it is a melancholy feeling to find oneself enriched by another's demise." He looked solemn for a moment, then brightened. "But that reminds me, there is a small bequest for you, Cousin Kate, a peculiarly feminine bequest."

He smiled at Kate's enquiring look and passed her a flat oblong packet. She looked at it for a moment, puzzled, then opened it and gasped in surprise and pleasure. She looked at Jack, her eyes wide with delight. "Jewellery." She turned back to her cousin. "My grandmother's?"

He nodded. "Yes, she left one or two pieces to you as a keepsake."

Jack frowned, remembering his grandmother's belief that Kate would have been left well provided for. It seemed she was wrong, for there was not much of it—just a string of pearls and one of garnets, some earrings, a ring and a brooch or two.

He suddenly noticed that Kate had gone very silent. She sat, her head bowed, staring at the jewellery on her lap, her hands gently touching the pieces, turning them over, running the pearls slowly through her fingers. Of course, he realised, she must be disappointed that there was nothing there of any value. He could not see her face, but he knew how she must be feeling. Frustration and anger grew in him as he noticed a tear roll down her cheek. She must have hoped for the sort of things other women wanted, and which she deserved to have more than any of them—diamonds, emeralds, rubies. He silently called a curse on the heads of all her thoughtless relatives.

She looked up. Her eyes were filled with tears, but her smile was radiant. "Thank you, Cousin Jeremiah, thank you. You don't know how much it means to me that my grandmother left these to me," she said in a soft, husky voice that told Jack she was very moved. Mr Cole shifted uncomfortably in his seat. She stood up abruptly and smiled mistily at the two men. "If you don't mind, I would like to look at my grandmother's bequest in my chamber. Will you excuse me, please?" She held out her hand to her cousin. "Will I see you again, Cousin Jeremiah?"

"Of course." He smiled, bending over her hand again. "You don't think I will go away again, just when I have discovered a charming little cousin all of my very own? I will seek accommodation in the nearest town and with your permission, Cousin, will call again tomorrow."

She nodded happily and left the room, cradling the packet to her bosom. Jack stood staring after her, flabbergasted. To see her face, one would have thought she had been given the Crown Jewels, not a small collection of trumpery beads. The girl never failed to amaze him. She was like no other female he had known. He turned and looked at Mr Cole. He was smiling to himself in a very satisfied manner. Damn the man. Jack didn't like him one little bit.

"The front door is this way, Cole."

"It has been a pleasure to meet you, Mr Carstairs," said Mr Cole politely, disregarding the glowering look his host was giving him. "I look forward to furthering our acquaintance. I collect you are one of our gallant heroes from the Peninsula. I would be delighted to discuss it with you at some future time."

The gallant hero, nauseated by the description, managed not to throw Kate's cousin down the steps and contented himself with slamming the door instead.

Jack needed a drink, so he went into the library and stopped dead. Kate was sitting in a wing chair. She looked up. "Millie is washing the floor in my room," she said by way of explanation of her presence in the library.

He nodded. "That fellow has left."

"It was very good of him to come all this way," Kate said quietly. "He could have just sent these to me by mail."

Jack watched the way her hands stroked the packet that still lay in her lap. There was a long silence.

"You seemed pleased to see him," he said at last.

Kate sighed. "Yes, it is so wonderful to discover that I am not utterly alone in the world, after all."

"You are not alone at all."

"But I am, Jack," she said softly. "Or at least I was."

"You have my grandmother—" he began. *And me.*

"Oh, Lady Cahill is a dear," she interrupted, "but in truth she is no kin of mine. I am a charitable project she has taken on for the sake of my mother's memory, that is all. She has been very kind and generous, and I am grateful to her for it, but you must see that I have no real claim on her. It is different to know that someone is part of your family, that you belong to them."

Jack objected to that in the strongest terms. "You do not belong to that overfed, overdressed, fawning puffbag!"

"Mr Carstairs," Kate reproved him coldly, "I will thank you to speak politely of Cousin Jeremiah in my presence. He is well built, not overfed in the least and I find his taste in clothes impeccable." The look she cast on Jack's stained buckskins was not lost on him. "Moreover, he has a kind heart and he came all the way here from Leeds only to meet me and to give me my grandmother's jewellery."

"Trumpery beads," he snorted.

Kate bridled at his tone. "They may be trumpery beads to you, but they are all the jewellery I possess, and they belonged to my grandmother, whom I never met."

She clutched the small packet of jewellery to her breast.

"My mother died when I was born and I never knew her.

All I had of her were her pearls and her eyes. The pearls I had to sell, to pay our debts.'' *And her eyes cost me my father's love.* ''You cannot understand what it means to me to know that my grandmother remembered me, for my father fell out with my grandparents before I was born and they never contacted us as far as I know.'' Her eyes shimmered with unshed tears.

The bequest was far greater than its size or monetary value. Kate had only known her mother through others' eyes—and the image had been tarnished with her own guilt. But now Kate had something tangible, from a grandmother who'd thought of her with love instead of blame. Who'd cared enough to send her a keepsake—one which was not tainted by her father's resentment of Kate's existence.

''You call them trumpery beads, but my mother may have worn these as a girl, don't you see?'' Her voice broke and she turned and fled upstairs.

Jack swore under his breath and ran his hand angrily through his hair. Damn him, did he always have to speak before he thought? He hadn't meant to sneer at her pathetic little collection of jewellery; it had just been too much for him. First Francis had put him in a temper, with his damnably impertinent plans for Kate's future, and then to come home and find Kate beaming with delight on some oily Cit…it was too much! And besides which, his leg was hurting him. It was his own fault too, showing off before his friends. He would have to have it massaged again before it stiffened up on him any more.

''Carlos!'' he bellowed. ''Carlos!'' He stumped his way morosely upstairs.

Chapter Thirteen

"Damn it all, Francis," Jack exploded. "At least Tubby and Drew had the decency not to outstay their welcome. Haven't you got anything better to do than to hang around here for weeks on end, eating me out of house and home?"

Francis chuckled. "Not the least, dear boy. I like it here. The fresh air, the scenery..." he raised his eyebrows significantly in the direction of the terrace, where Kate was strolling with her cousin "...the charming company."

He took another sip of port and added ironically, "Oh, and of course you are a superlative host, Jack, old man. Make a chap feel so welcome."

Jack growled under his breath. "A man can't take a step in any direction without tripping over you or that damned Cole fellow." He glared at a hapless vase of flowers. "And the place is so cluttered up with these stinking weeds! Haven't either of you anything better to waste your blunt on? I don't know which of you is worse—that blasted Cit bleating platitudes all over Kate and kissing her hand until it must be quite soggy—or you, mouthing flowery compliments at her like a blasted poet."

"I do pride myself on my poetic talents, and little Kate seems to enjoy them too."

"Little Kate? Miss Farleigh to you! I'll thank you not to treat my grandmother's ward with such familiarity, Francis."

Francis's grin broadened. "She asked me to call her Kate, dear boy, and I hate to refuse a lady's request."

Jack muttered something unintelligible and stomped out of the library, leaving Francis chuckling. Jack had been acting like a bear with a sore head for several weeks now, snapping and snarling at his guests for no good reason. Or no reason he could be brought to admit to.

Francis's gaze sharpened on the pair on the terrace. His own so-called courtship posed no danger to Jack, but that Cole fellow was a serious contender. He had visited Kate morning and afternoon for the past three weeks, bringing her flowers, books and sweetmeats, though where he found the flowers at this time of year, and in the countryside, was more than Francis could guess. The man was obviously very plump in the pocket.

Francis frowned. He liked the fellow no better than Jack, though not for the same reasons. There was a pushiness about him that Francis disliked. Cole had pursued Kate from the moment they met with a single-mindedness and determination that to Francis's eye smacked of the calculating, rather than the lover-like. His possessive attitude towards his "charming little cousin' was increasing daily, and Francis suspected that Kate was finding it uncomfortable.

However, Jack's open hostility to the man made it difficult for Kate to repel her cousin's over-familiarity, for they all knew Jack was just itching for any excuse to toss Cole out on his ear and forbid him the house. Cole was Kate's cousin, after all, and her only living relative, and she wanted to be able to see him, even if she might not relish his possessive attitude towards her. Francis sighed and poured himself another drink.

"My dearest cousin," Jeremiah Cole began.

Kate felt her stomach sinking. She'd known for some time

that this was coming, and no amount of hinting had managed to dent her cousin's obvious determination. Perhaps it was better to allow him to speak, and then it would be over. He took her hands in a moist grip.

"Perhaps you have been aware these last weeks of my desire, my very ardent desire, to make this relationship of ours a closer one."

"Cousin Jeremiah, I am very happy to have you as my cousin—"

"But *I* am not," he interrupted. "You must know, Kate, how I feel about you." He pressed her hands against his broad chest. Kate tried to pull them away, but he only held them more tightly. "I am in love with you, Kate—madly, desperately—and I want you for my wife."

"Cousin Jeremiah," she said gently, "it is very kind—"

"Kind! It is not kindness I feel for you, my beloved. It is love! I want you to be mine. You are all alone in the world. Allow me to care for you, to protect you, to love you for the rest of your life. Only give me your hand, sweet Kate."

Despite the seriousness of the moment, Kate's sense of humour got the better of her. "Indeed, Cousin Jeremiah, you seem to have taken it whether I will or not," she said, tugging to release her hands from his grip. He did not let go, but smiled, almost angrily, at her.

She said more firmly, "Please let me go, Cousin Jeremiah. You are hurting me."

"And you are hurting me, Kate, by not answering. I asked you a question, one of the most important questions you will ever be asked in your life. Will you be my wife?"

"No, Cousin Jeremiah," she said gently. "I am sorry."

He frowned at her disbelievingly. "I don't believe it!" he said, releasing her hands only to take her shoulder in a tight grip. "I don't believe it!" he repeated, shaking her quite hard. "I love you and I am sure that you love me." His tone softened. "That is it, isn't it, Kate? You are teasing me." He pulled her hard against him and though Kate tried to push him away he was far too strong.

"Naughty girl to tease your Jeremiah like that," he crooned, and before Kate realised what he was about he had planted his lips firmly over hers and was kissing her with a wet determination that filled her with revulsion. She struggled in vain as his hands stroked down her body and his thick tongue probed to enter her mouth.

Suddenly she found herself released. She staggered back against the balustrade as Jack thrust himself between her and her cousin.

"You filthy swine, keep your paws off her!" he roared, and let swing a punch that sent Cousin Jeremiah sprawling inelegantly on the flagstones. Jack stood over him, rolling up his sleeves, the light of battle fairly blazing from his eyes.

"How dare you maul a decent girl, you cowardly scum?"

Cousin Jeremiah scuttled backwards.

"Come on, you scurvy blighter. It's one thing to bully a helpless female, and another to stand up to a man, isn't it? Subject an innocent girl to your filthy lust, will you? Not on my property, you won't. I'll teach you a lesson in how to treat a lady—one you'll never forget."

Jack stepped forward, murder in his eyes, oblivious to Kate's frantic jerking on his sleeve.

"Jack, stop it! You mustn't. He didn't hurt me. *Jack!*" she cried, but he was determined on his course. He moved purposefully towards Cousin Jeremiah, his fists bunched, blue eyes glittering with rage.

"Jack, he asked me to marry him!" screamed Kate in his ear.

At that Jack came to a dead halt. He swung around and stared at her in shock. The angry colour died from his face, leaving it a bleached grey.

"He what?" he croaked at last.

"He asked me to marry him," repeated Kate quietly, belatedly realising she'd given Jack the wrong impression, but seeing no immediate way out—except violence. She'd seen enough violence.

"So that's why…" Jack choked. He wrenched his eyes from her face and turned away. "I…see," he muttered. Without looking at either of them, he left.

Kate gazed after him, biting her lip. There had been pain in his eyes. Because he thought she was to marry Cousin Jeremiah? She wanted to run after him and tell him she'd refused, but she was afraid that if she did Jack would return to his former rage and do Jeremiah a grave injury. And now that Jack had stopped her cousin she felt she could handle things herself. She might be angry with Jeremiah for the way he had forced his embraces on her, but much could be forgiven a man rejected in love, and he was still her cousin, after all.

She turned. "I think you'd better leave, Cousin Jeremiah. I'm sorry it had to come to this."

He had struggled to his feet by now. His fright had passed, and was fast turning to indignation at the way he had been treated. "I must tell you, Cousin Kate, that I am deeply offended by that man's treatment of me. I have a good mind to report him to the nearest magistrate. He is clearly a dangerous lunatic."

Kate's temper finally exploded. "How dare you say such a thing? If you must know, I think you got off lightly, for if I were a man I would have knocked you down much sooner. How dare he? How dare *you?* To force your kisses on me, and think to overcome my refusal by brute force! Report him to a magistrate if you dare, Cousin Jeremiah, and you will find yourself reported for assault—on me!"

Cousin Jeremiah blanched and calmed down immediately. "Now, now, Kate, my dear, I did not mean it. I…I was upset. I think you must allow me the right to feel angry at being attacked so violently, but of course if it will upset you I will take no injudicious steps to have the matter followed up."

Kate was mollified. She spoke more softly. "I am sorry it had to come to this, Cousin Jeremiah. If you please, we will never speak of this matter again."

"No, no, of course not," he agreed eagerly. "But now, my dear, I would like to have the matter of our marriage settled as soon as possible."

Kate stared at him incredulously. Was the man utterly impervious? "Cousin Jeremiah," she said firmly, "all this happened because you refused to listen to me the first time. I am sorry, but I will *not* marry you."

"But I love you," he insisted.

"Then I am sorry for you, but I do not return your love."

"Love can grow after marriage," he persisted.

"Not in this case," said Kate bluntly. She had endured enough of his florid compliments and hand-kissing to last a lifetime.

"I do not mind if you don't love me; I will marry you anyway," he declared nobly.

Kate gritted her teeth and began to wish that she had let Jack give him a thrashing after all.

"But I do not wish to marry you."

He took several steps towards her, and she backed away. Good God, he was going to try to embrace her again.

"Cousin Jeremiah, I am *not* being missish!" she almost shrieked in her frustration. "I said I will not marry you and I meant it. *Nothing* will make me change my mind."

"How sweetly shy you are," began Cousin Jeremiah, advancing on her, a determined smile on his face.

"I am not shy!"

"I think you'd better listen to the lady," said a quiet voice from behind them. "My friend Mr Carstairs has already introduced you to the rather crude fighting methods of the Coldstream Guards. I would like to demonstrate the techniques favoured by gentlemen of the 95th Rifles." Francis began to roll up his sleeves, then paused. "That is, unless you apologise to the lady and leave before I finish rolling up my sleeves.'' He continued rolling them back, very deliberately and precisely.

Cousin Jeremiah eyed the sinewy forearms that were emerging. He already had a massive headache and a cracked jaw from just one frightful punch from Carstairs. He began to mutter indignantly about violence being offered to a man whose only crime was to woo a lady too ardently, when he caught Colonel Masterton's glittering eye. It bore a disturbing similarity to the look that he had seen in Mr Carstair's eye a few moments before. Hastily Cole gabbled an apology to Kate and left, almost running across the lawn in his desire to be quit of the place.

Despite the comical sight he made, Kate had no desire to laugh. She felt like a wrung-out rag. Nor did she feel up to discussing it with Francis.

"Thank you, Francis," she said quietly, and turned to leave.

"Are you all right?" he said.

"Oh, I'll be as right as a trivet," she said, attempting a cheerful smile that failed miserably. "I just need to rest for a while, I think." She turned and ran upstairs to her room.

Later that evening she went downstairs to supervise the preparation of dinner. Jack had taken himself off somewhere. The tavern, no doubt. Kate didn't feel up to dining with Francis, so she ate in the kitchen with the servants. It was too ironic, really. Here she was, a girl who knew herself unable to marry, being courted by two gentlemen, neither of whom she wanted...

Kate sighed. For a short while, her life had been so pleasant. Now it was all changed. She still felt Jack's eyes on her a hundred times a day, but instead of protectiveness and a lurking tenderness there was suspicion and brooding disapproval in his gaze. Whatever she did, he seemed to be furious with her. It was confusing, hurtful—and more than a little annoying.

She had no idea what his intentions or feelings towards her were. There was no denying that his kisses moved her like nothing she had ever experienced, but it was a feeling she knew she ought to fight. Even if by some wondrous chance he came to feel something deeper than lust for her, an alliance between them would not be possible. Anyone with a grain of sense would realise that in his position Jack would have to marry money.

Kate wondered what sort of a man his father had been to disinherit his son so callously. Had he not been playing cards the day he died, and won the deed to this property, Jack would be living…heaven knew where. At any rate, if he was to make anything further of his life, Jack would have to find himself an heiress, a well-born heiress—not a poor clergyman's daughter with nothing but a tawdry scandal for her dowry…

"Miss Kate." Florence interrupted Kate's train of thought. "Are we goin' to have the next bit o' that story soon?"

Kate smiled. While cleaning the library a few weeks before, she had discovered some of Mrs Radcliffe's novels. The vicar's daughter had been utterly forbidden "rubbishy novels', so naturally Kate had become addicted to them. Now, each evening, while Martha and the girls sewed and mended they also gasped with horror and delight as Kate read the heroine's adventures aloud.

And Kate's audience had grown. The girls' sisters and brother, hearing each thrilling episode of *The Mysteries of Udolpho* retold at the farm, had soon decided that Millie and Florence needed to be escorted home. Each evening, the six Cotter siblings, Martha, Carlos, Francis's groom, and even his very superior valet, "accidentally" arrived in the kitchen in time for the next episode.

Glancing around, Kate saw that her audience had assembled already. She hadn't realised it was so late. She took out the book, sat down near the fire and began to read. An hour later, she closed the book, to the sighs and protests of her audience.

"Eh, Miss Kate," said Millie's brother, Tom. "That Sinner Montoni, 'e's a proper villain, ain't 'e? Our Dad allus says you can't trust foreigners." He tossed a dark look at Carlos.

"Sí," said Carlos immediately. "Me, I never trust Italians…never! That Signor Montoni is a bad man. Poor Miss Emily."

There was a chorus of agreement. The girls shuddered eloquently and chattered about the story as they filed out.

"Coming up to bed now, dearie?" asked Martha.

"No, not yet." Kate wasn't at all tired, after her earlier sleep. "I think I'll just sit here for a bit in front of the fire, Martha. You go up, though." They exchanged their goodnights and Kate was soon left alone with her thoughts.

"How many more hidden talents do you have, I wonder?" The deep voice coming out of the shadows made her leap in fright. She turned and perceived Jack leaning casually against the scullery wall, half hidden by the gloom.

"How long have you been there?" she gasped.

He moved forward out of the darkness. "Twenty minutes or so. They were all so entranced by your reading that no one noticed when I came looking for you, so I decided not to disturb things. You read well, li'l Kate." His voice was mocking and he stumbled over a chair.

Kate's stomach clenched. He was drunk.

"Quite the li'l actress, aren't you?" He loomed over her. Kate pressed back in her chair as far as she could. He reached out a long finger and brushed her nose lightly. "Spot o' flour. Damned if I ever saw a woman so inclined to messiness."

Kate jerked her head away from his hand. She did have a tendency to splash things around when she was working, and

despite all her best efforts to remain neat she usually found
a splatter of flour or a smear of dust on her face or hands
when she went to have her usual nightly wash. But she was
sure it was not nearly as bad as he implied. She rubbed her
nose vigorously with her sleeve, watching him swaying
gently on his feet.

"You're foxed," she said bluntly.

"And what if I am? 'Tis none of your business what I
do."

Kate frowned. "Where is Francis?" she asked.

"So it's Francis now, is it?" he sneered. "Very familiar
you are with my friends."

Kate did not reply. There was no point in arguing with
him when he was in this state.

"Have you told him yet of your little arrangement with
that greasy Cit?"

Kate had no doubt of whom he was speaking. "Please do
not call Cousin Jeremiah rude names. I know you do not like
him, but he is my only living relative, however distant."

"And soon to become even closer, eh?" he jeered. "So
much for all your pious talk of not marrying! All it takes is
a wealthy Cit to smother you with flowers and greasy compliments, and all your res'lutions go down the drain." He
snorted in contempt. "Women! You're just like all the rest
of them. Let some fellow dangle his moneybags in front of
you, and you're all sweetness and compliance."

He imitated her voice mockingly. "Oh, Cousin Jeremiah,
I would be delighted. Dear Cousin Jeremiah, you wish to kiss
me? Please do. Oh, yes, Cousin Jeremiah, I will wed you,
will allow you to put your greasy paws all over me, to plant
your disgusting fishy lips on mine!" He was enraged by now.
"How you can have the stomach to consider wedding such
a loathsome upstart is beyond me."

Kate glared at him. She had initially opened her mouth to
inform him she had refused her cousin's proposal, but by the

time he had paused for breath, and she had an opening, she was so incensed that all thoughts of telling him had flown from her head. His close proximity was rather overwhelming, though, so she wriggled out of the chair and faced him across the kitchen table.

"How dare you speak to me in this way?" she spat. "It is no concern of yours what I do, Mr Carstairs, no concern at all. If I wish to see my cousin I will, if I wish to embrace him I will, and if I wish to marry him I will! It is nothing whatsoever to do with you!"

She stamped her foot on the hard flagstones and continued. "And how dare you impugn my honour in that way? A person's wealth or lack of it has nothing—*nothing*—to do with my attitude to them, and it's outrageous of you to suggest otherwise. It is quite irrelevant to me whether Cousin Jeremiah is wealthy or not. I have not the slightest interest in a person's financial standing, and only a completely vulgar person would think it could ever be important."

"If the cap fits…" he began.

"Then *you* must wear it," she snapped, "for such considerations have never been mine!"

"You cannot mean you love that contemptible creature." His voice was scornful, but his body was tense as he waited for her answer.

She tossed her head at him. "That, Mr Carstairs, is none of your business!"

"It damned well is!"

"Why?" she demanded, her mouth dry.

They glowered at each other, then he moved with unexpected speed, dragging her against him. He stared down at her for a moment, then crushed his mouth on to hers.

It was a stormy kiss, full of passion and desperation and anger. He gripped her hard, and if she had been aware of his grip she might have told him he was hurting her. But Kate too was lost in the roiling waves of passion and she returned

his kiss with equal anguished desperation, clutching him
fiercely, returning his every caress with interest.

Eventually they separated and stood there staring into each
other's eyes, breathing heavily. Kate's lips were bruised, but
she was oblivious of anything except him. She swallowed,
trying to recover her poise. He watched her silently. Eventually the silence became too much for her.

''What did you mean by that?'' she said in a low voice.
She wondered if he could hear her heart thudding, it sounded
so loud to her.

Jack stood, breathing heavily, slowly gathering his wits.
He'd given her the chance to repudiate Cole and she hadn't.
Nothing was changed. She was still betrothed to her wealthy
Cit. He'd be damned if he exposed himself to gratify a
woman's vanity. He had done quite enough of that already.
He looked down into her eyes. He could see her waiting,
willing him to say the words, so she could throw them back
in his teeth, no doubt. She was no different from any other
woman.

''What did it mean?'' he said. ''What did it mean? Why,
nothing, my dear Kate. A pleasant interlude, that's all.'' He
licked his lips suggestively. ''I did say you are talented, did
I not?''

Kate felt her throat close as the eyes, which had been blazing with fiery passion a moment before, iced over.

''You beast!'' she whispered. His words were a timely
reminder. It was the old story of the dog in the manger. But
it had been a long, exhausting day, and for once Kate didn't
have the energy to deal with the hostility and the anger she
saw in his eyes. She was feeling so miserable herself that all
she wanted to do was to throw herself against his chest and
sob her heart out. Only the mood he was in, he would probably rip it out of her chest and devour it. Or had he done
that already?

He laughed harshly. ''Haven't you heard, my dear girl? I

would have thought a parson's daughter would have been warned many a time that all men are beasts. That's why you like us so much.''

''On the contrary, my father taught me to love all mankind, as he did,'' said Kate dully. *My father, who loved all mankind—except me.*

Jack took her unconscious expression of pain to be caused by his words. He recoiled and his hand reached out to her half pleadingly, but she did not notice.

Kate did not look at him again. She quietly left the room, and went upstairs to bed. She was just blowing out her candle when she realised she hadn't made it clear to Jack that she was not going to marry her cousin. If only he would get it into his head that she would never marry! Stubborn, wretched man! And why was he drinking again? Surely not because he thought she had accepted her cousin? No—why would he, when he had been urging her to go to London and find a husband there?

Oh, well, it was cold, she was tired, and she certainly had no intention of seeking him out when he was in the state he was in, and she in her nightrobe. He would probably kiss her again, and she was feeling so lonely and miserable tonight that she would probably do absolutely nothing to prevent it, and that would be fatal.

She'd had enough accusations of impropriety in her life—she needed no more.

''Have you seen Kate today?'' Francis asked Jack.

''No,'' Jack mumbled. He continued reading a newspaper that had been sent by a friend. He did not even want to think about Kate. It was too distressing, imagining her wedded to Cole, forever out of sight, out of touch. It was no concern of his what she might be doing. He didn't care. He was reading the news instead.

The paper was out of date, but it contained a detailed description of the army's retreat from Spain back to Portugal. Both Jack and Francis had found the news very depressing, containing, as it did, news of dreadful casualties. Jack was particularly affected by the horrendous losses suffered by Anson's brigade. They had fought together at Salamanca, and Anson and many of his officers were friends of Jack's.

The paper criticised Wellington for allowing it to happen. The press were fair-weather friends to Old Hookey, Jack decided. He was a hero when he was winning, and a bungling fool when things were difficult. Disgusted, he tossed the paper aside. After a few moments, he recalled Francis's question about Kate. He hadn't seen her at all that day. No doubt she was avoiding him again, after their clash in the kitchen the previous night.

"She's probably in the kitchen." He got up to pour himself a glass of madeira, but was annoyed to discover the decanter empty. "Carlos!" he bellowed.

Carlos arrived and was dispatched to fetch a new bottle. As he was leaving Francis spoke. "Carlos, have you seen Miss Kate?"

"No *señor,* she went off for a drive with Señor Cole this morning."

Both men frowned. "But it is now well into the afternoon. Are you sure she has not returned?" asked Francis.

Carlos nodded lugubriously. "*Sí, señor,* for Mrs Martha and the girls have been waiting for her to come back all afternoon."

The two gentlemen exchanged glances. Jack sullenly shrugged, endeavouring to conceal his concern. "If she wants to spend all day with her betrothed, then it is her concern. She clearly has no concern for her reputation."

"Her betrothed?" said Francis. "She is not betrothed."

Jack shrugged again. "She neglected to inform you? That greasy Cit had the confounded impudence to propose to her yesterday and the stupid chit accepted him."

Francis frowned. "When exactly was this?"

"Yesterday, on the terrace. I caught him with his greasy paws all over her, kissing her. Gave him a leveller." He clenched his fists. "Wish I'd knocked his teeth clear out the back of his head. I would have too, but the wretched girl hung off my arm, screeching that they were to be married, so then there was nothing left for me to do but go away and leave the happy couple to plan the wedding."

Francis's brow cleared, and he tried to hide his twitching lips. His friend was trying very hard to sound indifferent, with scant success. He took pity on him. "She didn't accept him, you know."

"Yes, she did."

"No, she did not. I was here, in the library, when you knocked him down." Francis chuckled. "I was just about to go out and intervene, but you beat me to it, for she was no willing participant in that embrace, I can assure you."

Jack looked doubtful. "Well, she must have changed her mind later."

Francis shook his head. "Not a chance, old boy. After you left, the fellow had the infernal cheek to persist with his suit. I heard Kate refuse him in no uncertain terms, several times. He would have forced himself upon her again if I had not intervened and sent him to the rightabout with the offer of a little of my own home-brewed." He grinned reflectively. "You should have seen him scuttling off across the lawn. I expect his coachman caught up with him by the time he reached the front gate."

Both men burst out laughing at the thought.

Then Jack sobered abruptly. "Then why the devil did she go driving with him this morning?" Their glances met. "And why has she not returned by now?" He ran his hand through his hair.

"I have to tell you, Francis, that I taxed her with it last night and she never denied that she and Cole were betrothed."

"I suppose you did it in your usual tactful manner, didn't you?" said Francis.

Jack grimaced.

"In a filthy temper, were you?" said Francis. "Doing your level best to pick a quarrel?" He shook his head. "The best way to make a woman do the opposite of what you want is to try and bully her. Especially a woman as spirited as Kate. She probably told you she was betrothed to her cousin to pay you back for your impudence."

He met his friend's eye. "Depend on it, Jack, it was all a hum. If yesterday was anything to go by, the little Farleigh has nothing but dutiful family feeling in her heart for that fellow, and it was pretty strained at that, after the way he tried to push her into marrying him."

"So where the devil is she?" Jack headed for the kitchen, shouting for Carlos, Martha and the two girls. He questioned them as to why Kate had gone for a drive with her cousin when they had not parted on good terms the day before.

"'E came around this morning," said Martha, "with an 'angdog look on 'is face and a bunch of flowers. Said 'e were sorry and would she forgive 'im and let 'im take 'er for a drive." She wrung her hands in her apron. "But that were hours and hours ago, sir, and it ain't like Miss Kate to stay out so long, 'specially with a gentleman."

"Did she take anything with her, Martha?"

Martha looked puzzled. "What do you mean, sir?"

"A portmanteau, a bandbox, something like that."

Martha shook her head firmly. "No, sir, nothing like that." She peered suspiciously at him. "You bain't be thinkin' as Miss Kate's run away, sir? Not Miss Kate. She wouldn't worry us all like that."

She caught his look of doubt and shook her head again. "I've known that girl since she was a tiny babe, Mr Jack, and it's simply not in 'er to sneak off behind people's backs."

He looked sceptical, but Martha would have none of it. For once her beloved Mr Jack was wrong, and she, Martha, would put him right. "Oh, I admit, she 'as a temper, when it's roused, sir, but to do somethin' like that—never! I'm worried, Mr Jack, summat awful, and I don't like 'er cousin, not one little bit. She shoulda been home long since." Her old face crumpled with concern, and she clutched Jack's coatsleeve.

"Find 'er, Mr Jack. Find 'er and bring 'er 'ome."

"Carlos, saddle my horse," snapped Jack.

"Perhaps the curricle would be better, Jack. Your leg wouldn't stand up to riding for hours, would it?" said Francis.

"Damn my leg. A horse is faster than a curricle. Saddle the roan, Carlos."

"And my chestnut," added Francis.

"Does anyone know which direction they were headed in?"

"Sir, I saw the carriage turn at the gate and head north," said Florence.

"North?" Jack turned and looked at Francis grimly. "Are you thinking what I am thinking?"

Francis nodded slowly. "He was damned persistent yesterday. Seemed almost desperate when she refused him so adamantly. But would he force her?"

Jack swore. "If that bastard lays as much as a finger on her, I'll kill him!"

Chapter Fourteen

Darkness was falling rapidly as the two men neared the outskirts of a village. Francis deliberately reined in his mount and after a moment Jack, too, slowed his horse, with obvious reluctance. He'd set a killing pace. Their horses were nearing exhaustion. As the pace slowed, his tension increased—this village was probably their last chance.

Jack's shoulders slumped. His face was grey with pain and anxiety. He'd expected to catch Cole long before now. The longer the search, the less chance they had of catching up. The consequences of that were too appalling to even think of. And of course he could think of nothing else. They must be on the right track; they had to be!

Enquiries had revealed that Cole had exchanged his gig for a hired closed carriage and was heading north. Informants had further disclosed that Cole had his sick sister with him and was conveying her home. Armed with a description of the carriage, Jack and Francis had ridden furiously onwards, enquiring at every village.

The moon rose; its pale beams silvered the countryside. Francis cast a worried look at Jack. It was perfectly obvious that Jack was almost at the end of his tether, and in a great deal of pain. "We should rest up for a short time, old chap. Give the horses a break, you know."

"And leave her a moment longer than necessary in the hands of that fiend?" Jack's tone brooked no argument. "He has kidnapped her to force a wedding. He cannot possibly reach the border in less than two nights. That means he intends to force her, Francis. Tonight. Do you think I can rest, even for a short while, while she is in the hands of that madman?"

"Ah, don't torture yourself, Jack. I agree, the direction seems to indicate he is making for Gretna, but he has no reason to know he is pursued. He has no reason to force her tonight."

Jack opened his mouth to reply when something caught his eye. He wrenched his horse to a halt, backed up and peered down a narrow lane. "Do you see what I see?"

Down the lane, silhouetted against the silver sheen of a small pond, was a shape which could have been that of a travelling carriage. Beside it was a small cottage. Exchanging silent glances, the men quietly walked their steeds down the lane.

The cottage was old and run-down. It was clear from the weeds that surrounded it that no one had lived there for years. They dismounted and crept closer. A figure moved inside, illuminated by a candle. It was Cole, bending over a motionless shape on a pallet on the floor.

The door crashed open. Cole swung round in fright. The high colour drained from his face and his lips began to writhe in a ghastly attempt at a smile as he perceived the face of the large black shape in the doorway. "Er...ah..."

"Get away from her," said Jack in a soft voice that chilled Cole's bones to the marrow.

Cole scuttled sideways as far as he could.

"If you have touched so much as a hair on her head, you're a dead man," Jack said in that same chilling tone, moving towards the pallet. He laid a gentle hand on Kate's cheek, smoothing the hair back from her forehead. Her eyelids fluttered and she moaned.

"What the devil have you done to her, you blackguard?"

"Nothing, nothing on my life, I swear it!" gabbled Cole. "She is not hurt, only drugged."

"Drugged!" said Francis from the open doorway.

Cole started and turned towards the door. "Only a little laudanum, I swear it...it was just that she strugg—" He found himself grabbed by his collar and flung against the wall.

"Struggled, did she, you filthy swine?" snarled Jack. "And do I have to ask why she felt the need to struggle?" A rock-like fist slammed into Cole's stomach, and he doubled over, gasping for breath. Another one crashed into his jaw with a resounding crack. Then he was ruthlessly dragged up by the hair and shaken like a rat. Blazing blue eyes met his.

"I'll teach you to abduct innocent girls!"

Two more punches smashed into Cole, almost simultaneously. His nose felt as if it had exploded. Cole collapsed.

"Get up, you blackguard," roared Mad Jack Carstairs. "I haven't finished with you yet! Not by a long shot!" He reached down and grabbed the blubbering Cole by the throat. He smiled, a peculiarly sinister smile which sent the blood draining from Cole's face, and said softly, "I'm going to kill you, you know that?"

Cole had always thought himself a big man, but now he found himself dangling by the throat, being slowly choked to death by an enraged madman. He struggled, but it was as if he was a rabbit in the grip of an eagle. His face began to turn purple and his eyes bulged as the powerful hands tightened their relentless grip around his throat.

"Jack...?" The faint, wavering voice came from the pallet.

Cole was tossed aside like a bundle of rags. He lay on the

floor, gasping for breath like a beached and battered fish. Jack bent solicitously over Kate, his arms lifting her off the dirty pallet until she lay cradled against his chest.

"Are you all right, sweetheart?" A gentle hand smoothed back her tangled curls with infinite tenderness.

"Oh, Jack, I feel so strange," she murmured, trying to sit up.

"No, no, don't try to move, sweetheart. It's all right. You're safe now." He pulled her more closely against him. His arms were hard around her, holding her protectively, whilst he crooned soothing nonsense in her ear, interposing it with small kisses on her hair, her ears, whatever he could reach.

Kate, bewildered, ill and dizzy from the effects of the drug, burrowed into his chest and lay there, clutching him, understanding nothing except that Jack was there, holding her, and that everything was therefore perfect.

Francis watched them, a soft look in his eyes, then a movement to his left caught his attention, and his gaze hardened as he took in the sorry sight of Cousin Jeremiah. Blood was oozing from cuts over his eye, and gushing from his nose and lips. His jaw was beginning to swell and both eyes were puffing up.

Francis's lip curled contemptuously as he took in the snuffling, sobbing creature. Silently he opened the door, and curtly jerked his head. Casting fearful glances towards Jack, who was still wholly absorbed with Kate, Cole lurched to his feet and tottered out. Francis followed.

"Not the carriage, I think," he said softly as Cole headed towards it. "We will need that to convey Miss Farleigh home."

"But how will I get home myself?" Cole whimpered. It was a freezing night.

"I have not the least notion," said Francis coldly, "but

once my friend realises you are out here I have no doubt that you will return home snug and cosy enough—in a coffin.''

Cole gasped in terror and set off down the rough track towards the main road, stumbling and crashing, casting frequent fearful glances behind him. Francis watched until he was out of sight, and out of earshot, then quietly re-entered the ruined house.

Kate was curled up almost in a ball, cradled in Jack's lap, nestled against his chest like a child. She seemed to be asleep. The eyes of the two men met. Francis's eyebrow rose in a silent question and Jack nodded imperceptibly. Francis heaved a sigh of relief. She was all right, then. Cole had drugged her, but no violence had been done.

He glanced at the pair on the pallet and sighed. Neither of them were in any condition to move tonight. Kate was exhausted by her ordeal and still partly drugged; as for Jack, he might have had enough strength to give Cole a thrashing while his body had been functioning on rage, but now that his anger had died away Francis would hazard a guess that Jack would barely be able to walk.

''I'll see to the horses,'' he said quietly, and left the room. Jack did not appear to hear him. All his attention was on Kate. She murmured something in her sleep and his hold on her tightened.

Over her head Jack stared blankly at the wall. What a fool he'd been. He'd thought he could give her up, convinced himself that she would be better off without him, that the best thing he could do for her was to send her to his grandmother...

He didn't want to send her anywhere. He wanted to hold her like this for the rest of his life. He shifted slightly and winced as his bad leg reminded him of his uncomfortable position. Well, not exactly like this. Not on a grubby pallet on a hard cold floor in a squalid little tumbledown cottage.

Kate shifted and wriggled against him, and despite his discomfort he felt his body respond to her. No, he didn't want to hold her like this for the rest of his life. Hold her, yes. In his bed. Caressing her and loving her and introducing her to the delights of passion. Oh, yes, she had passion in her, his little Kate. He felt his body tighten just thinking about it as it had so many times recently. Too many times. He had barely been able to control himself. The slightest look or movement of hers had been enough to force him to battle with his body's response.

She shivered and moved against him again. Damn his stupidity, she was cold, he realised. Blasted fool that he was, thinking of himself when all the time the girl was cold. It was his body warmth she wanted, not his body. Selfish, bloody, stupid, insensitive fool! Gently, trying not to disturb her, Jack shrugged himself out of his greatcoat and wrapped it snugly around her.

"Mmm, nice," she muttered, and he grinned wryly, realising that she had indeed been cold. Carefully he moved, gritting his teeth at the jarring pain, tenderly manipulating her until he was lying half on his side, half on his back, with her small body tucked into the warm curve of his. He opened his jacket and shirt to pull them more closely around her and give her more of his body warmth. Instantly she snuggled her arms around his bare torso and moved closer on top of him, nuzzling her mouth against his throat.

Steadfastly ignoring his body's tumultuous response, he closed his shirt and jacket over her and tucked the greatcoat carefully around her. She would be warmer now, with his body and his coat sheltering her from all possible draughts. He could feel his pulse thundering. His body throbbed for release. He was torn between savouring her closeness, the feel and scent and touch of her, and battling the demands of his body to further that closeness. An electric jolt passed through him as she wriggled again. He swore silently and gritted his teeth, willing his body into obedience.

Damn it all! He was little better than Cole, he thought. She was drugged. She didn't know what she was doing. He should be protecting her, not lusting after her like a mindless beast! She had just come through a dreadful ordeal and all he could think of was how desperately he wanted to make love to her. He stared at the stained and sagging ceiling and tried desperately to think of other things.

He was failing miserably at this task when Francis reentered the cottage, staggering under a load of wood. Swiftly he cleared the grate and soon had a fire crackling briskly. From his position on the pallet Jack grinned approvingly. Francis left again, and soon returned with several rugs.

"Found 'em in the carriage." He tossed one over Jack and Kate. "Brought you something else, too." Grinning, he produced from his pocket a substantial flask of brandy.

"Good man!" whispered Jack, and reached out. He took a long pull on the flask and sighed, feeling the liquor burn a cosy trail through his body. "Ah, that's better."

"Leg paining you much?"

"Not too bad."

Francis grunted. "Always were a shocking bad liar, old man. Have another drink. It's going to be a long, uncomfortable night for you. She's all right?"

Jack nodded. "Just cold and the after-effects of the drug—filthy swine. I gather you let the bastard go."

"Couldn't have you clapped up for murder, old thing. You gave him a good enough hiding and I sent him out into the night. Bloody cold at that. Might not survive. If not, no bad thing. If he does, well, he's still been punished."

"Not enough."

"Try and get some sleep, old man. Or worry about young Kate if you must, not Cole. I'll sleep in the carriage, keep an eye on the horses."

The cottage fell silent, the only sound the occasional crackling of the fire and the blowing of the wind in the trees outside.

Kate was the first to waken next morning. She came slowly to consciousness, her mind still fuzzy from the drug she had been given. Despite a slight headache and a stomach that was insisting it be fed, she was aware of a tremendous feeling of rightness. Still with her eyes closed, she inhaled slowly, moving her cheek sensuously against its pillow. She stopped. Her pillow felt...odd.

She opened one eye. Her pillow was a naked male chest, lightly sprinkled with dark hair. Good God! Cautiously she lifted her head and looked at the owner of the chest. Jack? She had slept with Jack? Swiftly, with a minimum of movement, she glanced around the room. She had never seen this place in her life.

The last time she had wakened with no recollection of the previous day she had found herself in the hands of the French. But Jack was here. Grimly she forced her mind to recall its last memory. Arguing with Cousin Jeremiah...and drinking that bitter coffee. Had she been drugged? Or had she passed out for some other reason? It was no use. She couldn't answer. She would have to wait until Jack woke.

She looked down at Jack as he lay sound asleep and her mouth curved in a tender smile. He looked so young and boyish and handsome, the harsh bitterness wiped away in sleep. Gently she stroked the lines of his face, smoothed the tousled thick dark hair. Unable to help herself, she touched her lips to his in the lightest of kisses. She froze as he stirred, then relaxed as his breathing returned to its previous regularity.

She watched the broad chest moving up and down with each breath and marvelled that she had slept all night on it without realising it. She bent and kissed the warm, slightly salty skin. She feathered tiny damp kisses up his chest, over his throat, along his jaw and back to his lips. She spent long moments tasting and caressing him, all in the lightest of gossamer touches so as not to disturb his sleep, revelling in the contrast of texture of his darkly rugged jaw, scraping her soft lips against its harsh texture, then placing her mouth gently against his soft, relaxed lips. Greatly daring, she touched his lips with her tongue, just to know again the taste of him. He moaned and shifted slightly and she froze again, watching him, but he was still asleep, and she returned to her illicit explorations.

Kate's heart was pounding. She knew she should not be doing this, lying so with a man, exploring his unconscious body like a thief in the night. It went against every principle she had been raised by, every tenet of the proper behaviour for a lady—but she couldn't help herself. She would never have this opportunity again. This was not simply a man—it was Jack, the man she longed for with every fibre of her being, the man she loved but could never have. Surely God would forgive her this once.

She gazed at his sleeping face, her body tingling all over. Oh, but he was a beautiful man. Gently she ran her hand over his naked torso, marvelling at the smoothness of his skin, the contained power in the relaxed muscles of his chest. Delicately she ran her fingers through the soft curls of his chest hair. His flat brown nipples were ringed with whorls of dark hair. She kissed them and he shuddered under her touch.

She lifted her head, waiting for signs of him awakening. Her eyes ran over his face, his dear battered cheek, his long aquiline nose, the deep grooves that ran from nose to mouth. Her gaze stopped on his open mouth and slowly she lowered her mouth to his, seeking that incredible, wonderful sensation she had experienced before, when her tongue had touched his.

Jack silently groaned as he felt her mouth come down on his again. He couldn't take much more of this without responding. His body was aflame with the desire to hold her, return her sweet, tentative caresses, to take her and bring them both to glorious crescendo. But he couldn't, not here, not now, not in silence and stealth, for he was too aware of their situation: the filthy cottage, the sagging ceiling, the hard floor. And Francis could walk in at any moment. No, it would be too sordid.

When he took Kate and made her his, he wanted it to be utterly perfect. But for now he would take what he could. And what he had was the most exquisite torture he had ever experienced.

He had come awake almost instantly, as soon as he had felt her stir, but had not moved, allowing her to escape from their embarrassingly intimate position if she wished to. He had waited for her to move away from him, feeling the cold rush of air as she lifted her body away from his, feigning sleep to make it easier for her to leave him.

He'd been unprepared for the shock of the first feathery caress on his skin. So light, he had almost not believed it was happening, but it had been followed by another and then another, and it had taken all his will-power just to lie there instead of gathering her hard against him in a passionate embrace. Such a thing had never happened to Jack Carstairs before. To lie still, and to all intents placid and unaware, while the little creature that had wound herself around his heart planted the tiniest, most delicately moist kisses all over him.

His pulse pounded with the effort of remaining relaxed under her innocently questing sensual onslaught. He had no choice. He had to lie here in tormented bliss, treasuring each tentative, seductive caress, as if he had no more feeling than a block of wood. It was that or lose the precious moment to sordid reality. No choice at all.

God, but she was sweet. Oh, Lord, she was kissing him on the mouth again. He braced himself for the ravaging temptation as her small pink tongue reached in and delicately touched his. The jolt of sensation swamped him, and with silent anguish he felt his tongue responding, curling around hers. He felt her alarmed withdrawal but he could not help himself and his tongue followed hers. She jerked away in panic. Gently but firmly his hand cupped the back of her head and, blue eyes blazing into hers, he pulled her mouth back to his.

The kiss was long, sweet and intensely passionate.

Outside the cottage, Jack could hear Francis getting the horses ready. He released Kate and after a moment she drew back, a dazed, bemused expression on her face. Jack yearned to pull her back into his arms and kiss her arousal into passion. Instead he smiled, an odd, twisted, tender smile.

"Morning, sweetheart," he whispered. "That's the nicest awakening I think I've ever had."

Kate blinked, then blushed rosily. Good God, she was lying full length on top of Jack Carstairs in the most immodest position, legs entwined, her breasts resting on his naked chest and his...his manhood pressing into her. And he was awake!

Hurriedly she scrambled off Jack and stood, tugging frantically at her clothes, desperately attempting to achieve some semblance of decency and composure. Heavens! How long had Jack been awake? Had he known all that she had done?

Deeply embarrassed, she busied herself with tidying her clothes and her hair, unable even to look in his direction, let alone meet his gaze. She wanted to break the fraught silence with words, but could think of nothing to say. Behind her she could hear Jack moving; presumably he was closing his shirt, buttoning his waistcoat, shrugging himself back into the coat she had found herself wrapped in...

"Morning, all. Sleep well?" Francis entered the cottage with a stamping of boots. "Brrr, it's cold out there. I think we should try to get moving as soon as possible. Kate, how are you, m'dear?"

Kate murmured something unintelligible and slipped outside the cottage, her face flaming. Francis here as well? Who else knew of her shame? Bad enough that she had allowed herself to be kidnapped by her cousin, but to have two witnesses to it—and then to have behaved in that manner with Jack! What must he think of her, to have touched him that way...with Francis somewhere about too? It was all too mortifying.

She went in search of water in which to wash. She could find no well, nor any pump or stream. The night had been a bitter one and the small pond beside the cottage was frozen over. Kate tried to smash through the ice with a rock, but it would not break. She rubbed some icicles over her skin until they melted and dried her tingling face on her petticoat. She tore a ribbon of lace off her petticoat and tied her hair back as neatly as she could. Then she returned to the cottage, shivering in the morning chill.

By the time she returned, both Francis and Jack looked presentable, if not their usual immaculate selves. She avoided Jack's eyes and knew her face was flaming, but hoped it would be put down, by Francis at least, to the nip of the frigid air outside.

"Good morning, gentlemen," she said brightly, smiling impartially at a space somewhere between the two of them. "Anything to eat? I'm utterly ravenous."

Francis chuckled. "The lady is hungry, old man. We can't have that. Shall we adjourn to the nearest hostelry and obtain some breakfast? I fancy there is an inn in the next village which can accommodate our needs tolerably well."

"Oh, yes, let's," said Kate immediately, beaming at him. She still could not look at Jack.

"In that case, ma'am, I shall fetch your carriage at once!" said Francis, bowing like a flunkey. Kate giggled as he left the cottage, bowing repeatedly like a Cit facing royalty.

She turned to find Jack leaning against the wall, glowering at her. "Must you flirt with him so early in the morning?"

Kate flushed and looked away. She felt his gaze scorching her.

"I wasn't flirting." Her heart plummeted.

Jack grunted disbelievingly.

Kate turned her back on him and walked to the open door and looked out. There was nothing she could do. He would think whatever he wished to. She could not change his mind. She shivered in the bitter cold and folded her arms against her chest then jumped as a heavy coat was dropped over her shoulders from behind.

"Here," he said curtly. "Wrap this around you."

The coat was still warm and smelled faintly of him. Kate didn't move. She felt his hands coming over her shoulders, tugging the coat more firmly around her. She tried to shrug it off. "No, no. I don't need—"

"Don't be so stupid," he growled. Strong hands came down on her shoulders and turned her around. She looked up at him, but he concentrated on buttoning the coat firmly over her.

"Thank you," she said softly.

He glanced at her briefly, a hard, unreadable look, muttered something under his breath, then pushed past her and went to help Francis with the horses.

He was limping heavily, she realised with dismay—his leg must be paining him dreadfully. White lines of pain were back around his mouth, deeper than they had been for months—he had hurt himself rescuing her. She wanted to run after him, do something, but she knew she could not. Hadn't she done enough? He was clearly embarrassed by that morning kiss, and angry with her because of it, or why would he be so cross with her for responding to Francis's nonsense? Although pain did nothing for anyone's temper.

The carriage arrived. Francis acted as driver, and the two

horses he and Jack had ridden were tied behind. Kate got in and waited while Jack and Francis had a brief altercation about who was to drive. Eventually Jack conceded, but said in a surly manner that he would sit up with Francis.

"Don't be ridiculous, man," said Francis acerbically. "Your leg is in no condition to be climbing up here and, in any case, you haven't got a coat and you'll freeze in this weather. Now shut up and get into the carriage before Kate thinks you have conceived a distaste for her company."

Kate swallowed. Francis had been joking, but he had inadvertently hit the nail on the head. Jack didn't want to be in the carriage with her. It was obvious.

Jack climbed into the carriage. Kate gazed out of the window.

Wordlessly he seated himself and stared moodily out of the opposite one.

They travelled the short distance to the next village in silence and pulled up before a small, neat inn. The innkeeper looked them over with a practised eye, taking in their crumpled clothing, the men's unshaven chins, Kate's loosely tied-back hair, and a knowing look crept over his ruddy features.

"Two chambers, landlord, if you would be so good," drawled Francis. "One for myself and my friend and the other for…my sister."

Kate flushed at the landlord's glance. He clearly disbelieved the tale and took her for quite another sort of female. She put her chin up proudly, defying him to judge her.

Jack had noted the exchange. "My *wife* will want hot water and a maid to assist her," he snapped. "Her maid and our coachman were injured in the accident we had last night. We have no time to delay, landlord. Shall we say breakfast in forty minutes? Oh, and hot water for my friend and myself as well and shaving implements."

The landlord responded to the haughty tone of command and leapt to obey, calling his wife to come and help the young lady, a look of deepest obsequiousness replacing the sleazy gleam.

Kate blinked. *His wife?* She sighed. Sister, wife—it was all the same—a tale fabricated to protect her non-existent reputation. She followed the landlord's wife upstairs in silence.

After a hearty, though not exactly jolly breakfast, during which Francis and Kate chatted while Jack ate in morose silence, they set off again. Mile after mile passed in uncomfortable silence, both passengers brooding and thoughtful. The impasse continued until the countryside began to look familiar.

Kate finally spoke. "You didn't need to tell that man that I was your wife, you know. Francis's sister would have been quite sufficient."

"That's all you know," snapped Jack. So she would rather appear as Francis's sister than as Jack's wife, would she? Had this morning meant nothing, then? Women! He would never understand them.

"What do you mean?" asked Kate.

"Well, after last night, you'll have to marry one of us, and as you slept in my arms the whole night it might as well be me," he snarled ungraciously. Oh, God, he thought. I've botched it. I hadn't meant to put it like that. Oh, you fool, fool, fool!

Kate went white. So that was why he was in such a furious temper. It wasn't his leg or her so-called flirting with Francis at all. He thought she had trapped him into marriage.

"I don't see that there is any need to marry you at all," she said. "After all, nothing happened."

A blazing blue glare forced her to drop her eyes. What did he mean by that look? He had kissed her before and not felt compelled to offer marriage.

Jack's fingers itched to grab the little hussy and shake her until her teeth rattled. So nothing had happened, had it? How dare she lie to him like that? He could still feel the tiny moist kisses travelling slowly and delicately over his naked skin, leaving behind them a trail of fire.

"The fact remains that you were known to have been abducted by one man, and then spent the night in the company of two others, neither of whom was related to you. You have no choice. If you can't stomach the thought of marrying me, then Francis will oblige, as I am sure you are well aware. He is a much better catch—we both know that." His bitter sarcasm flayed her.

"There is no need to be so horrid," she said with quiet dignity. "And there is no need to marry either of you. I have no intention of wedding anyone, as I have told you before, only you are so stupid you refuse to believe me," she concluded, her temper getting the better of her. How dared he speak to her like that? As if she would care two hoots whether or not a man was a good "catch', as long as she loved him! Stupid, stupid man! Did he know her so little?

"Your so-called intentions have no relevance any longer, my dear," Jack said in a withering voice. Call him stupid, would she? "The fact remains that your reputation is now in shreds, and you have no choice but to marry one of us. I, at least, know the ways of the world, even if you do not."

"Well, you know nothing at all!" she flashed. "My reputation cannot be destroyed by the events of last night."

He snorted in mocking disbelief.

"You cannot destroy something that was in shreds months ago!" she snapped. "And believe me, Mr Carstairs, my reputation was utterly destroyed long before last night."

"Don't be ridiculous. You had my grandmother's maid and then Martha with you the whole time. It may have been a trifle unorthodox, but you were well and truly chaperoned the entire time—my grandmother made sure of that!"

Kate gestured impatiently. "The damage was done long before I even met your grandmother." Her voice broke.

She felt sick to her stomach. She had hoped never to have to tell this story ever again in her life, and now here she was, obliged to tell the one man in all the world she wished not to tell.

But he could not be allowed to sacrifice himself for the sake of her non-existent reputation. He needed to marry well, she knew. Some girl with no dark shadows in her past, who would bring her innocence to her marriage. Innocence, an untainted name, and wealth—wealth so that he could rebuild his shattered life. Kate had none of these to offer him, nothing but herself and her heart—small, pathetic offerings at best.

Innate chivalry, despite his gruff manner of expressing it, was forcing him to offer her the protection of his name. It would be rank cowardice for her to put off the inevitable...

Kate shivered. She felt like some small sea creature which had had its shell ruthlessly peeled from it and was now open and vulnerable to every hurt. The sensation was devastating.

"I will explain, Ja— Mr Carstairs, but before I do I must ask you not to say anything, either while I am explaining or afterwards, particularly afterwards. It...it is very difficult for me to tell you this, but I know I have no choice, and...if you look at me or touch me or say anything to me at all...it will destr— Well...you must promise me you will not."

Jack stared at her, puzzled. Deep foreboding filled him—she was in deadly earnest. "And if I do not promise?"

Kate looked despairingly at him. "Well, if you do not, I suppose I must tell you anyway...but it will be much worse, much more painful for me."

"Then I promise," he said quietly.

Kate took a deep breath and looked resolutely out of the window, staring unseeingly at the countryside flashing past. She turned her face away, hunched his big warm coat around her and in a hard little voice related the events of her last few months in Spain and Portugal, leaving nothing out, making no excuses, making it totally clear why she had no reputation to destroy and why she could marry no one.

Jack was oblivious to the jolting of the coach and the pain of his leg. He moved not an inch towards her, but his eyes dwelt on her averted profile with passionate intensity. He regretted nothing more than that last promise he had made her, wanted desperately to pull her into his arms and kiss her grief and pain away. But he could not. He had given her his promise.

His eyes were sombre and his throat filled as he realised the desperate courage that had made her lay her life bare for his edification. His eyes were soft and heavy as they took in the brave tilt of her chin, the resolute carriage of her slender frame as she destroyed herself in his eyes. Or so she thought, his little love. Did she not know how wonderful she was, how brave and gallant and beautiful?

She finished just as the carriage was drawing in to Sevenoakes. The carriage pulled up. She gave a shaky little laugh and said, "So there is no need for you—or Francis or anyone—to put yourself out to save my reputation or defend my honour. You cannot save what has already been destroyed, nor protect what was lost long ago."

He made an inarticulate sound of repudiation deep in his throat and reached out a hand to her, but she flinched away from him. Francis, unaware of the drama which had taken place inside, jumped down, shouting for brandy and hot food. He threw open the carriage door; Kate scrambled out and fled blindly into the house. Francis looked after her, frowning, then turned and saw the haggard face of his friend.

"Come on, old chap," he said softly. "I'll give you a hand."

As Jack limped slowly up the front steps of the house, a vehicle swung in through the front gates. It was a smart travelling carriage. Jack recognised it. It bore his grandmother's crest. It drew to a halt and an unknown man alighted and walked briskly towards the two waiting men.

"Mr Carstairs?" he said.

"Yes," said Jack.

"My name is Phillips. I have the honour to be Lady Cahill's man of business. I have come with important news for Miss Farleigh, whom I understand to be staying here." He beamed at the two men, then faltered at the look on Jack's face. "She is here, is she not?"

Jack frowned. "Yes, she is here, but I am afraid she will not be able to see you immediately. She...she is indisposed." With an effort he gathered his composure and said wearily, "Please come inside and I will have some refreshment brought to you. I'm sure you'll need it after your journey."

Chapter Fifteen

"She's an heiress, isn't she?" Jack could restrain himself no longer. Already he'd had to wait until he and Francis had changed and refreshments served to Mr Phillips.

The elderly lawyer looked momentarily shocked at his bluntness, but after a moment seemed to come to a decision. He allowed a discreet smile to transform his face.

"Yes, sir, you have guessed correctly, although I must say no more until I have informed Miss Farleigh of the whole. But it is wonderful news indeed."

Jack turned to Francis. "According to my grandmother, Kate's Delacombe grandparents were extremely wealthy. Undoubtedly they have left her a legacy," he said, feeling unaccountably low.

"That should please Kate. Girl deserves a bit of good fortune," Francis said.

"Wait a minute…" said Jack slowly. "I thought all the money went to that cousin of hers."

"That's right," said Francis, sitting up.

"What cousin is that?" said Mr Phillips, frowning. "I investigated the matter very thoroughly, and to the best of my knowledge there is no living cousin."

"Fellow called Cole."

"Cole!" snorted Phillips rudely. "He is no cousin of hers. I've sent Bow Street Runners after him!"

"What?" Both men leaned forward, riveted.

"Well, if it is the same man—Jeremiah Cole, big fellow with sandy hair?" They nodded. "He's the rascally solicitor that I caught with his hands in the honeypot, so to speak. He slipped out of my hands a few weeks ago and disappeared."

"Good God!"

"Fellow has been discreetly helping himself to funds from the Delacombe estate for some time since his father, the previous trustee, died."

"Good God!" exclaimed Francis again.

"Do you mean to say that swine was embezzling Kate's money? And that he's no relation at all to her?"

Phillips nodded. "Yes, indeed. But how do you know of him?"

Jack exchanged a long look with Francis. The motive for Cole's abduction of Kate was perfectly clear now. Had he forced Kate to marry him, her entire inheritance would have legally belonged to him. But there was no need to let Phillips know of the abduction attempt.

"He was here," said Jack grimly. "Posing as Miss Farleigh's cousin and attempting to get her to marry him."

Mr Phillips gasped in amazement. Jack glanced at Francis. "You should have let me kill him, you know," he murmured.

"The Runners will get him, old man. He'll hang, or be transported at the very least."

"If they catch him."

"Oh, they'll catch him, no fear of that," said Mr Phillips confidently. "I have no doubt at all. None at all."

"They'd better," growled Jack.

"I don't suppose he got his greasy paws on too much of Miss Farleigh's inheritance?" asked Francis diffidently.

Jack shot a look at him. Francis had no need of a rich wife.

"No, no. Fortunately the great majority of her inheritance is tied up so he could not touch it, and the whole is of such a size that it makes Cole's depredations almost negligible, a fact I expect he was counting on, should the heirs ever have been discovered," said Mr Phillips, rendered indiscreet by the generous quantity of brandy his host had pressed upon him.

Jack's heart sank. She was rich, immensely so, from what Phillips had inadvertently revealed. She would not stay here long, in that case. With a fortune she would have need of nothing, nobody.

"I gather there's some significance to your arrival in my grandmother's carriage," he said heavily.

"Yes, so very kind of her ladyship," agreed Mr Phillips. "I am to convey Miss Farleigh to London as soon as may be convenient. Lady Cahill has great plans for her, I believe, great plans."

"I'll wager she has," muttered Jack sourly.

"Perhaps Miss Farleigh will have her own ideas about that," suggested Francis. "She may not wish to leave here."

"Not wish to leave here!" Mr Phillips was astonished. He glanced around the shabby room. "Not wish to live in a fine London house, to go to balls and routs? Why would she not?"

"Why not, indeed?" murmured Jack. "If you will excuse me, I must go upstairs and have my man see to this curst leg."

He stumped wearily upstairs, almost relishing the distraction of the pain of his leg. He stopped at the door to Kate's room and stood there for several minutes. There was something to be said for purely physical pain, after all. An hour or so of massage, a half-bottle of brandy and it was cured.

Neither of those remedies would help the other sort of

pain. In fact, they only served to intensify it; massage invariably conjured up the memory of the time when Kate first laid her small, strong hands on his leg, kneading, stroking, caressing... And as for brandy—there was neither pleasure nor forgetfulness for him in getting drunk now, for the very scent of alcohol recalled that night when she had stormed into his sanctuary like a small avenging angel, smashing all his decanters and bottles. He would never forget the look on her face that night...nor what occurred afterwards...the pleasure, the madness, the bitterness.

He had to let her go. She had no future with him. Not now. Not since she had become a rich woman. She might have agreed to take him on in exchange for a home, shabby as it was, for security, for his protection for the rest of her life. He hadn't dared to speak of love. That would have remained his secret. But a home—that might have been enough for a girl who had lost everything. That and the promise of a family. To an orphan, the promise of a family might have been appealing.

None of those things held any significance now. She didn't need to marry now—she could choose. She would go up to London and choose. He would never ask her now—he would not have her think him a fortune hunter. He cursed the Delacombe inheritance. He cursed Mr Phillips. Had the man not arrived when he did, Jack might have had her agreement to wed him already. And he would have wasted no time, would have had her to the village church the very next day.

He glanced up and down the corridor, then leaned his ear against her door and listened. Nothing. He could smell the beeswax she had used to polish the timber panelling. Beeswax. Another reminder of Kate. Reluctantly he brought his cheek away from her door, and headed towards his room. There were flowers on a side table in the corridor, small, insignificant blue things in a mass of green spiky stuff. He bent down to smell them, closing his eyes in anguish. They smelt of Kate's hair. This must be rosemary, then. He pulled out a sprig, crushed it in his long, strong fingers, and inhaled the fragrance.

"Carlos." He absent-mindedly tucked the sprig of rosemary into his shirt.

"*Sí señor.*"

"Do something about this blasted leg, will you?"

"At once, *señor.*"

As Carlos clattered downstairs to heat the massage oils, Jack began to shrug off his coat. He paused for a moment, then stepped back into the hallway. He gazed down at the vase of fragrant greenery. Carefully he picked it up, carried it into his room and set it down beside his bed, where the morning sun would catch it.

"No, it is very kind of Lady Cahill, but now that I am able to support myself there is no need for me to go to London."

"But Lady Cahill was most insistent—" The elderly lawyer tried to keep the frustration out of his voice. The heiress was being extremely difficult. He had tried every persuasion, painted pictures of the marvellous things she would see and do, of the shops, theatres, concerts and balls, of the cultural wonders, the famous places and people she would see. Nothing had the slightest effect.

Mr Phillips cast a tense look at Mr Carstairs. Her ladyship's grandson had observed the entire argument, arms folded, looking sardonic and bad-tempered. He had said not a word so far.

Mr Phillips felt very put out. Having a romantic soul underneath his dull exterior, he had envisaged himself as a kind of knight, who would escort the lost princess back to her rightful milieu. Only the princess was unaccountably resistant and unfemininely sharp of tongue and wit, and nothing he said could move her.

And, what was more, he thought, with a growing sense of injustice, when he had told her of the immense fortune which was at her sole disposal she had reacted quite as if she had other things on her mind. When he had repeated himself, thinking she was too overcome to take it in, she had replied, "Yes, yes, I heard you the first time. It is very nice, thank you."

Nice! Mr Phillips might be a mere solicitor, but there was something downright insulting about referring to such a huge fortune as "nice'. He began yet another attempt to persuade her, but his remarks were cut across by the harsh, deep voice of his client's grandson.

"I've had quite enough of all this nonsense. Kate, you are going to London and no argument. Carlos!" he called, moving to the door.

"*Sí,* Major Jack?"

"Tell Martha to have Miss Kate's things in that carriage within the hour. She and Mr Phillips will accompany Miss Kate to London, to my grandmother's house."

"She will do no such thing!" snapped Kate, meeting his eyes for the first time.

He looked back at her, his expression unreadable. "No, you are right, of course. Carlos, tell Martha to pack only what she and Miss Kate will need for the journey. They will be purchasing all new clothes and what-have-you in London." He ignored Kate's gasp of indignation. "Oh…Carlos, have the girls pack some food and refreshments in a basket in case Miss Kate gets hungry on the way."

"Do no such thing, Carlos!" said Kate in a voice ringing with indignation.

Carlos met her gaze sheepishly. "I am sorry, *señorita,* but I must obey Major Jack."

Jack laughed at her infuriated exclamation, a harsh, humourless laugh. "I see I am still master in my own house," he said dryly.

"Yes, but you are not my master and I refuse to do your bidding!"

"I'm not asking you to do my bidding," said Jack coldly.

"I...I don't underst—"

"I'm telling you. This is my house and I choose who I have in it. You know perfectly well I was reluctant to have you here in the first place. Well, now there is no reason for you to stay on any longer. You're going to my grandmother, all right, and will leave here today—if I have to toss you in the carriage myself." He snapped out the orders crisply, every inch the military officer. "Do you understand me, Miss Farleigh?"

Kate flinched, then turned away, hiding her distress.

Only Jack saw the expression on her face. He ran his hands through his hair in frustration. Damn it, he couldn't bear that wounded look on her face. What the devil did she think his grandmother was going to do to her? Torture her? It was the opportunity every young woman dreamed of. She didn't know what she was turning down. Oh, he knew what was stopping her, all right. But his grandmother would soon set her straight.

A scandalous accident in the past would mean nothing in the face of her huge inheritance. She would find she had the pick of the eligible bachelors—only the stuffiest would quibble at her lost virginity. It wasn't as if she had done anything wrong, after all. Kate Farleigh was honourable to her fingertips; any fool could see that. The biggest problem she was likely to face was fortune hunters, and he could rely on his grandmother to deal with those.

Best to have it over with quickly. He hated long goodbyes. And he did not know how much longer he could stand that look on her face without hauling her into his arms. But the last thing Kate needed was to be tied to an embittered cripple. With this fortune she had a glittering future ahead of her, a future he would have no part in.

"Then shall we all agree to meet in the front hall in, say, half an hour to make our farewells? Good." He nodded to the astounded observers and left the room.

"What a splendid fellow!" said Mr Phillips after a moment. "Such decision, so masterful! I'm sure he was an excellent officer. He is more like his grandmother than I realised."

The travelling chaise jolted and bounced along the road; Mr Phillips had bespoken rooms at an inn in readiness for the return journey and he was anxious to reach their destination before dark. Kate hung on to a strap, staring out of the window, oblivious of the passing scenery, the state of the road and her companions in the vehicle. She felt utterly wretched, desolate, shattered. Tears dripped unheeded from her eyes.

When Harry had abandoned her, she'd thought she could never be hurt so terribly again. She was wrong. This was a thousand times more painful. Harry she had loved with a schoolgirl's light-heartedness—Jack she loved with all of a woman's heart and body and soul.

It was her own stupid fault—she had allowed herself to care, to hope, to dream, and now, as she had told herself a thousand times would happen, all was in ashes.

He despised her. The man she loved despised her.

She'd gathered up her courage, told him all about Henri, about Lisbon, hoping against hope that it wouldn't matter to him. Oh, she hadn't expected him to renew his offer to marry her, not really—though her foolish heart had hoped a little. No, she knew it was impossible. The most she had hoped for was that he would finally understand why she didn't wish to go to London with his grandmother, why she would never be on the marriage mart. She'd hoped he would let her stay, let her live in his house as long as she could...

But he'd heard her story and the very next morning he'd ordered her belongings to be packed.

He hadn't been able to rid himself of her polluted presence quickly enough, had bundled her into the coach without so much as a by-your-leave, had given his farewells as if she were a complete stranger. He hadn't even looked her in the eye then, but had murmured goodbye in a voice devoid of emotion.

Kate bit her lip, tasting blood as she recalled the way he had taken her hand in the lightest of touches, fingers barely meeting as if he couldn't even bear to touch her. Francis at least had bowed over her hand, kissing it lightly, as he had that first day—he, apparently, still thought her a lady. Kate supposed that Jack had not yet enlightened him.

It was almost impossible to reconcile herself to the change in Jack. Only twenty-four hours previously she had woken in his arms. Even sleeping, his powerful arms had held her possessively, cradled her gently. She savoured the memory: the taste of his skin, the rough delight of his stubbled cheek against hers, the tremulous excitement of her body spread full length on his. The glory and the wonder of that secret, stolen kiss, the tentative tasting that had blazed into passion. And then, when he'd opened his eyes, those blue, blue eyes, and smiled that wonderful, crooked smile of his— ''Morning sweetheart''—it had been one of the most beautiful moments of her life.

At that moment she'd known—had believed—in the deepest part of her heart and soul that she loved him and that, miracle of miracles, he loved her in return. Her lonely, battered heart had at last found safe harbour. She had allowed herself the momentary dream that this was how she would wake up every morning for the rest of her life... ''Morning sweetheart.''

Oh, how she wished it could be so...but wishing was futile, racking her body with empty, echoing pain. It was not to be. She'd known it, deep down; she'd never believed otherwise. Like a hungry child, knowing herself doomed to a life of starvation, she had risked all to snatch at a morsel, knowing she'd never taste such nectar again.

Was it that which had made him reject her now? Her behaviour in the cottage? Did he think that the Lisbon gossips were right about her? What irony. She had never in her life felt wanton except with Jack Carstairs. But how was he to know that?

Being kidnapped once could be seen to be an accident. But twice? First Henri, then Jeremiah. A half-hysterical giggle rose in her throat—thrice—even his grandmother had kidnapped her. She clearly attracted such attention. Of course he would blame her.

The cruelty of his denial burnt into her heart now like acid into flesh…but she could not yet regret her moment of foolishness, her taste of bliss. Would it have been easier in the long run had she never known his embrace? she wondered. Perhaps. But now her dreams had substance to sustain themselves through the long grey years ahead.

The past was an ocean of pain; the future lay before her. Kate contemplated the thought. One day at a time; that was the way to go. First she must endure the rigours of "the Season".

Endure? No, she decided. There would be endurance enough to come; if there was pleasure to be had, she would have it while she could. She would make the most of her opportunities, experience the best that society could offer her. Sooner or later her secret would be out and she would have to leave town in disgrace, but it could not hurt her if she did not let it. Forewarned was forearmed, after all.

She would make no friendships here that she could not bear to be severed. She could build that much ice around her at least. She would not allow herself to think of this as anything other than a temporary treat. That way, when the time came to leave, she should be able to do so, if not without regrets, then without pain.

She could never be hurt as badly again. By the time she reached London, Kate silently vowed, her armour would be well and truly in place. When the time came, she would disappear quietly, none the worse, to take up her life elsewhere. At least this time, with a substantial income at her disposal, she would not starve.

Not for food, anyway.

She focused back on the scenery flashing by, becoming aware that her hands were very cold. Fishing around in her small travelling bag, she pulled out a pair of gloves. Kate looked at them. They were a very large pair of gloves, well-made leather, worn and soft, fur-lined. A gentleman's gloves. Only yesterday Jack had noticed how cold her hands were and had given her his gloves to wear. She must have forgotten to give them back to him.

Small frozen hands slipped into the big furry gloves, taking comfort from the size, the scent, the warmth of them. She rested her cheek in one gloved hand; the other was cupped against her heart. She leaned against the hard corner of the travelling chaise and closed her eyes. Finally, cradled in Jack Carstairs's gloves, Kate slept.

"Quiet, ain't it?" murmured Francis. He glanced across at his companion. Kate had left almost a week before, her face white and set, her eyes tragic. Since that day, Jack had spent his time furiously riding about the countryside, pushing himself to the absolute limit, galloping recklessly as if invisible demons were pursuing him. And in the evenings he got silently, determinedly drunk.

Francis had accompanied him in all things, understanding Jack's need to purge himself of the excess energy, to tire himself out, to blot a certain woebegone little face out of his memory, to try to drown his guilt. For a time at least.

"Got something to say to you, old man. Don't think you'll like it. Going to say it anyway." Francis drained his glass.

Jack glanced at his friend in disgust. "You're foxed."

Francis nodded. "Probably. So are you," he said. "Still going to say it."

"Well, for God's sake just spit it out, then, instead of rambling on."

"All right, then. Think you did the wrong thing. Shouldn't have forced her to go."

Jack swallowed the contents of his own glass and slammed it down on the table at his elbow. "Oh, God, not you too. As if it isn't bad enough, the whole household looking at me as if I'd taken the girl out, slung a brick around her neck and drowned her in the river. Damn it all!" he exclaimed. "It's for her own good! Not a blasted Cheltenham tragedy... Anyone would think I'd sent her off to her own execution!"

"Well, you just might have, old man," said Francis, after a pause.

Jack swung round in his chair. "What the devil do you mean by that?"

Francis didn't answer immediately. He got up and poured another measure of brandy into both glasses. He caught Jack's eye. "Planning to get us both stinking drunk," he said. "Tell you something in strictest confidence, old chap. Delicate matter. Concerns Kate."

Jack frowned. "If you mean what happened to her on the Peninsula, I know about it."

Francis nodded thoughtfully. "Told you in the carriage, didn't she? Thought that was it when I saw your faces that day."

"So full marks for observation," muttered Jack sourly.

"Brave little soul. Very painful to bring that sort of thing up again." Francis added, "Probably frightened that you'd despise her, too."

"Despise her? *Despise her?*" Jack's voice was angry. How could anyone despise Kate? "What the devil do you mean?"

"Not saying *I* do," interjected Francis pacifically. "Not saying anyone should. On the contr'ry. I'm talkin' about what *she* thinks. Thing is, it damned well looked like you couldn't wait to get rid of her. Less than twenty-four hours after you find out she's been...sullied...by a Frenchman, you bundle her out of the house. Girl probably thinks you *do* despise her. What else is she to think?"

Jack whitened. "She wouldn't...she couldn't..."

"Nothing to indicate she don't," said Francis quietly. "Didn't exactly make it clear to her, did you? Threw her out, not to put too fine a point on it."

"But I..."

"Oh, yes, *I* know what you were about, but did *she?*"

Jack groaned and clutched his hair in anguish.

"Expects to be despised, you see. Happened before. Lost her betrothed for that reason. Not saying that was a bad thing, mind you—chap wasn't good enough for her. He'd known her all her life, childhood sweetheart sort of thing. Didn't stop him despising her after the scandal. Fellow called off the wedding on account of it. And most people thought he did the right thing."

Jack groaned again. "I didn't know...didn't think..."

"Thing is, the story got out and all the cats got stuck into her in the most appalling fashion."

"My God."

"Things some of them said to her would make your hair curl. Ha! The gentler sex! Bitches carved young Kate up in the most vicious and cold-blooded fashion, and all the time with the sweetest smiles on their faces. Held her to be a traitor because she nursed wounded French soldiers. Claimed she went with them willingly. Called her a whore behind her back...and a few said it to her face. And all with such smiling politeness and seeming sweetness... I tell you, Jack, it almost put me off women for life. The gentler sex.'' He shuddered.

The beautiful, hypocritical face of Julia Davenport appeared in Jack's mind. "I know just what you mean," he muttered grimly. The two men sipped their brandy. The flames danced in the grate.

"Thing is, same thing could happen in London. Some of the tabbies in Lisbon last year are bound to be in London now. Even if they aren't, you know what women are like for writing letters. Bound to be someone who knows the story. Come out sooner or later, I'd say—just a matter of time."

Jack was too appalled to speak. He felt as if his stomach had dropped out of his body. Oh, God, no wonder she'd looked if she was going to an execution; she would have an axe suspended over her head the whole time she was in London, and it was only a matter of time before it would fall.

Jack groaned and clenched his fist. There was a snap as his glass shattered in his hand. Francis sat up, exclaiming at the blood dripping from Jack's fingers. Jack waved him aside impatiently.

"Going to London," he said. "Can't leave her to think that— Oh, shut up, Francis, what's a damned scratch? I'm off to London in the morning. Are you coming with me or not?"

"Oh, absolutely, old man, absolutely."

Chapter Sixteen

"Your young protégée seems to be doin' rather well, Maudie."

"Thank you, Gussie," replied Lady Cahill. "I couldn't be more pleased with her if she was my own daughter."

Lady Cahill and several of her cronies were doing what they called "taking tea and cakes'. The tea trolley was laden with dainty cakes and elegant little savouries. Steam curled languidly from the spout of the teapot, and each lady sipped delicately from a fine eggshell-thin teacup. The sherry decanter was half empty.

"Charmin' gel, quite charmin'." The speaker, wearing an enormous feathered turban, reached for a fourth crab-and-asparagus patty.

Lady Cahill beamed. Kate had taken to her new life like a duck to water, hadn't put a foot wrong. Lady Cahill had, at first, been rather anxious lest Kate reveal herself as a true scholar's daughter—it would be fatal for her to gain a reputation as a bluestocking.

However, to Lady Cahill's pleased surprise, Kate had proved to be almost as delightfully ignorant as any anxious sponsor would wish her protégée to be. She seemed to take more pleasure in a visit to the Pantheon Bazaar or Astley's

Amphitheatre than she did in an afternoon at the British Museum or a viewing of the archaeological sensation, Lord Elgin's Marbles. She knew nothing of famous thinkers, writers or philosophers. Her conversation was not weighted with dull pronouncements from weighty tomes, and she was in no danger of frightening gentlemen by spouting screeds of poetry at them. It seemed that the only topics on which Kate was knowledgeable were horses and the Peninsular War—and since the *ton* was full of horse-mad military gentlemen that was not held to be a disadvantage.

Lady Cahill basked in her protégée's praise.

"A sensible, well-bred, pretty-behaved gel, Maudie. Poor Maria would have been delighted to see how charmingly her daughter has turned out."

The others nodded.

Kate's success was only to be expected, Lady Cahill told herself complacently. Kate was a sociable girl, and a sympathetic listener. Moreover, a life of ordering her father's household and her experience of having had to adapt to extraordinary conditions had given her an indefinable air of assurance, taken by many to be a sign of good breeding.

And, from having spent most of her life in male company from all walks of life, she was neither shy nor coy nor odiously missish with the London gentlemen she met. She seemed to listen as happily to the dull military pronouncements of an elderly general as to the stammering confidences of a young man in his first season or the practised compliments of a rake.

Lady Cahill's granddaughter, Amelia, had introduced Kate to her more dashing set, made up largely of young fashionable matrons. They had noted her elegant, modish appearance, her mischievous sense of humour, her quick wit and her complete lack of interest in their husbands, and pronounced her to be a sweet and charming girl.

* * *

"*Very* popular with the soldier laddies," said one elderly lady waspishly, holding out her teacup to be refilled.

"And you know why, Ginny Holton, so you need not sneer!" snapped Lady Courtney. "You know perfectly well what that dear sweet girl did for my Gilbert."

The others nodded. Lady Courtney's grandson, Gilbert, had barely set a foot outside his home, until Miss Farleigh had teased him into going about in society with her, apparently oblivious of the awkwardness of his missing arm and the ominous black eyepatch.

"Told him he looked like a wonderfully sinister pirate and that it would help protect her from unwanted attention." Lady Courtney wiped her eyes.

"And *then* she told him that he must not blame her if they were mobbed by young ladies because he looked quite disgustingly romantic, and, while *she* knew him to be odiously stuffy, other girls were not as discriminating as she… And he laughed—my boy actually laughed—and consented to take her out. He hasn't looked back since."

"Yes, shame on you, Ginny," agreed another elderly lady. "If Maudie's Kate is popular with military gentlemen, it is not to be wondered at. You are only being uncharitable because your Chloë is without even a sniff of an offer! A pity to be sure, but no reason to snipe at others!"

It was true. Kate's unselfconscious attention to the wounded had done her no disservice in the eyes of the more fortunate of the military. The polite world soon noted that little Miss Farleigh had a court of large, protective gentlemen, led by Mr Lennox, and Sir Toby Fenwick and other military types, who seemed equally delighted to fetch her a glass of ratafia, escort her to the opera, take her driving in Hyde Park at the fashionable hour or depress the pretensions of any too assiduous suitors.

There were many of these, as word of her inheritance had

leaked out. She was being courted by several gazetted fortune hunters, as well as men of substance and position.

Lady Cahill sat back in her chair as the talk turned to more general topics. She was almost satisfied. One factor, however, was missing from the equation. She hoped he would bestir himself soon and get himself to London before Kate was snapped up by some fashionable fribble who didn't deserve her.

''What do you think of this, miss?'' The maid held an elegant spray of artificial flowers to Kate's hair and looked enquiringly at her new mistress in the mirror.

Kate stared. She almost didn't recognise herself. Her hair had been cropped in the latest style and feathered curls clustered round her face, doing amazing things to her appearance, things Kate would never have dreamed possible. For the first time in her life, she felt elegant, and, though the Reverend Mr Farleigh's daughter knew it to be an immodest thought, almost pretty. The new face and hairstyle were enhanced by the gown she was wearing—a soft shade of green that brought out the colour in her eyes and minimised the slight unfashionable golden tone of her skin, brought about by too much time outdoors.

Lady Cahill and Amelia had subjected Kate to a rigorous regime of crushed strawberries—to refine and clarify the skin—buttermilk baths—to soften it—and, for general toning and nourishing, slices of raw veal laid on her skin for hours at a time while Amelia read to her. In addition there were twice-daily applications of distilled pineapple water—for clarity and beauty and to erase wrinkles—egg and lemon face packs—to fade that dreadful tan and nourish the skin—and oatmeal masks—to brighten and refine the skin.

Kate laughed, complained they made her feel rather like the main ingredient in a strange and exotic stew, and admitted her complexion had improved under their ministrations. But it was still a terrible waste of good food.

And then there had been the shopping, a positively sinful orgy of it, in Kate's eyes, but "the merest necessities' as far as her female mentors were concerned. Kate tried to remain sensible and practical, but the fizzing excitement that rose in her at the sight of the exquisite, dashing outfits that Lady Cahill and Amelia had bullied her into purchasing was irresistible to a girl who had had very little opportunity to indulge in fashionable feminine frivolity.

Kate's head had been spinning at the end of that first day, which had begun at the silk warehouses. Delicate and lovely fabrics were draped, compared, contrasted, swathed, discussed, discarded and selected, mostly without reference to Kate, who was far too easily pleased, according to her companions. Then it was off to see Amelia's modiste, Madame Fanchôt, who, well primed as to the state of *mademoiselle*'s finances, went into professional Gallic raptures about *mademoiselle*'s face, her figure, her air of *je ne c'est quoi,* then flew into genuine raptures when Kate responded to her in fluent French. Then there were hours spent poring over issues of *La Belle Assemblée* and *Ackerman's Repository,* with dozens and dozens of plates, all of the most elegant outfits.

In the end Kate had spinelessly allowed Madame Fanchôt, Amelia and Lady Cahill to decide everything and left to them the meticulous planning and endless discussion which went into every choice. For her part, Kate could not have cared less whether, for instance, the lemon muslin was cut to drape *so,* enhancing the lovely line of *mademoiselle*'s shoulders and neckline, or like *so,* to enhance her bustline, or like *so,* to give her height. Her only contribution to that discussion had been to suggest that perhaps the neckline was rather too low, a suggestion that was ignored by all three ladies as too nonsensical even to warrant a response.

So now Kate stared at her reflection, exposing more of her

chest than she had ever done in her life. She became aware of her maid still holding out the artificial flowers, awaiting her response, and smiled apologetically.

"I think not, Dora. To be quite honest, I am terrified that it would fall out of my hair." The maid bridled, assuring her that such a thing was quite impossible.

Kate interrupted the flow. "It is just that my head feels so strange and light since my new crop, and I cannot but feel that something is missing, so although I am sure you would place the flowers most securely you do understand how I feel, don't you?"

Dora relented after a moment and said that of course she did, and miss looked very elegant and lovely and would be sure to be a success again tonight.

Kate wrinkled her nose. Yes, of course, "success' was what was important. How could she have forgotten? She had tried not to let herself think of other things, or wonder what might be happening at Sevenoakes. That was one benefit of such hectic socialising—one didn't have time to brood. To-night, for example, she was going to a ball and it would be surprising if she had time to think of Jack even once.

Jack leant against an elegant column, arms folded, a black frown on his face, staring, glaring, unable to tear himself away. It had been Francis's idea to come to this ball on the evening of their arrival in London and Jack had regretted it the moment he'd arrived and clapped eyes on Kate, utterly transformed from the shabby little starveling he had first met. She was dancing, her head thrown back, mischievously laughing up into the eyes of a fellow Jack had been to school with, and knew to be titled, rich and eligible.

"Blast it!" he exclaimed to Francis. "What the devil is she doing dancing with that fellow Fenchurch? And in such a dress!" Jack could hardly take his eyes off the creamy curves revealed by the fashionable low-cut neckline of Kate's dress, and neither, he noticed, could Kate's partner. Nor a number of other so-called gentlemen.

Francis glanced from his friend's black frown to Kate's laughing visage and back again. He controlled his twitching mouth and said innocently, "Nice chap, Fenchurch. Kate would do well to encourage his advances. Couldn't do better, in fact."

"Fellow's a complete bounder!" snarled Jack.

"Good heavens, is he?" said Francis placidly. "How very shocking. News to me, I must say. Always thought he was a friend of yours, old man. A bounder? Well, well. I must say, I am surprised. Still, he's a dashing-looking chap, and there is the title. I dare say that accounts for his popularity with the ladies."

Jack grunted. There was nothing particularly dashing that he could see in the tall Viscount's regular even features, thickly curling blond hair and tall, muscular physique. Fellow was addicted to sports, that was all. Damn it, what the deuce was he saying to make her blush like that? Jack found he was clenching his fists and thrust them into his pockets to hide the fact.

"Stand up straight, boy, and stop lounging all over the wall like a looby! How many times have I told you to get your hands out of your pockets? Not that I can see how on earth you can have pockets in such indecently tight garments."

Jack sighed. "Good evening, Grandmama." He turned to face her. He bowed, and she ran her eyes over him assessingly. A marked improvement from the last time she'd seen him.

"Have you seen my little protégée?" she said, grinning.

Jack grunted.

"Looks charming, doesn't she? Gel's done me proud. I wish her mother could see her." She raised her lorgnette and peered short-sightedly at the dancers. "Who's she dancing with now? Eh, Jack?"

"Fenchurch."

Lady Cahill smiled. He hadn't even turned to look. And what was more, she thought delightedly, he was so taken up with Kate's activities that he had forgotten to be sensitive about his altered appearance, his shattered cheek and his limp.

"Fenchurch? Ah, yes, fine, big, handsome chap, ain't he? Not that that signifies. All her beaux seem to be. Gel's mighty popular—her dance card was full before she'd been here ten minutes. I doubt she could give you even a country dance, Jack. You could ask her, though."

He snorted.

Lady Cahill smothered a chuckle and continued. "Oh, look, the dance is finished and see how they rush to procure her a chair and refreshments. Can't leave the girl for a moment but she's surrounded by admirers. Taken very well, Maria's girl. But, there Jack, you're not interested in an old woman's ramblings. Tell me, what has brought my favourite grandson to London?"

Her favourite grandson mumbled something inaudible and stumped away, scowling. Kate was undoubtedly a social success. And he was unaccountably infuriated. He'd rushed up to London in a state of high anxiety, ready to rescue a poor little waif from social ostracism and humiliation. He'd found her apparently in the highest of spirits, with any number of fellows underfoot, making complete cakes of themselves over her! Her dance card too full to allow him even a country dance! He snorted again. He had no intention of joining the ranks of her admirers, begging for a moment of her attention! He retreated behind another pillar and scowled at her from there.

Kate saw him arrive. For a moment her heart seemed to stop. He looked worn and tired and the broad shoulders of his plain dark coat glittered from the hundreds of candles that lit the ballroom. He had come in the rain. His hair too was damp and clung to his brow in dark wild curls. She longed to run across the room and fling herself into his arms. She longed for him to stride out across the ballroom floor and sweep her into his embrace. She longed to kiss him.

She continued through the cotillion mechanically, finding in the performance of the stately measure the control she needed. Her heart was ablaze with excitement. Why had he come? How long would it be before he noticed her? Would he like the way she looked now? Would he ask her to dance? Oh, how she had missed him!

She forced herself not to look at him, not trusting herself to do so. She responded to Viscount Fenchurch's sallies, laughing and smiling automatically, having no idea of what he was saying. The dance would finish soon and then Jack would come over to her. Unable to restrain herself any longer, she used the movement of the dance to dart another quick shy glance at him.

And froze. He was staring right at her. His gaze scorched her…and she froze. There was nothing but the strongest condemnation in his face. He was staring right at her as if he despised her. Her steps and smile faltered, and as she stumbled her partner gathered her smoothly up, concern in his handsome face. Kate recovered herself and continued.

The dance felt like the longest one in history. Somehow she got through it, smiling blindly at her partner whenever his face swam into view. She had thought she had come to terms with the pain of Jack's condemnation, but the sight of him had been so unexpected, her response so joyful, that his obvious disgust had slid through her icy armour like a hot knife through butter, straight into her heart. Again.

The dance finished, but before she could excuse herself and seek solitude in which to deal with her desolation the band struck up again and she found herself being whisked back on to the floor. Pride alone carried her through it, and if her partner found her to be a little inattentive and *distraite* he found nothing amiss with the dazzling smiles she flashed him.

By the time the second dance drew to a close, Kate's temper was rising. Jack had continued to prop himself against the wall, glaring at her throughout the dance, black fury and total disapproval on his face.

How *dared* he follow her here and stand there sneering at her? It was *his* fault she was here in the first place. She hadn't wanted to come to London. And if she had made her entrée to society under false colours, as he obviously believed, then it was his grandmother who'd made her do it. And *he* had delivered her to *his* grandmother, so *he* was as much at fault as anyone. How *dared* he look at her like that?

Kate's anger enabled her to sweep through the next dance in glittering style and to parry the flirtatious compliments of her small court of admirers with wit and panache. For the next hour she danced, flirted, smilingly declined an offer of marriage and added a dozen new members to her circle of male admirers, all in the most furious of tempers and under the scorching long-distance glare of Mr Jack Carstairs.

Jack forced himself to stay for an hour or so longer, seeking out all the most beautiful women. She would not think he had no female admirers! Look at her—responding to the gallantries of the biggest collection of rakes and downright gudgeons he had ever seen—and they called themselves his friends!

Finally, unable to stand the sight any more, Jack left, turning abruptly from the sight of her, pushing his way through the glittering throngs of people.

Kate watched as he disappeared out into the night. He hadn't even looked at her for the last half-hour. Suddenly she realised she had the vilest headache. She sought out Lady Cahill and asked to be taken home.

"Mr Carstairs called again this morning, Lady Cahill," announced the butler, an edge of disapproval in his voice.

The old lady frowned. "And I gather from your tone, Fitcher, that Miss Farleigh was 'out' to him again."

Fitcher assented with a dignified half-bow.

"The foolish child! I suppose I will have to talk to her about it. Ask her to step down for a moment, will you?"

"Now, missy, I'd like to know why my grandson has been haunting this house for the last week or so but not, apparently, finding anyone home, and I do not refer to myself."

Kate flushed. "I've been so busy..." Her voice trailed off under Lady Cahill's sardonic gaze. "Well, if you must know, I have no wish to speak to him."

A well-plucked eyebrow rose.

Kate's voice warmed in indignation. "Well, and why should I subject myself to more of his tyranny?"

"Tyranny?"

"Yes, ma'am. As if it is not impossible enough having him glaring and glowering—and gnashing his teeth at me from across every room I enter, whether it is at Almack's, or a concert or a private ball. He is making me—and himself— ridiculous. I wish he would return to Leicestershire and leave me alone. He has nothing to say to me that I have not heard before...or, if he has, I do not wish to hear it, for I know what it will be."

"You think so, eh?"

"Yes, ma'am." *He despises me.*

"As I understand it, you have barely spoken with my grandson since leaving Leicestershire."

Kate flushed again. "There has been no need," she said in a low voice. "He made it perfectly clear then what he thought of me. And his behaviour since then only reinforces it.''

Jack's behaviour made a horrid kind of sense to Kate—he thought she was some sort of immoral lightskirt, and he was there to prevent her from disgracing his grandmother. That was why he glared at her every time she so much as looked or smiled at a man, no matter who the man. He didn't trust her an inch, that was obvious!

The old lady observed the tense way her young protégée fiddled with the fringe of her shawl.

''And there is no possibility that you could be mistaken? Young men, and young women too, often say foolish things that they do not mean, especially when they are in love.''

''In love! No, indeed, ma'am, you are quite, quite mistaken there!'' The fringe tore in Kate's fingers. Unaware, she moved restlessly around the room.

Lady Cahill heaved herself off the sofa. ''My dear, foolish child, when you are as old as I am, you will learn that young men, particularly young men of my grandson's cut, do not generally make cakes of themselves following a young lady around only to glare at them from a distance, unless their emotions are *very* strongly engaged. And only one emotion prompts that sort of behaviour.''

She held up a hand to forestall Kate's reply. ''No, that's quite enough. The subject is becoming tedious and fatiguing. I beg you will think about what I have said, but we will speak no more of it now. I intend to repose myself for a few hours before I ready myself for the ball tonight.''

She paused at the doorway and looked back. ''I expect you will find that my grandson will be present at the ball tonight—Wellington is guest of honour. It is to be his last social appearance before returning to the Peninsula.''

Chapter Seventeen

"Good God, how has *that* young woman managed to insinuate herself amongst decent people? Do our host and hostess not know she is a traitress and a whore?"

The penetrating voice was overheard by dozens in the tightly packed ballroom. As one, heads turned.

"Who do I mean? Why, that Farleigh chit, of course. Look at her, dancing as if she had not a care in the world, the shameless hussy. And at a ball in honour of our brave and gallant Marquis of Wellington; the gall of the woman!"

The voice lowered itself slightly, and continued to a gathering crowd, avid for gossip.

"That little tart betrayed our brave soldiers to the French, lived with a Frenchman *as his mistress!* I know, for my husband was one of the officers that captured her. Her father would be turning in his grave—he was a man of the cloth, you know. Mind you, I always wondered why he never looked at her—he must have known..."

The crowd pressed closer.

Something was wrong. Kate knew it. So many looks, sideways glances, whispered comments followed by significant stares.

"Miss Farleigh, our dance, I believe." An elegant young fribble bowed over her hand and led her into the next set.

"Have you heard, Miss Farleigh? 'Tis monstrous exciting. Apparently some little whore has been passing herself off as a lady, when all the time she played spy for old Boney and whored for his officers. *And she's here tonight!*" Her partner glanced around the room, speculating.

Kate glanced away, a sick feeling in her stomach. Let me just finish this dance, she prayed silently, then I can leave inconspicuously.

But it was not to be. As they moved through the stately steps of the cotillion she noticed her partner eagerly whispering his news to the others in the set. At one point he faltered, stopped and stared at Kate, aghast. He turned back to his source, whispered something and resumed the steps.

Only now he would not look her in the eye. His fingers did not so much touch hers as gesture disdainfully in her direction. The dance continued. Kate felt the ice surround her. No one looked at her. No one touched her. No one spoke to her.

Bitterness rose in Kate like bile. She had known how it would be. *This* was the reason she had never wanted to appear in society ever again. Had she been allowed to go her own way, she would not be experiencing this. Again.

"Ceddy, please escort me to my mama. I cannot think she would wish me to associate with a traitress!" Nose held high, a young lady abandoned the set in mid-movement.

In seconds, the ordered progress of the dance collapsed, as each of the ladies in Kate's set marched righteously off the dance floor, escorted by their partner. Kate looked at her partner in mute appeal. If he would only escort her from the floor, she would be able to leave with a shred of dignity.

His face twisted in contempt. "My brother was injured at Salamanca!" he snarled, and stalked away.

Kate stood in the middle of the dance floor, frozen. She

knew she had to move, to get away from all of the eyes, from the whispering and pointing. From the hate. The loathing. The avid speculation. But she couldn't move.

Around her she felt the rest of the dancers faltering, the rising hum of gossip and conjecture. The music petered out in mid-tune as the last of the couples left the floor. It had the effect of focusing all attention on Kate. She felt the crowd gathering into a dense barrier, the seething, greedy stares of bored aristocrats, eager for sensation to alleviate their safe, pampered, dull lives.

Lions and Christians.

The thought gave Kate the strength she needed to move. She turned, seeking Lady Cahill with her eyes, but there was no sign of her. Kate moved slowly towards the circle of watchers, trying to ignore the barrage of eyes upon her, probing, malicious, scornful.

She had nothing to be ashamed of. She would not give them the satisfaction. She stiffened her spine. The way before her parted reluctantly. Ladies, who only hours before had claimed friendship, turned their faces coldly away. No one would meet her eye; a hundred eyes bored into her.

"Little better than a camp follower!"

"The cheek—to try to pass herself off like that in decent company!"

And one, less elliptical than the others. "Traitorous whore!"

Her body began to shake. She could do nothing. There was no standing up to insubstantial whispers from people who would not even look her in the face. She forced herself to keep walking, desperately hoping the trembling of her body was not visible to the observers.

Was there ever a room so long? Only four more steps. Three...two...

A powerful black-clad arm snaked out of the dense crowd and pulled her into the centre of the circle again.

"What—?"

"I think you must have forgotten me, Miss Farleigh," said Jack. His normal tone of voice carried in the watching hush.

Kate blinked up at him.

"My dance, I believe. Did you forget it?" He smiled down at her bewildered face, his casual manner belied by the implacable grip on her arm.

"But..." With everyone listening, Kate couldn't say it. She *hadn't* promised him a dance. He didn't dance. Not since he was wounded, anyway. He only leaned against walls and columns, glaring at her. So why would he seek her out now? Now, when the world was turning against her again and she wanted nothing more than escape. Kate tried to pull away, but his hold on her was too powerful.

Ignoring Kate's glance of pathetic entreaty, Jack moved steadily back through the crowd, towing her beside him, greeting acquaintances in a cheery tone as he went, for all the world as if they were not in the very heart of a major scandal, their every movement watched by hundreds.

His uneven footsteps echoed as he led her out on to the deserted dance floor. He finally released her arm, but took her hand instead. Bowing, he kissed it lightly. Kate stared at him in a daze. He grinned at her, a wicked, tender grin.

"Courage, love," he whispered as he straightened up. "Let's show them that an old cripple and a gallant war heroine are not beaten by a paltry bit of gossip."

He nodded to the band. Kate followed his glance. Sir Toby was standing over the band in a very determined manner. He smiled and waved, then turned back to the band. The music started.

Kate's eyes misted as she looked up into the handsome face bent over her. She had been prepared to withstand anything—scorn, mockery, disgust, revilement. His kindness had undone her.

Jack determinedly stumped his way through the intricate

steps, his bad leg making a clumsy mockery of the movements. Kate gracefully performed her part, making adjustments for his limp where she could.

Jack's eyes never left her face. Her head was held high, but she danced blindly. No one in the audience could see the tears which trickled down her cheeks unheeded. Jack wished he could take her in his arms, wished that strait-laced English society would bend their rules sufficiently to adopt the scandalous Viennese dance which was all the rage in Europe. Jack smiled at her tenderly. Yes, it would be wonderful to hold Kate in his arms for a waltz.

The ballroom might have been deserted, the audience silent ghosts. Only the strains of the band playing, the clumping of Jack's shoes and the faint shuffle of Kate's tiny satin slippers could be heard at first, then the murmuring started again.

The dance ended, but under Tubby's supervision the next one started almost immediately. As the second dance drew to a close, Jack bent over her hand again and murmured, "Two dances are my limit, I'm afraid. A third and people will begin to think you are fast."

Kate stared at him, stupefied. She was being pilloried as a whore and a traitress, and he was concerned that three dances with the same partner would label her *fast!* A bubble of hysteria rose in her throat. The music started again.

"My dance, I believe, Miss Farleigh. Off with you now, Carstairs. This lady is promised to me." The whole room heard him, but without waiting for a reply Francis swung Kate into a country dance.

There was still no one else on the dance floor.

"Miss Farleigh, would you do me the honour of partnering me in the next dance?" A young man bowed over Kate's nerveless fingers. He was dressed in immaculate evening attire, one empty sleeve pinned neatly back. Kate stared at him dumbly.

"You may not remember me, Miss Farleigh, but we met at Badajoz. Arnold Bentham at your service. Francis's cousin."

Kate glanced at his empty sleeve. The young man smiled. "No, Miss Farleigh, that arm I lost at Salamanca. You saved the other one at Badajoz, and I offer it now at your disposal. Shall we?" With his one remaining arm, Arnold Bentham swept Kate into the next dance.

Two other couples joined them on the dance floor—Francis and Andrew Lennox and their partners. There was no sign of Jack.

"Miss Farleigh, may I present my son as a desirable partner? He…he is a little out of practice, but I'm sure you will not mind that." The well-modulated voice broke.

Kate turned, then stopped dead. Her prospective partner stood very still, smiling in her general direction, his hand resting on the arm of a middle-aged woman.

Kate's face crumpled. It was too much. All this unexpected kindness. All this support. And now this.

It was Oliver Greenwood. Oliver Greenwood, whom she had first met as a terrified young lieutenant at Torres Vedras, with blood gushing all over his face. She had visited him several times since she had come to London, but he was the last person she'd expected to see at a ball. Oliver Greenwood was blind.

"Miss Farleigh, I would be most honoured if you would stand up with me," said Oliver Greenwood, bowing in her direction.

Kate glanced at Mrs Greenwood. His mother's face was working with emotion. She nodded at Kate, her eyes filled with tears.

Kate curtseyed. "The honour would be all mine," she whispered through a mist of tears, and took her place.

Immediately they were surrounded as others joined the set.

Francis, Tubby, Andrew Lennox and others, unknown to Kate, some whose faces were vaguely familiar to her, others who were clearly friends of Oliver Greenwood. And their partners, girls for the most part unknown to Kate, girls who smiled encouragingly at her and nodded their heads.

Somehow they got through the dance, Oliver being gently steered in the right direction by his fellow officers, and Kate too, for by this time she was completely blinded by her tears.

And by the time it finished she was not the only person with wet eyes.

"May I escort you to your guardian, Miss Farleigh?" said Oliver Greenwood.

"Not yet, young Greenwood," a bluff voice boomed heartily from behind them. "I want to talk to this young lady."

"Sir!" All the young officers snapped instantly to attention, Oliver Greenwood included.

Kate turned. Jack and a man in a plain, neat, dark blue coat were approaching her—a smallish, thin man, whose blue eyes twinkled at her from over one of the most famous noses in all Europe.

"My Lord!" she gasped, and sank into a curtsey.

"So it's little Kate Farleigh who's got my officers in knots, is it?" said the Marquis of Wellington. He smiled again at Kate, bowed and kissed her hand. A gasp ran round the room.

"Knew your father, m'dear. Very fine man he was. Sorry to hear about his death. Your brothers, too. Brave boys, brave boys. Know they would be proud of you."

He took her hand and tucked it into his arm. "Shall we take a turn about the room?" Without waiting for a reply, he moved off, lowering his voice so that only she could hear.

"Young Carstairs filled me in. Pack of worthless gabble-mongers. But we'll fix them. Face 'em down, what? Show 'em for the cowards they are, eh?"

Wellington moved slowly towards the crowd which

pressed forward, eager to speak with the great man. As he did so, he introduced Kate, mentioning to this person that he was a friend of her family, to that person that she was a gallant young heroine, to another that she was a brave little lady, one of England's finest.

They were soon joined by a group of older ladies, one of whom linked arms with Kate, clearly declaring her support. Kate blinked at her. The woman was a complete stranger.

She bent towards Kate. "Lady Charlotte, my dear. I'm so terribly sorry this happened. If I'd known...but we were all in the card room, I'm afraid, and only just heard what was happening." She indicated the rest of her party. Kate recognised Lady Courtney and several others, but this glittering matron was a complete stranger.

Seeing Kate's continuing puzzlement, the lady added, "I'm Arnold Bentham's mother—you know my nephew, Francis." As Kate suddenly nodded in comprehension, the lady continued, "You saved my Arnold's life, Miss Farleigh. For that, you have my undying friendship and support, and that of these other ladies too."

Kate slowly circled the room; on one side of her, the Marquis of Wellington, on the other, a collection of society's most formidable matrons. She was dazed by the turn in her fortunes, unable to comprehend quite what was happening. She nodded, curtseyed and smiled, oblivious of whom she was meeting, who was shaking her hand.

Jack was there, a pace or two behind her, hovering protectively. She could feel his presence, sense his strength. She wanted to touch him, but she couldn't. She turned to look at him over her shoulder. Their eyes met, caressed, clung, but she was moved forward inexorably, and they were separated by the crowd, pressing closer, eager to meet the Great Man and his protégée.

Kate could hardly believe it. She had been snatched from

her worst nightmare, and now was engaged in an almost triumphal procession on the arm of England's greatest living hero. But it was Jack who'd saved her. He had risked social ostracism, had stood up with her in the most public of places, had declared his support of her for all the world to see. Jack, who'd been a recluse, hiding his wounds from the world—he'd come out and danced with her, when no one else would even look her in the eye.

And it was Jack whose arm she wanted to be on, whose arms she wanted to be in.

Kate glanced back. He was no longer there. Her eyes scanned the room anxiously. Where was he? She could see him nowhere. He had stood up for her in her hour of need. Surely he wouldn't desert her in her moment of triumph? Didn't he know it would mean nothing to her if he was not with her?

She caught Francis's eye across a dozen heads and asked him the silent question. He returned a sombre look, then shrugged and shook his head hopelessly. Kate's face dropped. Jack had left. But why?

With a leaden heart, Kate returned to the hollow greetings of well-wishers and sycophants.

"What do you mean, she's gone? Gone where? She hasn't been seen since that blasted ball, and let me tell you, Grandmama, nothing could be more ill-judged. She needs to be out there, circulating, seeing people, showing them she's nothing to hide. We've scotched the worst of it, but if she's hiding herself away..."

"I said she's *gone,* Jack. Gone away. Left."

"Left where? What do you mean?" Suddenly Jack turned white. He sat down in a rush. "You mean gone? She's left London?"

Lady Cahill looked at him in some compassion, then hardened her heart. He'd been acting like a fool.

"Gone where?"

"Back to that village I found her in."

"Good God, how could you let her do something so...? What is there for her anyway? Why would she do such a thing?" He rose to his feet again and paced about, raking his fingers through wildly disordered locks. Suddenly he looked up sharply.

"Who is escorting her? How is she travelling? And who is to meet her?"

His grandmother shrugged.

"You mean you let her go alone!" he roared.

"I was not exactly consulted, Jack, and do not take that tone with me. I'm as worried about the dratted girl as you are!" snapped his grandmother. "The foolish child slipped away at dawn."

"So how is she travelling?"

"I don't know, Jack, the Mail or stage, I presume!"

"Good God! Mail or stage! Rubbing shoulders with God knows who! Doesn't she know the dangers? Footpads, highwaymen! Doesn't she know how often accidents happen? Pray God she took the Mail; at least they have a guard!" Swearing, he rushed from the room.

Lady Cahill sat back, a satisfied grin on her face.

"What the *devil* do you think you're doing?"

The roar, which seemed to echo from the heavens, almost startled Kate into dropping her basket. It was, however, a very familiar roar. She looked around. There, on a horse flecked with foam, its sides heaving, legs trembling, sat Jack Carstairs, glaring at her yet again.

He looked dreadful. Covered with mud, his jaw unshaven, his neckcloth all awry. Her eyes softened. She glanced around. The narrow country laneway in which she'd been walking was by no means deserted; several farm workers were within earshot. She smiled up at him for the benefit of their observers.

"Good afternoon, Mr Carstairs," she said in a clear calm voice. "As you see, I'm just off to the village."

"Just off to the village, are you? And with no thought for how others might be worried about you?"

She looked up at him in silence. Why would he be worried? And why so angry?

"How the hell did you get here anyway?"

"I hired a chaise and outriders."

"A chaise and outriders? A chaise and outriders!" He seemed outraged by the notion. He was breathing heavily, his eyes positively crackling with blue rage.

"Well, and what is so wrong with that?"

"Only that I stopped every bloody stage and Mail coach between here and London, searching for you!"

"Oh, no. You didn't, did you?" Kate looked up at him, her eyes wide, imagining the scene. She giggled.

As far as Jack was concerned, it was the giggle that did it. With a groan of fury he leaned down, grabbed her under the armpits and dragged her up on to his horse. Ignoring her outraged squeaks, he clamped her to his chest and moved off. Kate struggled, but as the horse moved faster she clung to Jack to save herself from falling. The farm labourers came closer, several of them carrying sticks and cudgels.

In a trice Jack clamped his mouth over hers. Kate's struggles suddenly ceased as the familiar magic of his kiss washed over her. She was, after all, where she most desired in the world to be. One hand slid around his neck, her fingers tangling in his wild, damp hair. The other hand gently stroked his rough, unshaven jaw. Abandoning all defences, she opened her heart and allowed herself to simply love him.

By the time the kiss had finished, they had left the grinning farm workers long behind. Kate sighed, nuzzling her face against the underside of his jaw. She leaned against him, relishing the taste of him on her lips, the strong embrace of his muscular arms around her.

"There was no need to run away, you know," he said after a time. "We had everything under control. You will be completely accepted in society, no shadow of a doubt. There was no need to hide here."

"Run away?" she said quietly. "Did Lady Cahill not tell you?"

"Oh, she told me all right. How else do you think I knew where to look?" He swung her round to face him, eyes blazing, hands gripping her hard. He shook her. "What is there here for you? A small dirty village? A falling-down cottage? The company of rustics? You cannot possibly prefer this to London!"

Her eyes clung to his. "Everything I want in the world is right here," she said slowly. "Nothing I want or need is in London." She leaned back into the curve of his body.

He turned ashen. His hands loosened their hard grip. He looked away, staring blankly across the top of her head. "Nothing?" he said at last.

"Nothing in London. Everything I want in the world is right here," she repeated.

He sagged in the saddle. "So be it."

Defeated, he turned his horse back towards the village. They rode in silence, the only sound the twittering of birds and the slow clip-clopping of the horse's hoofs. Kate lay back against his chest, rocking against his hard, warm body in rhythm to the horse's gait. She could say no more. How could she, not knowing how he felt? She had told him as much as she dared.

Why had he come after her? Had his grandmother sent him? Was it duty? Or a constitutional dislike of being crossed? He'd saved her reputation, but then made it clear that he wanted nothing further to do with her. Oh, he desired her all right, but she wanted more than that.

They drew closer and closer to the village until at last the cross on the spire of the tiny stone church was clearly visible. The horse stopped.

"Damned if I do, damned if I don't, so I bloody well will and damn the consequences!" Jack suddenly growled. He wrenched the horse around and started to gallop in the opposite direction. Kate clung on for dear life.

"Where are we going? This is not the way to the village," she shrieked. His only response was to clamp her more tightly against his chest and spur the horse onwards.

"The cottage is in the other direction!" she shouted, bouncing up and down.

The horse galloped on. Jack said not a word. Kate thumped at his chest in frustration. "Jack! Where are we going?"

His arms tightened around her. "I'm kidnapping you."

Kate was stunned. *Kidnapping her?*

"Everybody else does, so why not me?" he shouted into her ear.

"Oh, Jack, no. Not you, Jack, please, not you," she cried tremulously. She began to weep.

Appalled, he wrenched the horse to a halt. Awkwardly he slid off it and lifted Kate to the ground. Her legs buckled under her and she crumpled on to the grass. He followed her, gathering her into his arms. "No, Kate, don't, please don't," he said brokenly. "Don't cry, please."

He pulled out a large handkerchief and clumsily started blotting her cheeks with it. "Don't cry, sweetheart. I can't bear it if you cry."

Kate just sobbed harder.

He held her against him, rocking her gently. Finally her sobs shuddered to a halt. He continued to hold her in his lap, her face pressed against his chest, stroking her tumbled hair with a gentle hand.

After a time she pulled away. "Why?" she whispered.

He took a deep breath and shook his head despairingly.

"I...I just thought that if you really had decided to live in rural obscurity..."

"Go on," she prompted.

He looked deeply uncomfortable. "Well...I thought...you might..."

"Might what?" she prompted again.

Suddenly he exploded. "Well, if you must know, I thought that if you wanted to bury yourself in obscurity the least you could do is do it with me! There, now you have it! I am a despicable rogue, am I not? An arrogant fool, who thought you might consent..."

"Consent to what?" Her heart was thudding uncontrollably. This was the crux of the matter. What had he thought she might be willing to do? Consent to be kidnapped? To be his mistress? His doxy? Consent to have her heart broken?

There was a long silence. Finally he reached into an inner pocket of his coat and drew out a folded document. He stared at it a moment, his mouth twisting ruefully, then tossed it on the grass between them.

"See for yourself. There it is, documentary evidence of what an arrogant, desperate fool I am. Go on, open it, see for yourself. Just don't laugh in my face."

With shaking fingers Kate reached out and picked up the parchment. Opening it, she read it several times, her mind struggling to come to terms with the meaning of his having obtained this document.

"It is a special licence," she said at last. "And not so very new, either." He'd obtained it before she'd been kidnapped by Jeremiah Cole, Kate realised, with a thrill.

"Yes, fool that I am, I thought I could get you to marry me." He laughed, a harsh, dry laugh that ended abruptly.

"Why did you not simply ask me?" she said softly.

"Ask you?" His voice was bitter. "Why ask when there's no possibility of acceptance? What woman would consent to marriage with a fellow like me, a cripple, and a bad-tempered, ugly one to boot? And with barely a penny to my name. What sort of a bargain is that for a woman?''

''Some women might think it a very good bargain.''

He looked at her then. ''Perhaps…if the woman had lost everything—her family, her home, her…her good name. Such a woman might have thought it sufficient. She would have had no other options.''

And yet he'd lent her his family, given her a home and saved her good name. Kate felt a spurt of anger grow inside her. How dared he think himself such a poor bargain? And herself so mercenary!

''But a woman who had been left a fortune?'' she said. ''A woman whose good name had been retrieved by a bad-tempered, poverty-stricken cripple—such a woman must needs be tricked, kidnapped, coerced?''

He looked stricken. ''Only because you ran away. You didn't seem to want the London life, so I thought…''

''I came down here to redeem the things I sold when I had no money. Some of my mother's jewellery, my father's books, things like that. Lady Cahill knew that very well. She expects me back on Tuesday. I wasn't running away from anyone or anything. You should know me better than that!''

''I didn't think…'' He shrugged despairingly.

''No, you didn't think!'' raged Kate. She moved closer and thumped him on the arm. ''You *are* bad-tempered and poor, and also quite stupid! You great brainless clod! You don't talk to me for weeks and weeks—''

''But you wouldn't—''

''—and you glare and spit blue fire at me across crowded dance floors—''

''What do you mean, blue fire?''

Kate ignored that. If he didn't know the power of his beautiful blue eyes, then she wasn't going to enlighten him. She thumped him again, this time on the chest.

"And then you must drag me up on to your poor, smelly..."

"Smelly?" One arm went around her.

"Smelly, exhausted horse in front of men who I've known since I was a child, and then, with not a shred of shame about you, you must kiss me in front of—"

"It seemed to me you were doing a bit of kissing of your own," he said, catching one small fist as it sailed perilously close to his jaw.

"And then, you great lout, as if that isn't enough, you must bounce me over miles and miles of countryside—"

"And very beautifully you bounce, too," he interjected wickedly.

"And *then* you decide I don't even deserve the courtesy of a proposal! When I'd already told you I loved you!" She collapsed furiously against his chest with a final thump.

He snatched her away from him and stared into her face.

"You what? You did no such thing!"

She blushed. "I did too."

"When?"

She blushed a deeper, rosy pink. "When I told you I had everything here I wanted."

He stared at her, dumbfounded. Then his eyes started to twinkle. "And I was supposed to understand from that that you love me?"

She nodded, embarrassed.

Suddenly he laughed, a joyous ringing laugh. "Oh, what a clod I am indeed! So clear you made it, and, stupid great lout that I am, I didn't understand!"

"I did kiss you back," she mumbled, aggrieved.

He stopped laughing and she could feel the warmth of his smile as he leaned close and gathered her back in his arms. Kate wouldn't look at him. "Yes, you did, didn't you? And very nice it was too." He bent his head towards her, seeking her lips.

Kate pouted. "I'm not kissing any horrid kidnapper."

He laughed and rolled back on to the grass, pulling her down on top of him. "Then, my little spitfire, will you kindly consent to kiss a man who is utterly mad for love of you? A man who has nothing but his heart and a run-down but very clean house to offer you. And, though he does not deserve you, he asks you most humbly and desperately to be his wife."

She stared down at him for a moment and Jack was horrified to see tears welling in her beautiful eyes again. "Oh, no, my love, I'm sorry. Whatever I said or did wrong, I'm sorry. Oh, God, I'm such a clumsy fool, but I love you so much. Oh, Kate, darling, please don't cry."

The tears dripped harder, landing on his face. He kissed her wet cheeks, her wet eyes, her wet mouth. "Don't cry, my little love. I can't bear it."

She looked at him through the shimmering veil of tears. "I'm sorry..."

His heart contracted unbearably.

"Sorry, Jack, darling... It's just that I'm so happy..." she wailed.

It was so wonderful to be held like this, safe and warm in his arms, her cheek resting against his heart, her head tucked beneath his chin. She rubbed her cheek softly against the rough bristles along his jawline, and sighed with pleasure. She looked up and met his eyes, and the tenderness she saw in them warmed her clear down to her toes. After some time Kate forced herself to push him away. Reluctantly he allowed it. She sat up and straightened her dress. He lay there watching her, a tender, proud smile on his face.

"I've just thought of another reason for you to marry me," he drawled.

"Hmm?"

"Valet service. I never knew a woman who was so good at getting into a mess," he chuckled, picking pieces of grass out of her hair. She slapped his hands away and pushed him back on to the ground. Her hands rested on his chest, partly to ensure he kept his distance, partly so she would not lose the contact with his body.

Her face grew serious and her eyes darkened with anxiety. "I have to ask this, Jack. Do you truly not mind about what happened to me, in Spain?"

His eyes softened. "On the contrary, I mind it a great deal...but not for the reasons you're worrying about, my love." He pulled her down into the curve of his body. "I mind that you were hurt, that you were frightened and abused, that you were hungry and in danger and that you were alone with no one to protect you. I mind that you did not get the support and assistance you needed, that you were subjected to gossip, cruel impertinence and worse. I mind that you came home to nothing and no one, facing destitution, and I mind that to earn a living you had to scrub my floors and put up with my vile temper..."

His voice came to a shaky halt and he held her tight, trembling with emotion. After a time, he stopped shaking, his grip altered and his mouth came down over hers, infinitely gentle, infinitely loving. "I give you my word, Kate, that you will never again suffer hunger, fear, pain or loneliness, not while I am alive to prevent it. And I vow to dedicate the rest of my life to loving and protecting you."

She was weak with relief and joy. "And I to you, my love," she whispered. It was all she had time to say before his mouth came down over hers again.

After a long, tender interval, he added, "Besides which, it is my firm belief—" he moved against her in an unmistakably erotic fashion, his face coming alive with wicked humour "—my very firm belief, that virginity has absolutely no place in marriage."

Distracted by the feelings engendered by his movement, Kate was a little slow in realising his meaning, but gradually she became aware of his wickedly quizzing look, the laughter, and deep, passionate love and acceptance in his eyes. In relief she began to giggle, and his lazy chuckle joined hers as he swept her into his arms and hugged her tightly against him.

After a time, Kate pulled his chin down so she could look him in the eye. There was a hint of mischief in the loving look she gave him. "So you promise to love and protect me always…"

"Always, sweetheart."

"And to make sure I never go hungry again?"

"Of course."

"And kill spiders for me."

"As many as you want."

"And never make me scrub your floors."

"Baggage!" He flicked her nose teasingly. "If you recall, it was not my idea in the first place."

She nodded wisely. "Oh, yes. I recall now. You prefer your floors dirty."

A low mock-growl and a swift, hard kiss was her only answer.

"And you promise I will never have to put up with your 'vile temper' again?" She reached up and curled a lock of dark hair around and around her finger until it was held tight. She gave it a little tug to make her point.

A baleful look from glittering blue eyes made her giggle.

"That depends," he said sternly.

"On what, dearest?" she murmured, fluttering her lashes innocently.

"Oh, on such things as whether coffee pots and vases remain on tables or come flying through the air."

She dimpled. "Oh, I do not know if I can possibly promise such a thing. Coffee pots are so unpredictable, you know."

"Mmm," he agreed dryly. "I see it will take me at least twenty or thirty years to understand the ways of coffee pots."

"Oh, no," she said dulcetly.

He looked quizzically down at her. His heart thudded at the blatant adoration that poured from her eyes.

"Much longer than that, my darling, much, much longer," she murmured, reaching up and pulling his mouth down to hers.

Epilogue

"**O**h, mind you do not drop me, you wretch!"

"Silence, baggage! And stop that infernal wriggling or I will!"

Laughing, Kate was carried over the threshold. Jack kissed her long and hard, and set her on her feet, smiling down at her. His bride of three weeks looked radiant. So radiant, in fact, that he found he had to kiss her again. And then again.

Carlos, Martha, Millie and Florence looked on, beaming. Eventually Kate became aware of their audience. Blushing, she tugged Jack's sleeve and pointed. Immediately they were surrounded by well-wishers.

Refreshments were brought in, congratulations were exchanged and the girls clustered round, admiring Kate's frock. After a time, Martha came forward with a bulky letter, an apologetic look on her face.

"I'm that sorry to interrupt everything, Mr Jack, but this letter has been here for a couple of weeks now and it's been worrying me. It's from London and looks very important."

Jack took it and turned it over in his hands, frowning.

"From *lawyers!*" said Martha darkly. "Never any good news from lawyers. Sorry, sir." She left, ushering the other servants out of the room.

Jack opened it and began to read through the papers. After a moment he sat down, an odd look on his face. Kate, worried, ran to him.

"What is it, Jack? Is it bad news? It's not your grandmother, is it?"

"No. Not bad news," said Jack in a strange voice. "Here, read it for yourself."

Kate took the sheaf of papers. The first was a letter from a solicitor, saying he had instructions to forward this letter when certain conditions had been met. Kate frowned. It was very puzzling. She turned to the next letter and glanced at the opening.

"Jack!" she gasped.

"Read it out, love," he said. "I'm not sure I believe it myself yet."

Kate read:

Jack, my beloved son,

When you receive this letter, either my lawyers have been convinced that you have finally and irrevocably broken with Julia Davenport, or it is a year and a day since I have died. I hope it is the former.

Either way, you will inherit everything you ever expected to. I never intended you to be poor. My will was a dying man's ploy to free you from That Woman.

My doctors tell me I shall be dead in a matter of weeks, so I have done what I can to give you the best chance of happiness. I know my actions will cause you pain, my son, and I am sorry for it. But I believe it is for the best.

Julia Davenport is a Harpy, Jack, and a Faithless, Greedy Harpy at that. I am counting on her to abandon you when she discovers you inherit nothing. I hope it does not hurt you too badly, my boy.

I hope also that you can forgive my apparent rejec-

tion. It is cruel, I know, for you have always been a loving son, even when we quarrelled. But I want so much to see you happy, Jack. There is nothing as important as true love—your mother and I were so very happy and my heart went with her when she died. You are the image of her, my beloved son, and I know she would never forgive me if I did not make a push to secure your happiness.

Find another woman to love, Jack—one with a true and loving heart, who will love you for yourself—not for your fortune or your position. And when you find her, Jack, marry her at once and never let her go.

I will carry five hundred pounds and this damned deed to Sevenoakes wherever I go from now until my death, so that you will not find yourself entirely destitute. And I know your grandmother and sister will look after you. You are much beloved, my son.

I hope you can find it in your heart to forgive a father's meddling. May God protect you.

Your loving father...

"Oh, Jack, he did love you after all..." Kate was in tears.

Jack could not reply; he just reached out and gathered her into his arms. After a long moment he said in a cracked voice, "I found my true and loving heart, Father. Here she is..."

* * * * *

ANNE GRACIE

was born in Australia, but spent her youth on the move, living in Scotland, Malaysia, Greenland and different parts of Australia before escaping her parents and settling down. Her love of the Regency period began at the age of eleven when she braved the adult library to borrow a Georgette Heyer novel, firmly convinced she would, at any moment, be ignominiously ejected and sent back to the children's library in disgrace. She wasn't. Anne lives in Melbourne, in a small wooden house, which she will one day renovate.

HHIBC557

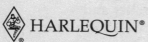

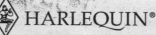

HARLEQUIN®

bestselling authors

Merline Lovelace
Deborah Simmons
Julia Justiss

cordially invite you to enjoy three
brand-new stories of unexpected love

The
Officer's
Bride

Available April 2001

HARLEQUIN®
Makes any time special ®

Harlequin truly does make any time special. . . . This year we are celebrating weddings in style!

A Walk Down the Aisle
WEDDING CELEBRATION

To help us celebrate, we want you to tell us how wearing the Harlequin wedding gown will make your wedding day special. As the grand prize, Harlequin will offer one lucky bride the chance to **"Walk Down the Aisle" in the Harlequin wedding gown!**

There's more...

For her honeymoon, she and her groom will spend five nights at the **Hyatt Regency Maui.** As part of this five-night honeymoon at the hotel renowned for its romantic attractions, the couple will enjoy a candlelit dinner for two in Swan Court, a sunset sail on the hotel's catamaran, and duet spa treatments.

Maui • Molokai • Lanai

To enter, please write, in, 250 words or less, how wearing the Harlequin wedding gown will make your wedding day special. The entry will be judged based on its emotionally compelling nature, its originality and creativity, and its sincerity. This contest is open to Canadian and U.S. residents only and to those who are 18 years of age and older. There is no purchase necessary to enter. Void where prohibited. See further contest rules attached. Please send your entry to:

Walk Down the Aisle Contest

In Canada	In U.S.A.
P.O. Box 637	P.O. Box 9076
Fort Erie, Ontario	3010 Walden Ave.
L2A 5X3	Buffalo, NY 14269-9076

You can also enter by visiting www.eHarlequin.com
Win the Harlequin wedding gown and the vacation of a lifetime!
The deadline for entries is October 1, 2001.

HARLEQUIN®
Makes any time special ®

HARLEQUIN WALK DOWN THE AISLE TO MAUI CONTEST 1197
OFFICIAL RULES
NO PURCHASE NECESSARY TO ENTER

To enter, follow directions published in the offer to which you are responding. Contest begins April 2, 2001, and ends on October 1, 2001. Method of entry may vary. Mailed entries must be postmarked by October 1, 2001, and received by October 8, 2001.

Contest entry may be, at times, presented via the Internet, but will be restricted solely to residents of certain georgraphic areas that are disclosed on the Web site. To enter via the Internet, if permissible, access the Harlequin Web site (www.eHarlequin.com) and follow the directions displayed online. Online entries must be received by 11:59 p.m. E.S.T. on October 1, 2001.

In lieu of submitting an entry online, enter by mail by hand-printing (or typing) on an 8½" x 11" plain piece of paper, your name, address (including zip code), Contest number/name and in 250 words or fewer, why winning a Harlequin wedding dress would make your wedding day special. Mail via first-class mail to: Harlequin Walk Down the Aisle Contest 1197, (in the U.S.) P.O. Box 9076, 3010 Walden Avenue, Buffalo, NY 14269-9076, (in Canada) P.O. Box 637, Fort Erie, Ontario L2A 5X3, Canada.

Limit one entry per person, household address and e-mail address. Online and/or mailed entries received from persons residing in geographic areas in which Internet entry is not permissible will be disqualified.

Contests will be judged by a panel of members of the Harlequin editorial, marketing and public relations staff based on the following criteria:

- Originality and Creativity—50%
- Emotionally Compelling—25%
- Sincerity—25%

In the event of a tie, duplicate prizes will be awarded. Decisions of the judges are final.

All entries become the property of Torstar Corp. and will not be returned. No responsibility is assumed for lost, late, illegible, incomplete, inaccurate, nondelivered or misdirected mail or misdirected e-mail, for technical, hardware or software failures of any kind, lost or unavailable network connections, or failed, incomplete, garbled or delayed computer transmission or any human error which may occur in the receipt or processing of the entries in this Contest.

Contest open only to residents of the U.S. (except Puerto Rico) and Canada, who are 18 years of age or older, and is void wherever prohibited by law; all applicable laws and regulations apply. Any litigation within the Province of Quebec respecting the conduct and organization of a publicity contest may be submitted to the Régie des alcools, des courses et des jeux for a ruling. Any litigation respecting the awarding of a prize may be submitted to the Régie des alcools, des courses et des jeux only for the purpose of helping the parties reach a settlement. Employees and immediate family members of Torstar Corp. and D. L. Blair, Inc., their affiliates, subsidiaries and all other agencies, entities and persons connected with the use, marketing or conduct of this Contest are not eligible to enter. Taxes on prizes are the sole responsibility of winners. Acceptance of any prize offered constitutes permission to use winner's name, photograph or other likeness for the purposes of advertising, trade and promotion on behalf of Torstar Corp., its affiliates and subsidiaries without further compensation to the winner, unless prohibited by law.

Winners will be determined no later than November 15, 2001, and will be notified by mail. Winners will be required to sign and return an Affidavit of Eligibility form within 15 days after winner notification. Noncompliance within that time period may result in disqualification and an alternative winner may be selected. Winners of trip must execute a Release of Liability prior to ticketing and must possess required travel documents (e.g. passport, photo ID) where applicable. Trip must be completed by November 2002. No substitution of prize permitted by winner. Torstar Corp. and D. L. Blair, Inc., their parents, affiliates, and subsidiaries are not responsible for errors in printing or electronic presentation of Contest, entries and/or game pieces. In the event of printing or other errors which may result in unintended prize values or duplication of prizes, all affected game pieces or entries shall be null and void. If for any reason the Internet portion of the Contest is not capable of running as planned, including infection by computer virus, bugs, tampering, unauthorized intervention, fraud, technical failures, or any other causes beyond the control of Torstar Corp. which corrupt or affect the administration, secrecy, fairness, integrity or proper conduct of the Contest, Torstar Corp. reserves the right, at its sole discretion, to disqualify any individual who tampers with the entry process and to cancel, terminate, modify or suspend the Contest or the Internet portion thereof. In the event of a dispute regarding an online entry, the entry will be deemed submitted by the authorized holder of the e-mail account submitted at the time of entry. Authorized account holder is defined as the natural person who is assigned to an e-mail address by an Internet access provider, online service provider or other organization that is responsible for arranging e-mail address for the domain associated with the submitted e-mail address. **Purchase or acceptance of a product offer does not improve your chances of winning.**

Prizes: (1) Grand Prize—A Harlequin wedding dress (approximate retail value: $3,500) and a 5-night/6-day honeymoon trip to Maui, HI, including round-trip air transportation provided by Maui Visitors Bureau from Los Angeles International Airport (winner is responsible for transportation to and from Los Angeles International Airport) and a Harlequin Romance Package, including hotel accomodations (double occupancy) at the Hyatt Regency Maui Resort and Spa, dinner for (2) two at Swan Court, a sunset sail on Kiele V and a spa treatment for the winner (approximate retail value: $4,000); (5) Five runner-up prizes of a $1000 gift certificate to selected retail outlets to be determined by Sponsor (retail value $1000 ea.). Prizes consist of only those items listed as part of the prize. Limit one prize per person. All prizes are valued in U.S. currency.

For a list of winners (available after December 17, 2001) send a self-addressed, stamped envelope to: Harlequin Walk Down the Aisle Contest 1197 Winners, P.O. Box 4200 Blair, NE 68009-4200 or you may access the www.eHarlequin.com Web site through January 15, 2002.

ntest sponsored by Torstar Corp., P.O. Box 9042, Buffalo, NY 14269-9042, U.S.A.

PHWDACONT2

Got a hankerin' for a down home romance?
Pick yourself up a Western from Harlequin Historical

ON SALE MAY 2001

CIMARRON ROSE
by **Nicole Foster**
(New Mexico, 1875)
An embittered hotel owner falls for the beautiful singer
he hires to revive his business.

THE NANNY
by **Judith Stacy**
Book 2 in the Return to Tyler historical miniseries
(Wisconsin, 1840)
A handsome widower finds true love when he hires a
tomboyish young woman to care for his passel of kids.

ON SALE JUNE 2001

THE MARSHAL
AND MRS. O'MALLEY
by **Julianne MacLean**
(Kansas, 1890s))
A widow wishes to avenge her husband's murder, but
soon loses her nerve—and then loses her heart
to Dodge City's new marshal.

Available at your favorite retail outlet.